THE
NUN'S TALE

THE OWEN ARCHER SERIES
BOOK THREE

CANDACE

The Owen Archer Series
The Apothecary Rose
The Lady Chapel
The King's Bishop
The Riddle of St. Leonard's
A Gift of Sanctuary
A Spy for the Redeemer
The Guilt of Innocents
A Vigil of Spies

The Margaret Kerr Series
A Trust Betrayed
The Fire in the Flint
A Cruel Courtship

Diversion Books
A Division of Diversion Publishing Corp.
443 Park Avenue South, Suite 1008
New York, New York 10016
www.DiversionBooks.com

For more information, email info@diversionbooks.com

First Diversion Books edition July 2015.
Print ISBN: 978-1-68230-103-6
eBook ISBN: 978-1-62681-977-1

ACKNOWLEDGMENTS

I thank Lynne Drew for being an insightful editor with inexhaustible patience and a sense of humour; Jeremy Goldberg and Pat Cullum for fielding questions about everyday life in the 14th century; Karen Wuthrich for reading the manuscript with a critical eye; Charlie Robb for taking on a plethora of supporting jobs, including outline doctor and mapmaker; and Jacqui Weberding for navigating the North.

Additional thanks to the talented professionals who smooth the way: Evan Marshall, Patrick Walsh, Victoria Hipps, Rebecca Salt, Clare Allanson and Joe Myers.

GLOSSARY

bedstraw: a plant of the genus Galium

corody: a pension or allowance provided by a religious house permitting the holder to retire into the house as a boarder; purchased for cash or by a donation of land or property

fulling mill: a mill that cleanses, shrinks and thickens (fulls) cloth by means of water and pestles or stampers

houppelande: men's attire; a flowing gown, often floor length and slit up to thigh level to ease walking, but sometimes knee length; sleeves large and open

lady chapel: a chapel dedicated to the Blessed Virgin Mary, usually situated at the east end of the church

leman: mistress

liberty: an area of the city not subject to royal administration; for example, the Liberty of St. Peter is the area surrounding the minster which comes under the archbishop's jurisdiction

mazer: a large wooden cup

minster: a large church or cathedral; the cathedral of St. Peter in York is referred to as York Minster

nones: between 2:00 and 3:00 p.m. (varied with seasons)

pandemain: the finest quality white bread, made from flour sifted two or three times

Petercorn: income supporting St. Leonard's hospital, dependent on the harvest (Peter's corn)

prime: between 6:00 and 7:00 a.m. (varied with seasons)

routiers: see Author's Note

sext: noon

solar: private room on upper level of house

trencher: a thick slice of brown bread a few days old with a slight hollow in the center, used as a platter

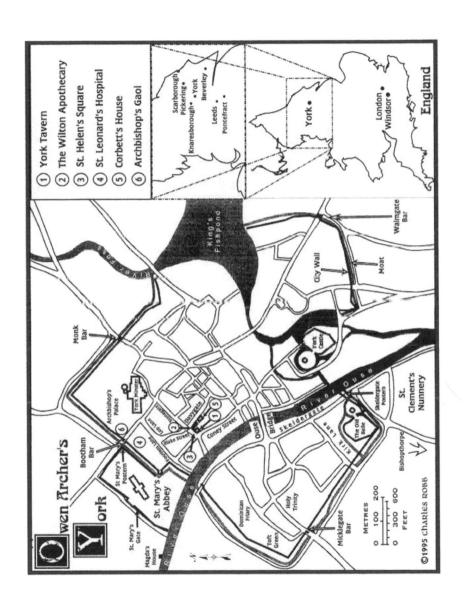

Owen Archer's York

1. York Tavern
2. The Wilton Apothecary
3. St. Helen's Square
4. St. Leonard's Hospital
5. Corbett's House
6. Archbishop's Gaol

England

Scarborough
Pickering
Knaresborough • York
Beverley
Leeds
Pontefract

York •

London •
Windsor •

River Foss
King's Fishpond
City Wall
Moat
Walmgate Bar
Monk Bar
York Castle
River Ouse
Skeldergate Postern
St. Clement's Nunnery
Archbishop's Palace
York Minster
Petergate
Stonegate
Davygate
Blake Street
Coney Street
Ouse Bridge
Skeldergate
The Old Bailie
Kirk Lane
Bootham Bar
St. Mary's Postern
St. Mary's Abbey
St. Mary's Gate
Magda's House
River Ouse
Bishopthorpe
Dominican Friary
Toft Green
Holy Trinity
Micklegate Bar

METRES
0   100   200
0   300   600
FEET

©1995 CHARLES ROBB

PROLOGUE

JUNE 1365

Joanna hoisted her pack and trudged through North Bar, entering Beverley as the bells of the great Church of St. John rang out. She had been walking since sunrise; the sun was now overhead. The coarse weave of her habit chafed at her clammy skin. The city's streets curved snakelike along the Beck and Walkerbeck, and as she walked Joanna glimpsed the becks through the houses. She imagined shedding her clothes and sinking into the cool, rushing water as she and her brother Hugh used to do in the river near their house.

It was a damp, cloying heat. Though this day was sunny and hot, it had been a summer of torrential rains and the dirt streets were waterlogged. Where the sun shone down between the houses, steam rose up, creating a fog that blurred Joanna's vision. She found the dreamlike effect disorienting. The houses shimmered; lines dipped and spun. She clutched her Mary Magdalene medal and whispered prayers as she walked.

Laughter and the merry sound of singing tempted her as she passed a tavern. She yearned to enter and wash down the road dust with strong ale, but she must not call attention to herself in such a way, a nun traveling alone.

Not far past the tavern she spied a churchyard with a shaded well. Surely this was a safe refuge. Joanna slipped through the open gate, set her pack down under a shading oak that thrust a root up through the mud. Glancing round to check that she was unwatched, she shed her veil, her wimple, her gorget, folding them neatly on her pack, then unclasped the Mary Magdalene medal and set it on top.

She drew up a bucket of cool water, cupped her hands to drink, then splashed her face, head and neck.

A sound made her turn. A boy in tattered clothes held the medal and chain in the air above Joanna's pack. Joanna shouted. The little thief went running.

Damnable cur! Grabbing up her skirts, Joanna took off after the thief. "Give me the medal, you Devil's spawn. A curse on your mother and all your kin!" She threw herself at the boy, tackling him to the ground. He kicked her in the face and wriggled out of her grasp, throwing the chain at her as he took off.

Pushing herself up onto her knees, her habit now heavy with mud, Joanna crawled awkwardly over to the silvery treasure. Sweet Heaven, no! She found an empty chain, no medal. Her heart pounding, she crawled round in the mud and weeds, searching for her precious Magdalene medal. Her brother Hugh had given it to her on another journey to Beverley six years before, and Joanna treasured the medal. It was all she had from her beloved brother. And the cur had taken it. Tears of anger and frustration blinded her. She gave herself up to weeping.

"My child, what troubles you?" A priest stood over Joanna, his expression one of curious concern.

Her hand went to her bare head. "*Benedicte*, Father."

"What has happened here, my child?"

"I have been traveling since dawn and your well tempted me. I thought you would not begrudge me water." She smiled into his kind eyes.

"Of course you are welcome to drink. I see that you wear the habit of a Benedictine. Where are your companions? Surely you do not travel alone."

Joanna scrambled to her feet. "I strayed from my companions. I must hurry to catch them." She could not allow him to accompany her or she would be discovered.

He gestured toward her wet, soiled skirt. "Why were you sitting in the mud?"

She glanced down at her habit, dismayed. She tried to brush off the mud, but succeeded only in smearing it. "'Twas nothing, Father.

God bless you." She fumbled for her head coverings.

"Perhaps you should come within to dry off. If you tell me where your companions are headed, I could send someone after them with news of you."

Joanna picked up her pack. "No need, Father. Thank you for the water. God go with you." She fled through the gate and on down the street, taking no notice of her surroundings, reprimanding herself for such stupidity. A wall suddenly stopped her, and she stared round, confused. Sweet Jesu, she had lost her way. She fought back tears, weary, frustrated, frightened. The medal was lost, there was nothing to protect her. She breathed deeply, trying to still her panic. She must find her way. She must reach Will Longford's house before dark.

Slowly she groped her way back to North Bar and began again. It was now mid afternoon and clouds gathered overhead, deepening the gloom of the narrow streets. The air had grown heavy, pressing on Joanna's chest. Her head pounded. It felt as if she had been walking for an eternity. At last the heavens opened, but instead of a refreshing shower the rain thundered down, turning the streets to rivers of mud. Joanna would not allow herself to stop and take shelter. She must not leave a trail. Her habit clung to her. Her veil slapped against her face. She fought for each step, pulling her feet out of the sucking mud. She wept for her lost medal, but trudged on. She had not come so far to be drowned by a summer storm.

At last, as the rain turned to a gentle shower, Joanna recognized the way. Round a corner, and there. The house with the whitewashed door. Will Longford's house.

A skinny serving girl answered, stared at Joanna's bedraggled clothes. "Surely you've taken the wrong turning, Sister. This be no place for nuns."

Joanna tried to adjust her sagging wimple and veil. "I would speak with Master Longford. I've business with him."

The girl scratched her cheek with a chapped hand. "Business? I warn you, there's but one sort of business the Master has with women, and afternoon's not the time for it. Nor does he endanger his immortal soul with brides of Christ." She glanced behind her nervously.

Joanna reached out and grabbed the girl's apron, pulling her forward. The shock on the girl's face was rewarding. "Tell your master that I've a treasure to trade."

The girl nodded. "I meant only to warn you."

Joanna let her go.

"What name shall I give the Master?"

"Dame Joanna Calverley of Leeds."

The girl scuttled away.

Shortly the doorway darkened. Will Longford was a huge, hairy man, his coarse black hair now streaked with white, a white beard—he had aged in six years. He wore a chemise that brushed the ground, but Joanna knew what it hid, a wooden peg that had replaced his left leg. Arms folded across his chest, Longford leaned against the doorjamb, formidable even when one knew he was crippled.

"You are a Calverley? From Leeds?" He did not so much speak as growl. His dark eyes glittered with hostility.

"I accompanied my brother Hugh when he sold you the right arm of St. Sebastian six years back."

The dark eyes narrowed. "Ah. The little sister." Longford scratched his beard and studied her face. "St. Sebastian. His arm, you say?" He grinned. "Have you come to offer me more of Sebastian? His other arm, perhaps?"

Joanna stood up straighter. She did not like the emphasis on *little* sister, or the nasty grin. "I offer you something more sacred still. The milk of the Virgin. From St. Clement's in York."

"The milk of—God's blood, what's the bastard up to?" Longford looked her up and down. "You are a nun of St. Clement's?"

"I am. This has naught to do with Hugh."

Longford stepped forward, peered up and down the street. "Your kind are wont to travel in groups. How do you come to be alone?"

Joanna's knees knocked together from cold and weariness. "Might I come within and get dry by your fire?"

Longford grunted and stood aside. "Come within before the Lord God drowns you."

He closed the door behind her. "How fares your brother Hugh?"

"I have had no news of him in six years. But I hope to find him."

"Ah." Longford scratched his beard again. "I remember something about you. What was it? You were off to learn housewifery from your aunt. You were betrothed then." He touched her veil. "I thought your betrothed was a mortal husband, not our Lord God.

Joanna stepped backward, discomfited by the man's nearness. "I changed my mind."

"Hm. I reckon you do not represent St. Clement's in offering this relic. You've had another change of mind, eh?"

Joanna hesitated. It seemed too soon to come to this point. But she had little choice. "I have stolen the relic. I need funds to travel. I mean to find my brother, Hugh."

Longford raised an eyebrow. "Do you now?"

He gestured for her to sit by the fire. "Wine, Maddy," he yelled. He sat back and nodded at Joanna's muddy habit. "You'll never get warm in those damp clothes. Maddy will loan you something dry." He grinned at her.

Joanna thanked him. But his grin did not have a comforting effect.

It had been a year of deluges, and August was no drier. John Thoresby stared gloomily out the window at the muddy Ouse rushing along the lower garden, the heavy rain pommeling the flowers so that they floated limply in the water pooling in the beds. Of the palaces that had come to Thoresby as Archbishop of York, Bishopthorpe was his favorite. But this summer it was more ark than palace; the roof leaked in almost every room and the water level had risen to threaten the undercroft. Thoresby had rushed back to Bishopthorpe to preside over the Lammas Fair, looking forward to a rest from the endless politics of the royal wedding which had kept him at Windsor. He had been anxious to doff his Lord Chancellor's chain for a few months, get back to the business of God. But the rain had done its best to ruin the fair, he felt imprisoned in this great, leaking palace, and no one had good news for him, including the two men sitting by the fire.

One was his nephew, Richard de Ravenser, provost of Beverley Minster. Prominent bones, deep-set eyes, strong chin, a face that might be handsome with more flesh. It was as if Thoresby gazed at his own reflection with years erased. Did his sister look so like him? Or had she stared at him too intently when she carried Richard?

Ravenser's news was an administrative headache. A nun of St. Clement's, York, had run away and the prioress had not reported the incident. An irresponsible prioress could cause continuing problems.

Across from Thoresby's mirror image sat a dark-haired, broad-shouldered man with a patch over his left eye. Owen Archer had spent July searching for the murderers of a mercer whose body had been found in the minster liberty. Archer reported no luck—discouraging news, because if he could not find the guilty parties, they would not be found.

But Richard and Archer were not to blame for their news. Thoresby resolved to put aside his gloom as best he could. "Come, gentlemen, it is time to join the other guests for dinner."

Owen gave Thoresby a questioning look. "You are certain you wish me to dine with your friends, Your Grace?"

Thoresby sniffed. "Not friends, Archer. We traveled together from Windsor. Nicholas de Louth and William of Wykeham are canons of Beverley, returning with Richard to satisfy their terms of residency. I could hardly refuse them hospitality when their provost is my nephew."

Ravenser bowed to his uncle. "I am grateful for this, Your Grace. I know that Wykeham is hardly a welcome guest in your house."

Thoresby lifted his Lord Chancellor's chain and let it drop against his chest. "The man who seeks to relieve me of this weight? Perhaps I should thank him for it. But I confess I smile at him with my teeth clenched. I have got the habit of power."

Nicholas de Louth and William of Wykeham stood near the hearth in the great hall, warming their feet by the fire, their insides with wine. Both men lived mostly at court, Nicholas de Louth as a clerk in the service of Prince Edward, William of Wykeham as Keeper of the Privy Seal and King Edward's chief architect. Louth, a fleshy man, elegantly dressed, chatted amiably with Wykeham. The latter did not call attention to his appearance, but dressed soberly, in shades of gray and brown, and had no marks of distinction in his appearance. He was soft-spoken, with an earnest intentness about his eyes that might pass for intelligence.

As the five settled at the table, Thoresby spoke. "Forgive me if I seem distracted this evening, gentlemen. I have just learned that a nun from St. Clement's Priory in York has died of a fever in Beverley, a nun who had no permission to travel. She disappeared on St. Etheldreda's feast day." He watched Louth and Wykeham tally up the days from 23 June. "She had been missing more than a month, and the Reverend Mother had not reported her disappearance, nay, had excused Dame Joanna's absence with a story of illness, a convalescence at home."

"She was ill when she fled, then?" Wykeham asked.

"No. Though she had a pallor that might be mistaken for illness from fasting and praying through the spring."

"Ah. Lovesickness," Louth said. He smiled into his wine.

"On the contrary," Thoresby said. "Dame Isobel claimed the nun was the sort of young woman who believes that excesses of devotion bring her closer to God."

The company grew quiet while servants laid out the fish course. As they withdrew, Ravenser shook his head. "A serious discrepancy in the story, Your Grace. A devoted nun does not run away."

"Where in Beverley?" Louth asked, obviously caught up in his own thoughts.

Thoresby nodded to his nephew to continue the tale.

"A man kindly took her in when she collapsed in the street outside his house. She sank into a fever and died. The vicar of St. Mary's church agreed to bury her at once, fearful she might poison the air." Ravenser shook his head, sipped his wine. "But the priest wished me to inform His Grace and ask whether the family would want her body brought home to Leeds or whether the convent wished to claim her remains."

"Beverley needs occasional excitement to wake it up," Louth said with a cheerful grin. He chewed contentedly, his eyes half-closed, a man who enjoyed food and wine, particularly such excellent fare as one was served in Thoresby's household. "Who was the kind soul took her in?"

"Will Longford."

Louth leaned forward, suddenly wide awake. "Longford. A one-legged bear of a man?" He dabbed the grease from his chin.

Ravenser shrugged. "I have not had the honor of meeting him."

Thoresby was interested. "You know him, Sir Nicholas?"

"I have had occasion to question Longford for the Prince," Louth said with a dismissing shrug. "He fought in the Free Companies under du Guesclin."

"A peculiar good Samaritan," Owen said. "I wonder what inspired such a man to tend a sick nun?"

Thoresby found that curious indeed. The Free Companies were bands of renegade soldiers with no national allegiance—though most were abandoned English soldiers—who terrorized the French countryside and then extorted protection money from the frightened people. A most unlikely source of charity.

Louth lifted an eyebrow. "An odd sympathy indeed from a man who has most like raped and killed nuns across the Channel."

Ravenser nodded. "I daresay she was a piteous sight." His posture toward Louth indicated an impatience with the man's behavior.

Wykeham sat pensively holding a piece of bread in mid-air. Thoresby wondered what he was thinking. Sensing the archbishop's eyes on him, Wykeham turned to his host. "What drew her to Beverley?"

Thoresby gave a fleeting smile. "An excellent question to which I have no answer."

"An unfortunate story."

"Perhaps her family can enlighten us," Louth suggested. "What was her name?"

"Joanna Calverley," Thoresby said. "I have asked Dame Isobel de Percy to inform her family. Perhaps she will learn something more."

"Of Leeds, you said?" Louth asked.

Ravenser nodded.

"It is curious," Louth said. "Why did she flee to Beverley, not Leeds?"

"Why indeed." Thoresby sipped his wine. There was more to this than a runaway nun. He felt it in his bones. The others went on to more amiable topics through the two meat courses while Thoresby brooded.

As the servants cleared and brought out the brandywine, Thoresby returned to the subject. "Why is the Prince interested in Longford, Sir Nicholas?"

Louth tapped his fingers on his cup and looked around at the company, weighing how much to say. "Now that du Guesclin is a captain in the service of King Charles of France, Prince Edward would like to know all he can about a man he will inevitably face in battle."

"And was Longford helpful?" Ravenser asked.

Louth laughed. "Helpful? You would not ask had you ever met him. A slippery man, Will Longford. Much to hide. Oh, he told us a few things, but nothing to compromise du Guesclin."

Owen leaned forward, his good eye turned to study Louth. "So it was not just information you wanted."

Louth squirmed under the hawklike regard. "I have the house watched."

Wykeham was interested. "What do you think he does for du Guesclin?"

Louth shrugged. "I have proof of nothing. But men who might fight for our King have been taking ship to the continent to join the Free Companies."

"Thus weakening us." Thoresby nodded. "So you watch Longford's house, and yet no one reported the arrival of a solitary nun."

Louth sighed. "I know. What else have my men missed, you wonder. So do I."

Wykeham noticed Thoresby's brooding expression. "You think there is more to this nun's death than an unhappy runaway struck down with fever?"

Thoresby met the eyes of the man who was positioning himself to take over as Lord Chancellor. Perhaps they were intelligent eyes. He shrugged.

"A nun runs away to a lover. 'Tis always the story," Louth said, pouring more brandywine, though his face was flushed by what he had already imbibed. "Think no more of it."

Thoresby closed his eyes, weary of idle speculation. He would like to know more about the dead nun, yet what would be the gain? She was dead, buried. He tapped his fingers impatiently in time with the steady plop of a new leak behind him, near the window. Perhaps the ominous ache in his bones was just the rain and his too many years of living.

1

LAMENTATIONS OF THE DEAD

LATE MAY 1366

Nicholas de Louth dropped his work and hurried out to the hall to greet Maddy, Will Longford's servant. Surely she would not have come to Louth's house unless she had gotten word of her master.

Longford had disappeared in March, slipped away in the night. When a few days passed with no signs of activity in and round the house, Louth had his men break in. They found not a soul, not even the servant, Maddy. She was discovered at her parents' house, complaining of her abandonment. She said one evening Longford had told her to leave, that he and his man Jaro were going away. "With no more notice than that. He might have told me sooner. I might have arranged for work. I've no wages now." Longford had said he would come for her when he returned. "He left that night. I've heard nothing since."

A search had revealed that someone had gone through Longford's house before Louth's men, scattering things everywhere. They had found more than a dozen daggers, several swords of French make, one of Italian, and—the prize—a letter with Bertrand du Guesclin's seal acknowledging monies owed Longford. It was not proof of treason, not even signed, but it was a link with du Guesclin, however ambiguous. Louth would be less gentle in questioning Longford next time. They had also found some puzzling items, including a bottle of Italian glass that held a white powder. Maddy recognized it. She said the nun who had died at Longford's the previous summer had brought it with her, offering it to Longford as a relic. Louth had taken it home with the weapons and the letter.

A generously hefty bag of coins had convinced Maddy to stay at the house. She was to alert them if Longford returned or anyone else showed up.

Had Maddy come to Louth to report visitors this morning?

He found her sitting in a chair by the fire, a thin young woman clutching a mazer of mulled wine in trembling hands. When he greeted her, she lifted up to him eyes red-rimmed and frightened. "I cannot go back there, Sir. I dare not!"

"What is it, Maddy? Has your master returned?"

She shook her head. "'Tis the ghost of poor Dame Joanna. She's come back for the milk of the Virgin. Weeping and wailing and beating her chest and praying that she should die. She's not at rest, Sir."

Louth did not absorb Maddy's story at once, so far was it from what he had expected. "Dame Joanna? What can you mean, child?"

Maddy took a gulp of wine. It did not ease her tremors. "Please, sir. 'Tis just as they say, the dead walk when they are not at peace. 'Tis Dame Joanna—she's come back because of the relic. She must have the bottle she brought to my master."

By now Louth had caught the drift of the girl's story. "Dame Joanna, whom your master buried last summer? She has returned? She is at the house now?"

Maddy crossed herself and nodded. "I came to you straight away. I'd come in from the kitchen to open the shutters. I do it midmorning everyday, to keep it fresh in there in case the master returns. There she was, in the corner by the shelves, wrapped in a blue shawl, whispering about the milk of the Virgin. Such a ghostly voice. Like angels' wings aflutter. And when she'd searched all the shelves she fell to her knees and wept and beat at her breast. Oh, sir, the lamentations of the dead are not for us to hear unless we may help them! You must return the bottle!"

Louth was not one to believe in the dead walking, but until now Maddy had seemed to him a sensible and trustworthy young woman, not one to lose her head. "You think this apparition seeks the relic Dame Joanna brought from St. Clement's?"

Maddy nodded and took another gulp of wine.

"Was she in the house when you left?"

Maddy nodded again and crossed herself.

It was not what Louth had hoped. Nor did he believe that the dead would walk for the sake of a lost relic. Men with far more reason to lie unquiet in their graves stayed put. But Maddy had stuck to her post until this moment, and she deserved his attention. Could this be a clever ruse to get Maddy out of the house? After more than a month of close watch, had someone fooled them to get inside? The thought propelled Louth to act.

He instructed a servant to hurry to the provost's house and ask him to come to Longford's. "Sir Richard might be at Mass at the minster. Do your best to get him as quickly as you may." Louth called for his squire.

"Now, Maddy, do you wish to come or stay here where it is safe and warm?"

Maddy glanced at the fire with longing, but shook her head. "'Tis my place to come, sir. And I must see for myself what you see. I will not rest if I am not sure what happened."

Louth admired her pluck. "Then come along. We must not keep her waiting."

Though it was beyond mid morning on a sunny day, the light was dim inside Longford's house. Louth heard the woman, alternately weeping and whispering, before he made out her form in the shadowy corner. He could not understand what she said. As his eyes grew accustomed to the dark, he noted that the windows across the room from the apparition were still shuttered. He motioned for his squire to open them. The apparition threw up a slender hand to protect her eyes from the light. A decidedly physical gesture, Louth thought. He doubted that a spirit's eyes would be sensitive to light.

Louth crept up to within a few feet of the blue-draped figure, close enough that he could reach out and touch her head. He could see little more than a light blue mantle or shawl, stained and torn, wrapped about a slender form. The hand held up to the face was dirty. The figure had a strong, moldy scent, but it was the odor of unwashed flesh and clothing, not decay. So, Louth reasoned, neither a spirit nor a corpse.

"Who are you, Mistress?" He spoke in a gentle tone, but loudly enough to be heard over her whispering.

She pounded her chest thrice and murmured, "*Mea culpa, mea culpa, mea maxima culpa,*" then sobbed and crumpled to the floor. Louth did not know what to make of it. He was relieved when Ravenser slipped quietly in the front door and joined him. The provost crouched by the inert figure, sniffed, rose quickly, putting a handkerchief to his nose. "Who is she?" he whispered.

Louth shrugged. "I know not. But she is a fleshly apparition, I think." He knelt down and gently pulled the mantle back, uncovering greasy, matted hair. The woman seemed unconscious. Louth cautiously turned her over and touched the delicate, tear-stained face. "Come, Maddy," Louth called softly. "She is warm to the touch, a living being. Tell us if this is Dame Joanna."

Maddy tiptoed forward, a hand stretched out in front as if to protect herself from a sudden attack. When she was still too far away to see the woman's features in the dim light, she said, "She was not so thin as that, sir."

"Come closer. I have touched her and have not suffered." Louth reached back to Maddy. "Come. Tell us if it is she."

Maddy crept close, then recoiled.

Louth nodded. "It is the smell of unwashed body, unwashed clothes, Maddy, not decay. Come. Look at her face. Is this Dame Joanna?" The woman lay still, her eyes closed.

Maddy leaned close, then jumped away, nodding. "'Tis her."

"Are you certain?"

"As much as I can be. If I saw the color of her eyes, I should be certain. I have never seen the like. Clear green, if you can imagine."

Louth sat back on his heels, wondering how to proceed. "Is there a fire in the kitchen, Maddy?"

"Aye, sir."

Louth's squire, John, crouched down beside him. "Shall I carry her there?"

Louth nodded.

John scooped up the woman and stood. Maddy hurried before him, leading the way to the kitchen. Louth pulled two benches together near the fire and John gently laid down his burden. The woman stirred, eyelids fluttering.

"Some brandywine, Maddy!" Louth called.

The serving girl brought a cup. As Louth lifted the woman's head, he noted that her hair was pale red. He was more and more confident that this was Dame Joanna. He put the cup to the woman's mouth and whispered, "Drink slowly." Some of the wine spilled down her chin. A hand fluttered up to the cup, touched it. The lips parted. She drank, then coughed. Louth helped her sit up. Her eyes opened, but did not focus. Clear green eyes stared out into the distance.

Maddy nodded. "You see the eyes. 'Tis her."

Louth held the cup to Dame Joanna's lips and she drank again, then pushed it away. "Can you understand me, Dame Joanna?" The green eyes glanced at Louth with no expression. He was uncertain whether she even saw him. "You are in Will Longford's house in Beverley. Can you tell us what happened to you?"

The pale brows came together in a frown. Then the eyes cleared and focused on his. She grabbed his shoulder. "The milk of the Virgin. Is it here?"

"It is close by."

"I must return it."

"You must return it to St. Clement's?" Louth asked.

"I wear Our Lady's mantle, you see." She clutched the blue shawl to her. "I have risen from the dead—as did Our Lady. But it should not have happened so. I am a Magdalene. Our Lady said I must return to die."

"Our Lady told you that?"

The eyes opened wide, guileless, innocent. "The Blessed Virgin Mary is watching over me."

Louth glanced at the provost, back to the nun. "You had a vision?"

The eyes filled with tears, the head drooped backward against Louth's arm. "I must return," she whimpered, her eyes fluttering shut.

"Dame Joanna?" Louth whispered.

Joanna muttered something incoherent.

Louth lay her back down on the benches, looked up at Ravenser. "What do you think?"

Ravenser frowned down at the nun, pursed his lips, shook his head. "I do not like such things—Our Lady's mantle, rising from the dead."

They both gazed down at the woman, dirty, ravaged by hunger. "She is lovely, even in this condition," Louth said with a sigh.

Ravenser glanced up, surprised by the comment. "A peculiar thing to be thinking."

Louth shrugged. "She touches something in me. Her delicacy. Her desperation." He shook himself and pulled himself up straight.

"We shall take her to Nunburton Abbey," Ravenser said. "There she can be tended and watched."

Maddy looked from one to the other. "She is truly alive?"

Ravenser smiled. "Yes, Maddy, truly alive. Now tell me. Did you actually see her dead?"

Maddy thought, shook her head.

"But you prepared her for burial?"

"No. I was at market. I came back and she was wrapped in a shroud."

Ravenser glanced at Louth, back to Maddy. "Dame Joanna died while you were out?"

Maddy stared down at her feet, tears welling in her eyes. "It was so sad. I wouldn't've gone if I'd seen she was worsening."

Louth did not like this new information. "You thought she was improving?"

Maddy nodded. "She'd been up and dining with them."

"Longford and Jaro?"

Maddy nodded. "And their two visitors."

Visitors. All this time Maddy had mentioned only Will Longford and his man Jaro. But then, Louth had been interested only in

Longford. "I will send for you tomorrow, Maddy. You must tell me everything you remember about Dame Joanna's days in this house."

"But who's to watch the house while I'm gone, sir?"

"I will set a watch, Maddy. I am more anxious than ever to find your master."

Richard de Ravenser left Dame Joanna, still in a faint, in the competent hands of his housekeeper and rode out to the Abbey of Nunburton. The abbess returned with him and took charge of Joanna. It occurred to Ravenser as he watched the litter and escort depart that he should write to his uncle, the archbishop, who had shown an interest in the nun's story last summer. But what could Ravenser report? Perhaps he should wait until he and Louth had talked to Maddy again.

Maddy did not like being alone in the house. She had heard Dame Joanna say she had risen from the dead, no matter that Sir Nicholas said it was untrue. Maddy knew the stench of the grave—its odor lingered in the rooms. And the way Dame Joanna had wept—that was not a holy vision. More like the dead returning to haunt the living.

Maddy distracted herself with fantasies about John, Sir Nicholas's squire. So courteous and handsome, so richly dressed. Maddy imagined lying in John's arms, close to his heart, as Dame Joanna had. John had shown such tender concern for Joanna, gently cradling her head to help her drink. Oh, that it had been Maddy! She went to market for a blue mantle, found a large shawl that sufficed. Back at the house, she draped the blue shawl round her and danced about the hall. In her imagination John came in, found her a breathtaking vision. He scooped her up in his arms and carried her up to the master's bedchamber.

At sunset, Maddy's dance was interrupted by the creak of the hall door. She had not yet latched it for the night, nor had she fastened the shutters. The gray twilight was the only light in the hall. She held her breath, listening. She heard nothing more, but she sensed someone in the shadows.

"Who is there?"

No answer, but now she could hear breathing, quick and excited.

"This is Master Longford's house." Maddy tried to sound stern. "You cannot just walk in off the street."

The intruder laughed, a sharp cackle of a laugh that echoed weirdly in the darkening hall.

Maddy crept toward the door that led out back to the kitchen. She could run out into the street if she could get there first. Her way brought her into the silvery light from one of the open windows. She pulled the shawl tighter and hurried.

Someone grabbed at the shawl, pulled her backward. Maddy screamed, fumbled with the knot she'd made to fasten the shawl beneath her chin. An arm squeezed her waist. "So slender," a voice hissed in her ear. The man stank of onions and sweat. This was nothing like Maddy's imaginings. She gave up on the knot, tried to pull free of his grasp. His other arm came round her neck, then eased, feeling the knot. He yanked the shawl down off her head, twisted it so the knot pressed into her throat. Her screams were choked into desperate coughs. Maddy's eyes hurt from the pressure in her head. She could not breathe. Her legs gave out. The knot pressed in, tighter, tighter. Sweet Jesu, it had been but an innocent fantasy…

Louth showed Sir Thomas, the vicar of St. Mary's, into his parlor. He hoped to learn more about the events surrounding Dame Joanna's time in Beverley. The priest seemed a likely informant, having given Joanna the last rites and buried her; but past experience with Sir Thomas prepared Louth for a difficult time. The man was devoted to his own self-preservation, nothing more. "Longford's servant mentioned two visitors, Sir Thomas. Did Longford have any companions other than Jaro at Dame Joanna's grave?"

The priest frowned down at his muddy boots. "Two men." He raised his dull eyes to Louth. "Yes. I remember them."

"Had you ever seen them before?"

The priest shook his head.

"Describe them to me."

"I am afraid I can be of little help." Sir Thomas mopped his forehead with a large handkerchief. "My eyes have failed me of late."

Louth thought the blank stare bespoke a slothful nature rather than failing eyesight. Would he not squint more in an effort to focus? Louth sighed. He had a critical, uncharitable streak for which he continually did penance. "Tell me what you can, Sir Thomas. Anything will be most appreciated."

The priest's face contorted in a childish fashion as he bit the inside of his mouth. Louth averted his eyes. "Longford is a dangerous man, Sir Nicholas. Much feared in Beverley."

"All I ask is that you tell me what you recall," Louth said with increasing impatience.

The priest mopped his forehead again as he glanced round the room. "One was tall, fair-haired. He spoke like a foreigner. A Dane. Perhaps a Norseman. The other was of average height, sturdy build but not overly muscular. Thinning hair. Gentle spoken."

"Were they referred to by name in your presence?"

Sir Thomas shook his head. Too quickly for Louth's taste. The other questions had not been answered with such speed.

"You gave Dame Joanna the last rites. Did you believe she was dead?"

"Oh no. No. Longford said she was dying. And she did seem weak and pale. Her hands were cold, her forehead, too, as I recall."

"You buried her in haste. Why was that?"

The priest squirmed under the intent regard. "It was to be temporary, until her family came for her. We worried it might be plague, you see."

"Who suggested plague?"

The priest chewed the inside of his mouth and thought. "Jaro. 'Twas he suggested it. Said the body stank of plague and he would not have her in his kitchen. You cannot know how I prayed over it."

Louth had no trouble believing that the priest had prayed—but for his own health, not for guidance.

"Has there been any—disturbance—around her grave?"

The priest looked nervous. "What sort of disturbance?"

Louth pressed his fingers together and closed his eyes, calming himself. "Does the grave look as if it has been untouched since the so-called funeral of Dame Joanna?"

Sir Thomas took a deep breath. "I tell no tales, but since I heard of her return, I went to look, and, I must say, something has been at the grave in the past year. Though not so recently as Dame Joanna's resurrection. Then again, would a body disturb the earth as it rose from the grave? Seems to me—"

"She did not rise from the dead," Louth said sternly.

"No. No, of course not." The priest blotted his forehead.

"Did Dame Joanna wear a blue mantle when you attended her?"

"Our Lady's mantle? Alas, no. I did not have the good fortune to touch it."

Louth sighed. "Yes. Thank you, Sir Thomas." He rose with the priest, escorted him out, called for his squire. "Come, John, let us visit little Maddy and ask her about the two men."

John knocked on the whitewashed door of Longford's house. It swung open. He glanced back at Louth, puzzled. Louth nodded. They drew their daggers. John stepped inside, Louth followed. The afternoon sun poured through the unshuttered windows, illuminating overturned chairs and benches. An oil lamp lay on the floor next to a scorched chair. The house was silent but for a bird that took fright at their entrance.

"Maddy?" Louth whispered. He cleared his throat, repeated her name loudly. No answer. He moved slowly toward the door that led to the kitchen, stepped through, stopped with a sense of dread at the bloodstains in the courtyard, an uneven trail that connected the hall with the kitchen. He opened the kitchen door. "Sweet Heaven."

Cooking pots lay shattered on the stone floor, the remains of a stew coagulated in a pot over the pale embers of the cook fire, wine pooled on a trestle table, dripped onto the floor. "Maddy?" A curtain was drawn across an alcove. Probably Jaro's pallet. John reached it first, pulled back the curtain, turned away with a strangled cry.

Louth crossed himself and joined his squire. Maddy lay on the wide pallet, coins on her eyes, her hands folded neatly on her breast, fully clothed, draped in a blue shawl. But the swollen face, split lip, the blood on her skirt and hands, and most of all the ugly dark bruise on her throat made it plain that Maddy's death had not been peaceful, much as someone carefully arranged her afterward. Poor little Maddy. Louth fell to his knees and wept.

Louth's round, usually ruddy face was pale the next morning, his eyes shadowed. Ravenser invited him out into his garden, where the sun might draw the chill of death from his bones.

"What have they done with Maddy's body?" Louth asked.

"I have claimed it. The bailiff and the coroner will deliver her to me."

Louth leaned forward to touch Ravenser's hand. "God bless you, Richard. Pray, let me bear the expense of her burial."

Ravenser withdrew his hand, discomfited by the canon's emotion. "Why should you bear the expense?"

"In Heaven's name, it is my fault that she is dead. What was I thinking to leave her there alone?"

Ravenser bowed his head to hide his agreement. "Did you notice the blue shawl, how like Dame Joanna's it is?" Best to engage Louth in searching for answers. The peacock would have made note of the bright shawl.

"The blue shawl." Louth nodded. "Yes, I did note how like it was."

"I wonder why she wore it? The day was warm."

"It must have happened last night."

"Yet she was fully dressed."

Louth raised a dimpled hand to dab at his eyes. "I shall never forgive myself. Maddy looked to me for protection while Longford is away. He may be a mercenary, and all the unsavory things they say of him may be true, but Maddy was safe under his care."

"You do not think it might have been Longford who killed her?"

"What?" Louth looked puzzled.

"Might he have walked in, thought she was Dame Joanna in that blue shawl?"

Sweat beaded on Louth's fleshy face as he considered it.

Ravenser did not like the heavy man's pallor, his shallow breathing. "Now that I think of it, we do not know whether Joanna had that mantle when she was here with Longford."

Louth blinked rapidly. "Of course. It need not have been Longford. Perhaps someone else mistook her for Joanna Calverley. Or perhaps—do you suppose they wrapped the shawl round Maddy as a warning?"

The possibility made Ravenser uneasy. He wanted a simple solution, involving as few people as possible. "We have no proof of it, Nicholas."

Louth sighed, dabbed at his upper lip. "Has the abbess learned anything from Dame Joanna?"

A safer topic. "She says the nun speaks dizzying nonsense." Ravenser stood up. "I see no choice but to open the grave they dug with such haste, see whether it reveals aught."

Louth crossed himself. "You do not mean to bury Maddy there?"

Ravenser looked at the canon askance. "Do you think me a monster?"

Louth rubbed his eyes. "Forgive me. I shall attend you at the grave, if you do not mind."

"I welcome your company, I assure you. It is not a thing I do lightly. I would also like you to send out your men to stir up gossip, see whether they learn anything new about Will Longford. Or Maddy. Let me know tomorrow morning what you've heard."

• • •

What Louth learned from his men about Longford's reputation surprised neither him nor Ravenser. Longford was universally disliked, distrusted. His appetite for women had led most folk, upon hearing of the death of the nun in his house, to surmise that Longford had abducted, raped, then rejected the poor young woman, and she had died of shame or fear for her immortal soul. Some even suggested he had poisoned her. Now, with the news of Dame Joanna's return, the consensus was that she had run away with Longford (no matter the delay in his departure) and now he had rejected her. Some cynical souls even hoped that the nun had killed him.

"*Not* a romantic figure," Louth said.

Ravenser leaned back, his slender hands behind his head, and stared at the ceiling. "Eight months before he followed her. What if she was with child and he went to meet her after the birth? Then something happened to separate the happy family?"

"Then where is the baby?"

Ravenser sat up. "Dead? Might that be why the grave has been disturbed?"

"Or perhaps she lied about being with child. He discovered it. Rejected her."

Ravenser smiled. "We spin a good yarn."

Louth did not smile. "As I see it, Dame Joanna ran away to be with a lover, who may or may not be Longford, and something went wrong. Perhaps so wrong that he followed her back here to kill her."

"But why would he have raped Maddy?"

Louth closed his eyes, shook his head. "My men heard nothing ill of her. A hard worker, bit of a dreamer." He dabbed at his eyes. "The poor, sweet child."

Old Dan took off his dusty cap and scratched his bald head. "A man buries so many as I have, can't recall 'em all. But I remember Master Longford buryin' someone, aye."

"Do you remember anything else about it?"

The old man wriggled in his ragged clothes as if the question made him itch. "Not as such, Sir."

"Is that a yea or a nay?"

"I remember the ale, Sir. A wondrous brew, thick and strong. The kind you chew before you swallow." He grinned at the memory.

"Someone brought it while you filled in the grave?"

Old Dan crushed the hat in his hands, stared down at his dirty boots. "I shouldn't've touched it before 'twas done, but dear Lord, it was one of the sunniest days of that wet summer and steam come up at me with every spadeful of earth. It near boiled me. A thirsty man will drink."

"I am not judging you, Dan. Who brought you the ale?"

"Master Longford hisself."

"Do you remember filling the grave while you sampled the ale, Dan?"

A dirty hand crept back up to the bald head, scratching. "Now there's the problem, you see. I can't say as I remember the filling in, but I've been digging graves all my life and I'm sure I did it right."

"Did anyone help you? Longford, perhaps?"

Old Dan shrugged. "To speak truth, I can swear to naught once I tasted that wondrous brew."

"You know what you're to do now, Dan?"

"They spoke true, then? You want it dug up?"

"It must be done. Have you the stomach for it?"

"Don't know till I do. But if it must be done—" Dan shrugged. "Can't say as I wouldn't welcome company."

"I shall accompany you." Ravenser wished to keep this incident quiet if possible. "And Sir Nicholas, also."

It had rained in the night. The morning was dry but overcast, the air heavy. Old Dan and his son fell to the task in silence, but soon they cursed the saturated earth. As they dug, water seeped in to fill the hole and make the soil heavy to lift.

Ravenser slipped into his own thoughts. What if they found the real Dame Joanna rotting in her shroud? Then who was the woman at Nunburton who claimed to be the Virgin resurrected? The Abbess of Nunburton had noted that the woman's French was genteel and her clothes, though travel-stained and torn, were new, not mended, and of costly wool. She also noted that the supposedly ancient, sacred mantle looked like good Yorkshire wool. Why would someone claim to be a dead person? What was to be gained? Was she dangerous? Or just confused?

"They have reached the body," Louth said quietly.

Ravenser apologized for his inattention. "I have been pondering this strange case."

"Here we are," Old Dan called out. "Knotted up in her shroud, just as I remember. Shall we lift her out, Sir Richard?"

Ravenser knelt down and slipped his knife through the upper knot, blinking back the tears the odor brought to his eyes. "I should think we can come to a conclusion with a peek."

"Lord ha' mercy!" Old Dan covered his mouth and nose with a dirty kerchief as Ravenser peeled back the sheet. "Don't like the looks of 'em when there's still flesh. Nor the stink."

"What have we here?" Ravenser muttered. "Much too much flesh for a year-old corpse, and it is not Dame Joanna, but a man with a broken neck. A huge man."

Louth held a scented cloth to his plump face and leaned down, examining the face and body. "Unmistakable. That is Jaro, Longford's man." Louth pointed to an amulet on the chest. "The tooth of an animal he killed in the Pyrenees. Proud of it, he was. But his girth is enough to identify him." He turned quickly away.

Ravenser's gut burned. How in God's name had Will Longford's man wound up in this grave? He rose. "Fill it back in, Dan, and say nothing to anyone. I must notify the mayor, the coroner, the bailiffs"— he passed a hand over his eyes, sighed—"and the Archbishop of York."

As they walked away, Louth asked what Ravenser meant to do with Dame Joanna.

"I shall ask my uncle to allow me to escort her back to her convent. Perhaps she will be more coherent with her Mother Superior, someone familiar. But after all this, the escort must be well guarded."

"I shall attend you. With my men."

"You, Nicholas?"

"I feel responsible."

As well he should. Ravenser agreed.

2

TO YORK

Five days later, Ravenser, Louth, and company set off on a slow journey to York. Dame Joanna was still weak, so she rode in a cart with two sisters who would see to her needs along the way. Traveling with a cart slowed them, but June had begun with fair, mild weather that almost made Ravenser glad of the excuse to go journeying. As the sun warmed him and the smells and sounds of the countryside cheered him, he grew more confident that the prioress of St. Clement's would find a way to reach Dame Joanna and learn her story, and the archbishop's men would soon discover who had killed Maddy and Jaro. The mayor of Beverley had been relieved to hear that Archbishop Thoresby had offered his aid.

Ravenser fell back behind his companions, thinking about his uncle and the one-eyed spy he had met at Bishopthorpe. He wondered what sorts of inquiries Archer made for a man so powerful as his uncle—Archbishop of York and Lord Chancellor of England. Was he watching Alice Perrers and William of Wykeham? Or would Archer consider helping out on a matter such as this? Ravenser gazed about him, focusing on nothing, until a movement off to the side of the road, in a stand of trees, caught his eye. Two horsemen, riding neither toward the road nor away from the road, but pacing Ravenser's company. Ravenser reigned in his horse. So did the horsemen.

"Ho, there!" Ravenser called. Two of Louth's men reigned in and turned at his cry. Ravenser nodded to the still figures in the trees. Louth's men took off. So did the horsemen, who had the advantage of their own plan.

It was not long before Louth's men came riding back to the shady knoll where the rest of the company waited. "We lost them," John, Louth's squire, said, "but we did see that they had friends with them, waiting for them farther back. I counted five more. And well armed."

Dame Joanna stared about her, agitated, clutching at the tattered blue shawl she insisted on wearing over her habit. "Who? Who follows?"

Louth lounged in the shade near her. "I thought you might tell us, Dame Joanna. Your lover, perhaps?"

"My lover?" She laughed, an odd, hysterical sound. Her eyes were wild, haunted. "Oh, indeed, if Death be now my lover. Yes. Death shadows me. Only my lover Death can come for me now."

Ravenser raised an eyebrow in response to Louth's puzzled glance. So Dame Joanna saw her dilemma as a morality play. It did no harm. "Shall we continue?"

Louth ordered his men to prepare to move on. They fell back to guard the rear of the party. It was a much subdued, anxious company, aware of the armed men behind them, unseen. The women did not protest the armed guard that accompanied them when they washed or relieved themselves.

The wind from the arrow's flight ruffled Owen's hair. Much too close for comfort. He'd seen the trainee's aim go astray when the messenger entered the yard. Owen had stood his ground, wanting to make a point, that lives were at stake. But he had not meant to make it so dangerously—he had miscalculated the arrow's trajectory. It had happened time and again since he lost the use of his left eye.

Gaspare yanked the bow out of the trainee's hands and hit him across the stomach with it. "What are you, a dog after a hare? Captain Owen comes all the way from York to teach you how to save yourself in the field and you'd be killing him? Because a messenger caught your eye? What manner of cur has Lancaster sent us?"

The young man clutched his middle and said nothing.

Gaspare crossed the castle yard to retrieve the arrow, slapping Owen on the back as he passed. "You've not lost your nerve, that's clear." He grinned crookedly because of a scar that puckered the right side of his face from ear to chin, creasing the corner of his mouth. "So what am I doing wrong, old friend? Why can't the cur resist gawking at the world?"

"You're right to call him a dog after a hare," Owen said. "If he cannot ignore everything round him and see only the arrow and its target, he cannot be an archer."

Gaspare slapped the arrow shaft against his leg, a motion that the young man in question watched anxiously. Broad shouldered and well-muscled, when Gaspare acted on his anger, he caused considerable pain. "I need to know. Is it me, or has Lancaster sent us a pack of fools?"

Owen said nothing. The messenger, now within earshot, wore the livery of John Thoresby, Archbishop of York and Lord Chancellor of England. *What now?* Owen wondered. Thoresby had encouraged Owen to take up his present task at the Queen's castle of Knaresborough, helping two of his old comrades-in-arms, Lief and Gaspare, develop a strategy for training archers in a mere two weeks. The Duke of Lancaster was to sail for the Aquitaine in the autumn with one hundred trained archers—if attempts at negotiating the restoration of Don Pedro to the throne of Castile failed. Meanwhile, Lancaster did not want to feed a hundred archers any longer than necessary. Thus this experiment in training seven men in a fortnight. They were to be presented to Lancaster at Pontefract after their training, where he would judge whether their skills were acceptable.

"From His Grace the Archbishop, Captain Archer." The messenger handed Owen a sealed packet. "I'm to await your reply."

"Take yourself off to the kitchens. I'll find you there."

Gaspare noticed his friend's clenched jaw. "Likely to be bad news, coming from the mighty Thoresby?"

"More likely to be orders."

"You've no love for him, that I can see."

"I do not like being his puppet."

"You did much the same work for the old Duke."

"Henry of Grosmont was a soldier. I understood him. I trusted him."

"Ah." Gaspare glanced over at the waiting trainee. "So. What am I to do with this 'archer' who shoots his captain by mistake?"

Owen scratched the scar beneath his patch with the Archbishop's letter as he thought. "We have not the time to change his character. Nor the one who swatted a fly earlier. Release them. Expend your effort on the other five."

Gaspare nodded. "With pleasure." He tapped the letter. "Think you Thoresby means to call you back so soon?"

Owen looked down at the packet in his hand. "It is the sort of thing he would do. I had best go and read it."

Knaresborough sat on a precipitous cliff over the River Nidd. The trees that grew on the cliff were oddly twisted and stunted by their lifelong struggle to cling to the soil and sink their roots in horizontally. Owen stood atop the keep gazing down to the rushing river, remembering another precipitous cliff, another river. He had climbed the mountain with his father and his brother, Dafydd. At the top, Dafydd dared Owen to walk to the edge and look down. Their father had laughed. "To look down is nothing, Dafydd, for your eyes can see it is far to fall, and you will not be tempted." Owen's father had made them sit close to the edge and look down, then told them to shut one eye and look down. "You see how God protects us? He gave us two eyes that we might see the depths of Hell and seek to move upward." It was one of Owen's best memories of his father, a rare moment when he had time to take a day with his sons.

But now Owen gazed down a precipice with but one working eye, and it looked as if he could reach down and scoop up the river water in his hands. Folk made light of his blinding. But as an active man, Owen felt the loss every day. Balance, his vision to the left of him, and judgment of depth, distance, and trajectory, were all crippled by it. And his appearance made people uneasy. Owen would like to teach his child things such as the value of two eyes. But hearing the words from a scarred and crippled man, would the child listen?

Irritated with his self-pity, he tore open the letter from Thoresby, read quickly. The runaway nun from St. Clement's had reappeared. Odd, but no more than that. He read on. The rape and murder of Will Longford's maid, and his cook buried in the nun's grave with his neck broken—now those were more troublesome. Thoresby expressed an uneasiness about the business and ordered Owen to return to York. Owen could finish training the archers on St. George's Field; the archers could stay at York Castle. Meanwhile, Owen could begin inquiries into the matter. Meanwhile? What did he think, training archers occupied a few moments of his day?

Inquiries into what? Folk ran from unhappiness every day. So the nun stole a relic and went to Will Longford—that signified nothing unless he was a relic dealer. The fact that he had not sold the relic in a year suggested that he was not.

Well then, that raised the question of why he helped Joanna. No one had described her yet. Perhaps she appealed to Longford. But why the two murders? And where was Longford?

Owen shook himself. He was being drawn in.

A hand clamped down on his right shoulder. "This place suits Lancaster, eh?"

"A treacherous keep for a treacherous man, my friend." Owen would know that strong grip anywhere. How did Lief use those meaty hands to carve such delicate figures and sweet-voiced flutes?

Lief shrugged. "I meant it in a more complimentary way, but no matter." He followed Owen's gaze down the precipice. "Can you imagine the pitiful prayers of the poor souls who built this?"

"Aye, that I can. I have heard some of the men say Gaunt lusts for this castle. He shall have it in the end. Nothing stands in his way."

"And the tenants will be better for it."

Owen snorted.

"The Duke is not the tyrant you think him. Neither is he the old Duke. There will never be Henry of Grosmont's like again. But

Gaunt is a fair man, and wants the best for England."

Owen had been captain of archers to the old Duke and would gladly have laid down his life for the great warrior and statesman. The present Duke had yet to win his respect. "Lief, you are a fool."

"Well, when you meet the Duke at Pontefract you will see I am right." They were to deliver the archers to Pontefract Castle in a week.

Owen shrugged.

"What news from York?"

"His Grace orders us to York, where we may continue training while I look into the tale of a runaway nun who leaves a trail of corpses behind her." Owen scowled. "Does the man think I live only for him?"

Lief pressed Owen's shoulder. "I am relieved to hear it is a summons from the archbishop, not news of trouble at home. With Lucie expecting a child…" Lief sat down in a watchman's alcove, patted the stone ledge beside him.

Owen sat down. "He says nothing of Lucie."

"He's stirring up trouble again that will take you from your home, eh?" Lief drew a knife from a sheath at his waist, made the first cut in a block of wood he carried. "In my mind, that's the trouble with forbidding priests to follow their nature. If they had wives and families, they'd understand."

Owen had an odd grin on his face.

Lief frowned. "I'm happy to make you smile, but I'm damned if I know what I said to do it."

"My friend, you sounded philosophical just then."

Lief chuckled. "'Tis all the time I spend with you. You're such a thinker. Worse than ever, you are. A regular worrier."

"Aye, you're probably right about that." Owen had let the letter drop down beside him, and sat with his forearms on his thighs, his hands folded, his head drooping.

Lief whittled for a while. "And so why is that, Captain? Why are you ever in such a dark study?"

Owen shrugged. "I have more to worry about."

"The Archbishop, you mean?"

"Lucie and the baby."

Lief glanced over at his friend, surprised by the answer. "You cannot mean to say you are not happy to have a child on the way?"

"I thank God that He has blessed us."

Lief frowned. "Then is it Lucie? You do not love her?"

What were all these silly, wrongheaded questions? "I love her beyond measure."

"Then what ails you?" Lief asked, exasperated.

Lief would never change. Life was very simple to him, a handful of absolutes. "What if she dies in childbed? What if the child dies? What will a child think of me, scarred as I am? Will I frighten it?"

"Good God, man, you *do* think too much. It's ever been your problem. You have all the best in life—strength, honor, a beautiful wife, and soon the fruit of your union. Any other man would be puffed up with pride and giddy with joy."

Owen rubbed his scar beneath the patch. It was difficult to explain. "Lucie had a child once, a boy, Martin. He died before he could walk. Plague."

"Ah." Lief nodded over his energetic whittling. "So she's gloomy and fretful, eh?"

Owen shook his head. "No. That is not Lucie's way. She is determined that all will go well. But it is not up to us, is it? It's God's game in the end."

Lief paused, studied his friend's face. "Here's another piece of philosophy, then. It's no use worrying about what might happen. God's will is unknowable to the likes of us."

How true. And how maddening. If ever there were something Owen would give anything to control... "You are right. And you were right before when you guessed it was Thoresby making me worry. Before you sat down, I'd been wondering about the nun who ran away. She or someone else went to great lengths to make it look like she'd died. She was helped by a man, Longford. Had he gone after her, and she ran back to the convent for protection from him? Or was he kindly? Why is Longford's man buried in the nun's grave, his neck broken? Why was his maid murdered? Why was she wearing a blue shawl like Joanna's?"

Lief shook his head. "Is that what you do for the Chancellor? Make up questions?"

Owen laughed. "It amounts to that, indeed. But that was not my point. I was showing you how I must think to do Thoresby's work. Of course I'm thinking about all that could go wrong with Lucie. I've trained myself to think that way."

"No wonder you hate him."

Owen shrugged. "I don't know that I do hate him."

Lief glanced over at Owen. "God's blood, but you are a hard one to figure. Well, think about hating the archbishop for a while and give your family a rest, eh?" He handed Owen the carving, a featureless figure in an archbishop's robes.

Owen laughed, slapped Lief on the back. "Good advice, my philosophical friend. And a clever reminder." He picked up the letter and rose from the stone bench, stretching. "I should go back. Gaspare will think I've already ridden off to do battle in Thoresby's new cause."

Lief nodded, already absorbed in another piece of wood. "I'll join you later."

Owen stopped in the kitchen to inform Thoresby's messenger that he would start out for York on the morrow with his men.

3
LADY'S MANTLE

St. Clement's Nunnery was a small claustral establishment compared with St. Mary's Abbey, but the setting was pleasant, nestled among gardens, orchards, meadows, and small arable and pasture closes, separated from the west bank of the Ouse by a commons. A Benedictine house, St. Clement's had the customary church and chapter house, cloister, guest house, and even a staithe on the Ouse. The priory's church was the parish church of the residents of Clementhorpe; beneath its stones were buried not only nuns and their servants, but parishioners as well, and the nunnery was often remembered in the parishioners' wills. As prioress, Isobel de Percy strove to instill in the sisters, boarders, and their domestics the importance of the community's respect. Even the smallest scandal might convince potential benefactors to take their largesse elsewhere.

This present situation distressed the prioress. She was not fool enough to think Joanna Calverley's story would not spread among the people of York, but hoped in time Joanna's notoriety would fade. Isobel intended to keep close watch on Joanna from now on.

She had given orders to be notified at once when the party from Beverley arrived. She meant to settle Joanna without fuss and with only the essential people knowing. As soon as word came, Isobel hurried to the gate to escort the company into the priory. She would announce the prodigal's return at the evening meal; it would cause an unpleasant stir, she had no doubt, but the sisters must be told. She would savor these last few hours of peace. As Sir Richard de Ravenser and Sir Nicholas de Louth took seats in the prioress's parlor, the subprioress and the infirmaress hurried in to help Dame Joanna to the infirmary.

Isobel entertained Louth and Ravenser with the priory's best cider. Louth graciously praised the cider, the pleasant aspect of the lancet windows that looked out on the orchards stretching down to the river, the fragrant breeze. He told her what he could of Dame Joanna, how they had found her at Will Longford's, how little they could glean from her responses, her claim that she wore the mantle of the Blessed Virgin Mary, which had allowed her to rise from the dead, and her confession that she had stolen some of the Virgin's milk from the priory church.

Ravenser presented her with the stolen relic. "Beyond these facts, there is little we can offer you, Reverend Mother. The infirmaress at Nunburton wrote this down for you," he handed her a letter. "It is everything that she noted about Dame Joanna's condition when she arrived."

Dame Isobel liked least the part about the Virgin's mantle. "Does she speak freely about the mantle? Will anyone tending her be likely to hear this claim?"

Ravenser sipped his cider. "I do not think you can keep her silent on the matter. She does not like anyone touching the mantle. But as it covers her, it is difficult to avoid. At Nunburton she reportedly became quite upset when the infirmaress touched it. With loud voice she did protest. I think it impossible to keep it secret for long."

Dame Isobel debated whether to excuse herself and go warn Dame Prudentia, the infirmaress. But her rushing down the hall might call too much attention to the infirmary. She tucked her hands beneath her scapula and paced. "Joanna has ever been a difficult charge. I pray God I am able to cope with this. St. Clement's is so small. Word of her delusion will spread quickly." She paused, searched their faces as she asked, "It *is* a delusion?"

Ravenser smiled reassuringly. "We are as certain as we can be, Reverend Mother. The Abbess of Nunburton noted that the wool appeared to be Yorkshire wool, and certainly not of an age for it to have been owned by Our Lady. In truth, is it likely that such a thing would be bestowed on this troubled child?"

Although Isobel recognized Ravenser's attempt to reassure in his smile, she heard uncertainty in his words. "The Lord's purpose is not always clear to us, Sir Richard." Still, the Yorkshire wool relieved Isobel. It was a good sign.

And yet—such a relic would bring pilgrims from far and wide, with generous donations to the priory's empty coffers. Might this be a blessing? Should she consider that? Might the archbishop wish St. Clement's to become a popular pilgrimage site?

But the peace of the priory would be gone forever. Isobel sighed. "I am to speak with His Grace the Archbishop tomorrow morning," she said. "I shall ask for his guidance in handling Dame Joanna. It would seem wise to coax her into accepting that she is in error, that the mantle is merely a piece of clothing."

In the infirmary, Dame Prudentia sat on a stool beside Joanna's cot wondering what devils made the child so contrary. She studied the young woman's quiet face, the skin so pale the freckles stood out starkly, even on her closed eyelids. Prudentia knew Joanna from before, remembered the startling eyes, what a brilliant green they could be when the child was at peace—which was not often. She had never seen eyes so changeable as Joanna's. But then she had such narrow experience, only the thirteen or so sisters typically housed at St. Clement's, their servants and boarders. Perhaps some wise man had already discovered the meaning of such changeable eyes. Would Prudentia understand Joanna better if she knew more about the body and its workings?

Prudentia lifted one of Joanna's hands, pressed her fingernails. Strong, and with a healthy blush. Joanna appeared to be in better health than when she had first come to St. Clement's. At that time she had been starving herself, and her fingernails, pale and bloodless, had peeled away with alarming ease. Prudentia cautiously pushed back Joanna's upper lip, pressed her teeth. None loose, though one was chipped. Prudentia sighed. Well enough in body.

She called to her serving girl, Katie, to bring a bowl of scented water and a cloth.

"All the cloths are in the laundry, Dame Prudentia," Katie said. "They must be dry by now. Go and fetch some." The infirmaress lifted a corner of the blue shawl, hoping to peel it back from Joanna's neck without disturbing her.

The green eyes opened. Dark, almost moss-colored today. Joanna grabbed Prudentia's hand. "No!"

"Rest easy, child. I mean only to wash your neck and face. Make you comfortable."

"You must not touch it!" Joanna sat up, clutching the mantle to her, her eyes wild. "This is the Blessed Virgin's mantle. Did no one tell you?"

"The"—Prudentia frowned—"is this one of your stories, Joanna?"

"I rose from the dead. Did you not hear? How else might I have done so? She gave it to me."

Prudentia did not believe a word of it. "The Blessed Virgin Mary gave you her mantle?"

Joanna nodded. "So I might rise and return her milk to St. Clement's."

"Her milk?" Prudentia had not heard about this offense. "You stole our relic?"

"I have returned it." No guilt softened the eyes.

"Selfish girl!" Prudentia was horrified. "What of the pilgrims? What of their prayers at the shrine while the vial was empty? Were their prayers in vain?"

Joanna sighed. "I did not take it all. Even so, I have returned it. Now I may die and rest in peace. So you must not tend me."

Not tend her? "Nonsense, child." Prudentia spoke with a brusqueness she did not feel. Joanna's eyes were so dark, so intense, her skin so pale, the voice so certain. "I am the infirmaress here. It is my duty to nurse you."

"You must not. I was brought back to return the relic. I have done so. Now I must return to the grave."

Prudentia crossed herself and whispered a prayer for patience. "Perhaps you would just fold back the mantle so I can wash your neck and face, child." She looked round for the girl with the water and cloth. The infirmary door was just closing silently. Lazy child.

• • •

Katie scurried from the infirmary to the garden, where the cloths were spread over the lavender to dry. While gathering some up, she told the laundress what she had heard.

Dame Isobel spun round, interrupted in mid-sentence by a timid knock on the door. "Come in!"

Dame Alice, the subprioress, poked her head in. "Reverend Mother, forgive the intrusion, but I pray you come to the infirmary."

Isobel did not like the wide-eyed expression on the usually staid subprioress. "Is Joanna giving you trouble?"

"Not Joanna. The others."

"What do you mean?"

"Please, Reverend Mother. It is best that you come at once."

Dame Isobel excused herself and hurried out, exasperated. Dame Alice might have waited. Ravenser and Louth were going to the archbishop as soon as they left here. What would they say about such an interruption? But Isobel said nothing, just moved as quickly as her sandaled feet and significant bulk allowed. As Isobel and Alice approached the infirmary door, one of the novices tiptoed out, crossing herself as she closed the door behind her.

"Jocelin, what are you doing away from the kitchen?" Isobel demanded.

The novice bowed to Dame Isobel. "I took but a moment. Dame Margaret said I might." She bowed her head and hurried away before Isobel could ask more.

Isobel opened the door. Dame Margaret, the cook, knelt beside Joanna's cot, praying.

Joanna lay quietly, her eyes closed.

"Dame Margaret! Rise and come with me." Isobel turned to the infirmaress. "How did this happen? You were to tell no one of Joanna's presence."

"I told no one, Reverend Mother. I believe it was Katie. I sent her to the garden for cloths and shortly Dame Felice was in here."

Isobel should have guessed. The laundress was an unholy gossip. "And she of course stopped in the kitchen."

Prudentia looked to Margaret, who nodded.

"Dame Margaret, return to the kitchen and tell anyone who asks that Joanna's mantle is made of Yorkshire wool, *new* wool, and *cannot* be what she claims." Isobel glanced over at Joanna and caught her listening with a hostile glint in her eyes. So be it. Isobel would not have all the sisters of St. Clement's hysterical.

But Margaret did not rise. Instead, she pushed back one of her sleeves and thrust her bare arm toward Isobel. "Marry, look you, Reverend Mother. The skin is clear."

Isobel looked at the proffered arm. It looked reddened from scrubbing, but free of any blemish. "So it is. Why do you show me this?"

"It was *not* clear before I touched the mantle. Our Lady's mantle has worked a miracle, Reverend Mother. My rash is gone." Margaret bent low over the mantle once more, her hands pressed together in prayer. "Sweet Mother of Heaven, thou hast healed me, thy humble servant."

"You see?" the subprioress whispered. "When word of this miracle spreads..." She shook her head, her eyes wide, mouth pinched.

Sweet Mary in Heaven, why have you done this to me? Isobel took a deep breath. "Prudentia, did you examine Margaret's arm before she touched the mantle?"

The infirmaress looked confused. "No. I never thought—"

"Have you ever seen this rash of which Margaret believes she has suddenly been cured?"

Prudentia's wrinkled face lit up. "Oh, yes, Reverend Mother. Many times."

Isobel closed her eyes, clutched her hands beneath her scapula, thinking fast. She was no longer so firm in her disbelief. Perhaps it *was* Our Lady's mantle. But she must preserve the peace of the convent. "Dame Margaret, I order you to keep silent about this."

Margaret raised her head, her eyes dazed. "But, Reverend Mother, others might be cured."

Isobel drew herself up to her full height. "Remember your vow of obedience, Dame Margaret."

The cook bowed her head. "Yes, Reverend Mother."

Isobel turned to the infirmaress and the subprioress. "Not a word of this to anyone." They nodded and voiced their promise in unison.

Isobel did not for a moment believe she could stem the tide of rumor, but perhaps she could slow it to a manageable trickle.

Thoresby stood in the garden of his palace at Bishopthorpe, enjoying the mild morning and the company of his gardener. He liked Simon's quiet doggedness, the simple joy the gardener took in his accomplishments. This morning the talk was of lady's mantle, the beauty of the dewdrops caught in the furled, fan-shaped leaves, how the drops would dry as the leaves opened. "Mistress Wilton would collect the dew early in the day for her remedies. Apothecaries hold it in high regard."

"The dew? Why? What is its virtue?"

Simon sat back on his heels, took off his battered straw hat, and wiped his brow with a clean rag. "They say 'tis changed to the water of life as it sits in the leaves. A remedy is all the better for it."

"The plant grows wild in the Dales. The women dry it, but I never knew what use they made of it."

"Mistress Wilton says the plant dries and binds. Stops a wound from bleeding and seeping. And she told me the proper name for it, the one clerics use. *Leontopodium*." Simon pronounced the Latin carefully, with obvious pride.

"Lion's foot?"

Simon nodded. "For its spreading root leaves. 'Tis why Mistress Wilton believes in thinning the clumps. Gives them room to spread. I considered it a long while."

Thoresby envied the man his pleasant concerns. "And what have you decided? Will you be thinning these?"

"Oh, aye. You'll not find me wasting good advice. Mistress Wilton learned from the best of gardeners, Your Grace. Master Nicholas Wilton. Was never a man knew as much about gardens as Master Nicholas." Simon slipped his hat back on and bent to his work.

Nicholas Wilton had been dead for two years. Thoresby had not known him well. But Lucie Wilton's present husband, Owen Archer, was much on Thoresby's mind. He awaited Archer's return; he was just the person to look into this abysmal situation.

Thoresby could not complain of Archer's absence. He had been pleased when John of Gaunt, Duke of Lancaster, had requested Archer's help in preparing archers for the expedition to be led by Edward, the Black Prince, to restore Don Pedro of Castile to his throne. Last winter the French had helped Don Pedro's bastard brother, Don Enrique de Trastamare, usurp the throne of Castile and banish Don Pedro from the kingdom. King Edward and the Black Prince had vowed to restore Pedro, king by right of birth, and Edward's third son, John of Gaunt, was to aid his elder brother in this venture.

Assisting the Prince and Lancaster suited Thoresby, as he wanted their support in his efforts to rid the royal household of their father's new mistress, the upstart Alice Perrers. And Archer had been glad to oblige, welcoming the chance to spend time with his old friends, Lief and Gaspare.

But this uproar at St. Clement's nunnery—it was just the type of business Archer sorted out well.

"I was set against liking her new husband," Simon the gardener was saying. "Looks like a knave with that patch and his soldierly ways." He had loaded a handwagon with dirt and lady's mantle. With a grunt he began to move away.

Thoresby followed. "Archer's appearance does work against him." He had been surprised when he first encountered Archer in the old Duke's entourage, but Henry of Grosmont had been a keen judge of men, and Thoresby had never doubted that Archer must be a quick-witted, resourceful, trustworthy spy. "But his looks, patch and all, appeal to the ladies."

Simon shrugged. "I'll never understand it, but my wife says 'tis true. Captain Archer's a good man, no matter his looks. He's made Mistress Wilton laugh again. 'Tis a blessed sight to see a pretty woman laugh." Simon stopped in front of a freshly dug bed. Picking up the slips, he set them aside on the grass, then dumped the soil into the bed. He knelt down and began to place the plants at regular intervals. "I expect this is the first of many children."

"Children? Whose children?"

"Captain Archer and Mistress Wilton, Your Grace. They've been kind to Tildy and Jasper. It's good they're beginning their own family."

"I had not realized."

Simon shrugged. "Well, you were down at Windsor and up in the dales so much of the winter, weren't you?" He bent over the bed again, pressing mounds of earth around the new plants.

Thoresby did not like this piece of news. He did not like that Archer had not told him. "If I had known Mistress Wilton was with child, I would not have sent Archer away."

Simon squinted up at the archbishop. "He'll be back soon enough, won't he?"

"And gone again."

Simon shrugged. "Back by Michaelmas?"

"Long before that."

Simon nodded. "Then 'tis a good thing. Come close to her time, the Captain will be a help to Mistress Wilton, but before that he'd be fussing over her and she'd be pushing him away." Simon, the father of five, spoke from experience.

"Odd that Archer said nothing," Thoresby muttered. He looked up at the angle of the sun. "I must take my leave of you now, Simon. I have some unpleasant business to attend to."

"God go with you, Your Grace."

"And with you, Simon."

Thoresby had already spoken with his nephew and Nicholas de Louth, knew of the horsemen and Dame Joanna's odd behavior. He knew too that Dame Isobel had declared the nun to be Joanna.

Nicholas de Louth had certainly proved a bungling fool. How could he have left Longford's maid in such a vulnerable position? The man had not the wits for his post.

Louth had hung his head. "You are right to blame me, Your Grace."

"You are not my concern, Sir Nicholas. Whether Dame Joanna Calverley should be accepted back into the convent of St. Clement's and whether her disappearance and return are symptomatic of an incompetent prioress—those are my concerns. Why should a nun steal a relic, run away, arrange a false burial, then return a year later, seeking to restore the relic and herself to the convent? How are the deaths of Longford's cook and maid related to Dame Joanna's misadventure?" Thoresby had turned away from Louth's pouty penitence in disgust. He had expected more from someone favored by the Black Prince. Perhaps it explained Louth's being here instead of in Gascony with his lord.

Ravenser had entered the conversation with an uneasy clearing of his throat. "There is more, uncle."

"What else?"

"Someone gave Joanna a blue mantle which she believes is the mantle of the Blessed Virgin Mary."

Sweet Heaven. "I suppose the sisters of St. Clement's are kneeling to her?"

Ravenser winced. "There was a stir. And the cook believes she has been cured of a rash."

"*Deus juva me.*"

"But the Reverend Mother has everything under control."

"I daresay. Just as she has a tight rein on all of her charges."

Now Thoresby must speak with the annoying woman herself.

Dame Isobel entered his chambers much subdued. Shadows underlined her pale eyes. "*Benedicte,* Your Grace." She handed Thoresby a letter bearing the anchor seal of St. Clement's. "Joanna has signed this, Your Grace. She recants her sins and submits to her penance."

Thoresby made the sign of the cross over Isobel and motioned her to be seated. "I understand you have identified the woman as Joanna Calverley of Leeds." He tapped the letter against his left palm.

49

"I have, Your Grace." Isobel did not meet Thoresby's eyes, but focused on his hands and the letter.

Thoresby noticed, and put down the document. No need to look discomfited. "And you are satisfied that she returned and signed this willingly?"

"Joanna was most anxious to return, Your Grace."

"And when she signed it, was she Our Lady risen from the dead or Joanna Calverley?"

Isobel's pale eyebrows dipped in a puzzled frown. "She has not claimed to be the Blessed Virgin, Your Grace, just *a* virgin."

"And is that true?"

Dame Isobel blushed. "I think not, Your Grace. She has said things to Dame Prudentia that suggest—a loss of innocence."

"And God chose to bring this lying Magdalene back from the dead?"

"Your Grace, there is no logic to her delusion."

"Ah. So you agree she is deluded?"

Isobel looked surprised. "Of course."

"But she was lucid enough to write this letter and understand what it contained?"

Isobel blinked rapidly. "I wrote the letter, Your Grace. But she was fully aware of its contents and signed it of her own accord, as God is my witness."

"Indeed." Thoresby opened the letter, skimmed it. "Fully aware, you say?"

Isobel took a kerchief from her sleeve and blotted her upper lip. "I think she has moments of clarity."

Thoresby tossed the letter aside and folded his hands. "Can she explain her behavior?"

Isobel tucked her hands under her scapula. "So far she has said little that might be of use, but I shall ask again."

"Indeed you shall. And I trust you will not disappoint me."

The prioress blushed, but she did not drop her head meekly. "I shall not, Your Grace."

Thoresby liked the way her jaw stuck out with determination.

"How has Joanna been received at St. Clement's?"

Isobel sighed. "She has disturbed the peace of our house."

No doubt. Gossip was ever the bane of a closed community. "Her behavior is disturbing?"

"Only those caring for her witness her confusion, Your Grace."

"She plays the tragic heroine. She will tire of it."

"But the mantle, Your Grace—" Isobel stretched a hand toward him, imploring. "The rumor of it has spread through St. Clement's. And Dame Margaret's rash…"

"Sir Richard said you had put a stop to that."

Isobel withdrew her hand. "He was kind to say so. I have done my best, but once a rumor such as that begins—" she looked pained. "It is plain that something happened to Joanna, else why would she return after making such an effort to disappear forever? So the sisters take Our Lady's intervention as an explanation. The only one that has been offered."

But not the only explanation the sisters had considered among themselves, Thoresby was sure. "Sir Richard de Ravenser has a theory that she went off to have a child. Is there any sign of that?"

Isobel's pale face colored slightly. "Not that we can tell, Your Grace."

"Has she spoken of a lover?"

"Except for the comments to Dame Prudentia, no. At least— not a living one."

"What do you mean?"

The prioress looked uncomfortable. Her eyes met Thoresby's, then moved away, focusing on the floor. "Joanna speaks of dreams in which her one love comes to her. She said it was these dreams that led her to run away, but now she knows they were sent by the Devil."

"One love?"

"I believe Joanna had a vision and did not understand." Isobel held up her hand to stop the Archbishop's impatient interruption. "Have you read any of the mystics, Your Grace? They write of their love of God in terms of human love. It can confuse an inexperienced child like Joanna."

"Inexperienced?"

Isobel's stubborn chin jutted out even farther. "I stand firm in my belief that she left St. Clement's an innocent, Your Grace. And there is yet something else—something that frightens her. She was given the last rites in Beverley. She fears that in God's eyes she is dead. She wishes to profess her vows once more."

"You believe these ideas are connected?"

"I believe they reveal a soul in turmoil and confusion, Your Grace. I think that Joanna went out to seek the lover in her dreams and found an ordinary man."

"So you do believe a man was involved?"

Isobel shrugged. "It seems likely. In fact, a man has lurked about St. Clement's since she arrived."

A fact. Thoresby was pleased to hear a fact at last. "Horsemen followed Dame Joanna's company from Beverley, as you have no doubt heard. Do you feel threatened by this watcher?"

Isobel spread her hands. "How can I know?"

"Do you recognize him? Might he have visited Dame Joanna at St. Clement's?"

"She had no visitors, Your Grace."

Thoresby raised an eyebrow. "None? In six years? At least her family, surely."

The prioress looked down at her hands, dropped them at her sides. "No one, not even her family." A new note had crept into Isobel's voice. She chose her words with uneasy care.

Thoresby suspected they were now close to the nub of the problem. "Her family. Yes. Last time we spoke I sent you off to discover whether her family wanted to remove her body to Leeds. What was the outcome of that interview?"

Isobel once more tucked her hands beneath her scapula. Thoresby wondered whether she thought that hid her uneasiness. "They wished to have nothing more to do with her, Your Grace."

"Because she had broken her vows?"

Isobel, head bowed, said nothing.

"Whatever you are not saying, it will come out, do not doubt it, Dame Isobel. And it will be far better for you if I have heard it from your lips. I have ordered Richard de Ravenser to find out all there is to know about the friends who assisted Joanna in her escape and deceit. And Nicholas de Louth will talk to her family. So you might as well speak now."

A tense silence ensued. Silence did not bother Thoresby. He was content to let it lengthen until his visitor could bear it no longer. Indeed, it was to her credit how long Isobel held on to it. But at last she sighed and raised her eyes to his.

"I did not go to her family. When she entered St. Clement's we agreed that she was dead to her family from that day."

"It is a symbolic death."

Isobel shook her head. "It was a condition of payment, Your Grace."

He raised an eyebrow. "They paid handsomely?"

"I was not then prioress."

"But the Council of Oxford forbade this."

"St. Clement's is poor, Your Grace, and Joanna's family were keen to be rid of her."

"Did they explain why?"

"Her mother said she was impossible to rule."

"As Benedictines you take a vow of poverty."

Isobel bristled. "The money did not make our lives soft. It patched the roof and kept us warm in winter."

"Still, it is simony." Thoresby stood, clasped his hands behind him and, frowning, turned from her. "I am increasingly uneasy about the state of St. Clement's, Dame Isobel. I depend on you to watch over the sisters and rule them wisely. You have failed me." He stayed there a moment, letting her study his back, then spun round with a stern frown. "If you fail me again I must think what to do."

Isobel looked sufficiently disgraced. "Your Grace, please, it is an unfortunate—"

"Yes, it *is* unfortunate. This entire situation is unfortunate. And to prevent more misfortune, I want Dame Joanna taken to St. Mary's Abbey guest house. The abbey walls are better fortified than St. Clement's, the gates are more secure."

Dame Isobel's expression warred between shame and relief. "Considering the watcher and the rumors, I would be most grateful for such an arrangement."

"This does not relieve you of your duties. You will speak with Dame Joanna at St. Mary's. Find a way to inspire trust. I want to know what she knows of Jaro, the man in her grave, and Maddy, the maid who was murdered. I want to know why someone is following her and who it is. I want to know with whom she left Beverley. Sir Nicholas de Louth will tell you more. Speak with him."

"Yes, Your Grace."

"You may go."

She bowed to him. "Peace be the Lord my God."

"God go with you."

Thoresby thanked the messenger who had just ridden in from Knaresborough and bade him leave the door ajar as he quit the parlor. "Michaelo!" Thoresby bellowed a few moments later.

Thoresby's secretary presented his elegant self. "Your Grace?"

"Send Alfred and Colin to me. Captain Archer recommends them. I think they might manage to track down a man who is watching the nunnery."

"They might do," Michaelo said, "though you must not expect them to take him alive. They are thirsty for blood, those two."

Thoresby stared at his secretary. It was the most astute comment Michaelo had ever made to him. "I shall impress upon them that I wish to speak to the man."

Michaelo bowed and hurried off on his mission.

Thoresby drummed his fingers on the polished wood table and considered his departed secretary. He had appointed Michaelo to the post more to keep an eye on him than to make use of him. As a monk of St. Mary's, Michaelo had been led seriously astray by the former Archdeacon of York. But of late Michaelo had shown improvement. He was reliable, and kept his own counsel. Thoresby even detected some likable qualities in him—an amusing sense of humor. A quite unexpected development.

• • •

Dame Isobel paced her chamber. Her interview with the Archbishop had mortified her. It was plain he considered her incompetent. As well he might. But it pained her. She respected Archbishop Thoresby, admired his combination of worldliness and spirituality. She had read the lay catechism he had directed a monk at St. Mary's to write. It was an inspiration of elegant simplicity. And the Lady Chapel he was building in the minster promised to be a magnificent monument to Our Lady. Isobel must prove to Thoresby that she was worthy of her position.

But how? He wanted answers from Joanna, but the young woman spoke in riddles, gibberish. It was true she seemed occasionally lucid, but as Joanna's memories agitated her she lapsed into nonsense.

Isobel paced and prayed, but it was no use. Joanna's state required more than prayers; she was too agitated to think clearly. Perhaps Brother Wulfstan, St. Mary's infirmarian and said to be gifted, could be of help. Isobel resolved to speak with him when she accompanied Joanna to St. Mary's on the morrow.

Brother Wulfstan sat quietly in Abbot Campian's parlor listening to the prioress's description of Joanna's nervous state. Dame Isobel had been disappointed when the round faced, elderly man shuffled into the room. She knew the infirmarian only by reputation and had expected a commanding presence, not this meek serenity. But as she spoke and watched his age-dimmed eyes watching her, the round, tonsured head nodding and tilting as he considered her words, as he asked for details that she had not thought to offer, she relaxed and grew hopeful.

So she was puzzled when he said he would ask Mistress Lucie Wilton to assist him.

"Mistress Wilton," Isobel repeated, "but why?"

Wulfstan regarded her kindly. "You would remember her from her days at St. Clement's, but seven years have gone by, Reverend Mother. She is a master apothecary and quite skilled. Were this patient a man, I would have my assistant Brother Henry work with me. But it is more appropriate that a woman examine Dame Joanna, and I can think of no woman I would trust more. She might even teach me something." His eyes twinkled.

Dame Isobel looked down at her hands, thinking how to explain her concern. "Mistress Wilton was not happy at St. Clement's. She might not wish to cooperate."

Brother Wulfstan smiled sadly. "You made a vow to watch over the sisters in your care, did you not, Reverend Mother?"

"Yes."

"Would you break that vow because of an old grudge?"

"The Lord knows I would not," Isobel said, crossing herself.

Wulfstan nodded. "Mistress Wilton is a master apothecary, Reverend Mother. She performs her duties as faithfully as you do yours, and all for the honor and glory of God. She will do this as an apothecary; not as a favor to St. Clement's. Or even to me."

4

A CONSULTATION

A golden dawn found the chinks in the shutters and shone into the room. Lucie Wilton dreamed that her daughter took her first steps, safely supported by Lucie's hand under her left elbow, Owen's hand under her right. The child grew bold, rose on her toes, wobbled, and twisted to land in the soft grass with a cry of righteous indignation. She reached up to Lucie, her furry paw pressing against Lucie's chin.

Lucie woke. Melisende yawned in her face. "You confused my dream, you wretched cat," Lucie grumbled. Melisende lazily opened an eye, yawned again, drifted back into sleep.

Lucie closed her eyes and contemplated Owen's imminent return. He had written that he was on his way home, might reach York by this evening. Lief and Gaspare would accompany him, staying at York Castle with the archers they were training. Owen did not explain the change in plans, but Lucie was delighted he would be home, however briefly. Nonetheless, she wondered what had happened.

She looked forward to meeting Lief and Gaspare. Owen wrote that Lief spoke of little else but his healthy son. It was good that Owen was seeing a happy father; he seemed to dread the prospect of being one himself, much as he protested to Lucie that he thanked God they were at last to be blessed with a child. Gaspare, a bachelor, teased Lief and Owen about their virtuous devotion to their wives; in writing of this, Owen was quick to add that Gaspare could not lead him astray. Lucie did not fear that Owen would stray. It was the dark moods that had come over him since she'd told him she was with child that worried her. Perhaps Lief's enthusiasm would cheer him.

Idle thoughts. Lucie sat up. Melisende sat up, expectant. "Yes, we shall go down and stoke the fire. Let Tildy wake to warmth for a change." Lucie's serving girl, Tildy, had been pampering Lucie while Owen was away. With Owen returning tonight and Lucie's father, Sir Robert D'Arby, arriving by week's end, Tildy was about to become quite busy. "She deserves a treat," Lucie said, scratching Melisende's striped back. The cat blinked, as if in agreement.

Brother Wulfstan's summons arrived as Lucie and Tildy finished the morning chores.

"He is not unwell?" Lucie asked the messenger with alarm.

"Brother Wulfstan is well. He requires your assistance with an ailing guest."

Knowing that the infirmarian would not make such a request idly, Lucie instructed Tildy to ask customers to return in the afternoon and accompanied the messenger to the abbey, tingling with curiosity about the unusual summons.

Her haste was rewarded. When Lucie saw the prioress of St. Clement's in attendance in the patient's room at the guest house, she guessed the identity of the patient shrouded in the curtained bed. She had heard the rumors about Dame Joanna of Leeds.

Dame Isobel greeted her politely.

Brother Wulfstan came forward with open arms. "Bless you for coming so quickly, Lucie." He led her aside to explain the situation. His face darkened as he moved farther into the tale of Joanna's disappearance, reappearance, the two deaths that seemed linked to her, the rumor of her miraculous mantle, and her possible danger. "Forgive me for drawing you into such unholy concerns, Lucie, but I need a woman's help in this and I know you have the skill—and the discretion."

Lucie smiled at Wulfstan's dear, troubled face. "With such sweet words, how could I possibly be offended? Come." She took his arm. "Introduce me to this fascinating patient."

With a grateful smile, Wulfstan led Lucie over to the curtained bed. A table had been drawn up beside it. The infirmarian had assembled a wine flagon, some apothecary jars, a cup, spoons and measures, and a spirit lamp on which a bowl of water steamed. "The Reverend Mother needs Dame Joanna calm enough to answer questions. She hopes to discover what happened—what drove Joanna away, what brought her back."

Lucie could well imagine. She suspected that it was Archbishop Thoresby who motivated Dame Isobel.

"I thought to begin with something simple, valerian and balm in wine, a strong dosage. But I must know whether Joanna is in any pain. The sisters believe she has discomfort from cuts, scratches, bruises, but is otherwise sound. I hoped you might examine her and reassure me." Wulfstan turned at a noise from Dame Isobel. "Forgive me, Reverend Mother. I do not mean to question you. I am taking my normal precautions. A medicine for one can be a poison for another. We pray God to guide our hands, but He expects us to take care." He glanced over at Lucie uneasily, but she nodded, unoffended by the reference to her deceased husband's tragedy.

Dame Isobel tucked her hands beneath her scapula and bowed her acquiescence.

Wulfstan turned back to Lucie. "I shall be in the corridor while you examine Dame Joanna. I shall await your summons to return."

When the door had closed behind Wulfstan, Dame Isobel joined Lucie. Lucie opened the curtain. Dame Joanna lay with her eyes closed, her mouth moving as if in prayer, her hands pressed together on her chest. She was wrapped in a clean but shabby blue mantle. Her face was pale. Deathly pale.

"Dame Joanna," Lucie said, and waited for an answer.

The nun continued as she had been.

Lucie leaned over and touched Joanna's arm.

The woman jerked her arm away, opened her eyes, and stared up at Lucie with alarm.

Could she have been unaware of Lucie's presence until the touch and then respond so dramatically? Lucie was puzzled. "Please, do not be frightened. I am Mistress Wilton, an apothecary. I am to examine you so the infirmarian knows how to treat you."

The green eyes flicked over to Dame Isobel, back to Lucie. "Treat me?"

"Brother Wulfstan will prepare a remedy to calm you, help you sleep. But he must know as much as possible about you. Whether you are in any pain is important."

"Pain is unimportant."

Lucie glanced back at Dame Isobel with raised eyebrows.

Dame Isobel shook her head, dismissing Joanna's reply.

Lucie felt Joanna's forehead with the back of her hand. "You are not feverish, yet they tell me you have been talking as if you were. Why is that, Dame Joanna?"

Joanna touched the hand Lucie still held to her forehead. "I do not mean to be trouble. I would not mind so much if you would examine me alone."

"Without your Reverend Mother?"

Joanna nodded.

Lucie turned to Isobel. "Will you permit this?"

Dame Isobel did not look pleased, but she nodded. "Brother Wulfstan says I can trust you as I do him. Of course, Mistress Wilton." Dame Isobel gave Joanna and Lucie a little bow, then moved away to the far side of the room. She sat down with her head bowed, hands pressed together in prayer.

Lucie looked at Joanna's eyes, her mouth. Her teeth were in remarkably good condition except for a front tooth that was chipped. "Does the chipped tooth hurt?"

Joanna touched it with her tongue, nodded.

"Brother Wulfstan can give you clove oil to dab on it for the pain."

"I offer it up as a penance."

"But why, if there is a remedy?"

Joanna said nothing.

Lucie shrugged. "As you wish. How did you chip it?"

The eyes turned inward. "I fell."

Coupled with a fresh scar beside Joanna's mouth and a red streak in the whites of her eyes, Lucie guessed she had been beaten, and not very long ago. But her business was to examine Joanna's body, not her story. "You had a blackened eye recently?"

Joanna nodded.

"And a cut beside your mouth?"

A shrug.

"All from the fall?"

Another shrug.

Lucie patted Joanna's hand. "You can help me, if you will. I am not a physician, so I may miss something. If my touch hurts you, makes you uncomfortable in any way, please tell me."

"Your touch is gentle, Mistress Wilton."

Lucie wondered what all this talk of Joanna's state of mind was about. So far only the woman's inattention when Lucie first opened the curtain had been odd.

"I must lift your shift. Will you help me?" Lucie touched an end of the shawl.

Joanna grabbed it away from Lucie and unwound it, pulling it out from under her, carefully tucking it beside her. "You must not touch it."

"Is there anything else I must not touch?"

Joanna shook her head, then arched her body so Lucie could pull up the shift.

Joanna's feet and legs had the cuts, scratches, and bruises of an active child. The bottoms of her feet had healing sores, obviously already tended by the infirmaress at St. Clement's or Nunburton. Nothing unusual. She was missing a toe on her left foot, but it was an old injury. Still, it might be important. "How did you lose this toe?"

"Frostbite."

"How long ago?"

Joanna shrugged. "A few years."

Lucie found that quite plausible. Joanna's torso was bruised and scratched, but none of the marks were surprising.

Around Joanna's neck was a medal. "This is pretty." Lucie lifted it.

Joanna grabbed it from Lucie, holding it protectively in her cupped hand.

Lucie thought it best not to comment, just stick to her task.

"Please turn over on your stomach."

Joanna did so.

Here were puzzling injuries. Patches of scabbed abrasions, some still tender scars, yellowing bruises, almost gone. "How did you come by the cuts and bruises on your back?"

"I am clumsy."

Lucie doubted that was the cause. It was unlikely that her clumsiness would make her fall backward rather than forward. "They look almost healed." She pressed the worst spot gently. "Does this hurt?"

"Pain purifies me."

Wulfstan had warned Lucie that Joanna spoke thus. "You may pull down your shift."

Joanna pulled it down slowly, as if even this movement exhausted her.

"May I see your arms?"

Joanna pushed up her sleeves.

"So many cuts and scratches," Lucie murmured. "You have not been living a life of ease recently."

Joanna suddenly pressed Lucie's hand and looked earnestly into her eyes. "He was so kind. I thought he loved me."

Lucie stared at Joanna, puzzled by the shift in mood. "Who, Joanna?" She tried not to sound too eager.

Tears shimmered in the lovely green eyes. "How could I have been so fooled?" Joanna dug her nails into Lucie's hand.

"Who fooled you?"

But the moment died. Joanna withdrew her hand, turned her head aside. "I should be dead," she said in a matter of fact tone.

Lucie studied the tear-streaked face, the eyes staring blankly at the curtain. "Why is that?"

"I am cursed."

"By whom?"

"God."

"How do you know this?"

"The Blessed Virgin Mary told me."

"Then why were you given the great honor of resurrection?"

Joanna closed her eyes.

Lucie pressed a discolored spot on Joanna's left shoulder. Joanna jerked. "This hurts, doesn't it?"

"A little. It aches."

"Someone wrenched your arm out of the joint, I think."

Joanna stared at Lucie as if willing her to go away.

"It is difficult to do that with a fall."

The staring eyes blinked, betrayed by tears.

"And difficult, if not impossible, to pull back yourself. Was your arm useless for long?"

Joanna forced her eyes wide, trying to deny the tears.

Lucie dabbed at the tears already fallen. "I am finished. I will tell Brother Wulfstan what I've found. Trust him. He is a kind, skilled healer."

Joanna thrust out her hand, clutching Lucie's wrist. "I am not to be healed." Now her eyes, still wet, beseeched Lucie.

What on earth was she to make of this young woman? Not to be healed? "Why? Because of what you did? Running away, stealing the relic, arranging a funeral? Is that why you must do penance?"

"I am cursed." Joanna emphasized each word, though her voice still held no emotion.

Lucie pulled her hand from Joanna's grasp, smoothed the pale red strands from the woman's brow. "God be with you, Joanna." She closed the curtains and stood quietly for a moment, collecting her thoughts. As she moved toward the door, Dame Isobel stood.

"Joanna responded well to you, Mistress Wilton. You seemed to have a calming effect on her."

"She seems more secretive than agitated."

Dame Isobel shook her head. "No. She is different with you. When I ask questions, she becomes disturbed and incoherent. She answered your questions."

Lucie found Isobel's round, unlined, moon-pale face unnerving. Ageless. As if the girl Lucie remembered had merely grown larger, taller, but had not matured. "Joanna answered some of my questions. But she hardly gave me useful answers."

Isobel looked down at her folded hands, back up to Lucie's face with meek eyes. "His Grace the Archbishop wants me to interrogate Joanna, find out what I can about what has happened to her. Would you help me?"

Coming to Brother Wulfstan's aid was one thing, but to help Dame Isobel… They had not been friends at the convent. And last summer Owen had told Lucie that Isobel was much to blame in this case, that she had kept Joanna's disappearance a secret, being relieved to be rid of the strange young woman. "I am a busy woman, Reverend Mother. I have little time to spare."

"Forgive me." Isobel bowed her head and stepped aside. "God go with you, Mistress Wilton. Thank you for coming today."

Lucie found Wulfstan waiting anxiously in the corridor. She told him what she had found, the chipped tooth, the healing eye, the shoulder, the other inconsequential cuts, scrapes, bruises. And the almost healed abrasions and deep bruises on her back. "I do not know what to make of them. Her explanation was that she is clumsy. An odd sort of clumsiness, to always land on her back." As Lucie voiced the thought, she blushed, hearing echoes of jokes about women who conduct their business on their backs.

Brother Wulfstan did not seem to notice Lucie's discomfort. "Clumsy, yet no serious wounds or broken bones." He sighed. "So it is her soul, not her body that requires our help."

Lucie forced herself to concentrate on Wulfstan's concerns. "She will be a difficult patient. She believes God means her to offer up her pains as penance, and that she is meant to die soon."

Wulfstan looked unhappy. "I understand she has had a vision about this."

"She says the Blessed Virgin Mary guides her. Dost thou believe she had a vision, Brother Wulfstan?"

He lifted his hands, palms up, shrugged. "How can we ever know? But in my heart I think it more likely she had a nightmare, a fever dream—" He shook his head, sighed. "Did she say aught about her—Sweet Jesu, it sticks in my throat—resurrection?" He winced on the last word.

Lucie gently touched his cheek. "No. When I mentioned it she said nothing."

"What of the mantle? What had she to say of that?"

"Only that we are not to touch it."

Wulfstan sighed. "Put your feelings aside and tell me, do you think the child can distinguish visions from dreams?"

"I cannot tell. She says pain purifies her. She claims to be cursed. We have all heard such things before. If only her visions were more unusual. But even then, she might simply be a good storyteller." Lucie found it frustrating. "There are questions she will not answer, but I did not think that strange. Perhaps in time she will trust us and speak more freely."

Wulfstan took Lucie's hands. "You have been most generous with your time, Lucie. I am grateful. You have had better luck than most who have spoken with her. She babbled to me about stars winking out and much other gibberish I could not understand."

Lucie squeezed his hands affectionately. "I am happy to have been of help to you, my friend. But now I must get back."

Wulfstan nodded. "God bless you for coming. When does Owen return?"

"Perhaps tonight. For a short while, and then he will be gone again. Unfortunately, Sir Robert D'Arby comes later this week, to stay while Owen is in Pontefract."

Wulfstan searched Lucie's face. "Your father?"

Lucie nodded wearily. "Aunt Phillippa told him I am with child."

"You—" Brother Wulfstan's face lit up. "May our Heavenly Mother protect you." He made the sign of the cross over her. "How wonderful. It is a kind gesture on your father's part, to keep you company."

Lucie rubbed her eyes, suddenly tired. "It is foolish and useless. What does he know of my life? What does he know of me?"

Wulfstan put a hand on Lucie's shoulder, waited until she met his eyes. Hers shimmered with stubborn, angry tears. "He made a long pilgrimage to the Holy Land to ask God's forgiveness for what happened to your mother. I am certain that God forgave him. Why can you not try?"

Lucie looked into Wulfstan's sad eyes. She wanted to beg his forgiveness for distressing him, but she could not help how she felt. "It is not so easy."

Brother Wulfstan gave her a little hug. "You are a sensible woman, Lucie. You will do what is right."

She took a deep breath, calming her warring emotions. "I shall go about my business as usual."

"You must take care of yourself."

Lucie relaxed, seeing Wulfstan did not mean to argue. "Magda Digby and Bess Merchet are watching me closely. You need not worry."

Wulfstan pretended to be shocked. "Magda Digby, the Riverwoman? Could you not find a Christian midwife?"

"Magda brought me and so many other citizens of this city into this world, Brother Wulfstan. God guides her, no matter what she calls Him."

Wulfstan tucked his hands in his sleeves, gave her a little bow. "Well, she will have Bess to answer to if aught goes wrong. And myself. And Owen."

They moved outside into the bright June sunshine, Joanna forgotten for the moment.

5

THE WATCHER

Orchards surrounded St. Clement's, leafy and alive with bird song. But Alfred grumbled. "Where are the apples, that's what I'd like to know." Archbishop Thoresby, frustrated that Alfred and Colin had watched St. Clement's for two days without sighting the watcher, had ordered them to the nunnery at first light this morning, so early that they had not had time to break their fast.

Colin laughed. "Too early for fruit. When have you eaten a fresh apple before midsummer?"

"Can't say I notice when I eat what."

"Didn't you have fruit trees as a lad? Don't you look round you?"

"I'm not partial to trees and such. Just what comes off them."

"And I suppose you're proud of that."

"What's a soldier want with such things?"

"It's civilized to notice such things."

"I notice people is what I notice. And I've noticed that character pass the priory gate twice this morning." A stocky man in a russet cloak stained by travel. As the day warmed, he had removed the cloak and wide-brimmed hat. His clothes were those of a modest merchant. His balding head was tanned and weathered.

"So have I. *And* I notice when I eat what, too."

"So does that make you a scholar?"

Colin jabbed Alfred in the stomach. "Course not."

"He's eyeing the damage on the north wall, seeing whether he can scale it quickly, I'll wager. Look!" The man was indeed examining the height of the crumbling wall. "He's our man or I'm King of France."

"Lord help 'em over there, he'd best be our man." Colin hooted.

Alfred rolled his eyes. "Calm yourself," he muttered out of the corner of his mouth. "We must approach this cutthroat with caution."

"I doubt he's a cutthroat. Look at him. Clothes dusty from travel, but decent clothes, all the same. Clean shaven."

"What's he doing lurking round a convent, then?" Alfred demanded.

"You should need no help guessing what a man might want in a convent."

"Look at the dagger he wears at his waist."

"He'd be a fool to travel without one."

"You're becoming a regular Captain Archer."

"Wouldn't I like that? Pretty wife, nice house, an adventure now and then with enough danger to keep life interesting. I wouldn't say no to the Captain's lot in life."

"Don't go poking your eye out to wear a patch."

Colin groaned. "Shall we approach the man?"

"Lead on, Captain."

"God speed, stranger," Colin called out.

The man backed away from the crumbling wall. "God be with you two gentlemen."

"You seem uncommonly interested in that wall, stranger," Colin said.

"I thought I might find work fixing it."

"You're a stonemason, then? You don't wear the guild badge."

The man looked uneasy. "I have done nothing wrong. Nor shall I."

Colin glanced over at Alfred. Alfred nodded. "Glad we are that you mean no harm, stranger. And His Grace the Archbishop will be glad of it when you tell him so."

Colin gave a little bow. "If you will allow us to escort you."

The stranger frowned. "What is the need? I have told you I mean harm to no one."

Alfred grinned. "Then you have nothing to fear."

The stranger looked from one to the other. "I have no choice in this?"

Colin and Alfred exchanged glances. *Shall we seize him?*

The stranger sighed. "I shall come peacefully."

They led him away from St. Clement's, past the comfortable houses and orchards facing the city walls, and reentered the city through the gate by the Old Baile. As they headed down Skeldergate toward Ouse Bridge, the stranger asked, "Is there no other route?"

"'Tis the straightest route to the minster close," Colin said. "What do you fear?"

The stranger said nothing, but just beyond Bishophill he began glancing behind him every few steps.

Alfred and Colin began to check their backs, too. But the trouble appeared before them, four men blocking their way, shadowy figures standing with legs apart, arms folded. Their message was clear. The stranger gave a cry and took off down an alley, in the direction of the river.

Alfred and Colin hesitated. Neither was familiar with this part of the city.

Colin put his hand to the knife hidden beneath his jerkin and said quietly, "Could be a blind alley, and he's going to turn and fight. But he did not seem pleased to see these gentlemen."

"He might be a good actor, leading us into an ambush," Alfred said.

"And while we're arguing, it might not be a blind alley and he's got away."

Alfred groaned. "What about turning back?"

Colin glanced round. There were now several men at their backs. "No choice, I'm afraid."

With a nod, they took off after the runaway. The others pounded after them.

The alley was narrow and dark. The second story of the house on their left jutted out to touch the one-story roof of the building across from it. Odd to find a city street so deserted in late morning, so quiet but for the rats rustling through garbage in the shadows. A baby cried somewhere ahead. The two men groped their way along, coming once more into sickly daylight, a house to one side, a high fence to the other. Alfred and Colin kept alert to all sounds and shadows, but their prey eluded them.

"I don't see light ahead," Alfred whispered.

"So we're coming up on a bend. Is there a straight alley in all York?" Colin was as nervous as his mate, but they must go on, they would be fools to turn back into the arms of their pursuers. It was so dark he had to listen for Alfred's whereabouts. They passed under more jutting second and third stories. A sound of water lapping. The river was close.

But instead of the riverbank they encountered a stone wall.

"Devil take you, I was right!" Alfred hissed.

Colin had no time to answer. From behind came the sound of knives and swords being drawn, a hissed command. Alfred and Colin drew their daggers and turned, back to back, to face the attackers. Colin squinted, trying to make out the wavering shadows. He felt Alfred stiffen, then thrust, heard steel against steel. Alfred shouted, then fell away from Colin. They lost contact.

Colin lashed out at the attackers in front of him. A dagger came close to his face, he parried and heard a grunt. Something fell by his feet. He stepped on it. Another shadow loomed, thrust. Colin felt a searing pain in his left arm. He struck out with his right, found nothing. His invisible assailant got him in the waist. He doubled over, but fought the pain to force himself back upright, only to have his right leg kicked out from under him. He went crashing down backwards on something warm and bony. Alfred, he guessed. Colin twisted himself round so his back would be to the attackers. He did not want someone going for his eyes or his throat. A blow to his head, then his back, left him blind and breathless. He panicked, unable to get the muscles in this throat and chest coordinated to gulp air. *Jesu, forgive me my sins*, he silently prayed as he passed out.

Lucie tapped her foot as she listened to old John Kendall describe the pains in his joints in minute detail. She had measured out his salves and powders and put them in his hands several limbs ago. But she could not bring herself to be unkind. He had lost his wife and a daughter to the floods last winter and Lucie pitied him. The shop door's bell cheered her with the hope of release.

Until she saw who it was: Dame Isobel and a novice who stood meekly in her shadow. It had been one thing to see the prioress at St. Mary's, but Lucie resented yet another interruption in her day and the intrusion into her own house and shop... Dame Isobel conjured up unhappy memories.

Lucie's time at St. Clement's had been a purgatory. Her mother had just died, crumbling Lucie's world round her, and the nuns, reckoning her mother a sinner, had watched Lucie for signs of the Devil's influence. Isobel de Percy had been one of the most diligent in reporting on Lucie's missteps.

"*Benedicte*, Reverend Mother." Lucie did not bother to warm her voice.

Old John Kendall turned and bobbed his head at the prioress and the novice in tow. "I will leave you to your business, Mistress Wilton," he said to Lucie. "May the Lord smile on you for your kindness to a windy old man."

Lucie blushed as she watched John shuffle out; he must have heard her foot tapping.

Dame Isobel's pale eyes watched Lucie with an unexpected uncertainty.

"Dame Joanna should improve with Brother Wulfstan's ministrations, Reverend Mother."

"She already seems calmer, praise God." Isobel took a deep breath, glanced back at her companion. "Is there a more private place to talk?"

Lucie pressed her hands to her lower back. "I must watch the shop. I have sent my serving girl out on errands and I am alone this afternoon."

Isobel stepped closer, holding out her white, uncalloused hands in entreaty. "Forgive me. My troubles consumed your morning, and now I intrude on your work. But I could think of no one else who might be of help. I must convince Dame Joanna to confide in me and she seems determined to tell me nothing. You have a rapport with her. I thought you might advise me. And perhaps if I told you more of her past, you might see something I did not."

Lucie considered her backache, her plans to tidy up for Owen's homecoming, Isobel's past betrayals, all good reasons to bow out of any further involvement. And yet she was curious about Joanna Calverley... She stepped out from behind the counter. "Come. Let us go into the kitchen." Lucie nodded to the novice. "Make yourself comfortable on the bench. I can hear the shop bell in there. You've no need to come get me."

Lucie and the prioress sat down at a small table by the kitchen window, the shutters open to let in the summery breeze.

"I understand the archbishop is impatient for answers," Lucie prompted.

Isobel folded her hands on the table before her, fixed her eyes on her hands. An oddly meek posture for the prioress. "I also wish to know for myself," Isobel said. "I do care about Joanna. But, yes, Archbishop Thoresby is disappointed with me." She glanced up at Lucie, back down at her hands. "I bear the guilt of whatever happened to change Joanna so."

"She is changed, then?"

Isobel pressed her fingers to her forehead. "Oh, yes. The spirit has been leached from her."

"What do you think happened to her, Reverend Mother?"

Isobel shook her head.

Lucie stared out at the garden, thinking. "They say she stole a relic to pay for the funeral and her escape."

"A portion of the Virgin's milk. She claims that Our Lady saved her so she might return it."

"This man to whom she offered the relic in Beverley did not sell it?"

"No. When he disappeared, Sir Nicholas de Louth searched his house and found it."

An escape plan gone wrong. Lucie remembered her own unhappy time at St. Clement's, her ever more elaborate plans for escape, never carried out, but comforting. Dame Joanna had planned her flight, planned the theft as her source of money. A practical plan. Not everyone would accept a relic in payment. Only someone who traded in relics or knew of someone who did. So Joanna had planned this with the belief that Will Longford traded in relics, or would know who did. What else could she have been thinking? Such a trader would not have a stall at market. "How did Joanna come to know Will Longford?"

Isobel shook her head. "As I said, she has told me little."

The shop bell jingled. Lucie rose. "Shall I send in your novice to keep you company while I see to business?"

Isobel shook her head.

Lucie nodded toward a shelf with several jugs. "To the right, that is ale. The one beside it is water. Help yourself if you are thirsty."

The customer was one of Guildmaster Thorpe's children, come to collect several bedstraw pillows that Lucie had prepared. The baby was colicky and slept poorly. When her warm body heated the herb-stuffed pillow beneath her, the bedstraw would give off a soothing, relaxing honey fragrance and encourage restful sleep.

"How does your mother?" Gwen Thorpe had almost died delivering the baby.

Young Margaret smiled. "She's walking about. And this morning she yelled at Cook."

"And that made you happy?"

"'Tis the best sign she's mending right. But she coughs a lot."

"Has the Riverwoman been to see her?"

"Oh, aye."

Lucie picked up a small pouch and handed it to Margaret with the pillows. "I trust the Riverwoman is dosing her for her cough. But these herbs are my special remedy. Tell your mother to steep them in a pot and drink the tisane hot, so she breathes the steam. It will help clear out her chest after lying still so long."

"Thank you, Mistress Wilton."

The novice had fallen asleep on the bench and snored softly. Lucie took a cloak from the kitchen and spread it over the girl.

Isobel wandered about the kitchen, a cup of ale in hand.

"Tom Merchet's brew," Lucie said from the doorway. "You'd travel far to find better. This is nothing like the kitchen at St. Clement's, is it?"

Isobel blushed to have been found so blatantly snooping. "I confess my curiosity about the life you've led since you left us."

Lucie thought of the routine of St. Clement's, unvaried from year to year, the same schedule, the same faces, the same walls. "I have learned a trade, buried a husband and a baby, married again. It is a varied life."

"I noticed you pressing your hand to your lower back. Are you with child?"

Lucie had not thought Isobel so observant. "I did not know it showed much yet. I have four months to go."

Isobel smiled. "Some gestures are unmistakable. I will pray for your safe delivery of a healthy child."

"I can use your prayers."

Isobel gestured round the room. "You keep a tidy kitchen, well-stocked with herbs."

"The tidiness is thanks to Tildy, my serving girl. The herbs come from our garden. What we do not use in the shop, we use in our food." Lucie looked with satisfaction round the room, heavy oak beams, trestle table and chairs also of sturdy oak, well-scrubbed hearthstones in a fireplace with chimney. "My first husband's father rebuilt this part of the house. It is a comfortable room, even in midwinter, with the smoke going up the chimney."

"You have a good life, Lucie Wilton."

Lucie sat down beside Isobel. "You did not come here to rediscover me, Reverend Mother."

Isobel pressed her lips together, then relaxed them with a sigh. "In truth, I am not certain what I am asking of you. I hoped you would help me choose the right questions for Joanna. Find out what is in her heart." Isobel closed her eyes. "I admit that I do fear what might be there. I always have."

An interesting confession. "She was troubling before she left?"

Isobel fixed her pale eyes on Lucie. "Joanna has walked in her sleep ever since she came to St. Clement's. Walks and silently weeps. It is frightening to come upon a sleepwalker in the dark—silent, staring at something you cannot see. All of the sisters find it unsettling." Isobel dabbed her upper lip with a delicately embroidered linen square.

Lucie remembered her own trouble over much simpler vanities. "Tell me about Joanna before she left."

"We were much disturbed with her penances."

"Was that not a matter to take up with her confessor?"

"These were—I do not know what to call them. She claimed to have visions in which she was assigned the penances. Or were they self-imposed? I was never able to judge."

"What sort of penances?"

"She would force herself to stay awake, night after night, until she fainted with exhaustion; she would chant until she had no voice left; once she lay down to sleep at night in the snow—she lost a toe."

Frostbite. How innocent that had sounded. Yet true.

Dame Isobel shook her head. "If it were not for Dame Alice's watchfulness, we would have lost Joanna that time."

Lucie, remembering how small the nunnery had seemed, how a sound could travel the corridors, how eyes had followed her everywhere, could imagine how disquieting such behavior would be. "Joanna would indeed be a troubling presence as you describe her. For what was she doing penance before her escape?"

"She said she had dreams. Sinful dreams." Isobel blushed.

Lucie bit back a smile. "Did she describe these dreams?"

Isobel bowed her head. "No. Not directly. But—well, she came to me on several occasions to speak of visions of a heavenly lover, one who would possess her, burn away her sins with the passion of divine love and purify her." The prioress glanced up, then back down at her hands.

Lucie raised an eyebrow. "You have been reading the mystics in refectory?"

Isobel met Lucie's gaze, raised her hands, palms up. "It was ill-advised, I see that now. But some of the sisters found it inspiring, so from time to time I allowed it. I am afraid the allegory confused Joanna. She was such an innocent."

Lucie wondered whether Isobel knew how innocent she herself sounded. "Do you think she ran off to find such a lover, not realizing the mystics spoke of God?"

"I think it very likely."

"You blame yourself."

"I do."

They were both quiet for a while. Dame Isobel daintily sipped her ale.

Lucie broke the thoughtful silence. "Did Joanna seem secretive last spring? As if she were planning an escape?"

Isobel closed her eyes, her pale lashes almost invisible against her round cheeks. She sighed, as if the subject of Joanna wearied her. "Afterwards, I recognized the signs. She sought solitude even more than had been her custom. She paced the orchard—back and forth, back and forth, like an animal in a cage. But she performed her duties and prayed with us."

"If she ran off to a lover, where would she have met him? When?"

"That is what I cannot imagine."

"Did she have a confidante at St. Clement's? A particular friend?"

Isobel shook her head.

"A sadly solitary woman."

Isobel pursed her lips. "A difficult woman."

Lucie frowned at that. "More difficult than I was?"

Isobel had the courtesy to blush. "You did not take vows. You had not asked to come to St. Clement's."

"Joanna had claimed a vocation?"

"In truth, I believe she pretended a vocation to escape her betrothed."

"Ah." Lucie nodded. "Trapped by her own craft." She thought a moment. "So she had no friends, and there was no hue and cry when she disappeared?"

"I covered her absence with a lie. I told the sisters that she had gone home to regain her health." Isobel looked embarrassed. "I, too, was trapped by my cleverness. But worse than that. Had I told Archbishop Thoresby immediately, Joanna might have been found before—whatever happened to her."

Lucie leaned forward. "It was inevitable that you would be discovered. Her family would come to visit..."

Isobel shook her head. "The Calverleys never came to see her."

"Never?"

"Her family disowned her. When she came to St. Clement's she was more than symbolically dead to them."

"They paid you handsomely for that?"

Isobel nodded.

"Still, eventually someone would have asked where Joanna was. She could not stay away for her health forever. How did you intend to handle the questions then?"

"I planned to tell them she had been released from her vows because of her illness."

"And what if her family had suddenly reconsidered and come to visit?"

Sweat glistened on the prioress's face. "I would have told them she was dead."

"You were weaving yourself some difficult lies."

"Yes."

"To have it out in the open must feel like a chance at redemption."

Isobel looked away. "Perhaps it would be, if His Grace were not so angry."

"Yes. Back to that. How to proceed with Joanna." Lucie bit her lip. "She must believe that you are worried about her. You must not sound like an inquisitor. Be patient. Talk with her. Tell her something of yourself." Lucie rubbed her back, stood up. "I shall think about what you have told me."

Isobel rose, too. "You have been very kind. God bless you."

6

ALFRED'S TALE

As Owen passed through Micklegate Bar, he bade farewell to the fresh country air. The scent of forest and farmland gave way to the layered stench of the city—the mounds of composting manure on Toft Green, the sweat, smoke and onion of fellow travelers crowding through the bar to market, the rotten fruit and spoiled egg at the base of the pillory in the yard of Holy Trinity, the ammonia perfume of his own sweating horse, now that he must walk ahead of it, and, as he approached Ouse Bridge, the pungent scent of the fish mongers, all intensified by the strong midday sun. And flies everywhere. Only Lucie could lure Owen back to this city. But lure him she did; he could not wait to put his arms round her.

Gaspare nudged him. "You're thinking of your lady love, I can tell by the smile. Guilty pleasures."

At the Skeldergate crossing they were forced to the side of the street by a cart carrying two injured men. "I pray ye make way," shouted the driver. He squinted at Owen, then his eyes widened in relief. "Captain Archer, sir. Canst thou help me through this crowd to St. Mary's?"

"Not St. Leonard's Hospital?" Owen asked as he motioned to Lief, Gaspare, and the five new archers to surround the cart.

"Nay. St. Mary's, the one said. To Brother Wulfstan."

Owen peered into the cart. "Alfred?"

One of the men, bloody and bleary-eyed, tried to sit up. "Captain Archer. I cannot wake Colin. I thought Brother Wulfstan…"

Owen patted Alfred's shoulder. "Lie down. We shall get you there quickly."

The eight archers ploughed through the crowd on Ouse Bridge and then down Coney Street, the cart at their center.

Thoresby returned to the palace in the minster close thirsty, his feet aching from standing. He had spent several hours watching the masons at work on the minster's lady chapel, which would house his tomb. As Thoresby watched the masons raising the walls to Heaven, he meditated on his mortal body and his immortal soul. It humbled him, reminded him that for all his titles and power he was still just one of God's children.

The King did not like this humour; he thought the North Country was making Thoresby choleric. It was more to the point that King Edward saw Thoresby becoming more a man of God and less a Lord Chancellor, and that was what he disliked. But Thoresby was comfortable with the change. He was the Archbishop of York; he *should* be a man of God.

During the winter past, Thoresby had suffered a painful lesson in humility when he'd tried to remove the King's mistress, Alice Perrers, from Court. He had met his match in womankind. She had unearthed his most guarded secrets and unleashed emotions he had thought spent. Perrers. A month of prayer in the Cistercian peace of Fountains Abbey had not rid him of a taste for her blood.

Thoresby stopped in the kitchen, helped himself to some early strawberries, and warned Maeve that he would be wanting to bathe, she should begin boiling water. The thought of Alice Perrers made him feel unclean. And now he had heard that the King was campaigning for William of Wykeham, Keeper of the Privy Seal, to get the seat of Winchester when Bishop Edington died. With Perrers in Edward's bedchamber and Wykeham at his right hand, Thoresby's enemies were crowding him out, poisoning the King's mind against him. He wished he did not care.

He sought out Brother Michaelo, found him sitting quietly at his table outside Thoresby's parlor.

"Any word from Alfred or Colin?"

"Nothing, Your Grace."

79

"Where are the canons of Beverley?"

"Sir Robert and Sir Nicholas went out, Your Grace. I did not ask where."

"Good. I am going to bathe. See that I'm not disturbed."

Michaelo's eyes swept Thoresby from head to foot. "Bathe, Your Grace?"

Even the fastidious Michaelo could not understand bathing when clean. But Thoresby would be damned if he would explain to his secretary. "No interruptions."

Michaelo raised an eyebrow. "No interruptions, Your Grace."

Thoresby went into his parlor, checked through the documents Michaelo had arranged in order of urgency, judged none of them to require an immediate reply. He climbed the back stairs to his bed chamber. Two servants, Lizzie and John, balanced a large pot between them, tilting it toward a wooden tub. Steaming water poured out. Lizzie's face was red from the heat and exertion; John was soaked in sweat. An unpleasant task, lugging pots of boiling water up the stairs on a warm June afternoon.

The pot empty, the two lowered it to the floor, pausing to wipe their faces. Lizzie leaned on the canvas dome that extended over half the tub to protect the bather from drafts. She jumped as she turned and saw the archbishop. "Your Grace, we've only begun to fill it," she said breathlessly.

"Indeed. Carry on." He left them, headed for the hall. As he descended the stairs, he heard a familiar voice arguing with Michaelo at the outer door.

"They've been attacked while out on his business, you—I must see His Grace at once."

"Forgive me, Captain Archer, but that is impossible. His Grace is not to be disturbed."

A voice unfamiliar to Thoresby said quietly, "Leave it, Owen, just tell this man where they are and come away."

"Damn it, Lief, he'll want to know. It's why we've sped from Knaresborough. This nunnery business."

Thoresby had heard enough to be curious. "What is it, Michaelo?"

The secretary hurried in, sniffing with indignation to find Archer and two other men, obviously soldiers, at his heels. "Captain Archer has news of Alfred and Colin, Your Grace. I tried to tell him you were not to be disturbed, but you see—"

Owen pushed forward, his face grim. "We have taken them to St. Mary's infirmary, Your Grace."

"I take it they have been injured," Thoresby said quietly.

A flash of anger in Owen's good eye. "Both. Alfred has lost much blood from several wounds, but Wulfstan says he will mend quickly. Colin, however, is in God's hands. He has a head wound and cannot be roused. Brother Wulfstan says there is little he can do for him."

The watcher must have bested them. But with help, surely. "How did you come upon them?"

"Alfred and Colin were attacked down by the river. A good Samaritan saw Alfred dragging Colin into Skeldergate and took them up in his cart. We met them at the bridge, escorted them through the crowd." Owen gestured toward his comrades. "Lief, Gaspare, and the archers surrounded the cart and protected it."

Thoresby nodded. "I thank you for escorting them and bringing me this news. I shall go see them." He began to leave, then paused to add, "Lest you blame me for my ruthless use of my men, as you are wont to do, remember that it was you recommended them for this duty." He took satisfaction in seeing Owen's anger doused. "Now go home to your wife, Archer. I shall send for you tomorrow." Thoresby nodded to Lief and Gaspare. "The chamberlain has prepared quarters for you at the castle. You should be quite comfortable."

When the three had departed, Michaelo asked, "You will bathe first?"

"Later. Gilbert shall accompany me to the abbey. Call for him."

Owen escorted Gaspare, Lief, and the five archers to York Castle.

Gaspare had been quiet and glum as they left the minster liberty, but once on the crowded streets he perked up, looking round at the bustling humanity. "Tell me again why you chose to serve Thoresby rather than Lancaster—honor, was it?"

"Kind of you to remind me."

"Lancaster would treat you better than that bastard does."

"But he's right. I did recommend Alfred and Colin."

Lief shook his head. "He had no cause to speak to you in that way and you know it. Spiteful he is. Nasty."

Owen could not deny that.

Lucie had closed the shop by the time Owen reached home. He opened the garden gate and walked round to the kitchen door, but stopped as he saw Lucie kneeling by the roses, weeding. She wore a simple russet gown and her hair tucked up in a kerchief, a red-gold tendril curling delicately at the nape of her long neck. Owen leaned against the gate, enjoying the quiet moment, the anticipation of their first embrace. Tildy appeared at the kitchen door, grinning broadly. As she opened her mouth to greet him, Owen put a finger to his lips. She giggled and ducked within. Melisende rose from a sunny spot and stretched, padded over to rub up against Owen's legs and chatter, no doubt demanding some cream for her troubles. Lucie turned, saw Owen and gave a glad cry. She began to rise, one hand to her back. Owen hurried over, lifted her up for a kiss, then stood her on her feet.

"Are you well, my love?" he asked.

Lucie smiled and patted her stomach. "We are both in good health. And better now you are home." She glanced behind him. "I expected your friends."

"They agreed to leave us in peace tonight."

"Tomorrow, then. They must come to supper. And now come within and wash away the road with Tom's ale while you tell me of your travels."

The abbey infirmary was clean and redolent of herbs. A fire burned in the hearth and a small brazier warmed the air near the patients' cots. Brother Wulfstan was bent over Colin when Brother Henry opened the door to Thoresby. The archbishop put his finger to his lips, silencing Henry's greeting.

Brother Wulfstan pried open Colin's eyelids, brought a lit candle close to his eyes, moved it back. He called Henry over. "Watch closely." Once again the old monk moved the candle back and forth close to Colin's eyes. "What do you see, Henry?"

"The pupil still responds to light and dark."

Wulfstan nodded. "That is good. He is yet with us." He sighed. "But only just." He set the candle down, dabbed Colin's face with a cloth dipped in lavender water, and made the sign of the cross over him.

"How does he?" Thoresby asked, moving closer.

Wulfstan heaved himself up, with Henry's help. "Your Grace, I will do my best with him." His pale eyes looked sad. "But I must speak plain, we are close to losing him. It is difficult with such an injury. I can clean the flesh, apply cool compresses, but the injury is deep within. I cannot smell it, touch it, measure its extent. I can only make him comfortable and try to keep him with us until God calls him."

"I trust you to do everything possible, Brother Wulfstan. Whoever thought to bring my men here did me a good deed."

Wulfstan acknowledged the compliment with a bow.

"It was Alfred asked to be brought here, Your Grace," Brother Henry said. "He said Captain Archer has often spoken of Brother Wulfstan's skill, and when he could not rouse his friend he knew he must come here."

Thoresby knelt beside Colin, examined the bruised and swollen forehead, the blackened eyes, the crooked nose, dried blood in the nostrils. "He broke his nose?"

"I think he fell forward, Your Grace," Alfred said from across the way. His voice quivered with weakness.

Thoresby signed a blessing over Colin and moved to Alfred's bedside. "Tell me what you can, Alfred. Quietly. I can hear you."

Alfred raised himself up on his elbows. Brother Henry hurried over and propped him up.

"We approached the watcher…" Alfred described the man and

the attack, pausing often to lick his split lip.

"Can you guess how many attacked you?" Thoresby asked. "Two? Ten?"

"Half dozen, I think. Colin and me stood back to back. That's how I didn't see. Couldn't see in the dark anyway. I don't remember much more."

"Did they mean to kill you, do you think?"

Alfred shrugged. Henry helped him sip some wine, then dabbed Alfred's split lip with salve. Suddenly Alfred sat up straighter, remembering something. "A dagger. I found a dagger under Colin. Brought it with me." He looked round.

Henry put a hand on Alfred's shoulder. "It is over in the corner."

Alfred lay back on the pillow. "'Tis the dagger of Colin's attacker. I mean to find him."

They both started as Colin gave a loud, shuddering sigh.

"He goes deeper into sleep," Brother Wulfstan said with a worried shake of his head. "It does not bode well." He called Henry back over to Colin's bed. "I want you to sit here and talk to him, Henry. Talk about anything. And every now and then, call to him, ask him to open his eyes, to wake up. I will send for a novice to take over in a while. I want to give him no peace. I want to wake him."

Thoresby turned back to Alfred, whose eyes were closed, lips moving in prayer. "Sleep now, Alfred, and rest in the certainty that you did all you could for your partner. God be with you."

Thoresby asked Wulfstan to see him to the door.

"You have spoken with Dame Joanna?"

Brother Wulfstan nodded. "A most confused child."

"So you could make little sense of her speech?"

"Sadly, no. Neither can Dame Isobel. But Mistress Wilton had some speech with her that sounded lucid."

"Mistress Wilton?"

Wulfstan nodded. "So much so that the Reverend Mother thought she might ask Mistress Wilton to help her talk to Joanna."

"An interesting idea."

Wulfstan shook his head. "It is not Mistress Wilton's responsibility."

"Mistress Wilton refused?"

"I have not heard, Your Grace. But her father arrives in the city this week. And she is busy with the shop, Owen being away so often and Jasper here at the abbey's choir school learning his letters."

But Owen was back. Would he object? Thoresby must think how to finesse this. "Thank you, Brother Wulfstan. And I thank you and Brother Henry for your care of my men."

Brother Wulfstan bowed. "God grant we might see them both recovered, Your Grace."

"*Benedicte*, Brother Wulfstan."

Joanna spun round again and again, looking for a way out of the stony wasteland. But the rock outcroppings rose high on all sides of the sandy spot in which she stood. Above her was a gray sky, featureless. No wind. No sound. Not even her spinning broke the silence. She opened her mouth to scream, but nothing came. The air was so heavy it seemed to suck her breath away when she opened her mouth. She clamped her hand over her mouth. Tried to breathe. Could not. She could not remember how to breathe. Or swallow. The walls began to close in on her. She clawed at her throat, trying to open it to the air. Trying to breathe.

"Please, Dame Joanna, wake up. 'Tis but a nightmare you suffer. Please. You hurt yourself."

Joanna gasped for breath. It came. She used it to scream. "Hugh! Hugh!"

"Please, Dame Joanna, wake!"

All was darkness now. But there was sound and breath. A familiar voice. Joanna opened her eyes. It was the servant the Reverend Mother had sent to attend her, eyes round with terror. A scratch on the young woman's arm bled slowly. Joanna looked down at her own hands, held down by the worried maid. Joanna's fingernails were dark with blood. Something hurt. Burned. Her throat. She swallowed.

"Are you awake now, Dame Joanna?" the maid asked.

What was her name? "Mary?" Joanna whispered.

"Praise be God! I thought you would never wake." Mary looked back over her shoulder. "She is awake, Reverend Mother."

Joanna tried to move her hands. Mary let go, but stopped Joanna as she reached for the burning spot on her throat. "Let me clean it. You must not touch it. Let me clean you. Whatever were you fighting in your dream, Dame Joanna?"

Joanna closed her eyes. Hot tears spilled down her temples, into her hair. "The grave," she whispered. Would she ever be free of the dreams?

The Reverend Mother stepped forward, winced at the sight of the torn throat. "You are not in the grave, Joanna."

Joanna began to tremble. She hugged herself, trying to still the trembling. "No one deserves to suffer the grave before death's sleep."

"You said you had risen *from* the dead," Isobel said, trying to soothe her.

Joanna shook her head, moaned at the pain, closed her eyes. "He should not have done it. No one should suffer the grave before death's sleep," she whispered.

Isobel bent closer. "What did you say?"

Joanna rocked her head from side to side, whimpering. "He pays. But so dearly. It is not right. To be put there alive. He did not deserve that."

Isobel stepped back, crossed herself. "What do you know of Jaro's death, Joanna? Who killed him? Who put him in that grave?"

Joanna opened her eyes, grabbed Isobel's arm. "They opened my grave?"

"You knew Jaro was buried in your grave. How?"

Joanna squeezed Isobel's arm so hard the prioress cried out and pulled away. The green eyes were wild. "Jaro? Jaro was buried alive?"

Isobel rubbed her arm. "His neck was surely broken before he went in, Joanna."

The green eyes stared as the head snapped back and forth, back and forth. "No no no no no no no no no!"

Both Isobel and Mary worked up a sweat binding Joanna's hands to her sides, so she might not injure herself more. At last Isobel sent Mary for Dame Prudentia. While she awaited the infirmaress, Isobel sat as far from Joanna and her violent emotion as the room permitted.

Michaelo met the Archbishop with a note. "From the prioress of St. Clement's, Your Grace."

Thoresby took the note. "Follow me." The archbishop went into his parlor, poured two fingers of brandywine, drank it down, opened the note, read it to himself, threw it on the table with a curse.

"Your Grace?"

"Our intriguing Dame Joanna is now frightening the Reverend Mother with her terror of the grave."

"An experience one would remember keenly."

"She is a melodramatic woman, and speaks either nonsense or riddles. Dame Isobel is frightened. The nun ripped her own throat with her nails and keeps saying"—Thoresby picked up the letter—"'No one should suffer the grave before death's sleep.' A pronouncement, no more. According to both Brother Wulfstan and the Reverend Mother, only one person has managed to make sense of Joanna—or somehow inspires her to speak sense. Mistress Wilton."

Michaelo's nostrils flared. "Captain Archer will not like us drawing her in."

Thoresby glowered at Michaelo. "'Us'? You forget yourself, Michaelo. Go find out how long it will take them to warm my bath water." When he was alone, Thoresby picked up the letter and reread it. Dame Isobel begged him to use his influence to enlist Lucie Wilton's assistance, mentioning her interview with Lucie this afternoon. Thoresby poured himself another brandywine, sat down by the window, and sipped the delicate liquid while he pondered how to speak with the apothecary away from her protective husband.

At supper, Tildy mentioned seeing the prioress of St. Clement's leaving the shop as she returned from market. "Was it not enough that you saw her this morning, Mistress Lucie?"

Lucie frowned and shook her head, a tiny motion, obviously meaning only Tildy to see it. But Owen caught the exchange.

Tildy blushed and dropped her head, suddenly intent upon her soup.

Owen was intrigued. "What business have you with Dame Isobel de Percy? Is it Joanna Calverley? Have you met her?"

Lucie stirred her soup. "Briefly." She did not meet Owen's eyes. "Archbishop Thoresby has ordered Dame Isobel to learn what she can about the young woman's year away. Joanna has not been forthcoming. So Isobel thought I might suggest how to approach her."

Thoresby. Owen began to smell a rat. "Why you?"

Lucie shrugged. "Wulfstan sent for me. He wished a woman to examine Joanna. St. Clement's infirmaress had done so, but when she was moved to the abbey Wulfstan wanted to be doubly certain of her condition." Lucie pushed her soup aside, rose. "Shall we have the meat now?"

"Tildy can serve, Lucie. Go on."

Lucie sat back down with a sigh. "Isobel heard my discourse with Joanna, felt I had managed to get more sense out of her than she does. So she came to the shop this afternoon to ask my advice."

That sounded innocent enough. "You must tell me about her."

Lucie glanced up, saw that Owen had relaxed, grinned. "Poor Joanna. I of all people understand why she fled St. Clement's. And it must be all the worse now with God's ferret in charge."

"Is that what you called her when you lived there?"

"And worse! She was a sanctimonious informer."

Owen wished to hear more. Lucie seldom talked about her days at the convent. "And in what sinful acts did she catch you, my love?"

Tildy placed a trencher between Owen and Lucie and slipped back into her seat, leaning her chin on her hand, awaiting a good tale.

Lucie looked from Tildy to Owen and burst out laughing. "It was nothing so devilish, believe me. Snatching apples from the cellar, dancing in the orchard, climbing trees…"

"Her post was looking after the little ones?"

Lucie rolled her eyes. "Isobel is not that much older than I am. She simply took it on herself to torment me." The playful look darkened. "I have always believed it was Isobel spread the word that my mother was a French whore."

Tildy gasped. "Oh Mistress Lucie, that was never true!"

"Of course it was not true."

Owen did not like the color rising in Lucie's cheeks. "What was wrong with climbing trees?"

Lucie shrugged. "There were rules about everything. It seemed everything but prayer and work was a sin." Lucie suddenly laughed. "But Isobel now wears a silk gorget and carries delicately embroidered linen. I wish I knew to whom I might report her!"

"I hope you sent her away with bad advice."

"There was little I could tell her. But I shall tell you all you wish to know when you tell me why you are home betimes. Has Thoresby called you back to help him discover Joanna's story?"

Owen had known she would guess. He had purposefully not said, watching how long it would take. "You have found me out, wife. But while I was on the road, the circumstances became even more disturbing. I do not want you involved with this any more." He told her about Alfred and Colin.

When Tildy had gone off to bed, Lucie told Owen about Joanna's condition and what she had learned from Isobel.

"I want to speak with her tomorrow," he said as they climbed up to bed.

"Shall I come?"

Owen did not like the eagerness with which Lucie asked the question. "No. I have told you. People have been murdered round that woman. I want you to stay away from her." He stopped as they entered their bedchamber and turned to Lucie, tipping her chin up so she looked him in the eye. "Promise me you will stay away from Joanna Calverley?"

Lucie smiled, reached up on her tiptoes and kissed him. "Let us speak no more of nuns this night, Owen. I want my husband's full attention."

Much later, when Owen woke in the night with a full bladder, he shook his head at how neatly Lucie had sidestepped the promise. But, in faith, he loved her for that very willfulness.

7

SUBTLE MANEUVERS

Thoresby sent for Michaelo on rising. Usually he gave his secretary his orders for the day while breakfasting, but with the canons here there was no privacy. While the servants dressed him, Thoresby listed Michaelo's tasks, including summoning Owen Archer to the palace for a meeting. "Mid morning should suffice." He had an elegantly simple solution to getting Archer out of the way while he engaged Lucie Wilton in the task of communicating with Joanna Calverley.

By the time Thoresby descended to break his fast, Ravenser and Louth already sat before the fire in the great hall, dipping bread in honey and discussing their plans for the day.

"I shall spend the morning at St. Leonard's doing battle," Ravenser was saying. He was Master of St. Leonard's Hospital. "The monks oppose me in the sale of two corrodies, but they admit that there will be shortfalls by Michaelmas."

Louth sniffed. "Hospitals. I cannot abide such places. You were a saint to accept the post."

Ravenser laughed. "Hardly a saint, Nicholas. I rarely go in the infirmary. My business is with the brothers."

"Corrodies are an excellent source of income. What do they propose instead?"

"Economies, to get through the crisis." Ravenser nodded at Louth's laugh. "You see the folly of such thinking, why can't they? They refuse to admit that the Petercorn and the income from the manor farms are steadily falling. They shall not improve until we are free of pestilence and blessed with good harvests for a while.

Economies now will only prolong the problem."

Thoresby, tired of his nephew's frequent tirades about the backward economics of the Augustinians of St. Leonard's, made a noisy entrance as he joined them at table. "Are your retainers set to any tasks today, Nicholas?"

Louth straightened. "Doubling up the guard at the abbey gates as they have been doing, Your Grace."

"I would like two of them to talk with Alfred, learn all they can about where the assault occurred, and then go look round, talk to the folk who live there, find out if anyone saw or heard anything, knows anything."

Louth rose. "I shall see to it at once, Your Grace."

Ravenser dabbed at his sticky hands. "What about Owen Archer? Should he perhaps be with them?"

Thoresby shook his head. "I have other plans for him. He will be off to Leeds on the morrow. I want him to talk with the Calverleys. Find out all he can about Joanna. Why the family disowned her."

Louth had almost reached the door. Now he turned round. "Your Grace, might I accompany him to Leeds?"

Thoresby sat back in his chair, steepling his hands and peering at Nicholas de Louth over them. "Why?"

Louth returned to the table. He stood by Thoresby, his fingertips pressing into the table. "I feel responsible for much of this situation. I wish to do what I can."

"Archer is quite competent."

"Indeed." Louth cleared his throat and kept his eyes on Thoresby's hands. "I thought I might learn something by observing him, Your Grace."

Thoresby considered Louth's pampered paunch and fussy clothes. He could not imagine him riding with Archer. "I doubt he will be keen for your company."

Louth took a step closer. "I pray you suggest it. He can but refuse."

Thoresby shrugged. "I shall suggest it. Get your men to work at once—in case Archer surprises me and agrees."

Louth smiled, bobbed his head, hurried from the room.

• • •

The day was overcast, high clouds holding no rain, cooler than it had been of late. John Thoresby sat on the low wall separating the kitchen garden from the formal garden and looked back toward the house. The paths of the kitchen garden were edged in santolina and hardy lavender. Camomile blossoms gave off an apple scent even though they were closed up against the morning chill. Bees already buzzed among the borage blossoms. Thoresby looked up at the archbishop's palace, two stories of well-matched stone with small glazed windows, a third of whitewashed wattle and daub with wax parchment windows for the servants. It had been a beautiful house, worthy of entertaining even the King. Not so lovely now. Thoresby approved only essential repairs now that he stayed here infrequently. Because the dean and chapter of York Minster had become increasingly jealous of their autonomy, Thoresby usually chose Bishopthorpe as his residence when seeing to business in York—it was several miles south of the city, but close enough. And it was even lovelier than this, with gardens rolling down to the river.

He was a fortunate man to have palaces to choose among— he had even more, scattered about the countryside and even in Beverley. It was a great privilege to be Archbishop of York. He sat in the king's Parliament, ruled over a goodly portion of this great city of York, and through his archdeacons over all Yorkshire.

Yet it gnawed at him that William of Wykeham was poised to take the chancellor's chain from round his neck. Why? With his increasingly uncertain relationship with King Edward, it should please him to see an escape.

But it did not. He liked the power he wielded as Lord Chancellor. And he still hoped to guide the King in ruling his kingdom fairly and firmly. He had tasted too much power to be satisfied with just an archbishopric now.

• • •

Owen was puzzled to be shown out into the palace garden. Thoresby sat on a bench near the cloister wall, arms crossed, legs stretched out before him, chatting with the gardener. The scene struck Owen as false, set up for a purpose. He wondered what Simon thought of this sudden friendliness.

Simon looked up, saw Owen standing at the end of the path. "Captain Archer. Good day to you."

Owen nodded. "Simon. Your Grace." He strolled on down the path as Simon loaded his garden cart, prepared to make his escape. Lucky man.

"Godspeed, Your Grace," Simon said, starting forward. He grinned at Owen as he reached him. "Not too long now, eh? Mistress Wilton is in good hands with the Riverwoman." He trundled on by.

Thoresby drew in his legs and dusted off the front of his gown. "Is the training progressing well?" He gestured for Owen to sit on his left.

"Well enough," Owen said, settling down. Perverse of Thoresby to choose to meet in the garden on an overcast day.

"Can Lief and Gaspare continue on their own?"

Owen turned his good eye fully on the archbishop's face. He was up to something. "I've a few more things to show them."

"Might that be done today?" Thoresby turned to face Owen, shook his head with a mocking smile. "Why do you frown upon me with such ferocity?"

Owen had not been prepared for such a blunt question. "'Tis the light, Your Grace. Though overcast, there is yet a glare out here."

Thoresby chuckled. "Evasion does not become you. I thought it was the tasks I set you to, but I think not. You enjoy the challenge. So it must be me. You disapprove of me."

"You send me after the truth for the wrong reasons."

The archbishop's eyebrows rose. "And what reasons are those?"

Lucie would tell Owen to mind his peace, the archbishop had been generous to them. But Lucie was not here. "Ambition and pride. You care nothing for the victims, you merely wish to restore order."

Thoresby crossed his arms, leaned back again, stretched out his legs. "It is my duty to keep the peace in my liberty."

"No doubt that is true." A pointless conversation. "Why do you ask whether I can finish training Lief and Gaspare today?"

Thoresby chuckled. "Back to the matter at hand. Fair enough. I want you to go to Leeds, speak with the Calverleys, find out all you can about Joanna."

"What is your interest in the matter?"

"I must decide whether to order Dame Isobel to accept Joanna Calverley back in St. Clement's or whether to send the woman elsewhere. Before I impose the nun on anyone I must know whether she is in any way responsible for the deaths of Longford's cook and his maid. Or Longford's disappearance."

Owen nodded. He saw the sense in it. "Someone else might make the journey faster, Your Grace. I am off to Pontefract in a few days for the Duke of Lancaster."

"Leave tomorrow, stop in Leeds on the way."

Owen bit back a curse.

"And take Sir Nicholas de Louth with you."

"Who?"

"He is a canon of Beverley and clerk to Prince Edward. He had been watching Longford's house in Beverley for a long while."

"A Churchman? What use will he be to me? If I must be off to Leeds, at least let me choose my traveling companions."

"He has requested this, Archer. And it has occurred to me that it would be good to have him with you at Pontefract. Lancaster will be interested in what Sir Nicholas has to say."

"Why does he wish to come?"

"As I said, he has been watching Longford's house. It seems a natural extension of the work he has been doing."

"Do you order me to take him?"

Thoresby sighed. "If I must."

"Will he let me manage the Calverleys?"

"I trust he will."

Owen saw no use in further argument. Thoresby had arranged it all before approaching him. As usual. "You saw Alfred and Colin last night?"

"I did." Thoresby told Owen of their conditions, what Alfred had told him. "I have sent Sir Nicholas's men out to examine the site of the attack, find out what they can. Nicholas will give you a full account."

Owen rose. "Before I go, I should meet Joanna Calverley."

Thoresby gave a little bow. "Whatever you see fit."

Dame Joanna's sole companion this morning was a maid, spinning to keep herself occupied. The young woman clutched her spindle to her lap as she rose to greet Owen, but before he could introduce himself a nun hurried in, waving her hands and spilling smiles as she approached. "Sit down, child," she trilled to the maid, who did so gladly. The nun was of an age with the Reverend Mother, but much comelier, with laugh lines radiating out from her eyes and mouth. "God go with you, Captain Archer. I am Dame Katherine. I have been assisting the infirmaress with Joanna." She fanned her face and beamed at him. "Such a warm day. You are here to speak with Dame Joanna?"

Owen wondered at the wisdom of assigning this energetic woman to the infirmary. "I am off to see her family tomorrow. I thought she might have a message for them."

Katherine gave a little hop and clapped her hands. "How thoughtful! Let us see whether Joanna is awake. It is not always apparent." They moved toward the bed.

Dame Joanna lay quietly, her hands folded over the covers. A white cap controlled the red hair, which Owen could see was curly and thick. Her skin was stark white, which made her freckles seem like a spray of tiny blemishes. Owen still stood beside the bed when Joanna opened her eyes. The vivid green surprised him.

"Good morning, Joanna," Dame Katherine chirped. "You have a visitor. A Captain Archer."

Joanna boldly ran her eyes up and down, getting her fill of Owen. He felt oddly naked. A smile played round Joanna's full lips. "A soldier? Visiting me? To what do I owe this delightful courtesy?"

Owen thought neither of these women suited to the convent,

one boisterous, the other flirtatious. He sank down onto the stool Katherine had set behind him. "Tomorrow I travel to Leeds on business for the archbishop," he explained to Joanna. "His Grace thought you might wish me to carry a message to your kin." The moment the words were out, he remembered that her family had cast her out. Tripping on his own tongue again.

Joanna's smile froze. "My kin would hardly thank you for word of me, captain. You shall find that my mother denies giving me birth."

Surely not so far. "How could a mother be so cruel?"

Joanna made a dismissive sound, then smiled up at him. "How did you lose your eye?" She reached stubby fingers up to clutch the air at the height of his scar. The movement disturbed her covers and revealed the blue mantle wrapped round her. "I should love you to lie with me."

"Joanna!" Dame Katherine cried. "You forget your vows. And his. This is Mistress Wilton's husband."

Joanna pouted. "What a pity." She dropped her hand, drew the mantle up round her chin. "Why should such a handsome couple trouble themselves with a Magdalene?"

"A what?"

Joanna closed her eyes. "Tell the family of my burial in Beverley. That should cheer them."

Owen leaned closer. "What did you mean about a Magdalene?"

Joanna opened her eyes slowly, whispered something that Owen could not hear. He leaned closer. Her hand shot from under the covers, grabbed his vest, pulled him toward her. As Owen backed away, Joanna licked her lips.

"I am a Magdalene, my sweet captain," she murmured, and closed her eyes.

Dame Katherine hustled Owen from the room. "Pray God forgive her. My apologies, Captain Archer. I have never seen her behave so."

"No matter. I was forewarned that she was a strange young woman."

Dame Katherine looked truly embarrassed, her hands flitting about as if looking for a discreet perch. "What must you think! And Mistress Wilton was so kind to her, I hear. You must not tell her what a wicked thing Joanna did."

"Has she said anything to you about what happened to her?"

"She has spoken of the sea. And soldiers. What was it she said?" Katherine dropped her chin and hugged herself, thinking, nodded a few times, looked up. "One night she spoke of young soldiers being drawn to the sea. Gathered by the sea." She shook her head. "Just phrases, you know. Nothing you can be sure of."

"Anything else?"

"On several of the nights I sat with her she called for someone named 'Hugh.' I thought at first she shouted 'You!', but she was confused when I asked what she needed. 'Hugh.'" Katherine nodded.

"She said no more about him?"

"Nothing. And when she waked, she just frowned when we asked of whom she had dreamed."

"I noticed that she wears the mantle she claims to be Our Lady's."

Katherine glanced back toward the door. "Alas, we have not heard the last of that piece of cloth. Dame Margaret is convinced of her miraculous cure."

"Has she worked any miracles in your presence?"

The brown eyes studied him frankly. "Captain, you do not believe such a woman would be so blessed by Our Heavenly Mother, do you?"

Owen grinned. "I thought you might believe it."

The cheery face crinkled up in laughter. "Oh dear me no, Captain. And neither do these sober monks, praise God. But to answer your question as I believe you meant it, no, I have witnessed nothing that she has later claimed to be a miracle."

"And she has not tried to convince any of the monks?"

Katherine frowned. "That is a different question. Yes, she takes every opportunity to claim it is a holy relic. Foolish child."

"She is hardly a child."

"A child within is what I meant, Captain. I believe Joanna is— simple. God forgive me, but that is what I think."

"You have been most helpful, Dame Katherine. I thank you."

• • •

Owen left the guest house gladly and headed for the infirmary, hoping Alfred might be awake. But both Alfred and Colin slept. "Has Colin wakened at all?" Owen asked Brother Henry.

The young monk sighed. "We assault him with chatter—prayers, stories, songs, but God has deemed fit to sink him deeper and deeper into sleep. He rewards our efforts not at all; not even a flicker of his lids."

"Have Louth's men been to see Alfred?"

Brother Henry nodded. "They seemed pleased with his description of the street and hurried off to question all those who live nearby."

"How are Alfred's spirits?"

"Low. He feels responsible."

"Pity he is not awake. I could ease his mind on that account— 'Twas I recommended them for the duty."

Brother Henry shook his head, his young face solemn. "You must not blame yourself. Those who assaulted them are to blame, not you or Alfred."

Owen turned to leave.

"I pray you stay a moment," Henry said. "I have something you should see." He led Owen to a chest by the fire, took out a dagger. "Alfred clutched this when he came in. He says he found it beneath Colin. He says it belongs to Colin's murderer, though how anyone can say in such an assault which blow was—" Henry put his hand to his mouth. "Sweet Heaven, do you hear what we do? Both Alfred and I assume Colin will not wake." Henry crossed himself and bowed his head, murmuring a prayer.

Owen moved into the lamplight, examined the dagger. The handle was intricately carved, sea serpents. Dark, heavy wood, not metal. It was not a costly weapon. But worn, treasured. Perhaps the owner would return for it? "Keep it safe, Brother Henry. It might be of use to us."

Lucie shook her head at Master Saurian, who was launching into an account of a particularly grisly amputation he had performed at St. Leonard's Hospital. Jasper sat on a stool behind Lucie, ready to reach for jars. Lucie did not wish the boy to overhear anything that might give him nightmares. He had enough of them as it was.

Saurian sniffed. "The boy must learn about life, Mistress Wilton. You do him no favor sheltering him."

"He knows enough of life for now, Master Saurian." She stood poised over the scales on the counter with a jar of spice. "How much cardamom did you say?"

Back in the kitchen, the garden door opened and closed. Voices murmured. Owen. Lucie glanced back at Jasper. "Go on, now. Owen will be glad of your company."

Jasper needed no more encouragement. He had begged permission to skip classes today when he heard of Owen's return.

Lucie poured the last of the ingredients into a pouch.

Saurian hefted it in his palm as if weighing it. "They say you have been to see the resurrected nun."

"The prodigal," Lucie corrected him. "Her death and burial were an act."

Saurian looked down his long nose. "What of the miracles?"

Thank Heaven Jasper was out of the room. "I know of none."

Saurian shook his head. "You are a cautious one, Mistress Wilton."

"Was there anything else?" She smiled, but she knew it could not possibly look friendly.

"No. No, this will do." The physician gathered his pouches and departed.

The bead curtain rattled as Owen stepped through from the kitchen. His dark eye had an apologetic cast to it. "Bad news?" Lucie guessed.

Owen squeezed her shoulders. "I am off to Leeds in the morning."

"But you just arrived. And Sir Robert arrives tomorrow. I hoped you would be here." Owen hugged her to him. He smelled of smoke and fresh air and Owen. Lord, she did not want him to leave again so soon.

"His Grace is set on it," he whispered.

Lucie leaned her head against Owen's shoulder. "How vigorously did you protest?"

He held her away from him, lifted her chin so he might see her eyes. "Do you think I wish to be away from you so often?"

She shrugged.

"I miss you all the time I am away. And worry about you."

"But you enjoy the adventure." She stopped his protest with a finger to his lips. "Peace, my love. I do not blame you. I said from the beginning that you would chafe at the bit in the shop. But just now it is particularly hard. With Sir Robert coming. And the child..." She looked away as tears welled up. The damnable tears that were so ready to flow these days.

Owen pulled her back into his arms, but the moment was interrupted by the shop bell.

More than the moment, Lucie realized with dismay. Sir Robert had arrived a day early.

8

FAMILY TENSIONS

A house full of dinner guests on Owen's second and last night home. It seemed he never had time alone with Lucie except in their bedchamber. And it would be worse with children. Owen tried to dismiss the thought, but it persisted. What did he know of children, besides what he could remember of being one? He stared at the floor, his leggings half off, pondering. There was Jasper. He enjoyed Jasper. But the boy had joined their household just this year, at the age of eight. What would it be like with infants about?

Lucie bustled in the door, flushed from rushing about supervising Tildy's cooking, setting up the table, and checking that all was prepared in the extra chamber, where Sir Robert and his squire would sleep. She paused as she caught sight of Owen, shirt off, leggings half off. "I know that the day is warm, but really, my love, you must do better than that!" Then, with a worried, almost frightened expression, she asked, "What is it? What troubles you?"

It was no time to admit his doubts. Instead, Owen grabbed Lucie and toppled backward onto the bed with her squealing in his arms. Pulling off her cap, he let her soft hair tumble into his face.

Lucie tried to wriggle away, gasping for breath. "No time!" she managed. "Owen, please!"

With a sigh, he helped her sit up. "Could we not send word to Lief and Gaspare that your father has arrived, we have no room for so many at table?"

Lucie shook her hair, fluffing it, then went over to the small table where she kept her brushes and hairpins and a small mirror.

"There would still be Sir Robert and his squire. It is not possible to rid ourselves of them. So I should prefer your friends at least this night. Some cheerful company." She began to arrange her hair.

Owen lounged on the bed, watching her lazily. "Sir Robert seemed cheerful enough."

Lucie turned round to Owen, letting the coil of hair in her hands cascade down her back. "He *is* in good spirits." She rose, picked up the gown and surcoat Tildy had laid out, considered them, turning them this way and that. "Shall I wear this tonight? Or the blue?"

Owen frowned. The gown she held was a soft green, the surcoat gold and green, colors that brought the gold out in her hair. The blue gown—well, it did bring out her blue eyes. And the bodice was low cut... "This one, to be sure. Unless you mean to flirt with my comrades?"

Lucie pressed her thickened middle and laughed. "In this state?"

"Some men think a woman great with child is most delicious."

"You are wicked!" Lucie wriggled into the gown, turned to let Owen lace it for her. Then she spun round. "Truly. Am I presentable?"

How could she doubt it? "Most enchanting. Too tempting already." She kissed him on the forehead.

"So there is no remedy? I must dress?"

"Indeed you must. I certainly cannot entertain Lief and Gaspare without you."

"I met Joanna Calverley today. She tried to kiss me."

Lucie sank down on the bed beside him. "What had you said to her?"

Owen told Lucie of the incident. "Dame Katherine whisked me out of there, much embarrassed."

Lucie giggled. "I can imagine! But truly, what had you done to so delight Joanna?"

"I was my own charming self."

Lucie punched his bare chest.

"Dame Katherine believes Joanna is simple. Childlike."

Lucie shook her head. "Not at all. Her escape from St. Clement's took thoughtful planning. No. Not simple, Owen. And not innocent!"

Owen liked the way her hand lingered on his bare chest.

The evening began pleasantly. Sir Robert's squire assisted Tildy, allowing Lucie to relax and listen to Gaspare and Lief telling tales of their adventures in France. It was not until halfway through the meal, when Lief had gone on for a while about the pleasures of parenthood, that Sir Robert changed the mood.

Lucie's father had listened quietly to the banter. Owen liked his father-in-law, a retired soldier with a gruff, straightforward manner. When the older man lifted his cup to toast the gathering of friends and family, Owen knew something was up.

"My steward was in the city a while back and heard that your neighbor John Corbett had died and his house was empty," Sir Robert began. He tugged at his fashionably forked beard.

"Yes," Lucie said, sipping her wine, unsuspecting. "Poor John fell in the snow on his way to the privy one night. By the time a servant found him, he had frozen to death."

"They say 'tis a painless death," Lief said. "The chill makes you sleepy and you just lie down to sleep."

Sir Robert crossed himself. "I understand the Corbett children have offered the property for sale."

Now Lucie looked up, studied her father's face. "I have heard something of the sort. What is your interest in the matter?"

Sir Robert smiled. "It is a nice piece of property. And a sound house."

Lucie and Owen exchanged a look.

"I mean to purchase it for you," Sir Robert announced.

Owen's blind eye reacted with a shower of needle pricks almost before his mind registered the insult. Corbett's house was large, the house of a prosperous wine merchant. Sir Robert meant to give Lucie a house worthy of a knight's daughter, a house that Owen could not afford to give her. He was merely an apprentice and a spy, freeman though he might be. Even worse, he had no pedigree. He had not even given Lucie this house—it was hers from her first marriage. Owen looked round to see whether the others noted his humiliation. There was indeed an uncomfortable silence at the table.

Two spots of color stood out on Lucie's cheeks. Her slender

neck was poker straight. Her silk veil trembled. "*This* is our home, Sir Robert," she said quietly.

Sir Robert tilted his head and studied his daughter's face. His white brows drew together, then smoothed as he smiled and said, "Indeed. It is a lovely home, daughter, I meant no criticism. And the garden—I have seen no finer in all my travels. But with the child coming, and young Jasper about to begin his apprenticeship, and perhaps more children in the years to come, you will soon burst through the walls."

Owen, seeing Lucie's jaw freezing, jumped in. "We have talked of building a separate kitchen at the back, which would give us more room here."

Sir Robert nodded. "An excellent solution if it were not for the garden. Such a new structure would deprive you of some of the garden, which is vital to your business. Use Corbett's house to expand. Connect the houses, or at least take down the fence and make it all one property." Sir Robert dabbed at his beard, looked back and forth between Owen and Lucie. "I have done so little for you, I feel this is too little too late. But it is something…" He trailed off as he met tight faces.

The moment was saved by Gaspare, who chided them in a cheery voice for bringing family matters to the table with guests, and began the story of Owen's troubles with Lady Jocelyn, a lady in waiting to Blanche of Lancaster. Soon the table rang with polite laughter.

After Gaspare and Lief departed for the castle and Sir Robert and his squire retired, Lucie and Owen walked out into the garden and sat under the stars, silently regarding the dark bulk of Corbett's house.

"I am being selfish," Owen said quietly. "He is only offering you what he knows I cannot."

"The shop is doing well. And His Grace, for all your complaints about him, does reward you handsomely for your efforts on his behalf." Lucie's voice was still tight with indignation.

Owen turned to her, took both her hands in his. "Lucie, I do not understand. Why are *you* offended? It is *my* part to be so. But in truth, Lief is right; it is the generous offer of a fond father."

Lucie squeezed Owen's hands, lifted them to her lips, kissing one at a time. "Too little too late, Owen. He said it himself. You realize what he is about. He is bored with the manor and thinks to spend more time in the city. What could be more convenient for him than a house in the city, with a permanent staff?"

Owen had not even considered that.

Lucie nodded. "Grandchildren to bounce on his knee, an apothecary to see to his health—it is too perfect for him. But what of us, Owen? We shall have no peace. No privacy."

"We have precious little of that as it is."

Lucie pressed Owen's hands to her heart. "I know. And soon we shall be up all hours with the baby..." She sighed.

Owen's heart lightened. She, too, had misgivings about the coming event. He drew her into his arms and held her tight. She clung to him. When at last they went inside they were at peace.

Owen left early, after a quiet breakfast—Sir Robert had gone out riding. Feeling at odds, Lucie went out to the garden.

It was a cloudy, humid morning, hinting of a warm day to come. The air was heavy with the scent of early roses. Nicholas had loved those roses. With the little knife she wore at her belt with her keys, Lucie cut a few blossoms and placed them on Nicholas's grave. Then from the garden shed she got a basket, the old, rusty dagger she favored as a weeding tool, and the woven mat for kneeling, and settled herself at the edge of the mint garden to weed and think before she opened the shop. She did some of her best thinking out here, attacking the weeds and turning problems and plans over in her head. Her pregnancy made bending more awkward, but if she straightened often and stopped when the dull ache in her back became more noticeable, she still found this one of the most pleasant moments of her day.

Melisende, Queen of Jerusalem and the garden, came over to

see what Lucie meant to do in the mint bed. The cat was partial to mint and had the sweetest breath in York, so Lucie's pose above the bed, with dagger and basket, required careful watching. When Melisende verified that Lucie was not harvesting this morning, merely pulling the weeds that got in the way, she bit off a small sprig of peppermint and settled down beside Lucie to chew her snack.

Lucie rubbed Melisende's head until the cat began a rumbling purr and stretched her front paws out in contentment. Then Lucie fell to her work and her thoughts.

Sir Robert. She hardly knew him. What had possessed him to make this visit? And such an offer as the Corbett house? What was she to do with him while he was here? He said he would help with the heavy work while Owen was away, but he was a frail old man. And what did an old campaigner know of the work in shop or garden? Sir Robert's visit was the gesture of a father who wished to make amends for his neglect of Lucie and for his sins against her mother, Amelie, wresting her from her home in Normandy, leaving her with strangers in Yorkshire, blaming her for having but one daughter and no son, and by his neglect inspiring the despair that killed her. He was trying to work off his guilt.

It was his widowed sister, Dame Phillippa, who had impressed on Sir Robert the effect his behavior had had on his only child. Phillippa had stayed with Lucie when Nicholas was dying. When she returned to Freythorpe Hadden, where she was housekeeper for her brother, she had told Sir Robert how the torment of Amelie, Lucie's mother, had affected Lucie's life. Since that time, Sir Robert had prayed for Lucie and showered her with gifts.

But by then Lucie had not the habit of loving Sir Robert. To her he would ever be the loud soldier smelling of leather and horse sweat who had never remembered her name as a child, who had sent her to bed without answering her terrified questions the night her mother died, and who had sent her off to St. Clement's and forgotten her there.

What was she to do with him in the small house? He had no idea what her work as master apothecary entailed. He was not yet reconciled to her having married beneath her—and twice, at that. He could not understand her pride in being a master apothecary.

What would he think of her summons to St. Mary's to examine Dame Joanna? Or the Reverend Mother's plea for help?

Perhaps she should do more for Dame Isobel. Perhaps that was God's plan in having Sir Robert visit now: he would witness Lucie's service to the Archbishop of York and Lord Chancellor of England. He would realize that she had not wasted her life, nor was she her mother, dependent for everything on a man she hardly knew, terrified that if she did not bear him a son she would be discarded, and so destitute. He would see that she had no time to be his nursemaid.

Melisende's head jerked up. Lucie looked round. Sir Robert stood behind her, dressed simply. "Now, you see? I brought practical clothes. Put me to work!"

Brother Michaelo found Lucie in her garden, explaining the arrangement of the beds to a white-haired man who listened politely, occasionally stealing an odd, emotional look at the apothecary. Though old, the man had the bearing of a soldier. Michaelo saw something in the face that made him guess this must be Sir Robert D'Arby; there was a resemblance to Lucie, though he could not say exactly, perhaps—yes, the jaw. And the level gaze.

"Mistress Wilton, forgive the interruption," Michaelo said with a bow, "but His Grace the Archbishop requests the honor of your father's presence at supper this evening. He understands Sir Robert D'Arby is staying with you and, of course, extends the invitation to yourself."

Lucie's blue eyes widened in surprise. Her already straight back managed to straighten more. She touched the elderly gentleman's hand. "Sir Robert, this is Brother Michaelo, secretary to John Thoresby, Archbishop of York and the King's Lord Chancellor."

"Indeed?" Sir Robert glanced at his daughter with a puzzled frown.

"Brother Michaelo, this is my father, Sir Robert D'Arby."

Michaelo bowed to them both. "Sir Richard de Ravenser and

Jehannes, Archdeacon of York, also dine with His Grace this evening."

Sir Robert, recovering his poise, inclined his head. "We shall be honored to dine with the Chancellor."

After Brother Michaelo departed, Sir Robert turned to his daughter. "John Thoresby, Archbishop of York and Chancellor of England. I am honored—but why does he so honor me, I wonder?"

Lucie wondered, too. And so hard on the heels of Owen's departure.

Refusing to let the archbishop's summons fluster her, Lucie closed the shop at the usual time, deliberately making no change in her routine. So little notice. As if their plans for the evening were presumed to be nothing. But perhaps this invitation was for the best. She had dreaded the first evening alone with Sir Robert.

When Lucie stepped into the kitchen, she found her father already waiting down by the fire, grandly dressed. Tildy followed Lucie up to her bedchamber. "I've aired your blue dress and veil, Mistress Lucie, and heated water for you to wash."

"Tildy, I am not meeting the King."

"He is Lord Chancellor of all England, Mistress Lucie! 'Tis almost as much an honor."

"Owen never fusses when he eats at His Grace's table."

"Oh, Mistress, it *is* an honor, no matter what you say. And I must hear about everything. What you eat, how Lizzie serves, what hangings are in the hall—everything."

Lucie laughed, despite herself. "Would that I could send you in my stead. You would be a much more appreciative guest. But I *am* curious to meet Archdeacon Jehannes. Owen speaks of him fondly." Lucie lifted the blue veil, to be worn with a simple gold circlet to hold it in place. She frowned. "In faith, is this appropriate, Tildy?"

"He is accustomed to the ladies at Court, Mistress. This is most fitting."

Lucie fingered the soft wool of her gown, also a lovely pale shade of blue. Her Aunt Phillippa had had the dress and veil made for her on her last birthday. Fortunately, the slightly darker surcoat would hide the tightening of the gown round her five month waist. Not that she had reason to be embarrassed about her condition, but she did not care to flaunt it.

Tildy fussed over Lucie, winding her mistress's hair into coils on either side of her head, arranging the veil, adjusting the surcoat over the gown. As Lucie turned to let Tildy admire her handiwork, there was a knock on the kitchen door. Tildy hurried down, Lucie right behind her. Sir Robert had made no move to open the door himself, accustomed to a grander household with many servants.

A man in the Archbishop's livery stepped inside. With a bow, he introduced himself. "I am Gilbert, Mistress Wilton. His Grace has sent me to escort you and Sir Robert to his palace." A sword hung at his side, a dagger was tucked into his belt.

"Escort us? But it is not yet sunset. We can find our way. And we have Sir Robert's squire."

"His Grace insisted."

About to protest again, Lucie thought better of it. The weapons suggested that the Archbishop was in earnest about something. She extended her hand. "Then come, Gilbert. We must not keep His Grace waiting."

Tildy was proud of her pretty mistress as Lucie left on Gilbert's arm, her father and his squire, Daimon, walking beside them.

9

LUCIE DINES AT THE PALACE

Thoresby met Lucie and her father halfway across the hall.

"Welcome, Mistress Wilton, Sir Robert. You are most gracious to come."

Lucie curtsied. "Your Grace honors us." Her eyes were downcast, but he had seen how alertly she had glanced round the hall as she entered. She looked lovely, in a blue gown that matched her eyes. In carriage and grace, her noble breeding showed.

Thoresby turned to the white-haired gentleman. He had expected a somberly dressed man, knowing of D'Arby's long pilgrimage to the Outremer after his wife's death. But D'Arby surprised him, elegant in a green velvet gown with a jeweled belt hung with an intricately carved dagger. "Sir Robert, you are most welcome. I met you once, years ago, when you were in the King's service."

Sir Robert bowed. "I was honored then, and I am honored now, Your Grace."

"My man was an acceptable escort?"

Sir Robert bowed again. "Though there was no need, Your Grace. My squire Daimon is sufficient protection for my daughter."

"Perhaps I erred on the side of caution, but as Mistress Wilton undoubtedly knows, two of my men were attacked a few days ago. And I am in the midst of a puzzling situation involving two violent deaths. I worried that I might endanger you by asking you to come this evening. People know Captain Archer works for me, and in what capacity. And if the attackers knew that Mistress Wilton has spoken with Dame Joanna Calverley…"

Sir Robert looked puzzled. "I feel as if I have entered the room in the middle of a conversation."

Lucie, however, looked enlightened. "So this evening has to do with Dame Joanna?"

Seeing Sir Robert's confusion, Thoresby realized Lucie Wilton had told her father nothing of this matter. Perhaps this evening had not been such a clever idea after all. But he must make the best of it. He smiled at Lucie. "Brother Wulfstan and Dame Isobel de Percy both recommended I consult you in the matter."

Sir Robert glanced with alarm from the Archbishop to his daughter, back to the Archbishop. "Your Grace! Have you involved my daughter in some dangerous scheme?"

Lucie put her hand on her father's arm. "Peace, Sir Robert. I assisted St. Mary's infirmarian with a runaway nun who has returned a prodigal, that is all."

Sir Robert's dark look made it plain he was uneasy. Thoresby must quickly calm the man or the evening would be a waste. "Please, Sir Robert, I know your daughter's condition, and I have seen her husband in action. I assure you I would do nothing to incur his wrath."

Lucie gave a little laugh. "Besides, Sir Robert, it was not His Grace but my old friend Brother Wulfstan, and Dame Isobel de Percy, the prioress of St. Clement's, who approached me about Dame Joanna."

The uncomfortable moment was interrupted by the arrival of two men.

One, dressed in the robes of an archdeacon, bowed to the archbishop. "Your Grace!" He was of slight build with the sort of face that remains boyish until wrinkles or scars trouble the smooth surface.

The other gentleman was a startling twin to the archbishop, only younger.

Thoresby introduced Jehannes, Archdeacon of York, and Sir Richard de Ravenser, Provost of Beverley and Master of St. Leonard's Hospital. Noting Lucie's glances back and forth between himself and Ravenser, Thoresby added, "Sir Richard is my sister's son, Mistress Wilton. I see you note the similarities."

Lucie blushed becomingly. "It is remarkable."

Thoresby watched with amusement his nephew's reaction to Lucie Wilton. Ravenser looked Lucie over, then glanced quickly at his own attire and breathed easy, knowing he was fashionably and attractively attired in a green houppelande patterned with leaves, and gold leggings. "Mistress Wilton, you ornament the room with your beauty," Ravenser said with a little bow.

Two red patches of irritation showed high on Lucie's cheekbones. She leveled cold blue eyes on Ravenser. "Sir Richard."

Ravenser glanced with confusion at his uncle, who was not quick enough to erase the smirk from his face. "Mistress Wilton is a master apothecary, Richard. I have asked her here tonight to consult with us concerning Dame Joanna—not as an ornament."

Fortunately for Ravenser, Lizzie called them to table. Brother Michaelo already waited there.

Over the mawnenye, a delicately seasoned dish of lentils and lamb, Jehannes and Michaelo kept up a steady exchange of news about preparations for the Corpus Christi procession and pageants. A salmon and fruit tart followed. Sir Robert ate with enthusiasm while politely answering Ravenser's questions about the estate of Freythorpe Hadden. When the henne dorre was served, Brother Michaelo quizzed Lucie as to the virtues of cardamom and whether eating such a quantity of it in the chicken dish would invigorate them. Lucie was puzzled by the secretary. He had always seemed a disagreeable man, but tonight he was almost as charming as Jehannes, who proved as forthright and gentle as Owen had described him. What intrigued Lucie most, however, was how neither the present secretary nor the former made any effort to hide their admiration for John Thoresby. Lucie found herself watching the archbishop closely, wondering what it was about the man that inspired such loyalty in his secretaries and distrust in Owen. Ravenser she largely ignored—though it was difficult, he stared so. He was not an unpleasant looking man, with intelligent dark eyes and a sensitive mouth, but he obviously believed that, as ornaments, women welcomed stares. Lucie tried not to ruin the evening by fuming under his persistent regard.

After supper the servants arranged the chairs round the fire. Small tables held fruit and nuts, brandywine, claret and mead. Then the servants disappeared.

The company sat, and Thoresby picked up the brandywine, poured himself a cup, sat back, inviting the others to help themselves. Lucie, her father, Ravenser and Jehannes followed Thoresby's choice. Michaelo hesitated, looking uncomfortable.

"Shall I go, Your Grace? Do you want me part of this?"

Thoresby sipped his brandywine and studied his secretary over the rim of his cup. "Should I not trust you, Brother Michaelo?"

The secretary looked surprised by the blunt question. "I—you can trust me with your life, Heaven be my witness."

Thoresby nodded. "Then pour yourself a refreshment, Brother Michaelo, and prick up your ears." The archbishop nodded at Lucie. "I will let you speak soon. But first I must tell you of recent events. They convince me that we are faced with something far more serious than a love-sick, abandoned nun." He related Alfred's tale. "From the first, Will Longford's involvement has disturbed me, his having been in the Free Company of Bertrand du Guesclin. Is it possible that Dame Joanna fell among knaves who fear she will reveal their treacheries? Or was she one of them before she fled? I am uneasy about Longford's role in all this."

Thoresby turned to Sir Robert. "I gather Mistress Wilton has told you nothing of this circumstance?"

Sir Robert gave a little bow. "And, forgive me, Your Grace—but the more I hear, the more I dislike it." He turned to his daughter. "Not that I would interfere, but as your father I must be permitted to worry about you."

Lucie inclined her head, though she found Sir Robert's sudden enthusiasm for fatherhood ridiculous.

Sir Robert turned back to the archbishop. "Would you rather I did not take part in this consultation?"

"Not at all. You had much experience with the Free Companies. You might have some insight."

Sir Robert sat up a bit straighter. "I might. But it will bore your other guests if you must explain the situation."

"Not at all. Everyone knows pieces, not the complete story. It will do us all good to review it." Thoresby sipped his brandywine and recounted the details, which he had listed for himself earlier in the day. He ended with Dame Isobel's note requesting Lucie's assistance.

Lucie was puzzled by Joanna's remark about the grave, but saw nothing immediately alarming about it. Neither did the others. But the torn throat alarmed them all.

"She must be guarded at all times," Ravenser said.

"He is right," Lucie said. "Dame Joanna believes she is cursed. It is impossible to predict what she might do."

Thoresby nodded. "Dame Joanna has a fevered imagination." He turned to Lucie. "When you examined Dame Joanna, did you find any injuries?"

Lucie described the nun's condition. "Dame Joanna resolutely blamed her own clumsiness for all the injuries and says she is cursed and must not be healed."

"A stubborn woman," Ravenser commented.

Lucie closed her eyes so that she would not burn Ravenser with her look. She wanted to like him, but he tried her patience. How could such a man be Provost of Beverley and Master of St. Leonard's Hospital?

"What do you conclude from these injuries?" Thoresby asked.

"That she was beaten recently—perhaps a month ago. How many times I cannot say. It is possible that all the injuries are from the same attack."

Ravenser was shaking his head. "No man enjoys beating a woman. So the question is what Dame Joanna did to anger a man to such degree."

Now it was Sir Robert shaking his head at Ravenser. "The men of the Free Companies are notorious for raping and then brutally murdering women—nuns included."

Ravenser opened his mouth to protest, but Thoresby put up a hand to silence him. "So she has been in the company of someone who exhibits the behavior of a soldier in the Free Companies," Thoresby said.

"Perhaps Longford," Sir Robert suggested.

"Indeed," Thoresby poured more brandywine, sat back, studying the ceiling. "Joanna's family paid a generous sum to St. Clement's so that they might have nothing more to do with her."

Ravenser sniffed. "Simony."

Thoresby glanced at his secretary, who ducked his head under the Archbishop's regard. "It is not sanctioned by the Church to pay a monastery to take someone, but sadly it is not an uncommon practice, a family buying a place for an ill-favored member."

Lucie remembered what Owen had told her about Thoresby's accepting Michaelo as his secretary because of a generous donation by his family to the minster's Lady Chapel. Thoresby had described Michaelo as his hair shirt.

Thoresby, looking directly at Michaelo, added, "Sometimes such arrangements develop into workable relationships."

Lucie watched Michaelo's surprise. He did not look up, but she saw the ghost of a smile playing round his mouth. Something had changed between the archbishop and his secretary, that was plain.

"Still," Jehannes said, "her family wishing to dispose of her suggests that she has ever been difficult."

"Do you think Dame Joanna is mad, Mistress Wilton?" Thoresby asked.

Lucie shook her head. "I think she is burdened by a guilt that gnaws at her and gives her no peace."

"They tell me she spoke more clearly to you than she has to anyone else." Thoresby sipped his brandywine thoughtfully. "If you will agree, Mistress Wilton, I think it wise you speak with Dame Joanna."

Lucie clutched her cup. "I have the shop, Your Grace."

"You shall rule when the meetings occur."

"I have not agreed."

"No. But I beg you to consider it. Two men lie injured at St. Mary's infirmary, one perhaps mortally. A young woman was raped and murdered, Longford's servant was murdered and buried in the grave dug for Joanna. Something is amiss here, and we must discover what before more befalls us. The Reverend Mother has tried to gain

Joanna's confidence, but she has not been as successful as you. In truth, I have little faith in Dame Isobel at present."

"You are asking my daughter to place herself in danger," Sir Robert said. His voice was quiet, but angry.

Thoresby nodded. "I would not ask it of most women. But I also know something of Mistress Wilton's mettle. She will not fail me."

Lucie felt a confusing assortment of emotions. "You hope to convince me with flattery, Your Grace?"

He smiled. "You are as blunt as Archer. No. I ask only that you consider it."

"Owen asked me to promise not to become more involved in this."

Thoresby raised an eyebrow. "Ah. He anticipated me. He is angry that I sent him off so quickly to Leeds to speak with the Calverleys."

Lucie shrugged. "I did not promise."

Sir Robert interposed. "I do not understand, Your Grace. Why have you pulled Owen away from his work with the archers? Is not Lancaster's mission to Prince Edward of greater importance than a runaway nun and at worst a band of cutthroats hoping to silence her?"

Lucie was shocked by her father's boldness.

But Thoresby looked unsurprised. "To Lancaster it is certainly more important. But he might change his mind."

Sir Robert shook his head. "You cannot think that your concerns for York are more important than the welfare of all England. You are the King's Lord Chancellor."

"True enough. But I am not at all certain that England is best served by restoring Don Pedro to the throne of Castile."

"The King has pledged his support," Ravenser said softly.

Lucie wished to hear more, this being the mission Owen was helping prepare. "If Don Pedro is the legitimate heir, how can there be a question? And the French helped Enrique take Castile. Are we not at war with France?"

Thoresby studied the dregs of wine in his cup, placed the cup on the table beside him. He clasped his hands and pressed both thumbs on the muscle between his brows, then looked up at Lucie. "From time to time we are at war with France, yes. But as to the legitimacy of Pedro, the Pope himself has refuted that. He excommunicated Don Pedro and legitimized Pedro's half-brother. If one believes the Pope to be infallible, the French are in the right."

"Why did the Pope excommunicate him?"

Thoresby shrugged. "For no more than that Pedro is on good terms with the Moorish king of Granada. His Holiness might have found far worse with which to charge Pedro. There are rumors that would have him a tyrant of astonishing cruelty. They say he had his wife, a princess of France, murdered the day after he wed her. I find it difficult to believe such blatant evil. It is a fact that he repudiated her, and that she died shortly thereafter, but surely a king has advisors enough to be subtler. And yet he is said to have had many nobles of his country murdered."

Jehannes crossed himself. "Then why do Lancaster and the Prince support him?"

"Because of a treaty our King signed four years ago. Because the King believes Pedro is King of Castile by Divine Right. Because Pedro promises Prince Edward lordships in Castile. But perhaps most of all because the French support Enrique. You see why I question the wisdom of this dangerous campaign."

"This is treasonous speech," Ravenser said quietly. "Our King is already plagued with one treasonous blackguard in the York chapter."

"Heath is the Pope's man not because he believes in Urban's infallibility but because he has found the way to Urban's ear and makes money whispering into it for his countrymen. I am not such a weasel, Richard. Nor am I part of the chapter. Indeed, had the dean and chapter their way I should never venture closer to York than Bishopthorpe."

Lucie found this digression tedious. What cared she about the dean and chapter? She wondered how to bring this conversation to a close.

Fortunately, Thoresby came to the point. "Whether we are in the right or no, surely it should not take long for Archer to speak with the Calverleys. And then he will continue to Pontefract to present the archers to Lancaster. I am confident that Lancaster will be pleased and agree that Archer has trained his two new captains well. Besides, Sir Nicholas de Louth is to tell Lancaster of all that has happened, particularly concerning Will Longford, and Dame

Joanna's story of soldiers sailing out of Scarborough harbor."

Jehannes leaned forward. "What is this?"

"The Abbess of Nunburton recounted several versions of the nun's story," Ravenser said. "But the consistent items were soldiers and archers sailing away with men who spoke a variety of tongues. Luring away our fighting men to weaken us? It has the flavor of du Guesclin."

"Do you have proof of this?" Jehannes asked.

Ravenser shook his head.

"You see how the events surrounding Dame Joanna's reappearance concern me both as archbishop and lord chancellor?" Thoresby said. "And might change Lancaster's mind as to the importance of Joanna Calverley."

Sir Robert shrugged. "Regardless, our cause in Castile is just. Whether or no Pedro has earned the popular title 'the Cruel,' he is king by Divine Right."

"As an excommunicate, has he not forfeited that right?" Thoresby asked.

Sir Robert frowned. "You sound more the pope's man than the king's."

"As archbishop and lord chancellor, I have three lords, Our Divine Lord, the pope, and my king."

Disturbed by Sir Robert's growing agitation, Lucie rose. "Forgive me, but it grows late, Your Grace, gentlemen. I must thank you for your hospitality."

Thoresby rose and bowed to Lucie. "I hope you will see your way to helping us, Mistress Wilton. And that you do not pause too long over your decision."

"I am not in the habit of pondering choices overlong, Your Grace. I am already resolved to assist you."

Thoresby smiled. "God bless you, Mistress Wilton. I am in your debt."

"I shall go to St. Mary's tomorrow."

The archbishop himself escorted Lucie and Sir Robert to the door. While they waited for Lizzie to fetch Lucie's mantle, Thoresby took Lucie aside. "I wish to apologize for involving you in this, and for sending your husband away when you carry your first child."

Lucie studied his face, saw that he seemed sincere. "I thank you. It is not easy being away from Owen at this time. But I would not dream of using my being with child to keep Owen from his duties. Or to shirk my own."

"I would not expect you to," Thoresby said, and was about to say more when Lizzie returned with the mantle. Lucie could tell that he put aside what he'd been about to say and said instead, "You and your unborn child are in my prayers."

"I thank you."

"God go with you."

"And with you, Your Grace."

Sir Robert bowed stiffly.

Gilbert and Daimon appeared from nowhere to escort them home. This time Lucie was grateful for Gilbert's company—it delayed dealing with Sir Robert.

As soon as they were back at the house, with the door closed against Gilbert's ears and Daimon upstairs, Sir Robert spun round. "That arrogant cleric! To question the King and Prince Edward!" The voice that had been so soft all evening now boomed.

Lucie hoped he would not wake Tildy. "Is it not a wise check on the King that his counselors should have their own minds, Sir Robert?"

Sir Robert huffed with disgust. "Spoken like a woman. A man's duty is to obey his king!" His eyes flashed with anger.

Lucie closed her eyes, too familiar with that look from her childhood. "Please lower your voice."

"And to involve you, in your condition…" Sir Robert tugged at his belt and called for Daimon.

"Lower your voice, Sir Robert," Lucie said between clenched teeth.

He threw the belt on a bench. "Why do you always call me 'Sir Robert'? Why do you never call me father?"

Lucie sank down on a bench, yearning for her bed. What had he ever done to deserve her affection? Respect, yes, she gave him respect, as was his due. But affection… "I am not in the habit of saying 'father,' Sir Robert. You were seldom about in my childhood. And as soon as *maman* died you thrust me away, sending me off to the sisters at St. Clement's."

Sir Robert opened his mouth, closed it, bowed his head, his hands clenched tightly at his sides. In a moment, he made a fuss of picking up his belt, then yelled again for Daimon.

The squire came hurrying down the stairs. "Forgive me. I was turning down your bed, sir."

As Lucie followed them up, a great weariness came over her. It would be a long visit.

As Thoresby sat by the fire with his nephew, sipping brandywine, he studied the younger man. He realized he had never thought of Richard as a lusty man. He had been destined for the Church from birth. Thoresby's sister had never spoken of her son's having other ambitions. But after Richard's behavior tonight, Thoresby wondered. "I could not help noting how attractive you found Mistress Wilton. Your lust was quite evident."

Ravenser grinned into the distance, where he evidently held an image of Lucie Wilton. "An enticing creature. But I fear she found me a bore."

"You are content in the Church, Richard?"

Now Ravenser turned to his uncle. "Quite content. Why? Is it too sinful to appreciate beauty?"

Thoresby shook his head. "Merely a word of advice. A man of your rising fortunes must beware ill-judged passions. They can return to haunt you in unexpected and dangerous ways." He spoke from his experience of the past winter.

Ravenser frowned at his uncle. "I am but a man. I have appetites."

Thoresby downed his brandywine. "Satisfy them discreetly, Richard. And wisely."

"I meant nothing by it. I did not grab her, did I?"

"I felt the heat in you. Had you been alone with her…"

Ravenser looked shocked. "I am not a beast, uncle."

Thoresby relaxed. "The look on your face comforts me profoundly, nephew. I shall say no more."

10

OUR LADY'S MANTLE

When Lucie slipped down to the kitchen the next morning, hoping to break her fast with some bread and ale and be off to the abbey before anyone stirred, Sir Robert was already there, ale in hand, watching Tildy stoke the fire. Lucie cursed silently. On the walk home last night Sir Robert had insisted that he and Daimon would escort Lucie to meet Dame Joanna this morning. Lucie had countered with the suggestion that Sir Robert do some gardening for her. He had assured her that there was time for both tasks, he was here to do her bidding. But his first duty was to protect her.

And now Sir Robert was up betimes and eager to go. Tildy's smile was sympathetic as she set some breakfast before her mistress.

Lucie tried once again. "Sir Robert, I would prefer to do this alone."

"I would not think of it."

"The archbishop's man Gilbert will accompany me."

"It is best that Daimon and I are also with you. I shall not hover while you speak to the nun. I can be discreet."

Lucie sighed. "You are stubborn, Sir Robert."

When they left the narrow city streets, passing out through Bootham Bar, the sun shone down on the little party and lifted Lucie's mood.

Sir Robert, however, found the open sky threatening. "The abbey should have a gate within the city walls. It is unsafe for you to leave the protection of the walls."

"The postern gate is just here, Sir Robert." They were already upon it.

But Sir Robert continued to fret as they passed through the gate. "They do not post sentries along the abbey wall, and the outlaws know it."

Lucie made soothing noises and walked on, grateful for once to see Dame Isobel, who met them at the gatehouse, aflutter with gratitude. "God bless you for this, Mistress Wilton. I could not contain my joy when His Grace sent word you would come today. Every time I question Joanna she becomes more distant."

Lucie followed Dame Isobel. "Does she expect us?"

"Joanna looks forward to your visit." Isobel paused and turned to Lucie with a worried look. "But be forewarned, her moods are unpredictable." With a sigh, she resumed her heavy-footed march across the yard.

At the guest house, Sir Robert stopped and bowed to Dame Isobel. "I shall wait in the church. Come, Daimon." Sir Robert bowed again to Dame Isobel and pressed Lucie's hand, then walked away with a stiff dignity.

Lucie and the prioress mounted the guest house steps. Isobel turned at the top of the steps, her bulk making her breathless from the climb. She pressed her chest, motioning that she was catching her breath. "I shall accompany you, but if she prefers to speak with you alone, I am willing to accommodate her—are you?"

Lucie nodded.

The hospitaler opened the heavy oak door and bowed them in. His sandaled feet whispered across the wood floor as he led them to Joanna's room overlooking the garden.

The curtains of the great bed were open, the bedclothes straightened. Wrapped in the shabby blue mantle, Dame Joanna stood at an unglazed window, her back to her visitors, seemingly unaware of their presence.

"*Benedicte*, Joanna," Isobel said loudly.

Joanna started, then turned. "*Benedicte*, Reverend Mother." Her eyes flitted over to Lucie, her face warming. "Mistress Wilton, you were kind to come." The mantle dropped back from her head, revealing a cloud of unruly red hair that curled to Joanna's shoulders.

"How is your throat?"

Joanna touched the bandage. "It is nothing."

"May I see it?"

Joanna shrugged.

Lucie unwrapped the bandage around Joanna's neck. The skin had been scratched raw, not torn. Already it healed. "You are lucky someone watches over you."

Joanna said nothing.

Lucie replaced the bandage. "How do you feel otherwise?" Despite the scarred throat, Lucie saw a marked improvement in Joanna's appearance. The pale, freckled skin was no longer a sickly gray. The shadows under Joanna's eyes had faded. She stood up straight, her expression alert and friendly, though she had not yet actually smiled.

"Does an apothecary know remedies of the spirit?"

Lucie paused a moment, considering her reply. She did not wish to get off to a bad start. "We can do much to balance the humours. And we have remedies for simple maladies of the spirit. Rosemary and mint to wake up a sluggish spirit, balms, bedstraw, catnip and camomile to soothe an agitated spirit before sleep, lavender to cheer up a sad spirit."

Joanna clutched the blue mantle. "Rosemary helps the memory."

"Do you need a rosemary tisane to help your memory?"

Joanna shook her head. "I remember far too much."

"That mantle. Will Longford's maid wore something similar when she was murdered. Do you know why?"

"Murdered?" Joanna looked alarmed.

"You did not know?"

"I—" Joanna covered her eyes with her hands, shook her head.

"Maddy was wearing a blue shawl much like yours."

Joanna dropped her hands to the shawl, stroked it. Her expression was no longer one of alarm. She smiled. "Poor Maddy. We all long for a sign of favor from God's Mother."

"That is not an answer, Dame Joanna. I am not here to play games with you. I must open the shop after nones."

The half-shut eyes widened in surprise. Joanna sank down on a bench beneath the window. Lucie pulled a chair over and motioned to the Reverend Mother to do likewise.

"Now, please, Dame Joanna, tell us how you first came to Will Longford's house."

Joanna eyed Isobel, then dropped her gaze to her hands, clasped in her lap. "It rained. The streets were muddy rivers. My feet got cold. I got lost and walked in circles." Joanna glanced up at Lucie, back down to her hands.

Lucie wondered what that glance had meant. And the speech— it was as if she'd begun in the middle of her story. "Did you know Will Longford before you arrived in Beverley?"

Joanna shrugged.

"Joanna! Mistress Wilton deserves your respect!" Dame Isobel said.

Lucie saw a flicker of irritation in Joanna's eyes as she glanced at her prioress. This would not do at all. "Reverend Mother, might I speak with Joanna alone?"

Joanna glanced over at Lucie with a look of profound gratitude.

Isobel inclined her head. "This does not mean we shall now allow you to rule us, Joanna. But I shall leave you with Mistress Wilton this morning." Isobel rose. "God bless you for your patience, Mistress Wilton." With that, she left the room.

Lucie studied the nun's face. Except for the freckles, which were considered blemishes by many poets, Joanna was a comely young woman, with high cheekbones, pale lashes and brows, green eyes that shifted according to the light, from deep to sunlit. It was easy to imagine her catching a man's eye. "Perhaps we should just talk, Joanna. Do you know anything about me?"

Joanna nodded. "I have heard how you escaped St. Clement's and married a man who taught you a trade, and when he died you became a master apothecary and married for love."

Lucie winced. "Twice I married for love."

Joanna smiled. "I have met your captain."

Lucie waited for further comment, but Joanna said no more.

"So. You know something of me. Now tell me about you. You

speak of my 'escape' from St. Clement's as if you are unhappy there. Yet they say you performed heavy penances, so I would think you devout."

"Without God's love there is nothing."

"And you worry that God will cease to love you?"

Joanna twisted her head to look out the window. "I was betrothed to a fat old man who scolded me. I dreamed of a man like my brother, Hugh. Strong and courageous. Someone who laughed. Someone who loved me as God loves His chosen ones. I wanted my one love. Jason Miller was not he. Jason did not love me. He wanted a nurse for his children."

Hugh. It was her brother she called for at night. "So you asked to go to the convent."

Joanna nodded.

"But surely there was no need to take vows? By then Jason must have married someone else?"

The full lips pouted childishly. "I *am* devout."

"You felt you should take your vows?"

"My parents paid a great sum to St. Clement's for the promise that they would be bothered with me no more. I was dead to them."

"In a sense, that is the custom, is it not? You are a bride of Christ and finished with the passions of this world?"

Joanna fixed her green eyes on Lucie. "I *died*, Mistress Wilton."

"You mean the burial?"

Joanna's gaze seemed as if it could penetrate Lucie's eyes, look through them into Lucie's soul. "I received the last rites."

Lucie must ask the Reverend Mother what it meant to receive the last rites. She had a vague memory that it permanently altered one's standing in the eyes of God. "So the priest saw you before you were tied in the shroud?"

Now the gaze broke, the eyes moved over to the bed. "I lay there on the bed, my hands folded over my chest." There was something so focused about Joanna's gaze; Lucie wondered whether Joanna realized that was not the same bed.

"He must have touched your forehead in giving the blessing. You would not have felt dead to the priest's touch."

There was a flicker of annoyance in the eyes that moved back to Lucie. "I was dying, not dead then. But they had made me drink something to draw the warmth of life out of my hands and feet." Joanna touched her left shoulder with her right hand, a protective gesture, wadding the blue cloth of the mantle in her hand. "Nothing would warm me after I woke. That's when he gave me her mantle."

"Who? The priest?"

Joanna stroked the worn wool. "You can see the radiance of Our Lady's love. Would you like to touch it?" she asked softly, looking shyly through her pale lashes.

"So this is truly the Blessed Mother's mantle?" Lucie touched the cloth, then crossed herself. Was it wrong to pretend to believe? But how else was she to earn Joanna's confidence?

"You are protected now," Joanna said softly.

"How does it protect you, Joanna?"

"The Blessed Virgin watches over me. She keeps me from harm."

Now Lucie understood why Wulfstan and Isobel said Joanna was confused. Should Lucie challenge this theory by asking Joanna about the bruises? About her own ability to hurt herself? She decided she should not. "Who gave you this wonderful gift?"

Joanna's eyes darkened abruptly. "Why do you want to know?"

"It was a most loving gift. They tell me that two men visited Will Longford and were at your funeral."

Joanna looked down in confusion.

"You said 'he' gave it to you when you were so cold. Was it one of the visitors? Or Will Longford?"

"I was frightened. He put the mantle over my shoulders and told me it was the Blessed Mother's mantle. She would now protect me. I was a virgin risen from the dead—as Mary was."

"Joanna, do you truly believe that you died and rose from the dead?" The eyes challenged. "I did."

"And this man, the one who gave you the mantle, was with you when you—rose?"

"Stefan," Joanna whispered, her eyes focused on a memory, far away.

"He had been Will Longford's guest?"

"He was kind to me. He found my medal, too." She pressed a spot above her breast.

"He found the medal you wear about your neck?"

Joanna nodded. Her eyes were still far away.

"Tell me about Stefan."

Joanna looked surprised, then frightened.

"I am not here to judge you," Lucie implored. "I know what it is to love a man. I imagine it would comfort you to speak of Stefan. He was kind to you. He gave you something that must have been precious to him." Lucie touched Joanna's hand. "Tell me about him."

Joanna dropped her head, pressed her chest. "When I got to Beverley I was thirsty. I stopped for water in a churchyard. While my back was turned at the well, a boy tried to steal my Mary Magdalene medal. He dropped it when I shouted at him, but it was so muddy, and I was crying and so tired, and I could not find it. Stefan found it for me."

"You must have been very grateful."

Joanna drew the medal out of the neck of her gown, gazed at it. "My brother Hugh gave it to me when I was twelve."

Hugh again. "Mary Magdalene, the penitent. A curious choice for a young girl. Is your brother older than you?"

Joanna looked up through her eyelashes, an odd half-smile on her face. "My big brother Hugh. He said the Magdalene would understand if I wasn't perfectly good. He said she could forgive anything, so I need never be afraid to pray to her."

Lucie wished to find this merely charming, but the smile and the sentiment, spoken to a young girl—something about it disturbed her. "He knew you would be tempted to misbehave?"

"*Noli me tangere*," Joanna whispered.

Lucie recognized the words that Christ said to Mary Magdalene when she found Him outside His tomb. "'Touch me not.' What does that mean to you?"

Joanna's eyes changed from bright to wary, like a cloud covering the sun. "My parents said we were the children of Cain."

"You and your brother Hugh?"

Joanna nodded.

"You have other brothers and sisters?"

"One other brother, two sisters."

"Where is Hugh now?"

The eyes grew dark again. "That is who I wished to find."

"But you did not find him?"

Joanna bowed her head and gave a great, shuddering sigh.

"So you met Stefan at Will Longford's?"

Joanna hesitated.

"Is he handsome?"

A fleeting smile. "Oh, yes. Blond and strong like Hugh. But tall. With eyes that laugh even when the rest of his face tries to look grim."

"You love him?"

A vague frown. "I did."

"Was it Stefan who helped you get away from Beverley?"

Joanna hugged herself. "They bound me tight so I would feel more like a corpse." Her eyes were far away again, frightened. "When I woke I was so cold."

"And he gave you the mantle."

Joanna nodded, stroking the mantle with one hand, clutching the medal with the other. Stefan and Hugh, her saviors. Where were they now?

"Why did Stefan help you leave Beverley?"

"He had a customer for the relic. And he thought he knew where Hugh was. And Longford said he could not keep me in Beverley. Folk would know he was hiding a nun."

"Did Stefan find Hugh for you?"

Joanna turned to look out the window. "He did not really want to," she said in a small voice.

What did that mean? Lucie wished there were some way she might write all this down as she heard it. By the time she was home, would she remember all the twists and turns? "Was it Stefan's idea, your death and burial?"

Joanna shook her head. "Longford's."

"So why did Stefan get involved?"

Joanna pressed her arms down impatiently. "I *told* you. He could sell the relic. And he thought he could find Hugh. And Longford didn't want me staying there too long."

"Because Stefan was a relic dealer? Or Longford?"

Joanna shrugged.

"What made you think Will Longford was a relic dealer?"

Joanna looked down at her hem, then up at Lucie. "What happens to those who play God?"

Lucie breathed deep and prayed for patience. "Is that an answer?"

Joanna looked over toward the bed. "I am tired."

So was Lucie—yet she had a day of work ahead of her. Perhaps it was best to stop here for now. She rose. "I can see you do not wish to talk to me."

Joanna grabbed Lucie's arm. "Please. I—I knew. Hugh had taken me on the way to my aunt's seven years ago. Six?" She shook her head, uncertain. "I knew Longford sold relics."

Lucie faced Joanna, but did not sit. "Your brother Hugh also dealt in relics?"

Joanna shook her head. "Just once. Just to get some money to start his own life. He was to take vows. But he knew he was meant to be a soldier."

"Where did he get the relic?"

"From my father. Only part of it. My father will never know. He would never think to open the reliquary."

Lucie sat back down. "So you went to Will Longford, and he went to Stefan?"

Joanna nodded.

"How had you intended to leave Beverley?"

"I thought I would just walk away. Toward Scarborough."

"That's where you thought to find Hugh?"

Joanna closed her eyes. "He talked of Scarborough. I thought he hoped to become a guard at Scarborough Castle, but Longford it was more likely he had sailed from Scarborough harbor to join the Free Companies."

Thoresby would be keen to hear this. "Why would Longford think that?"

Joanna shrugged.

"So he convinced you that Hugh must be on the continent?"

"It sounded very likely." Joanna's voice sagged.

"You were disappointed?"

Joanna bit her lower lip. "It all seemed hopeless. I said I ought to just go back to St. Clement's."

"And what did Longford say to that?"

"He would not have it. They had a customer for the relic by then. They had it all planned out. I would leave with Stefan, wearing my habit, to convince the buyer that the convent was selling the relic through him."

"Clever."

"When we got to the manor it was noisy with soldiers and foreigners."

"This is the manor of the customer for the relic?"

Joanna looked confused.

"Where was this manor?"

"Near Scarborough. On the North Sea."

"Noisy with soldiers?"

Joanna shrugged. "Archers, they looked like. So I stayed at a cottage with Stefan."

"This is where you lived while you were away from St. Clement's?"

"Mostly."

"And the relic had never gone with you," Lucie said, more to herself than to Joanna.

But the stricken look on Joanna's face made it clear she had heard. "He lied to me. From the beginning he lied to me."

"You mean Stefan?"

Joanna bit her lip and frowned.

"Perhaps he just wanted you with him, Joanna."

She remained silent.

"Tell me about the manor."

Joanna took a deep breath. "Soldiers all over, all the time. Some of them I could not understand. They spoke in tongues. I sometimes thought they were devils, carrying off all those beautiful young men and dropping them off the edge of the earth."

It was the same story Joanna had told at Nunburton. "The young men would disappear?"

Joanna nodded. "I would meet someone and he would sail away." She shook her head. "No one returned."

"Were they going to join the Free Companies?"

Joanna closed her eyes. "I am cursed." Her teeth were clenched, sweat beaded on her upper lip.

Lucie studied the face, wondering whether these shifts were purposeful. "When you lived at the manor, did you live there as Stefan's leman?"

Joanna hesitated slightly before nodding her head.

"So you are no longer a virgin."

Joanna bit her bottom lip.

"Do you see why we wonder whether you are telling us the truth?"

"They did not want the King to know about them."

"Who, Joanna?"

"The archers."

"The ones who sailed away?"

"Not all of them left."

"Why did you leave Scarborough, Joanna?"

Joanna clutched her medal and began to rock.

"How did you get back to Beverley?"

"Walked."

"That is a long way to walk, Joanna. Had you no horse? No escort?"

Joanna said nothing, her eyes unfocused.

Scarborough. Stefan finding Hugh. The relic sale being a myth. All subjects that made Dame Joanna clutch the medal, turn inward. Lucie sat up, pressed her fists into her lower back. She was exhausted. "Shall we stop for today, Joanna?"

Joanna opened her eyes, let go the medal. "God bless you, Mistress Wilton."

Lucie rose. "Send word when you wish to speak with me again." She left with so many questions crowding her mind she almost walked right into Dame Isobel.

"*Benedicte*, Mistress Wilton," the prioress said. She was waiting right outside the room. You have been with her a long time."

"*Benedicte*, Reverend Mother."

"Did she make any sense?"

"I believe she did." Lucie rubbed her back. "I must think about it." Dame Isobel nodded. "I shall be patient."

In the nave of the abbey church, Lucie knelt beside Sir Robert and prayed to the Virgin. She prayed that at the end of all this, Joanna found a way to leave St. Clement's and find some happiness. If it was not too late. Lucie was less sure than she had been before this morning's interview that Joanna was untouched by whatever had befallen her. The inconsistencies, such as the mantle, the sudden changes in mood and subject, all suggested a woman under great strain. Because she hid something? Because she harbored guilt? She must die, she must be punished, she must not be healed. Guilt—that is what Lucie read in her. What had Dame Joanna done?

As she walked back into the city with Sir Robert, Lucie told him about the manor outside Scarborough, with the soldiers and the foreigners. It seemed a safe topic that would interest him enough to keep him from fretting about her involvement. It did distract him, and he left her in the shop and went out to work in the garden without further argument.

But it brought its own problems. Lucie had just finished with her first customer and was settling down to record her interview with Dame Joanna when Sir Robert came into the shop, frowning.

"What is it? You cannot find the right tools?"

"The garden is fine. 'Tis the soldiers. Archers. Archers sailing away. You heard the Chancellor. They are significant, Lucie. You must pursue that. You must learn where this manor is. And foreigners, she said."

"I intend to speak with her again, Sir Robert. I am well aware that there is much detail to fill in. I did not wish to press her and make her uneasy."

"A gathering of archers and foreigners. This might be treason, daughter. Pursue it."

"The garden, Sir Robert."

He nodded and departed, still frowning.

Lucie groaned. The shop bell jingled. It was mid afternoon before she was able to return to her notes.

As Lucie closed up the shop for the day, Bess Merchet poked her head in the door to invite her over for a tankard of ale in the kitchen of her tavern round the corner. Lucie accepted with pleasure. She was not ready to face Sir Robert across the table, and she welcomed Bess's opinion on the previous evening.

As the good innkeeper she was, Bess knew all the news of York, including Lucie's supper with the archbishop, and was eager for details. As a good friend of seven years, she could be trusted not to divulge anything that Lucie asked her to keep to herself, so Lucie was free to talk.

At the close of Lucie's summary, Bess sat back in her chair and squinted at Lucie over the rim of her tankard. "A passing strange story, indeed. But Owen will not be pleased by your involvement."

"No."

"He does not like his own work for the archbishop."

"You do not think I should do this for His Grace."

Bess shrugged. "I see no harm in it. Nay, I merely point out that you and Owen will be shouting at each other over this one."

Lucie stared down into her cup, imagining the argument. "I do not know how I would live if I avoided everything that might start an argument with Owen. He has a quick temper."

Bess chuckled. "And you do not?"

Lucie shrugged.

Bess laughed louder.

Lucie could not help but smile. In truth, she had a temper at least as hot as Owen's. She tapped tankards with Bess, and downed the rest of her ale. "Now that you know the tale, you might listen for any gossip in the tavern that might pertain?"

Bess nodded. "I shall do more than listen, I promise you."

Lucie hugged Bess. "You are a good friend."

"Come. I shall escort you out." Bess offered Lucie her muscular arm. Laughing, Lucie put her hand on it. They strolled out into the stable yard.

Lucie sighed at the sight of her father's horses. "'Tis good of you to stable Sir Robert's horses."

Bess eyed her with interest. "Never call him 'father,' do you?"

Lucie shook her head.

"He tries, you know. He's an old man to make this journey and offer help."

"Yes, he's an old man, and a soldier who knows nothing of the shop or gardening. What is he good for?"

"Those are spiteful words, not thoughtful. They're unworthy of you, Lucie. You're a fool to shun an earnest worker."

Lucie did not like being called spiteful. "I have put him to simple tasks in the garden. But beyond that, what can he do, Bess? Tell me that."

Bess shrugged. "Try him till you find out, woman. For pity's sake, when Nicholas first brought you to the shop, did he throw up his hands and say you could do naught to help?"

"That was different, Bess. I was to live here. I was his wife."

Bess grinned. "Well, God help you if Sir Robert stays above a week, eh?"

"He just might do that, Bess." Lucie told her of his offer of Corbett's house.

Bess rolled her eyes. "Well, that's a sticky one. If he meant to buy it for you and stay away, I would call it most generous. But if he means to visit often—" She shook her head. "Perhaps if you let him help you in these small ways—the garden, innocent things…"

She patted Lucie's arm. "You must not waste your father's good intentions. You must guide him to those favors you can accept."

Lucie found this conversation discomfiting. "Please, Bess. You know how busy I am. Busier now with the archbishop's request. To put Sir Robert to work in the garden or the shop would require instruction. In the same time I could finish the chore."

Bess had retrieved her arm and stood, hands on hips, looking stern. "True, you must train him the first time. But the next time he would do it without instruction."

"I hate to think of his staying that long."

Bess shook her head slowly, as if not believing what she was hearing. "Are you not at all curious about him? Have you never wondered whether you have any of his traits? Besides his stubborn chin."

Lucie touched her chin. "Sir Robert's chin?"

"'Tis a far stronger chin than your mother had. Look at your Aunt Phillippa. She has the D'Arby chin, too. And a backbone to match. Your father's family outlives its spouses, have you not noticed?"

Lucie crossed herself. "Don't say that, Bess. I do not want to outlive Owen."

Bess rolled her eyes. "That was not the point. Your father is not the frail old man you think him."

With a sigh, Lucie agreed. "I will put him to serious work in the garden on the morrow."

Bess pressed Lucie's arm. "You will not be sorry. You will be the better for it."

Lucie did not think so, but she was tired of the argument. And perhaps a little curious. She rubbed her chin as she pushed open her garden gate.

11

CALVARY

Owen was grateful when Nicholas de Louth grew quiet, winded from the long ride. And no wonder, with his flabby body and his ceaseless chatter, the man could not have a great store of breath. But for all his talk, he'd told Owen little of use. His men had found no witnesses to the attack on Alfred and Colin. One woman had noticed a group of men loitering on Skeldergate for several days. Only one had stood out in her mind, a fair-haired man with crooked teeth who shouted at the other men. But she had been at market when the attack occurred, and she had not seen the men since that day. An unhelpful harvest.

It was a quiet, solemn party that rode into Leeds.

The wool trade flourished in Leeds, apparent from the fine houses of prosperous merchants lining the north bank of the River Aire. The monks of Kirkstall Abbey to the northwest had begun the trade, the burghers had expanded it.

Owen and Louth stopped at an inn near the market square. As the innkeeper filled their tankards, they asked him to point them toward Matthew Calverley's house.

"Edge of the city, gardens and parkland surrounding it. For Mistress Calverley, who was highborn."

Owen caught the word "was." "Mistress Calverley is dead?"

The innkeeper nodded. "Aye. Drowned, she did." He tilted his head and squinted at Owen. "Queer your not knowing the story when you've business with the family. Are you gaming with me?"

"We are not acquaintances," Owen explained, "just messengers from the lord chancellor."

The innkeeper's eyes widened. "You're king's men, are you? Well well well. So Matthew's got business with the king?"

"His chancellor."

The innkeeper rubbed his ear, then snapped his fingers at them. "Law troubles, eh? Well, can't say as I'm surprised."

"You might sit with us and tell us Mistress Calverley's sad tale." Owen pushed his tankard toward the innkeeper. "Fill one for yourself."

The innkeeper poured, sat down. "Trot's the name. Trot the Taverner, my good gentlemen." He took a long drink, wiped his mouth on his sleeve, shook his head. "Poor Matthew. Thought he'd get noble blood in his line and wound up with a family ill fit for the world."

"Truly?"

"Aye. Mistress Anne Calverley was a comely lady, fiery hair and fiery temper. Once Matthew had set his eyes on her, there could be no other woman for him. She was the third daughter, so her family did not mind her marrying money instead of blood—Matthew had already made his fortune, though there were those who wondered how, with the king restricting the wool shipments across the Channel." Trot shrugged. "And quickly came two sons and three daughters."

Owen said a silent prayer of thanks for a talkative innkeeper. "Is Calverley's eldest son a merchant?"

"Oh, aye, young Frank. Plump and prosperous like his father. T'other son—Hugh—was a bad lot. Built like a warhorse. Fought like a wild dog. Went off to seek his fortune." Trot nodded. "Eldest daughter—Edith—cherry-cheeked and docile, married another merchant in this fair city, Harrison. Middle daughter—Joanna—was to marry a merchant from Hull, but she fled to the convent. Pity. Took after her mother, temper and then some. Her brother Hugh was her champion. Youngest daughter—Sarasina. Funny name. Mistress Calverley was already acting queer, you see."

"How long ago did the mistress drown?" Owen asked.

Trot screwed up his face, thinking. "Before Christmas." He

sighed. "Pity. Even after birthing eight children, five yet living, Mistress Calverley was still a beauty."

"Was her drowning an accident?"

Trot drained his tankard. "I'll repeat nothing I don't know as truth. All I know is she drowned in the river. How it happened, that I could not be saying."

An impressive house, an old hall with a new wing of stone, glazed windows, set in a meadow that rolled down to a line of trees through which the River Aire glinted. The day had warmed and the sun was strong. A burly man in a wide-brimmed hat put down his hoe and came from the kitchen garden to greet them. He wore a simple chemise, slit front and back, with the tails tucked up in his belt for easy movement in his work. His chemise and leggings were earth-stained.

Owen let Louth step forward, a more presentable stranger with his unlined face and guileless smile. "God speed. I am Nicholas de Louth, a canon of Beverley. Would your master be at home?"

The gardener's little pig eyes swept past Louth in his finery and narrowed at sight of Owen, whose patch always made folks uneasy. "What's a canon of Beverley want with Master Calverley?"

"It would be best to keep it between us and Master Calverley," Owen said.

"'Us', eh? And who are you?"

Impudent gardener. But Owen needed his good opinion. "I am Owen Archer, former Captain of Archers for the Duke of Lancaster, now a representative of John Thoresby, Lord Chancellor and Archbishop of York."

The pig eyes lit up. "Two Church men?"

Owen winced at that. "I am not a Church man."

The gardener shrugged. "As you will."

"We would speak with Master Calverley," Louth said.

The gardener grinned and stepped back with a little bow. "And so you are."

"You?" It was not just his gardening attire that surprised Owen—Trot's story had led him to expect a man in mourning. Matthew Calverley seemed quite cheerful.

Matthew chuckled. "I have handed most of my business over to my son for the summer. Let him sink or swim in the best tradition of ordeals. I must know at some point whether he is fit to take it over completely, mustn't I? And while he's flailing round in the pond of commerce, I am enjoying my garden."

Owen found the watery images disturbing from a man whose wife had drowned, but he put on a smile. "My wife is always happiest when she can spend some part of her day at work in the garden."

Matthew looked Owen up and down. "Married, are you? I wouldn't have thought." He shrugged. "So, men, what does the Church want with Matthew Calverley?"

"We hoped you might tell us a little about your daughter, Joanna," Owen said.

Matthew's expression grew pensive. "Ah. The poor little chit. Is she in good health?"

Louth shrugged. "Dame Joanna is recovering at St. Mary's Abbey from a long journey in unfavorable circumstances. The flesh improves each day; but the spirit—that is why we are here. We hope that if we learn more about her we shall be better able to help her recover."

Matthew glanced from one to the other with a puzzled frown. "A long journey? She took her vows at Clementhorpe Priory, last I heard. How's she been on a long journey?"

"She ran away," Owen said.

Matthew dropped his eyes, made an odd sound in the back of his throat, grabbed his hat off his head, and fanned his red face. "Dear me, she bolted, eh? Oh dear." He sighed, looked up at Owen. "Can't say as I'm surprised. Never did understand what turned that hot little filly into a nun—except Jason Miller's bald pate and hairy moles." Matthew threw back his head and laughed, but it was a nervous laugh, not sincere. He quickly grew serious and invited them inside. "Sounds to me like a story that requires fortifying. Come within. Welcome to Calvary House, as Joanna's mother used to call it."

A serving girl hurried off to bring refreshments as Matthew showed them through a high-ceilinged great hall into a smaller room with a lancet window looking out toward the garden Matthew had been tending. A writing table sat by the window to catch the south light, a basket of scrolls beside it on the plank floor. A brazier behind the writing chair would warm the room in most weather, though the air coming in the room today was mild and welcome. Matthew looked round, realized he had seating for only two, and hurried away with apologies to get a third.

Louth took the chair by the writing table, turning it to face into the room. He sat down. "He's full of smiles for a widower."

Owen walked over to the window to look at the garden. "Perhaps Calverley's cheerfulness is a mask to cover his true feelings. People—" He stopped as footsteps approached.

A procession entered the room. One man deposited a small table near the window, a second set a tray of bottles and cups on the table, the woman who had greeted them at the door set down a tray of bread, cheese, and apples. A third man lugged in an ornately carved chair, placing it to complete a triangle with the other chairs in the room. Matthew Calverley followed at the end with a small stool, the right height for a footrest.

After the servants had departed, Matthew settled himself in the ornate chair, propping his feet on the footrest. When he had adjusted the two items to his satisfaction, he rose and poured himself a mazer full of ale from a pitcher. "Come, help yourselves, gentlemen. Ale, wine, mead. Whatever is your pleasure." He had changed into an elegantly patterned gown and matching shoes with pointed toes.

Owen poured himself a cup of ale, tasted it, held the cup up to toast his host. "A fine brew. Second only to Tom Merchet's at the York Tavern."

Matthew nodded, busy settling back in his chair. Louth rose and poured himself some wine, tasted it, smiled at the cup. He, too, evidently surprised by the quality.

But then it was a substantial house, well situated, large, with adequate servants. Not as modern a house as another wool merchant's Owen had visited the past year, but quite impressive. The only thing truly surprising was the mood of the household. It did not feel like a house in mourning.

Perhaps the innkeeper had been having fun with them, feeding them a pack of lies.

"It might be advisable to include Mistress Calverley in this discussion," Owen suggested.

"Mistress? The mistress of this house is but a child, gentlemen." He laughed at their confusion. "My daughter, Sarasina, is mistress now."

"Your wife is dead, Master Calverley?"

"Dead?" The pig eyes moved up to the ceiling, rested there, moving side to side. "Well, I cannot say for certain, Master Archer. But she has been gone some time." He lowered his gaze to Owen's single eye. "So what has Joanna done to warrant your interest?"

Hiding his confusion as best he could, Owen said, "Your daughter ran away from the convent just before midsummer last year. Took a relic from the convent to buy help in her disappearance."

Matthew shook his head. "She was ever difficult, was Joanna. But to steal a relic..." He took a long drink. "And what happened? They caught her at it?" He shook his head. "But no, not a year ago. You would not be here telling me..."

"She arranged for a false funeral, then disappeared for almost a year." Owen watched Matthew's expressive face, saw there a mixture of admiration and distress.

"I suppose Anne was informed and neglected to tell me." Matthew suddenly stiffened, his eyes troubled. "If the Reverend Mother sent a messenger I did not see—Could that be what happened? Anne feared she had some part in Joanna's death?"

Louth shook his head. "The Reverend Mother said she did not inform your family—that you had given instructions that Joanna was never to be mentioned."

Matthew closed his eyes a moment, breathed deeply. "Anne's instructions, not mine." He looked up at Owen. "I am glad it was not that. So. Then what happened?"

"Last month Joanna suddenly appeared in Beverley, at the

house of a man called Will Longford. She sought the relic, hoping to return it to St. Clement's and be accepted back herself."

"Will Longford?" Matthew turned his head to the side, as if listening to an invisible person beside him.

Owen leaned forward, hopeful. "The man from whose house Joanna staged her funeral. Do you know the name?"

Matthew turned back to Owen, nodding slowly. "I believe I do. Yes. I do. And as was ever the case with Joanna, her trouble points back to Hugh."

"Her brother?"

Matthew dropped his head, as if deep in thought, then lifted it up with a wary look. "But why exactly are you here?"

"Since your daughter's return, Longford's maidservant has been murdered and the corpse of Longford's cook has been discovered in the grave dug for your daughter's false burial. Both deaths were violent."

Matthew looked alarmed. "God help us! You don't think Joanna murdered them?"

"No. But the fact that Joanna put such effort into getting away from the priory only to ask to be accepted back a year later is passing strange. We want to know just what her arrangement was with Longford."

"This Will Longford is no help?"

"He is missing."

Matthew crossed himself. "What has Joanna got into?" He rubbed his eyes. "She will not talk?"

Owen shrugged. "Will not talk or cannot remember, it is difficult to tell."

Matthew nodded again. "With Joanna that can be impossible. As with her mother." He was quiet a moment, then suddenly slapped his thighs, looked at each of his guests. "So you wish me to take Joanna back, is that it?"

The suggestion surprised Owen. "No. Though perhaps it will come to that."

Matthew gave a big sigh. "I would rather it did not come to that, Master Archer. Not that I don't love the girl, but it has lightened the burden of my advancing age to have those three gone. I had forgotten how quiet and sweet life could be."

Owen and Louth exchanged a look. "Three, Master Calverley?" Louth said.

"Anne and her little demons, Joanna and Hugh. They were purely of Anne's blood, gentlemen, as Edith and Frank are purely of mine. Sarasina"—he shrugged—"so far she has her mother's beauty but a placid spirit. God has been merciful." Matthew crossed himself again.

Owen found Matthew Calverley's reactions puzzling. He wished to slow down and study the man, but he must carry on while the man was in a good humour. "I know this must be painful to you, Master Calverley, but what exactly happened to Mistress Calverley?"

Matthew got up, poured more ale, held onto the little table while he gulped down a considerable amount, topped his mazer, and returned to his seat. "What exactly. Well, I cannot exactly say. She walked away one morning, a cold, dark day. When she had been gone too long for such cold, I went looking." He shrugged. "I never found her. She never returned."

Owen glanced out the window, remembering the river.

Matthew caught the look. "You are thinking she walked into the river." He frowned, nodded. "Her cloak lay not far from the riverbank, hanging on a branch, as if she had put it there to keep it out of the mud." Matthew was silent a moment, staring down at his feet. Then he sighed, looked back at Owen with a forced smile. "But I prefer to think she ran off with someone who shares her strangeness. You see, Joanna and Hugh shared their strangeness, and they were content in each other's company."

That brief moment of silence, then the forced smile, at last Owen felt he had glimpsed Matthew's suffering. Deep, forced down, kept down with a strong will. Might the drowning story have been told to stop gossip? "Was your wife sad that Joanna and Hugh had grown up and left her?"

Matthew rolled his eyes. "Far from it. By then Anne wanted nothing to do with either of them. She said"—an odd, dark look came over the round face, then passed—"no matter what she said. Anne saw the world sideways and upside-down. But I tell you, life has been quiet since the moon-mad Boulains have been out of the house."

"You have never searched the river?"

Matthew closed his eyes. "She was a beautiful woman, Master Archer. And the madness—it can be captivating, I tell you. The faraway look in the eyes, the half smile." He shook his head. "She had that look on that cold, gray morning. So beautiful she was." Tears crept from the closed lids. "I wish to remember her that way. It would—" His voice broke. He wiped his cheeks with his sleeves. "I do not want to know."

Owen rose and poured himself more ale, stared out the window, working to put down the image that wanted to darken his mind, of Lucie, bloated, lifeless. He had seen the bodies of the drowned. He understood why Matthew did not wish to see his wife so.

Louth's voice broke him out of his reverie. "Where is your son Hugh, Master Calverley?"

Owen returned to his seat.

Matthew Calverley brightened at the change in subject. "Hugh is at Scarborough Castle, working for the king's stewards there, the Percies. You see, that's where Will Longford comes in. Anne meant Hugh for the Church, but that was never right for him. He wanted to fight." Matthew shrugged. "Truth be told, he wanted to kill. Which did not sound like a vocation to the Church to me. It's the sort of mismatch that creates trouble. And Hugh was already trouble enough. So, being a father who would rather meet up with his children in Heaven some day, I reminded the Percies of a favor they owed me."

"What sort of favor?" Louth asked.

Owen could see that his companion was very alert now.

Matthew began to take another drink, but put the tankard down on the floor beside his footstool instead. Owen was glad of it. Their host's nose was already red from the drink. He did not want the man to get fuzzy headed and fall asleep before they had learned what they could from him.

"I offered to forget the balance of a loan I'd made them if they took Hugh into their service. They liked the terms, set him a task. They'd obtained a seal carried by a Frenchman whose ship went down in the North Sea. The Frenchman had drowned, but his squire traded the seal and information for a warmer cell in the castle dungeon. He told the Percies that his master's destination was Beverley, though he did not know for what purpose."

Louth rose, poured himself more wine, returned to his seat. "What was this seal?"

"St. Sebastian. The martyr with all the arrows stuck in him."

Owen nodded. "Patron saint of archers."

Matthew rose and cut some bread, nibbling on it as he stood a moment, gazing out the window.

"Forgive us for taking you away from your garden on such a day," Owen said.

Matthew flicked his free hand up, palm forward. "Do not apologize. In truth, I meander in my explanations. You must herd me to the gate, gentlemen, or you shall be here at Calvary till Doomsday."

Owen accepted the challenge. "What did the seal have to do with Longford?"

"There were reports that Longford was frequently in Scarborough, though no one knew where he stayed. The Percies believed he was still working with du Guesclin."

"So what was Hugh's task?"

Matthew put some cheese on the bread. "Hugh was to present the seal to Will Longford, tell him of the shipwreck, say he'd tried to save the envoy, who had paid him well to deliver the seal to Longford and had enticed him further with the promise that Longford would recommend him to one of the better captains in the Free Companies." Matthew bit off a mouthful of bread, chewed thoughtfully.

"They hoped Longford would be foolish enough to admit a connection with du Guesclin?" Owen asked.

"Some such. One of the younger Percies was in the city, awaiting a signal from Hugh." Matthew popped the rest of the bread and cheese into his mouth.

Louth snorted. "An impossible assignment."

Matthew returned to his seat, and took up his mazer, drinking deeply. "Though he's quite an actor, Hugh failed. Longford not only didn't slip up, he saw through him, Hugh could tell, and he got worried about Joanna—she was with him. He bundled Joanna off to her aunt at once. I doubt she ever forgave him that."

"Why was she with him at Longford's?"

"He was escorting her to my sister Winifred, near Hull—for instruction in the wifely arts. Anne was no good as a teacher. He should have gone first to Winifred, but Joanna begged to see Beverley."

"How did Hugh lose the seal?" Owen asked.

Matthew shook his head. "The fool left it at Longford's while he took Joanna to my sister's house. When Hugh returned, Longford had disappeared, and the seal with him. Nothing to prove, no trail to follow."

"Was Joanna privy to Hugh's purpose?"

"Nay. We had agreed he must not tell her the truth. It could be dangerous for her, she would be near Beverley. As far as she knew, he was supposed to escort her to Winifred's, then go south to Oxford, but his meeting with Longford was a secret plan to get some money and strike out on his own, escape the Church." Matthew frowned, scratched his cheek. "You say she stole a relic with which to trade? And went to Longford?"

Owen nodded.

"Poor little chit. She believed his story. He told her he'd stolen a relic and was trading with Longford. The arm of St. Hardulph of Breedon in a grand reliquary; our relic from the parish. Hugh was always frightening her with tales of St. Hardulph's bones, saying they did not rest easy, Hardulph missed his home. Once when he and Joanna found an arm on the riverbank, Hugh told her it was the arm of St. Hardulph, trying to get home to Breedon. For weeks Joanna begged us to send the saint back home."

Louth chuckled. "A wondrous spinner of tales, your Hugh."

Matthew sighed, stared into his mazer. "One of the Boulain gifts. But it is a cursed gift. They forget now and then what they made up and what is real."

"She seems confused at present about a blue shawl she wears. She says it is Our Lady's mantle."

Matthew shook his head. "You see? And after living with her

day in and day out saying it is, then it isn't, it is, then it isn't, you would not know what was true about it."

"So Hugh told Joanna he was taking St. Hardulph to Longford?"

"Yes. But they were to pretend it was St. Sebastian's arm, which would fetch far more money than St. Hardulph's. That was how Hugh twisted it round so he could say St. Sebastian at the door."

Owen thought it unnecessarily complicated. "And she believed it?"

"How else did she get the idea to try it herself? And it was a believable story. He would use the money to outfit himself as a soldier." Matthew rubbed his forehead. "You must understand. They played together, wove these tales, and I swear they believed half of them. When they were young, their mother would say it was all in fun, she had played so as a child, it was good to dream while young. But as they got older she did not think it so innocent." He frowned, clutched the mazer, drained it.

"How did the Percies feel about Hugh's failure?"

"It was the Percies wrote to me and told me the sad story. Hugh's poor judgment had cost them the seal; they might have put it to good use sending du Guesclin false reports. But they took Hugh on, said he had proved his courage and the mistake would make him try that much harder."

"Have you seen Hugh recently?"

Matthew shook his head. "Not since he and Joanna went to Beverley."

"How long ago was that?"

Matthew closed his eyes, tapped a finger on the arm of his chair, muttered to himself. "Seven years, thereabouts. Joanna was but thirteen." He shook his head. "Fool thing to betroth her to Jason Miller. I should have known such a dreamy child expected a prince, not an old merchant who wanted a nursemaid for his daughters."

"Tell us about that."

"Little to tell. Six, seven months later a letter came from my sister saying to expect Joanna in a week's time, she had insulted her betrothed and fasted until she was ill and mad with fever visions, and was begging to be sent to a convent."

"You were embarrassed by the broken engagement?"

Matthew rolled his eyes. "That is not the half of it. She was a vixen, gentlemen. Always flirting. Could not take her to a fair or procession, anything in the city, without having to break her grip on a young man and drag her home. Next day the young man would come calling, she'd refuse to see him. And she stared at herself. Polished little metal mirrors everywhere. We found her once in the river meadow running naked—at thirteen, mind you, and boats up and down the river all the time. She was—" He leaned back, head in hand. "When Jason Miller, a nice, stable widower, offered his hand, and a home in Hull, away from all the gossip, Anne and I could not resist the chance to be rid of her."

"Whatever made you agree to her entering the convent?"

Matthew shook his head. "When she returned from Beverley, so thin and whispering to herself about devils and dreams and God and the cross, we did not know what to think. All the bloom was gone. She had bald patches, her teeth were loose. I wanted to blame my sister, but in my heart I knew. After Anne lost our first babe, she sat in a corner of the hall and sang for days and days. I thought I would go mad. She would drink no water, her voice grew hoarse, disappeared to a whisper, and still she sang, sang, sang. And then one day a chapman came selling odds and ends. She heard his patter in the yard and went out. She touched a set of needles. One of them pricked her. She bought all the needles he carried and came in the house with them, went up to bed, slept for two days. When she woke, she said, 'My blood has come forth again. I am meant to live.'" Matthew shivered and crossed himself.

Owen and Louth exchanged puzzled looks.

"You decided Joanna was like her mother and might be better off in the convent?" Owen guessed.

"When madness begets madness, perhaps it is better to end the line, eh?" Matthew looked at their frowns, shook his head. "You cannot know, either of you. You keep hoping it is a passing mood, that tomorrow she will make sense, you will have a sensible partner. You rejoice when she wakes with clear eyes, practical worries, reasonable reactions to household problems. You mourn when the vagueness returns."

Louth lifted an eyebrow. "It is a wonder that your son Hugh is retained by the Percies if he behaves so."

Matthew shrugged. "Hugh embraces danger. That is desirable in what he does. And he seems merely a weaver of tales, not a liar, not mad. Just comes out differently in Hugh."

Owen grew curious to meet Hugh Calverley. "Why did your wife turn against Hugh and Joanna?"

Matthew frowned, stood up as if to get more ale, but just stood with his back to his guests, looking out at the garden. "It does not matter. She saw plots and transgressions in everything. I paid her no heed. Had I listened to Anne I would have gone mad myself."

"So you do not think that Joanna's flight from the convent and Mistress Calverley's disappearance are related?"

Matthew shook his head. "I do not say it lightly when I tell you Anne turned against them. I was at wit's end when the letter came from my sister, warning of Joanna's return. Anne said she would not let Joanna in the house. It was only after I exaggerated Joanna's reported vocation that Anne agreed to having Joanna in the house for a short time."

"Did Joanna know of her mother's feelings?"

"Joanna is seldom aware of the feelings of others."

Owen found it an interesting observation.

"The prioress of St. Clement's is a Percy," Louth said, changing the subject yet again. "Did she take Joanna as a favor to you?"

Matthew took a moment to answer. "A Percy?" He frowned. "Nay. Seven years back the prioress was not a Percy. Sir William Percy merely suggested the convent was poor, might accept Joanna with a generous dowry. He had placed a poor relation there. Perhaps she is the present prioress."

The shadows lengthened in the garden. Owen grew tired of sitting. He rose. "You have been most helpful, Master Calverley."

Matthew rose in haste. "But surely you will stay to supper?"

Louth followed Owen's lead and rose. "You are kind to offer, but we have men to see to, and a long journey tomorrow."

Matthew looked disappointed.

"There is one other piece of information that would be of use," Owen said. "Do you know where your son stays in Scarborough? Is he actually up at the castle?"

Matthew shrugged. "I imagine him there, but as I say, I have heard nothing from him in his new life. I address my communications with the Percies to the castle, but that means naught." He touched Owen's arm as he began to move toward the door. "If you see Hugh, tell him his mother has passed on, if you will. It seems right that he should know not to expect her if he ever returns. And tell him—tell him we are well."

Owen walked back out through the grand hall, turning his head this way and that to see around him, the lovely tapestries, the delicate tracery in the windows, the carved, high backed chairs, the solid table tops hung between the tapestries, ready to be brought down for feasts. Someone had worked hard to make the room pleasant. Anne Calverley on her lucid days? Was she aware of her changeable nature? Was Joanna? Had Joanna seen her mother's moods and wondered whether she would be the same? And if she had, had she feared it?

Owen, Louth and the canon's men were to spend the night at the guest house of Kirkstall Abbey. As they rode into the outer court of the abbey, Louth became animated, pointing out the tannery, the fulling mill, the brew house. "The Cistercians have perfected the self-contained community. They have everything here. They use every resource available. You will find all the latest techniques practiced here."

"You are thinking of giving up your prebends and joining the order?"

Louth looked at Owen askance. "Of course not. What gave you that idea?"

They rode through the inner gatehouse into the inner court, Louth still pointing out the wonders of the Cistercian design. Owen was glad when, after they were shown to a chamber in the guest house, Louth took his leave to go explore with his squire.

In the main hall of the guest house, Owen met a traveler en route to York with a scar on his hand that drew and bothered him like the scar on Owen's face. Seeing an opportunity, Owen gave the traveler a sample of the ointment he carried, specially prepared by Lucie, and promised him a jar of it if he delivered a letter to Lucie. The traveler found the trade more than fair. Owen found a quiet corner in the hall and spent the late afternoon writing to Lucie, telling her all he had learned today from Matthew Calverley. It helped him organize his thoughts.

12

WITLESS OR CUNNING?

Joanna stared with such ferocity that Lucie could not help but look away from the penetrating eyes. "For pity's sake, what have I done to warrant this?" Lucie asked.

Joanna just stared. This morning she made no other response.

Lucie tried to take Joanna's hands. Joanna pulled them away. "I come here as your friend," Lucie protested. "I want to help."

Now the eyes flickered. "You talk to me for *them*, not for me."

Lucie's heart pounded. Two spots of color high on Joanna's pale cheeks bespoke her agitation. Best not to lie to her. "His Grace and the Reverend Mother are worried about you."

Joanna shook her head slowly, tauntingly. "They are jealous of me. Not just those two, all of them. The abbot, Sir Richard, Sir Nicholas."

Lucie pressed her knuckle to her brow, searching for a reply that would not anger Joanna, but encourage her to talk. "Of what are they jealous?"

Tears welled up in Joanna's eyes. "I am alone but for Our Lady's love."

"We all mean to help you," Lucie said gently.

Joanna blotted her eyes with the sleeve of her chemise. Today the mantle was folded neatly beside her. "Do you remember what Christ said to Mary Magdalene when she saw him walking near his tomb?"

Lucie nodded. "You told me once. '*Noli me tangere.*'" But last time talk of Hugh had brought it up.

"After Mary Magdalene had loved Him so, mourned Him so, she was not to touch Him. He is cruel."

Good Lord. How had they come to this? "I do not think that

was the point," Lucie said. "He was risen. He—"

Joanna shook her head. "No! It *is* the point. It is *always* the point."

Lucie threw up her hands. "What are you telling me?"

"I am telling you nothing." Joanna folded her arms over her chest and turned away.

Lucie rose stiffly, walked to the window, massaging her left shoulder. When she spoke with Joanna it was as if she held her breath and tensed for a blow. She worried over each word, each gesture, hoping that what she said or did would not upset the awkward, fragile balance they had achieved.

Speaking with Joanna, picking her way with such care, drained Lucie of energy. And today Joanna seemed worse than ever. Dame Isobel had warned Lucie that Joanna's agitation had increased with frightening results. The past evening Joanna had thrown a heavy cup at the maid, Mary, cutting her above the eye.

Lucie felt lost. How was it that Joanna saw herself as both Mary Magdalene and the Blessed Virgin Mary? It was as unlikely a combination as Lucie could imagine. What was the point? *He is cruel.* Joanna's lover?

Lucie returned to her seat by Joanna. "Has someone told you not to touch him?"

Joanna cocked her head to one side. "You are with child."

Lucie realized she had been pressing her stomach with one hand, her lower back with the other. She clasped her hands behind her back. Letting Joanna know something so intimate bothered Lucie, which she realized as a hypocritical feeling when she was trying to discover such intimacies about Joanna. "Does what Christ said to Mary Magdalene remind you of something that happened to you?"

"Do you know about Saint Sebastian?"

Lucie closed her eyes, took a deep breath. She wanted nothing so much as to shake Joanna, make her stop playing this game. But they needed answers. "He is the patron saint of archers."

"What do you know of archers?"

"What do *you* know?"

"My brother Hugh had a seal that showed St. Sebastian with the arrows piercing his body."

"His seal was that of an archer?"

"Not his." Joanna frowned. "So? What can you tell me of archers?"

"The Welsh longbowmen have won many a battle for the king."

"How would you know that?"

"My husband is one. Was one. He was captain of archers for Henry, Duke of Lancaster. Who used the seal of St. Sebastian, Joanna?"

Joanna closed her eyes. "I thought I might go to France."

Lucie clutched her hands behind her, afraid she would strike Joanna in frustration. "Go to France with whom?"

A long pause. "Will Longford seemed a kind man. He gave me wine when I was so cold. I'd been caught in a storm."

"When you took the relic to him?"

Joanna sat up suddenly, her eyes wide open. "The wine was a sleep potion. So that I would sleep while he thought what to do with me. And what he gave me for my burial. To keep me still. It was too strong. For days they could not wake me."

"Who, Joanna?"

Joanna shook her head and suddenly lay down, pulled the covers up to her chin. "Must sleep now. It poisons me yet."

Lucie leaned against the door of the abbey guest house, letting the sun and the summer breeze caress her face. She was glad that she had followed her inclination this morning and rejected the wimple. She wore instead a short, light veil that let the breeze cool her neck. She felt the heat so much more this summer. The babe in her womb warmed her. She noticed Daimon up on the abbey's river wall. Without Sir Robert. Daimon must have tired of kneeling with his master in the abbey church. Lucie looked up at the sun. Quite early. Sir Robert would not be expecting her yet. If Daimon would agree to keep a secret from Sir Robert, he could escort Lucie to Magda Digby's house. Lucie could talk with Magda and return with enough time to get back to the shop. She needed Magda's advice about Joanna.

Lucie asked the hospitaler how she might get up to Daimon on the wall.

Brother Oswald looked at her with horror. "I shall send someone up to him."

Lucie smiled reassuringly. "There is no need. I would rather go myself."

The monk shook his head. "Forgive me, Mistress Wilton, but I cannot permit you to go up there."

In the end, Brother Oswald sent a boy up to Daimon, who came down chattering enthusiastically about the river traffic.

Lucie used his interest to coax him into going to Magda Digby's hut. "It sits on a rock at the edge of the river."

Daimon grinned. "I should like to see it."

"You agree that we need not disturb Sir Robert?"

Daimon readily agreed.

They were soon making their way down to the riverbank through the paupers' camps that clustered outside the abbey's beggar's gate. "I see why Sir Robert would not like us coming here. Why do folk live like this?" Having grown up on the manor, Daimon had never seen such poverty.

"The reasons are as countless as the stars, Daimon. Some come to cities to disappear, some have been given false hopes of riches, some have lost their land through no fault of their own, some have lived like this down through so many generations they know no other way. In a city it can be difficult to feed yourself. You must pay for food or trade for it. And there are so many people. Jasper de Melton, the boy who is to be my apprentice, could tell you how hard it is to find food on the streets of the city."

Daimon looked round at the makeshift huts, the rats that scurried underfoot, fat and aggressive, the ragged people, skinny and despondent, then back at the walls of the abbey and those of the city beyond. "But these people are not even in the city."

Lucie nodded. "And once they have lived here, it is difficult to find their way through the gates."

Daimon's shoulders slumped; his steps lost their spring.

Lucie was glad to see Magda's house up ahead. "Look, Daimon. There, just at the water's edge."

The queer home of Magda Digby crouched on a rock. The hut was built with the beams and planks of old boats, with an overturned Viking ship for a roof. The Riverwoman sat outside the door, in the shade of the dragon at the Viking ship's prow. The dragon leered upside down at the approaching visitors. Magda wore her usual patchwork gown. Her grizzled hair was tucked up into a cap, leaving her neck bare. As they drew closer, Lucie saw that Magda was mending a fishing net.

"Are you about to cast it out, Magda?"

"Nay. 'Tis late in the tide to catch a worthy fish this morning. Magda will fish by moonlight." The old woman's intense blue eyes studied Daimon. "Thou hast brought a soldier, eh? Dost thou carry such evil news thou'rt fearful Magda will attack thee?"

Lucie laughed and sat down on the bench beside the Riverwoman. Daimon stood and looked round, uncertain where to place himself.

Magda squinted up at the lad. "Thou'rt Daimon, son of Adam, steward at Freythorpe Hadden."

Daimon looked frightened. "How did you know that?"

"Magda brought thee into the world of men."

"But babies all look the same."

Magda shrugged. "Not to Magda. Thou also lookst the image of thy father."

Daimon relaxed. "You know my father?"

"Aye. A good, brave man. Magda made a salve for thy father's shoulder when first he came here from the wars. And she taught Dame Phillippa how to press and pull and loosen thy father's shoulder joint."

"Why have I never met you?"

Magda shrugged. "When Midwife Paddy lived upriver, Magda did not have as much work as now, got around more. Now Magda goes away for a day and a night, folk are camped out on the rock when she returns." She shook her head.

"Why do you use a ship for your roof?"

"Ever ready for a flood, eh?" Magda gave a barking laugh.

"Thou needst a stool. Hie thee within, bring out what suits thee."

When Daimon had gone into the hut, Magda put down her mending and touched Lucie's cheek. "Thou'rt hot-blooded with this child. A good sign."

"I was worried."

"Then cease thy worry." The sharp eyes studied Lucie. "How does Sir Robert?"

Lucie wondered what Magda read on her face. "He is well enough."

"And Joanna Calverley?"

Lucie glanced round for Daimon. She was uncertain how much to say in front of him.

Magda noted her hesitation. "The lad will tarry a while. He has the wide-eyed look of a child. He will explore Magda's treasures. Thou canst talk freely."

Magda had arranged a private talk just by sending Daimon in for a stool. Lucie smiled. "You are the one who should talk with Joanna. You would plot a course to coax more out of her than I shall ever hear."

Magda wagged her head from side to side. "Oh, thou'rt such a bungler, indeed. 'Tis of course why the crow and the squirrel wish thee to speak with Joanna."

Lucie paused. The crow, she knew, was the archbishop. The squirrel—ah! Dame Isobel, with her chubby cheeks and fussy little hands. Lucie laughed until tears blurred her vision and her stomach began to cramp. Magda watched her with a secret smile. "What is it?" Lucie asked.

"Thou dost so little of that. Laughter from deep within." Magda touched the thin veil. "This suits thee. Put off the wimple and gorget till thou'rt a crone, child. Thou hast lost one husband, but won another. Thou'rt neither a widow now nor yet a crone. Dance in thy beauty while thou mayest. But Magda wanders. What is the trouble with Joanna Calverley?"

What was the trouble? If Lucie could describe it, she would perhaps be on her way to helping Joanna. "I had a dream last night about how I feel. Joanna was a spider, and I followed her as she wove a web. She worked at it intently, ignoring me, though she knew

I was there. I would begin to see a pattern, try to guess where she would move next, and I was wrong most of the time. I predicted few of the strands."

Magda frowned and scratched beneath her cap with a bony finger. "Did she finish the web in thy dream?"

Lucie shook her head.

Magda looked out at the river, thinking. "Was the web well-ordered?"

Lucie closed her eyes and tried to see the web again. "There were strands that broke the harmony, but much of the web was well-ordered."

The Riverwoman nodded. "What dost thou think it means?"

Lucie groaned, exasperated. "I hoped that you would tell me!"

"Surely thou hast a thought or two, Master Apothecary?"

Lucie admitted it. But she expected laughter. What did she know of dreams? "I guess that Joanna knows what she is saying, that she deliberately confuses me."

Magda looked doubtful. "A spider does not set out to weave an imperfect web."

"So I am wrong?"

Magda leaned back against the house, looking up at the dragon's head. "Is Joanna a spider or a woman?" She shrugged. "'Tis the trouble with dreams. They seduce the dreamer with their seeming wisdom. Or is it trickery?" She smiled.

Disappointed, Lucie rubbed her temples, looked up at the sun. "I must return to the abbey for Sir Robert."

Magda squinted at Lucie and wagged a finger. "Be not petulant. Thou art not speaking plain. Thou didst not come to Magda to talk of dreams."

"No."

"What is so difficult about the woman?"

"She speaks a mixture of reason and confusion. I am exhausted when I leave her."

"Dost thou thinkst she is bedeviled?"

"Perhaps." Lucie shrugged. "In truth, I do not know. She told Dame Isobel that the Devil had tempted her with dreams of her beloved."

"Why should such dreams be the work of the Devil?"

"Because they proved false."

"Do you believe the Devil possesses her?"

Lucie shook her head. "I do not understand what she means by her dreams proving false, either."

"She was disappointed, perhaps."

"The beloved proved an ordinary man?"

Magda grinned. "Thou hast no such complaints."

"My problem is that my beloved is unhappy sitting still."

"Surely thou hast an idea what ails Joanna?"

"Today she said Will Longford served her wine seasoned with something that made her sleep, then gave her something more potent for her false funeral. Could all this work as a poison, not killing her, but tearing at her memory and her reason?"

"Was she well when she ran away?"

"She had fasted often. Harsh fasts. Once she had starved herself to the point that her fingernails peeled away and her teeth were loose."

"Foolish child." Magda frowned, her many wrinkles deepening, her grizzled brows pressing in and down over her hawk nose. Wise and fierce, she looked. Magda sighed, nodded. "Weakening her body, then piling poison on poison. Aye. Trust Apothecary Wilton to find such an explanation. Tidy. Reasonable." Magda patted Lucie's arm.

Lucie was not certain whether Magda agreed. She felt a reluctance to ask. "If I am right, I thought it might help if we sweat her, bleed her, and purge her."

Magda tapped her knee. "Unless like a slow-acting poison it has worked on her too long. Then a purge could well hasten the end."

Lucie had not considered that. "So I have not found a solution."

"Magda did not say that. Try it. But after thou hast cleansed her, she should have a long sleep. Magda will give thee mandrake wine for a long, healing sleep. After that, return to the herbs that calm her. Thou know'st the sort—catmint, bedstraw, and balms—nothing more. If that does not work, thou hast not found the proper solution."

Lucie saw a flaw in the plan. "How long is a long sleep?"

"Aye, thou art thinking 'twill be days without speaking with her. Nay. From sunset to sunset to sunrise—thou canst spare one day, eh?" Magda patted Lucie's hand. "Thou must not be overly hopeful. 'Tis but a theory. And though she may be calm and rested at the end of it, she may say little more than she has."

Lucie forced herself to ask the question that plagued her. "What would you do with her?"

Magda grinned. "Thou art alert. Thou hearest Magda's silences." She shook her head. "Thou wouldst not take Magda's advice."

"Please, Magda, tell me."

The old woman scratched her chin, frowned fiercely down at the sun-dappled river. After a long silence, she said, "Magda would leave the child in peace."

Lucie was certain she must have misunderstood. "Ask her nothing?"

Magda nodded. "And tell her nothing."

It was not like Magda to suggest inaction. "Why?"

Magda held out her wrinkled, sun-browned hands. "When storms blow down the dales to Magda's house, these old hands ache as a warning that the river shall soon rise."

Lucie frowned, then realized what Magda meant. "You have a feeling it would be best not to know what happened to her."

Magda stared at something beyond Lucie, a vision of trouble. "Aye. Keep thy distance, Magda would advise thee. But thou wouldst not abide by Magda's feeling. Nor shouldst thou. Thy task is to learn her secret. The Churchmen insist." Magda nodded toward the door. "Thou must retrieve the boy and make haste to St. Mary's."

Lucie looked up at the sun. "Sweet Heaven!" She stood up so abruptly she felt dizzy.

Magda jumped to her feet and held Lucie steady. "Stay. Magda will fetch Daimon."

Sir Robert met Lucie and Daimon at St. Mary's gate, sputtering with indignation that Lucie had sneaked away and taken Daimon with her.

"Would you rather I had gone alone?" she asked.

"Of course not. You need protection outside the city."

"Then it was clever of me to take Daimon?"

"You should have told me that both of you were leaving. Where did you go?"

"You are only angry because you feel you have been fooled."

"Where did you go?"

"To seek advice about Dame Joanna. Now I must speak with Brother Wulfstan. I would like you to go back to the shop and tell Tildy I will be there soon. Any customers can wait."

Sir Robert ordered Daimon to wait for Lucie and escort her home.

Brother Wulfstan frowned more and more as he listened to Lucie's prescription. "Bleeding, yes. Purging, perhaps. But this long sleep. Mandragora wine." He shook his head. "The Riverwoman is not a Christian. How can you trust her as you do?"

"Magda is a good woman, Brother Wulfstan."

"But she does not pray over her physicks."

"Then we shall pray over them. Please. I would like to try this. If it does not work, I promise to defer to you. Anything that you wish."

Wulfstan took Lucie's hands, looked into her eyes. "I think you have fulfilled your duty with Joanna. You have proven that she does not wish to be understood. What more do you hope to learn more from her? What is it you seek?"

Lucie looked into Wulfstan's age-clouded eyes. He relied more and more on Brother Henry's assistance. His round face was wrinkled, his voice crackled. She did not like to distress him. But she must. "I think something terrible happened in Scarborough." She did not like the sorrow she had brought to the cloudy eyes. "Perhaps I am wrong. Perhaps Joanna merely fell ill. If that is so, if we can bring her back to her senses, she might simply tell us that. Then we will know to leave her in peace to do penance at St. Clement's."

Wulfstan shook his head, his kindly face sad. "I do not think she merely fell ill, Lucie, and neither do you. But whether it benefits anyone to know what happened—" He shrugged. "Still, Jaro and

Maddy were murdered. It is best to make known the murderer."

Wulfstan let go her hands. "I will do as you wish."

"You are a good friend. I am sorry I burden you with this."

"Friends are blessed burdens."

Lucie hugged him. "I must get to the shop. I will return tomorrow morning."

Wulfstan put his hands gently on Lucie's shoulders and frowned sternly. "You are doing too much, Lucie. The infirmaress from St. Clement's—Prudentia, a promising name—she can help me bleed Joanna, and surely she can purge her. Leave the mandragora wine with me." Wulfstan smiled at her uncertain look. "I promise to administer it, Lucie. No matter what I think of Magda Digby, I have agreed to try your idea."

Lucie was exhausted by the time she opened the shop. A stranger had delivered a letter from Owen. From time to time, Lucie stole glimpses at it, learning gradually the odd story of Matthew Calverley and his missing wife.

13

AN ARCHER, A POET, A PRINCE

Owen had not slept well. What bothered him was Matthew Calverley's claim that he did not want to know what had happened to his wife. Such uncertainty about Lucie would drive Owen mad. He would be obsessed with finding her, either alive or dead. If dead, he would be devastated, but he would know, he would understand, he would provide for a grave nearby, where he could visit her every day. And if alive—well, he would not like to learn that she was happier without him. But he would know.

Matthew Calverley did not know. Did not wish to know.

But what of the rest of the family?

Indeed. What of the eldest son?

When Louth woke, Owen informed him that he was going back to Leeds to speak with Frank Calverley.

"Why, for pity's sake? We have spoken with the head of the family."

"I must ask him why no one searched for the truth about his mother's disappearance."

Louth, blinking himself awake, shaded his eyes from the dawn light and frowned at Owen. "Why? That is not your concern."

Owen paced, eager to be off. "I cannot explain, but I think it might be important."

Louth sighed. "So we spend another day in Leeds."

"Not 'we.' You go on with the men. Tell me your route. I shall ride hard to catch up to you."

"I should accompany you."

Owen noticed an edge in Louth's voice. "Why? You do not

agree that this is anything to be concerned about."

Louth struggled to sit up. He had slept hard on his left side and his face carried the impression of the wrinkled bedclothes. He yawned. "That is not the point."

"I shall not tarry."

Louth looked upset. "What if you are delayed?"

"Then you arrive at Pontefract before I do." Owen suddenly guessed Louth's concern. "You think I have no intention of arriving in Pontefract, that I mean to return to York."

Louth looked surprised, then smiled apologetically. "It had occurred to me." He swung his pale legs off the side of the bed, called for his squire.

Owen wished to be alone with his thoughts. Louth tended to chatter. "I will catch up to you on the road. I swear."

The servant brought in two tankards of ale for Louth and Owen to wash the night out of their mouths. Then he helped his master dress.

"For my soul's sake, I cannot let you go alone," Louth said as he tugged and pulled at his houppelande to make it hang just right. "Go along now," he said to the servant, watching him leave, checking outside the door that he was truly gone.

Owen found Louth's behavior more than a little puzzling. He acted as if he were about to divulge some terrible secret. But they had not been speaking of secrets.

Louth stood, hands behind his back, head bowed slightly so that his extra chin pressed forward, looking up through his thick brows. "Forgive me for pretending that I do not trust you. That is not the truth. It is in no way the truth." He took a deep breath, brought his head up straight and looked Owen in the eye. "Maddy—the serving girl who was murdered—would be alive if I had been worthy of my prince's trust. But I am not. I have made a mess of this Longford business from the beginning. And now a young woman is dead because of it. I mean to find her murderer."

Owen was torn between amusement at the thought of the softly rounded, pampered canon facing the murderer, and sympathy with the man's need to atone for his sin of omission. He chose to play with Louth. "I do not think Frank Calverley is your man."

Louth frowned in puzzlement. "I should not think so either."

"Neither does Mistress Calverley's disappearance have anything to do with the girl's death, I suspect."

Louth bristled. "Are you purposefully misunderstanding me?"

Owen bowed his head slightly. "Not at all, Sir Nicholas. I am trying to see what your confession has to do with my going back into Leeds alone to speak with Frank Calverley."

"It was not a confession."

Owen shrugged. "Call it what you wish. I appreciate your fine feelings about Longford's maid. But keeping Lancaster content is the issue as far as I am concerned, and I would appreciate your making it to Pontefract on schedule. If—and it is only an if—I do not arrive on time, you can assure him that I shall be there soon."

Louth closed his eyes. "I wish to observe your methods. That is why I wish to accompany you."

Owen did not try to hide his surprise. "What do you mean, methods?"

"How you question people."

"What do you think I am, an interrogator?"

It was Louth's turn to look surprised. "Is that not what you are?"

"God's blood, I am an apothecary's apprentice!"

Louth's red face turned redder, his breath expelled in a loud guffaw. But seeing the fury on Owen's face, he quickly grew serious. "Please forgive me, but you must indeed think me an ass if you expect me to believe that. What in Heaven's name are you doing here if you are an apothecary's apprentice?"

"I occasionally work for Thoresby." Owen was glowering and he hated himself for it. He should laugh and shrug it off. Of course he was a spy, and a damned good one, truth be told. Why was he always denying it? He forced a grin. Shrugged. "A spy never admits his calling."

Louth laughed. "Already you teach me. See how I need to observe you?"

Owen sighed. "Leave your men at the gates of the city, if you will. We do not want to call attention to ourselves."

• • •

As Owen and Louth rode along the River Aire to Leeds, sunshine warmed the river meadows and glinted off the water. Owen imagined Matthew Calverley bending over his garden, hoeing away the weeds, obliterating memories. He had noted certain silences yesterday. Some occurred around the issue of Mistress Anne Calverley turning against Hugh and Joanna. She seemed an unnatural mother to turn against the children who favored her. Was it *because* they favored her? Was there something about herself she did not like seeing again in her children? Something accursed in her? But would she not try to help them, teach them how to fight it?

It turned Owen's thoughts to his impending fatherhood. If he detected his child going astray, would he know what to do? Lucie would, most like. It seemed the sort of thing women knew about.

Was the problem in the Calverley family that Anne Calverley had been an inadequate mother?

Trot had given them directions to Frank's house in case Matthew Calverley was not about. They found it easily, a substantial stone house near the wharves. A logical location for a young merchant. Owen and Louth rode up just as the master of the house was striding out to begin his day.

"Captain Archer, representing His Grace, the Archbishop of York," Owen said, dismounting near the plump, brightly dressed young man. "And Sir Nicholas de Louth, Canon of Beverley." Owen gestured back to his companion, who was slow in dismounting. "Am I so fortunate as to find Master Frank Calverley with such ease?"

"You are indeed, Captain Archer. And doubly fortunate, for my father told me of your visit and I regretted not meeting you. I am glad to have news of my sister, good or ill."

"I wondered if you could spare us a few words before you begin your day."

Frank Calverley nodded. He was very much his father's son, the round, blunt features, the merry eyes. "Accompany me down to the wharves, if you will."

The street was shadowed by overhanging upper floors. With Owen's one good eye he must watch his footing to avoid night waste and keep a tight hold on his horse. He accompanied Frank in silence until they reached the wharf. Louth followed at the rear, forced into silence by his distance from Frank. The river breeze smelled fresh after the city street. Owen and Louth tethered their horses to a small tree outside Frank's warehouse door.

Frank turned to Owen. "So. You would know more about my sister Joanna?"

"It is another matter. I know it will sound as if I forget myself and grow too familiar with your family, but I am intrigued by your mother's disappearance."

Frank took off his felt hat and scratched his head, heaved a big sigh, the merry eyes growing sad. "Aye. 'Tis passing strange that a woman who lived so many years at the river's edge would fall in. But the bank was slippery and she was not strong. She had been unwell for a long while. I think it was the farthest she had walked since early spring."

"Your mother drowned, then?"

Frank frowned, tucking his chin in so that his jowls spread, aging him. "My father said otherwise?"

"He said that he did not know whether she drowned or ran away. He did not wish to know."

Frank put a meaty hand up to his face, covering his eyes for a moment, then, looking round, sat down heavily on a bale of wool. "Such a contrary way to mourn her. Edith and I have worked hard to convince our acquaintances that our father says such things that he may dream of seeing her again. Why he would want folk to think she had a lover... It is difficult for the family. I trust you thought it passing strange we would not have tried harder to find her." Frank kneaded his thick thighs with his fists. "It is simple to explain, impossible to cure. My father loved her so. He could not believe that she could be taken from him so suddenly after he had prayed so hard and sat with her so long in her illness. God had answered our prayers and spared her through the spring and summer, then took her in such a"—Frank held his hands out, palms up, and looked up at the sky for the words—"capricious manner."

"So you did find her body?"

"Oh, aye." Frank stood up as some men approached. "Gentlemen, I will be with you shortly. You are welcome to go sit in my office." The two men nodded and, with curious glances at the strangers, walked on into the warehouse.

"She drowned in the autumn?" Owen asked.

Frank nodded. "Just before Martinmas. She walked out, though the day promised rain and her nurse warned her that she was not up to it. Mother said she was restless, wanted to feel the wind on her face. There was no reasoning with her when she was determined. A Boulain trait. She slipped, got tangled in the river weeds." Frank wiped his brow. "Had she been stronger, I do not think she would have drowned. We found her right there beneath the bank. It took two of us to cut her out of the weeds."

"And your father decided he had not seen it?"

"Yes." Frank dabbed his upper lip. "God's blood, how could anyone forget it?" He pressed a hand to his gut. "My father is not mad, just determined not to remember how she looked, strangled by the weeds, bloated by the water." He shivered, as if the image had crept up from behind and surprised him. "My father found it more bearable to remember her as she had been in life. But he often spends a day—from sunrise to sunset—kneeling by her stone in the parish church, praying for her soul."

So much for the idea that the mother and daughter shared an urge to walk away from their lives. Or had met up somewhere. "One more question, if you would."

Frank shrugged.

"Your father said your mother turned against Joanna and Hugh. Do you know why?"

Frank glanced round at the warehouse, back to Owen. "There's a lot of foolishness spoken about my mother's family, the Boulains. Hugh and Joanna look like them. They were difficult to discipline. So mother thought they carried the Boulain curse."

"What was the curse?"

"Madness." Frank chuckled. "But in the end it is old Matthew

Calverley who acts out the madman, playing gardener, waiting for his dead wife to stroll up from the river."

"You feel neither Hugh nor Joanna is mad?"

Frank shook his head. "Hugh is a soldier born. As far as I know, we do not consider such a convenient passion madness. Joanna—her head has ever been silly with stories of handsome knights and princes. And, to be blunt, she discovered the pleasures of lovemaking too early to discipline her body. She was foolish to run from her betrothal to the convent. She was too fond of men to make that work. As a wife she might have found some satisfaction. Father says you told him Joanna ran away from St. Clement's, then came back."

"With an elaborate ruse to cover her tracks."

"When she made such a fuss about the convent, I thought she had found herself a man of the cloth who satisfied her and wished to be near him." Frank sat with head bowed, studying his hands. "Perhaps she wearied of him, went out into the world, found that men out here are no more exciting, and decided to go back to him."

Louth spoke for the first time. "The priest at St. Clement's is bald, portly, and knobby with age."

Frank shook his head. "Unless my sister is much changed, such a man would not lead her into sin. But convents hire men to do the heavy work. Joanna has an imagination and a way with men. Who knows what she might have got into and then run from? You'll find a man at the end of it, that's all I can tell you."

Louth turned in his saddle and hailed Owen to come ride beside him. Owen wished for peace and quiet, but he could not be so discourteous to ignore the man. He joined him.

"So Mistress Anne Calverley drowned and her body lies beneath the stone floor of the parish church."

"Aye. Sharing a roof with St. Hardulph of Breedon."

Louth nodded. "My lord Thoresby will be pleased by your thoroughness. But what does it tell you? What did you learn by it?"

"In truth, I did it for myself. I could not understand how someone who claimed to love so well could accept not knowing what had happened."

Louth studied Owen's solemn face. "You are an odd one, Owen Archer."

Owen shrugged.

"How do you get on with Thoresby?"

"Well enough." Owen leaned down and took a wineskin from his pack, took a drink. They had ridden hard to catch up with their planned arrival at Pontefract.

"So it was for your own curiosity that you spoke with Frank Calverley? There was nothing in the question about his mother that helped you?"

"Of course it helped."

"But you just said you did not do it for Thoresby."

Owen groaned inwardly. How to explain that Thoresby began the process, but once Owen's mind was engaged on the problem it was his own gut pushing him forward? Owen glanced at Louth, the fat thighs, the chubby hands, the bouncing double chin. The man did not want to know Owen's thoughts, he wanted to learn how Owen pleased Thoresby so that he might do it himself. Owen relaxed.

"It was an inconsistency that might have led me to suspect Matthew Calverley, indeed the entire family, were hiding something." Owen shrugged. "So it was my dissatisfaction that led me to question Frank, but in the end it helps me eliminate that worry as nothing to look into further."

Louth nodded. "There is a knack to all this that I fear may have more to do with character than method." He shook his head. "I fear I am too much a clerk, good at doing another's bidding, not thinking on my own."

A difficult thing to admit of one's self. "I should like to think less than I do, truth be told."

"We are what God makes us." Louth's face was sad. He fell silent then for a long while, leaving Owen to ponder the things he learned in Leeds.

• • •

The whitewashed walls of the great castle of Pontefract rose high above the town walls, which were partially obscured by the tents and cook fires of the markets of West Cheap. The markets were abustle as Owen, Louth, and company rode through to the city gates. There were some in the company tempted to linger. But Owen was anxious to complete his business and be off, so the word went out to ride on.

The castle was long and high. Even the revetments around three sides of the motte were whitewashed, the effect so brilliant in the sunlight it seemed a heavenly city. The height of the keep made Owen stare in wonder, though he'd seen many a castle in his life on the march.

Lief and Gaspare saw them riding into the yard and came out to greet Owen, who dismounted without the assistance of the grooms who came running out behind his friends.

"My lord duke is pleased with the archers," Lief said with a big grin and a slap on Owen's back. "So he has invited you to sit at the high table with Sir Nicholas this even."

Owen was glad the duke was satisfied. That meant he could soon return to York. But he did not look forward to sitting at the high table. "I am honored indeed. But where's the fun in it, I ask you? I came to visit my old friends."

Gaspare cuffed Owen's head in approval. "I see no need for you to be cleaning yourself up for supper right now. Come with us to the stables and wash down the road dust with a bit of our humble ale."

Louth had by now been assisted in dismounting. He gave Owen a little bow. "I look forward to further enlightenment at the high table this evening, Captain Archer." He nodded to Lief and Gaspare and turned to the castle.

"Come on, then," Gaspare said.

On a milking stool by the stable doors sat a handsome man dressed as a minor lord, wearing a deep, vibrant blue houppelande cut to the knees, belted in heavy silver and copper. His face was clean shaven, his hair trimmed just below his ears and curled under, a fringe covered his forehead. It was the soft brown doe-eyes that identified him.

"Ned!" Owen shouted, striding up to him. "God's blood, but you've grown grand!" Like Gaspare and Lief, Ned had been one of Owen's archers in the Old Duke's retinue. The talker.

Ned jumped up and strutted around good-naturedly. "Grand indeed, my favorite Welshman. And when is your speech going to roughen up to suit your scarred face? You still speak with the tongue of bards." He clasped Owen's hand. "We miss you."

Owen cocked his head to one side. "You cannot mean for me to think you are still an archer in those clothes."

"Nay. Bertold cuffed me on the head once too often and I took up the Duke's offer to serve as one of Master Geoffrey Chaucer's escorts to Spain this winter."

"Spain?"

Ned noted his friend's sudden interest. "We will speak of that by and by, with my lord duke. Now we must fill our tankards and toast to old friendships."

"Agreed."

Owen was escorted to the high table as promised, seated between Louth and a little round man with the look of a cleric except for his lively, alert eyes that seemed to take in everything round him.

"Geoffrey Chaucer," the man said lifting his cup of wine to Owen in greeting.

"Ah. Lancaster's ambassador to Spain."

A laughing bow. "And I know something of you, Owen Archer." He chuckled at Owen's surprise. "There are few well-spoken Welshmen with eye patches at the high table this evening, Captain."

"Sometimes there are several?"

Chaucer feigned surprise at the question. "Why, quite frequently, to be sure."

Owen wondered whether the man was silly on wine or his own wit. But he liked him. He played with conversation like a Welshman.

"I know that you were blinded in that eye by the leman of a

Breton jongleur whose life you had saved. Such a poetic blinding, but I can see you do not share my view."

"How can I, with but one eye?"

Chaucer clapped. "Splendid."

"Tell me, Master Chaucer, have you any Welsh blood?"

"Alas, no. A terrible lack for a poet, but it is my unfortunate lot. I must work all the harder."

Owen looked more closely at the man. The bards and poets he had met usually looked more imposing. "You are a poet?"

Chaucer shrugged. "I play with words. It helps me while away the dull hours envoys spend on benches at the edges of great halls, awaiting audiences."

"You have an intriguing variety of skills. I should think it hard to compose poetry while sitting amidst the courtiers who clamor for attention."

Chaucer nodded. "But a dabbler must live. And a wife must have money to set up a household."

"You are newly married?"

Chaucer nodded, but his eyes were on the tapestries behind the high table. The company in the hall fell silent as the duke came through them and took the center seat at the high table. John of Gaunt looked much as he had when Owen saw him last, at his grand castle of Kenilworth. Lancaster was in his mid-twenties, tall, broad in the chest, with a forked beard and full lips, a Plantagenet in his regal bearing, his height, his fair coloring. Owen wondered whether his temper was also true Plantagenet, quick to laugh, quick to take offense.

"Now there is a man blissfully married to the most beautiful woman in God's creation," Chaucer murmured, his voice full of yearning.

Owen looked at the poet with interest. A complex little man.

Lancaster did not linger over his food. He was the last to arrive at table, the first to leave. Owen, Chaucer, and Louth were soon summoned. They were led up a flight of stone stairs to a parlor.

The Duke of Lancaster stood at a table, studying maps. "Come, gentlemen," he called, beckoning them close. With a silver knife he pointed to the west coast of France. "Gascony, gentlemen, where Don Pedro is at present a guest of my brother, Prince Edward." Moving the knife to the right, he stopped at Castile. "Castile, where he should sit enthroned." The duke snapped his fingers and a servant took up the map and backed away into the shadows. Another servant brought forth a chair. Lancaster sat. Three more chairs appeared. His guests sat.

"Sir Nicholas," Lancaster said, nodding to Louth, "it is good to see you. If you are able to tie up your concerns in Beverley by autumn, the Prince wishes you to sail with me."

"I hope that I may do so, my lord Duke." Louth gestured toward Owen. "Captain Archer accompanied me to Leeds at my lord Thoresby's request. We spoke with Matthew Calverley, the father of the woman who has concerned us, Dame Joanna of St. Clement's Priory. Owen is a skillful questioner."

Lancaster studied Owen closely. "You are a man of many talents, Owen Archer. You have done well by me—the archers you trained hit the mark every time. Your service to me will not go unrewarded."

"Your Grace," Owen said with a little bow. "You have two able men in Gaspare and Lief."

Lancaster nodded. "Indeed. You trained them." He tucked the knife into a jeweled sheath at his waist, sank into a chair at the table. "And now I would hear you and Sir Nicholas on your visit to Leeds. Master Chaucer attends because I believe his business with me touches on this. He has read your letters, Nicholas, you need not begin from the beginning."

As Louth recounted the interviews with Matthew and Frank Calverley, Owen noticed an exchange of looks between Lancaster and Chaucer at the mention of the seal of St. Sebastian. When Louth was finished, Lancaster said nothing, but sat quietly, elbows on the table, fingertips pressed together, his brows drawn down in thought. At last he said, "Now, Master Chaucer, tell them of your mission."

Chaucer looked surprised. He smiled apologetically. "I pray

your patience, gentlemen. As one who is more at ease writing down his thoughts and then worrying them into a digestible form, I feel ill-prepared." He paused, studied his hands momentarily. "Shortly after the festivities of the Christmas court, I received orders to sail to Gascony and thence to Navarre. You know how King Charles, desperate to find an occupation for the ever growing Free Companies, used them in supporting Enrique de Trastamare's claim to the throne of Castile. What you may not know is that five Englishmen of renown were said to be planning to march with King Charles— or rather with Bertrand du Guesclin—against Don Pedro. It is a matter of misguided chivalry. They protest Don Pedro's rumored cruelty. In December, King Edward had sent letters to these men warning them that they would be punished if they proceeded. The letters failed to reach them. Hence was I sent to win the King of Navarre over to Don Pedro's cause, obtain from him a safe conduct, and travel into the mountains to intercept them."

"A dangerous mission for a poet," Owen said.

Chaucer smiled. "Dangerous for any man, Captain. The mountains themselves are unfriendly in winter, and the soldiers who had hidden in them were ravenous and wild, full ready to march into Castile and slaughter Don Pedro's men.

"But God was with me. I found four of the five English captains and delivered the letters. They were not eager to give up the fight; but when I assured them that there would be fighting aplenty on our side, with Prince Edward at their head in his glorious black armor, they agreed. Well, two of the captains agreed when the prospect was sweetened with gold.

"But the fifth captain had disappeared. Three of his fellows believed him to be in France, conferring with du Guesclin. One thought he had returned to England for more men. This fifth captain is the one called Sebastian."

Owen leaned forward. "Sebastian?"

Lancaster smiled a lazy smile.

Chaucer nodded. "Sebastian and Will Longford fought together under the Prince at once time, before Longford lost the leg. Sebastian uses his patron saint on his seal. About the time Longford returned to England, Sebastian joined du Guesclin's company of *routiers*."

Owen rubbed the scar under his patch. "Longford was of low rank, too low for the Crown to pay his passage home in peacetime. Having lost a leg and become unfit for soldiering, what are the odds that he suddenly had the money to return to England and establish a comfortable home in Beverley?"

"You have a good mind, Archer," Lancaster said. He paced the room, hands behind his back. "Go on."

"There's the letter with du Guesclin's seal that Louth found in Longford's house. And earlier, the Percies learned that a Frenchman had been carrying one of Sebastian's seals to someone in Beverley."

Chaucer sat back, content. "Longford will lead us to Captain Sebastian."

Louth and Owen shook their heads. "Longford is missing."

"Surely you will find him?" Chaucer looked naively confident. But was he actually baiting them?

Owen did not like it. "I was not aware that was our task."

"Indeed," Louth said. "What does Dame Joanna have to do with all this talk of *routiers*?"

Lancaster turned on his heels, stopped in front of Louth. "Come now, surely you see the tie."

Louth shook his head. But Owen saw it. "Longford must have remembered her, remembered Hugh Calverley, perhaps knew that Calverley was in Scarborough working for the Percies, a family seeking to stop the English soldiers from sailing out of Scarborough to du Guesclin. He used her to get to her brother?"

The lazy smiled reappeared. "Enough for tonight, gentlemen. We shall talk more tomorrow."

Owen did not like that. "Forgive me, my lord Duke, but I planned to leave for York early tomorrow."

"You are not to leave quite yet, Captain Archer. I have further need of you."

• • •

Owen sat on the bottom of the steps to one of the outer towers, glumly nursing the fist he'd put to a post in the stables. He had meant the pain to distract him from thoughts of Lucie's silken hair, the curve of her hips, her white breasts. It was not working. He was ready to put the other fist into someone's face.

"I should not like to cause such a dark look on such an obvious fighter," a voice said.

Owen focused his good eye on the approaching man, backlit by the sun. He recognized the short, round figure before he could clearly see the face. "Master Chaucer."

"Captain." He gave a little bow. "May I join you?"

Owen shrugged.

The little man settled on the step above Owen, bringing his line of sight even with Owen's. "Is it your beautiful, accomplished wife you are missing?"

"How do you know of her?"

"Sir Nicholas is a talker."

"He is a chattering jay."

Chaucer chuckled. "And Ned told me of her background, how you met. A fascinating story."

Owen frowned still. "I am attempting to forget my longing at the moment, Master Chaucer. Pray tell me something of your wife."

The poet gave a little bow. "Fair enough. You should know as much of me as I of you. Let me see. Something of my wife. We wed shortly after my father died this spring. She is Phillippa de Roet, an attendant of Queen Phillippa's chamber. Her father was a Flemish farmer, knighted on the battlefield. He died shortly thereafter and his daughters were taken in by our Queen, kindhearted and loyal to her fellow Flemings. My wife's sister, Katherine, young and sickly, was sent to the convent of Sheppey, but Phillippa already showed signs of formidable tidiness and practicality, so the Queen found her useful. Phillippa is round and plain like myself." He shrugged. "And she has little patience with my poetic endeavors. That is all there is to tell."

Owen did not detect much affection in the summation. "Do

you yearn for your Phillippa on your journeys?"

Chaucer considered it. "I was about to say that I am married too recently to answer that; but, now you ask, I do miss her—when a button goes astray or I misplace something. And the bed sport is to my liking." He slapped his thighs. "Faith, I nearly forgot my mission. I am to bring you to my lord duke. He made note of your desire for haste and wishes to give you your orders and send you off."

Owen was surprised to find Ned sitting with Louth in the duke's parlor, looking very pleased with himself. "We are to travel together, old friend."

"You are coming to York?"

Ned grinned. "I look forward to meeting your fair Lucie."

Owen glanced at Louth, but could read nothing in his expression.

The duke entered the room, looked round. "All present. Good. I shall be brief. This matter of Longford and Sebastian being tied together with your nun, I think it timely that you travel together to Scarborough, stopping in York to see whether anything new has been learned from the nun. Master Chaucer is needed back in London, so it must be just the three of you. Sir Nicholas will carry the King's letter for Captain Sebastian, in case you learn something that leads you to the rogue. He will also carry money with which to bribe the captain."

"I am to go to Scarborough?" Owen said.

"Indeed. I should think you will have more luck in ferreting out the weasel Sebastian than Master Chaucer. He is a poet, better at asking questions than finding the answers. Eh, Chaucer?"

The poet smiled and shrugged amiably, but Owen noted the man's heightened color. He was embarrassed by his failure, fool that he was. If Owen had failed more often he would be quietly measuring out medicines in York at Lucie's side.

14

A PILGRIMAGE OF DISGRACE

Summer was coming on. The lavenders were sending up flower stalks; on some the tightly closed buds were already visible. Both valerians were blooming, the delicately scented pink blossoms of the garden valerian and the intense, cloying white clusters of the true valerian. Melisende sprang out from the bushy balms and caught a butterfly drinking nectar from the pink blossoms. The comfrey bells trembled with bees, the starry borage blossoms bobbed in the gentle wind.

Lucie's head ached. When she bent over her growing stomach, the blood in her head pounded. She sat back on her heels, closed her eyes, took a deep breath.

She must have drowsed in the sun, for she thought she heard a familiar voice singing,

> "Heo is lilie of largesse,
> Heo is parvenke of prouesse,
> Heo is solsecle of suetnesse,
> Ant ledy of lealte…
>
> "Blow, northerne wynd,
> Sent thou me my suetyng!
> Blow, northerne wynd,
> Blou! blou! blou!"
>
> "For hire love y carke ant care,
> For hire love y droupne ant dare,

For hire love my blisse is bare,
   Ant al ich waxe won;
For hire love in slep y slake,
For hire love al nyht ich wake,
For hire love mournyng y make
   More then eny mon."

Lucie started as a hand pressed her shoulder. "Would you be grateful for a strong arm to help you rise up off your knees? Or shall I kneel beside you?"

She turned round and rejoiced to find Owen's voice had not been a dream. Her weariness gone, Lucie gladly grabbed his steadying arm and rose into a fierce embrace.

"Sweet Heaven, how I've missed you," Owen whispered into her hair.

Lucie began to cry. Confused by her reaction, Owen held her tight until the spell passed. Then he held her at arms' length and asked, "What is it? Are you not happy to see me?" His face was furrowed with concern, then puzzlement as Lucie smiled up at him.

"It is wonderful to hear your voice and see you here before me, to touch you. The tears were—" She shrugged. "Of late strong feelings conjure them." She hugged him hard.

"What does Magda say about the babe?"

"That all is as it should be."

Owen crossed himself.

"You are so soon from Pontefract. Did all go well?"

"Yes, but Lancaster has given me a task that will take me away again. He wishes me to go to Scarborough to look for Hugh Calverley."

"The Duke of Lancaster concerns himself with Joanna?"

"Longford, actually."

"Soon all of England will be caught up in Joanna's story."

"This reaches far beyond Joanna, Lucie. Longford may be scheming with King Charles to lure our soldiers into the Free Companies, to fight against Don Pedro."

Lucie caught herself as she was about to admit knowledge

of the possibility. The time was not right for confessing her continuing involvement. "But why you, Owen? Why must you go to Scarborough?"

He drew her back into his arms. "I shall hurry back to you. I promise."

With Owen's return, Sir Robert and Daimon moved to a room in the York Tavern, which Bess and Tom hastily readied. Sir Robert used the opportunity to repeat his offer of the house next door.

Lucie was glad of the privacy when Owen blew up at the news that she had dined with Thoresby and visited Joanna at the abbey. They managed to hold their anger in while they were downstairs in the kitchen with Tildy, trading their new information with courtesy, but Owen slammed the door when they went up to their bedchamber.

"Sweet Jesu, woman, you shall drive me as mad as Joanna."

"Owen, for pity's sake, lower your voice. All York will know you are home with such a ruckus."

He began to pace the room.

Lucie sat on the end of the bed, kneading her lower back with her knuckles. "I thought we were going to bed."

"My legs are stiff from sitting my horse all day." Owen's voice was not friendly. "God's bones, Lucie, I cannot leave you for a few days without your behaving recklessly."

Lucie wearily rose and began to unpack Owen's bag, seeing that there was to be no immediate rest. "You grow tedious. We have had this argument before. I am not a simpleton." Lucie regretted her sharp tone, but he treated her like a child.

Owen's scar stood out angrily. "Do you not want my baby? Is that it?"

Lucie blinked. Whence came that remark? "What does this have to do with our baby? Of course I want our baby. What are you talking about?"

"You should be resting."

"Sweet Mary and all the saints, there would be precious few

people on this earth if mothers must rest while carrying their babies. Who has the leisure to rest for nine months?"

Owen crossed the room to her, put his hands on her shoulders. "You put yourself right in the path of danger." His grip tightened.

Lucie shrugged away from him. "And you do not? Does our child not also need a father?"

"I do not volunteer for these things, Lucie."

"I did not volunteer either. I was asked."

They stood a few feet apart, facing each other down, mirror images with hands on hips, chins thrust forward.

"The archbishop himself does not know what to make of Joanna Calverley, whether he should admit her back into the convent. And why? Might it be because a man's neck has been broken, a woman has been raped and strangled, and Colin may die? Yet you go gaily about quizzing the woman who seems to be the center of all this."

"I have not done it gaily, and I have had an armed escort."

"I don't like it."

Lucie sat down on the bed and bent over to pull off her shoes. Anger and the ache in her lower back brought tears to her eyes.

Owen dropped to his knees and gently pushed her hands away, slipping off her tight shoes, then pulled her into his arms. "God's blood, why do we argue, my love?"

Lucie let the tears come freely, knowing it was futile to fight them. When she was quiet, Owen patted her eyes with the edge of the blanket, then covered her face with kisses.

Lucie put her arms around him and leaned her head on his shoulder. "I pray every chance I get that this baby will live and thrive and grow to be like his father," she whispered into Owen's ear. "I could hope for nothing better." She kissed his cheek.

He turned and kissed her on the lips, a long, lingering kiss, then held her away so he might see her face, smoothing back a stray lock. "And I pray that she will be just like her mother. Perfection."

"I have avoided asking Magda whether it is a boy or a girl."

"She would know?"

Lucie gave a little laugh. "What doesn't Magda know?"

Owen squeezed Lucie's side and she squirmed and giggled. "I'd wager she does not know where your ticklish spot is." He reached for it again. Lucie tried to grab his hand, but he kept snaking it out of her grasp. She dissolved into giggles. Owen pushed her back on the bed. She rolled over on top of him and tried to pin down his hands. "Shall we remove these clothes and have a real homecoming?" Owen was already unlacing the back of her shift. "Unless your condition...?"

"Magda says it is fine." Lucie wriggled out of her shift.

Dame Isobel gave Owen a little bow. "I fell on your wife's mercy and she has been my deliverance, Captain Archer. Joanna is much calmer." She turned to Lucie, took her hands. "I am most grateful."

"Let us see whether calming makes her more pliant," Lucie said.

Joanna had been brought down to the parlor of the guest house; she sat propped up with blankets and cushions in a chair by the window. Today she wore the mantle like a shawl. Owen was struck by her remarkable green eyes and the pallor that made her freckles look inky.

But when she turned to study him, Owen no longer thought her eyes beautiful. They seemed to see him and then continue through him, at once vague and intense.

"Captain Archer. You have returned."

"I bring news of your family."

Joanna frowned and dropped her eyes. "You labor in vain to please, for I would fain hear none of such news."

"You are not curious about your family?"

The green eyes looked him up and down. "You are not the first well-muscled man I have seen, you know." Joanna sniffed, dismissing him.

Owen halted on that change of subject. Lucie had warned him of Joanna's rapid shifts in thought, but it was still disorienting.

"You *do* know that, Captain?" Joanna asked, now teasing.

Owen had caught his balance. "I hear your brother Hugh is

quite a warrior. Is it he of whom you speak?"

Joanna glanced over at Lucie, then down at the Magdalene medal, which she proceeded to turn round and round in her hands.

"Is that your Mary Magdalene medal?"

Joanna took a deep breath. "They have bled me and purged me, these Christians, then poisoned me again. What do you think of that? Would you feel safe in such a place?"

Owen glanced over at Lucie, who gave an almost imperceptible shrug. She was not about to come to his aid. "Why would they do such a thing—purge you, then poison you?"

Joanna's pale lips curved into a smile. "An empty stomach drinks the poison faster. But I have tripped them up."

Owen might disagree that she had been poisoned, but he knew she would not accept his argument. "How did you trip them up?"

Joanna touched the blue mantle. "Our Lady protects me."

Owen wondered how she could put so much faith in such an ordinary piece of cloth. "Why would anyone wish to poison you?"

The eyebrows arched. "I am cursed," she stated, as if surprised he did not know.

"But you say that Our Lady protects you. Would she protect a cursed soul?"

The stubby hands clenched the medal until they trembled with the effort. The jaw clenched. Anger or fear? "You have been to Leeds?" Joanna asked suddenly. She did not look at Owen, but out the window. "You have climbed Calvary?"

"Yes. I met your father."

After a long pause. "He is a silly man."

"He is your father."

Joanna looked Owen in the eye. "More's the pity."

Owen tried smiling. "For him or for you?"

She did not return the smile, but leaned forward, frowning. "Do you go now to Scarborough?"

The abrupt question, such an excellent guess, made Owen wonder who might have told her. But he could think of no one.

Now Joanna smiled. It was not a friendly smile. Head down, eyes looking up through the brows, as if she had tricked him. "No one told me. It is the logical thing to do. You are on a pilgrimage of disgrace."

This woman was neither mad nor possessed of evil spirits. Why did she expend so much energy on clever avoidance? "If I go to Scarborough, whom shall I see there?"

"The Devil."

"And who is he?"

Joanna cocked her head to one side, still smiling. "Will the sins of the father be visited upon your child? Will she have but one eye?"

Owen jerked back as if slapped.

Lucie, who had been gazing out the window, lost in her own thoughts, looked up, first at Owen, then Joanna, back to Owen with a frown.

Joanna put a hand to her mouth, no longer smiling. "Forgive me. I do not mean to be cruel. There is naught to be won from cruelty. Christ should have known that."

Christ? Owen tucked that one away. He wished to return to the Devil. "Did you meet the Devil in Scarborough, Dame Joanna?"

She dropped her gaze to her lap again. "I am very tired."

Owen could not guess whether she was truly tired or just avoiding the question. He thought the latter. "Who is this Devil? Will Longford?"

Joanna shivered, closed her eyes. "Jaro's neck is broken."

"Who killed him?"

Joanna shook her head. "I did not like him. But no one should die like that."

"When you ran away from St. Clement's, did you run to a lover?"

Joanna looked up, laughter in her eyes. "And do nuns have lovers? St. Clement's is but a tiny priory. Where might I hide him?" She looked over at Lucie. "You are getting angry with me. You must understand. I cannot think about these things."

"Why?" Lucie asked.

"What things?" Owen asked.

Joanna shrugged. "Well surely if you do not agree what is important, I cannot judge."

"You play with us," Owen said. "Cleverly. But you ruin your own game if you mean to make us think you are mad. Such cleverness does not describe madness."

Joanna grew solemn. Her eyes turned inward.

"Joanna?" Owen touched her hand.

She jerked it away from him, eyes wide, staring into his. "*Noli me tangere.*"

"Why must I not touch you?"

Joanna did not reply.

"Please, Joanna, tell me what has happened," Owen said.

The eyes focused on him once more, studied his face, moved along his shoulders. Joanna reached out and took his hand, studied the palm, turned it over, studied the back of his hand, touched it to her cheek. "You are someone I might have loved."

"I am honored."

Joanna let go his hand. "But I am cursed now. I yearn for death."

"Then why complain that someone poisoned you?"

"I was not complaining."

"What, then?"

She shrugged. "Wondering is all."

"I wanted to tell you about Hugh and the arm of St. Sebastian."

"He sold it to Will Longford."

"No. He sold nothing to Will Longford. It was a seal he carried, from a French soldier."

Joanna giggled. "We lied to him. It was St. Hardulph of Breedon, not St. Sebastian."

"There was no arm," Owen said softly.

Joanna looked away. Her hands clenched the Magdalene medal. "Am I to understand that Hugh did not sell the arm of St. Hardulph to Will Longford?"

"That is right."

Joanna took a deep, shuddering breath. "It is still at the parish church in Leeds?"

"Yes."

"Poor Hardulph," she said flatly.

Owen closed his eye and pressed beneath the patch, where a shower of painful needle pricks gave physical form to his frustration.

Joanna leaned forward, gently touched Owen's scar beneath the patch. "Does it hurt?"

"Yes."

"May I see the eye?"

"No. Why do you think Christ was cruel?"

"Because He was. To Mary Magdalene He was. He took her love, then cast her aside."

"That is not the usual version."

Joanna bit her bottom lip, looked away. "How goes my mother?"

God's blood, Owen had almost forgotten. He had prepared a gradual approach to the sad news, but he wondered whether they would ever get to the point. Indeed, a shock might trip Joanna up. Lucie might not approve. But if he did not ask, she could not protest. "Your mother is dead."

Joanna started. "What?" She fluttered her hands as if swatting the thought away. "No." She leaned forward and peered into Owen's good eye for a long moment, then sat back, shaking her head. "The Boulains are mad. But that is no death."

"She is dead, Joanna. She drowned in the river."

Joanna looked frightened. She glanced over her shoulder, shivered. "Watery graves," she said softly.

"Who else has a watery grave?"

Joanna stood up abruptly. "Go away, you one-eyed scoundrel. You cannot have my body. It has been promised to the Devil. He shall devour me as—" She shook her head, sat down suddenly. Hiding her face with her hands, she began to sob.

Lucie knelt down beside her, felt her forehead. "Owen, call the Reverend Mother. We must leave now. Joanna needs to rest and calm down. Her spirit overcomes the physick."

"It is an excellent act."

Lucie met Owen's eye. "It is no act. She is feverish."

• • •

After they passed through Bootham Bar, Owen drew Lucie to the side of the street and paused, looking down at her, holding her hands. "I was clumsy. Sweet Heaven but I was clumsy. Can you forgive me?"

Lucie shrugged and gave him a halfhearted smile. "Your blunt speech *might* have worked. She *might* have responded more helpfully. As you have seen, Joanna is unpredictable." Lucie glanced round. "But let us speak of this at home, for pity's sake."

Owen, seeing she looked a bit pale, offered, "Shall I carry you? Are you feeling faint?"

"Conspicuous. Most couples do not pause at street corners for serious discourse."

Ned arrived, breathless, late in the day. Owen came round the counter in the shop to greet him and introduce him to Lucie.

"Charming," Ned said as he held Lucie's hand overlong, gazing into her smiling eyes. It was clear to Owen that Lucie found Ned charming as well. Not an auspicious introduction. But Ned at last dropped her hand and turned to Owen. "I have been sent to beg your presence at the abbey infirmary."

Ned a messenger? "Why?"

"One of the archbishop's retainers has died, and his friend is threatening to murder any man in the shire who looks even vaguely like the attacker."

"Colin is dead, then?" Owen said.

Ned nodded.

"God grant him mercy," Lucie whispered, bowing her head and crossing herself.

Owen kicked the doorway. "I've a cursed knack for getting folk killed."

Ned grabbed his friend by the shoulder and gave him a shake. "You were not with them when they were attacked."

Owen shrugged out of Ned's grasp. The man had no conscience. He would not understand. But it must be said. "I suggested they were just the ones to guard the priory."

Ned rolled his eyes and flashed Lucie a sympathetic look. "Your man never changes. He has ever been one to take on the blame. If evil befell anyone in his company, 'twas his fault, no matter the truth of it. It matters not a whit that His Grace might have chosen them anyway." He turned back to Owen. "Colin was Thoresby's man."

"Say what you will, 'twas I who involved them in all this. Colin was a simple soldier, obedient, eager." Owen saw Ned prepare for another argument. "Alfred will be thirsty for blood. I believe what he says."

"So what is to be done with Alfred?" Lucie asked.

"Ravenser wants to lock him in the archbishop's gaol," Ned said.

"Then Ravenser's a fool," Owen said. "What has the man done but obeyed orders and been a true and faithful friend?"

Ned shrugged. "So what shall we do?"

"Take him with us to Scarborough. Alfred can then trouble no one in York."

Ned folded his arms across his chest and gave Owen a murderous look. "He will trouble us."

"I take responsibility for him."

"Fool," Ned said softly as he followed Owen out the door, stopping to blow a kiss to Lucie before stepping out into the street.

Louth and Ravenser sat in the abbot's parlor with Alfred between them, his hands bound behind.

"Surely it is not necessary to bind him, gentlemen?" Owen said, though he saw in Alfred's face a dangerous mixture of grief and fury. "I should think him more in need of movement." He knelt down in front of Alfred. "Care to join me on St. George's Field for a round with the broadsword?"

Alfred stared ahead. "I knew it was an ambush, Captain. But I always gave Colin his way. Most times 'twas the right way. Wish to God he'd been right as usual." Alfred's eyes were dry, but glassy. Owen could hear the tightness in the man's throat, see the clenched jaw muscles.

"I want you to come with me to Scarborough, Alfred."

Now the dark eyes focused on Owen. "What for?"

"Never mind that yet. But I need you, and I need you clear headed. So how about the broadsword drill? Work up a sweat? Take it out on a wood dummy? For now, anyway. Clear your head for some talk and then the journey?"

"What will they do with Colin?"

Owen turned to Ravenser and Louth with a questioning look.

"Was he a York man?" Ravenser asked.

"Nay," said Alfred. "Lavenham."

"Then we shall bury him in the minster yard, I think. He died in service to the archbishop."

Owen turned back to Alfred. "Will that satisfy you?"

Alfred nodded.

"If I cut your bonds, you will not attack the first person who annoys you?"

"Colin would wish me to do your bidding without question, Captain."

Owen had once thought that a soldier's duty. That was before he'd begun to understand more about the world, through Thoresby's tutelage. Now he believed one should always question. But in Alfred's present state, blind obedience was advisable. "Good." Owen drew his knife and cut Alfred's bonds, stood up. "Come. Let us say goodbye to Colin, then go hack up some solid oak."

Ned joined them at the door. "Might I join you? I could use a good whack at my enemies."

Ravenser rose as the door opened. "You are dining with me tonight, gentlemen? To discuss the journey?"

Owen bowed to him. "And my wife and her father, as requested."

"Good. I should not want this incident interfering with the plans."

"Nothing will interfere with them, Sir Richard. Fear not. Ned and I shall be all the better for a good sweat." Owen grinned and stepped out the door, Ned and Alfred with him.

The two canons were left to puzzle out the strange ways of fighting men.

15

SCARBOROUGH

When Owen returned, dirty, sweaty, relaxed, Tildy put a cup of Tom Merchet's ale in his hands. He sat down with a contented sigh and drained the cup with one tilt of the head.

Tildy hovered. "Mistress Lucie is dressing, Captain. I would hurry if I were you. The provost of Beverley is expecting you."

Owen groaned. "I had forgotten."

Sir Robert came in from the garden. The elderly man wore a homespun tunic and breeches, spattered and caked with dirt.

"Have you been gardening, Sir Robert?"

Owen's father-in-law raked a hand through his white hair, streaking it with dirt. "I have indeed. A fine garden you have out there. Healthy." He eyed Owen's sweaty state. "You have not been idle this day either, I see."

Owen told him about Alfred. "We worked him hard. He will sleep till morning, I think."

Sir Robert nodded enthusiastically. "Just the thing for a fighting man. You must have been a good captain." He motioned for Owen to come away from Tildy's hearing. "By the by," he said, lowering his voice, "I wanted a word with you about Dame Joanna's stories of Scarborough. Have you heard about the soldiers who sail away, never come back? Archers, she said once. I told Lucie it was important, but I am not sure she appreciated the significance."

Owen bit back a grin. Lucie had told him of Sir Robert's attachment to this detail. "Lucie did tell me. After meeting the woman, I did not put much faith in my understanding of her meandering speeches."

Sir Robert held his hand up, palm forward. "Pray hear me, then. 'Tis not the sort of thing a young woman would make up. That is my point. You must see that."

Owen considered it. "Aye, 'tis true. But her brother is a soldier. If she did find him in Scarborough, and listened to him talking with his fellows, she might have heard something and misunderstood, or made it into a more intriguing story."

Disappointment rounded the old soldier's shoulders. "In faith, perhaps I make much of nothing."

"Not at all. Lancaster shares your interest in the story."

Sir Robert straightened up. "Excellent. Stealing our fighting men—it is the sort of small, sneaky maneuver King Charles favors. And du Guesclin."

Owen hoped he had as sound a mind at his father-in-law's age. "How do you find your daughter, Sir Robert?"

Sir Robert smiled fondly. "A formidable woman, Owen. Lovely as her mother, but much stronger. In spirit more like my sister Phillippa than Amelie. I am much relieved. I had thought Lucie's marriage to Wilton a terrible mistake—all my fault, of course, but still a mistake. Yet had she not married him, she would not have this life that contents her."

This was a new tone from Sir Robert. "I am happy you see that she is content."

"Owen!" Lucie called from the top of the stairs. "Did I hear you come in?"

"I must go to her." Owen tapped Sir Robert's sleeve. "And you must ready yourself. Ravenser seems anxious that we all attend."

Sir Robert patted Owen on the back. "You are a good man, Owen. My daughter chose wisely."

Lucie and Owen slept little, talking into the night after they returned from Ravenser's, wondering what Owen might discover in Scarborough, trying to organize what they knew about Will Longford and Joanna Calverley. Owen had proposed that they go first to

Beverley to speak with the vicar of St. Mary's and the gravedigger. Rather than find the suggestion an insult, since he had spoken with them several months before, Louth was in favor of doing so. He did not trust his talents in this endeavor. But Thoresby insisted that they follow Lancaster's orders and go first to Scarborough in hopes of finding Captain Sebastian. Lancaster sought to have Captain Sebastian back on his side before he left for Gascony in the autumn.

Lucie had been surprised by Thoresby's support of Lancaster. "I did not foresee His Most Arrogant Grace the Archbishop bowing to Lancaster's interests."

Owen wagged his finger. "You misunderstand, my love. It is a matter of priorities. Thoresby wishes to resolve the matter of Dame Joanna and the deaths surrounding her, surely. But his hatred for Alice Perrers takes precedence. And if he becomes Lancaster's ally in the matter of Captain Sebastian, Lancaster may become Thoresby's ally in the matter of ousting Mistress Perrers from the King's bedchamber."

"Ah." Lucie could hear the smile in Owen's voice. It irked her that he was in such good spirits when he must leave her in the morning. "I think you begin to enjoy taking part in these weighty matters of the realm."

Owen pulled her over on top of him, stroking her hair. "I prefer matters of the bedchamber. My own bedchamber."

Lucie kissed him and resolved to enjoy tonight, worry about the morrow on the morrow.

It required considerable noise on Tildy's part to wake them in the morning, and Owen had just finished dressing when one of the archbishop's grooms arrived leading a fine mount. Lucie watched Owen strap his pack to the saddle, check all the fittings. He hummed as he worked. She remembered his high spirits last night. It had not been her imagination—he was happy to be on the move.

"Will you be back for Corpus Christi?" She hated the yearning in her voice.

Owen heard it, turned round, pulled her to him. "Unless fortune shines on us, I think not, my love. But once back from this, I shall not leave your side until the baby comes. Thoresby be damned." He stroked her hair, kissed her forehead. "Promise to take every care, Lucie."

She held him, drinking in his scent, his warmth. She forced herself to smile up at him, not wanting him to remember her with tears in her eyes. "I have no reason to risk my life, and every reason to stay well, my love."

They kissed. Lucie handed Owen a cup of warmed, spiced wine. It was a damp, cool morning for summer. He drank, kissed her again, hugged her hard, and took his reins in hand.

"They await me at the minster gate."

Lucie nodded, not trusting her voice to speak. What was the matter with her? In their nineteen months of marriage she had seen him off enough times to be over this anxious care. He always returned. She touched his arm. He put his hand over hers, pressed it, and slowly led the horse out to the street.

"God go with you," Lucie called softly.

Owen did not hear over the horse's hooves.

Lucie watched his broad back until he disappeared beyond St. Helen's Square. She hugged herself and pressed her feet into the ground, resisting the urge to run up the stairs and hang out their chamber window for one last glimpse. It took all of her will to stay put.

What was the matter with her? A premonition of danger? Or was it merely her condition making everything difficult? She would go to the minster and say a prayer at Vespers.

Alfred sat stiffly in his saddle, fighting to keep wide the eyelids that preferred to close. Perhaps the workout had been too exhausting. But once they were on the move, he would perk up. Owen was glad to see Ned and Louth plainly dressed for the journey. They were headed into rough country and he did not relish attracting thieves. Ravenser saw them off, with Jehannes, as Archdeacon of York, giving the blessing.

It was a long, slow journey up onto heather-clad moorland. They spent their first night in the modest guest house of a Gilbertine priory in Malton. Owen and Ned rubbed Alfred's upper back down with hot oil to loosen his cramping muscles. Louth watched the proceedings, amused.

"I would fain pity you, but it was your own doing," Louth told Alfred. "The best remedy for sorrow is the solace of a head full of wine. What you chose was penance, not solace."

Owen scowled at Louth. "If Alfred had passed out last night with a head full of wine, he would have slept fitfully and been no good for the journey today." He grew weary of Louth's pampered paunch. Twice today they must needs halt for him to rest a while. Owen hated traveling with such folk. He might have said much, but seeing Louth's frown at his sharp tone and scowl, he stopped at that. For now it sufficed that Louth knew he did not agree, not at all.

The second day was an easy journey to Pickering Castle, one of Lancaster's, where the company were to be joined by a Percy youth who would escort them through the forests and bogs that stretched out from Pickering to the North Sea. The castle was often used as a grand hunting lodge for nobles taking their sport in the Forest of Pickering, and their accommodations, in the Old Hall, were much more comfortable than those of the previous night. Although the castle stood on a bluff overlooking marsh and moor and caught the northern winds, the Old Hall was built into the curtain wall and enjoyed a sheltered situation.

After a pleasant evening meal, the travelers shared wine and swapped travel stories. Owen thought he might learn something of Hugh Calverley from the young John Percy.

John grimaced. "Oh, aye, Hugh Calverley. Once met, not forgotten, unless you're a fool. Cross him and he butts you with his horns, make no mistake about it. *I* have been so unfortunate." The young Percy was fair, with a toothy grin and boyish features.

"You crossed him and he struck out?" At a boy? Owen found that surprising.

John nodded. "I greeted him out on the street in Scarborough. When next he came up to the castle he sought me out and beat me, said I might have revealed him to the enemy. I have never seen a man so angry for so little cause."

Owen thought it passing strange the Percies had allowed one of their own to be treated in such a manner by a merchant's son. "Your family did not punish Calverley for such behavior?"

John shook his head. "Nay. They looked the other way."

Ned nodded. "Thought it a good lesson, didn't they?"

John shrugged, but his eyes spoke of a festering anger.

Owen thought it best to speak of other matters. "How long have you been away from Scarborough?"

"I have spent two years at Richmond Castle sharpening my bones, as my father says."

"There are Percies at Richmond?"

"Nay. I have neither seen nor heard from my family in that time."

"Why are you now to Scarborough?"

John drew himself up straighter, puffing out his chest. "I am to be a customs warden, searching ships for wool and hides not customed and cocketed."

And confiscating the goods for the King. Owen knew of such wardens. They tended to have short, tragic careers or turn smuggler themselves. He wondered how much the lad understood about such a post. "'Tis dangerous work. Folk who have dared defy the King will not be shy of throwing a young customs warden overboard."

The cocky young man grinned ear to ear. "I am a Percy, Captain. I live for danger."

Owen and Ned exchanged amused looks over the lad's head.

Louth had no confidence in such a young, cocky guide. "Are you certain you remember the way from here to Scarborough? They say one needs a guide who knows the way well, so well that fog and mist do not turn him round. If it has been two years since you traveled there..."

The young Percy shrugged. "It will be different, for certain. The forests and bogs keep the trails ever changing. But I shall get us through."

"I have traveled this way with the archbishop in those years," Alfred offered.

His companions turned to him, surprised.

Alfred ran a hand through his coarse, sand-colored hair, making it stand up in random peaks. He seemed unaware that he should have offered this information long ago. "We twice came this way, once to join another party making for Whidby, once to meet with Sir William Percy at the castle. Between John and me, we can find our way to Scarborough."

"Twice over terrain does not make you sure-footed." Louth still had his doubts.

"Meaning no disrespect, Sir Nicholas, twice as one of the forward party teaches you much about the lay of the land."

Owen and Ned agreed. Louth shrugged. "I do not have another plan to offer, so I must be content. But I shall pray all the more fervently tonight."

Contrary to Louth's expectations, they passed through Pickering and Wykeham forests without mishap. John Percy did know his way, that was clear. And Alfred worked well with him. When the path forked and John hesitated, considering, Alfred would sniff the air and search the ground like a bloodhound. Between the two of them, the forks hardly slowed down the party.

The boggy moorland proved more difficult. The wayside was laid with stone slabs to support the horses and donkeys slung with panniers that carried loads across the moorland, the rocks and bogs being too treacherous for carts. The company followed alongside the slabs, walking their horses so that they might feel and sidestep any softness in the ground. It was slow going, and even worse when the slabs forked, for the road snaked round dangerous pools and outcroppings and it was not always the fork that seemed most direct that moved them toward their goal.

Once they chose the wrong fork and rode on unaware until young John Percy's horse reared. Concentrating on steadying his mount, John paid no heed to his footing and slid backwards into a bog. Alfred and Owen ran to his aid, fishing him out, while Ned calmed the horse and studied the cause of the near disaster. The horse had stepped onto a slab that teetered over the bog. The tip of what had once been the next slab could be seen sticking out of the muck. John wrapped himself in the blanket from his pack and gamely led the way back and onto the correct fork, determined to make it out of the bogs before dark. Louth pulled his own cloak closer about him and prayed for their deliverance from this hellish landscape.

At sunset they could see the castle of Scarborough rising far to the east, seemingly carved out of the rocky headland. A magnificent and comforting sight, but too far to reach tonight. "There is an inn just over the next rise," John said. "We should stop there for the night."

All agreed.

The innkeeper's surly greeting changed to a welcome when he recognized the Percy among them. "My father was groom at the castle as a lad. Sir Henry de Percy would let no one but my father touch the destrier that he rode against David the Bruce." He was even friendlier when he learned that the company traveled under Lancaster's protection. The innkeeper led them to an airy sleeping loft, relatively clean, where they stored their packs, then provided a simple but hearty meal for them.

Owen soon realized they were most fortunate for the man's interest. The inn filled quickly, and latecomers were given the bad news that there was no room. In fact, some earlier comers were being displaced by Owen's party.

Two of these unfortunates took exception to the news that they would be spending the night in the stables. A well scarred pair, their daggers notched and worn with use, they drew themselves up to full height and threatened the innkeeper, telling him they would upend everything not nailed down and skewer him on the signpost.

Owen and Ned rose to reason with them. Doe-eyed, elegant Ned whipped two daggers seemingly out of the air and threw one at the upraised arm of one of the men, nailing his sleeve to an oak beam. As Ned slowly approached the man, he tossed the other dagger from hand to hand and grinned lazily. Owen stretched out a long leg and tripped the other man, then grabbed him by the collar and lifted him until only his toes touched the ground.

Ned's man looked uneasily at his mate, dangling in Owen's grasp, then at the dagger that now rose and fell inches from him. "The stables will do us for tonight, gentlemen," he assured them.

"And what do you say to our host?" Owen asked.

"We meant no harm. 'Twas the ale talking."

Ned pulled his dagger from the oak beam, touched the man's startled face gently with the blade. "'Tis a wise man knows when he's had his fill."

Owen released his catch, who stumbled again but jerked away from Owen's steadying hand. Ned returned to the table, still tossing the daggers back and forth.

"I grow eager to pass through the town gates," Louth muttered, wiping his brow.

"Scarborough is a fair town, gentlemen," John Percy assured them. "My family are right proud to be stewards of the castle."

"I could see the great wall that snakes up the hill from the town and surrounds the keep," Louth said. "Perhaps it protects the castle folk from the town folk, eh? If it guards such a wild and lawless people…"

John Percy grinned. "Aye, you'd be hard pressed to find a worse lot all in one place. Pirates, every one of 'em. Even the Accloms and Carters, who take turns as bailiffs. Ask your lord of Lancaster about them. He has had to put them straight once or twice. But where is the honor in defending something that is never threatened? The Percies embrace the challenge." He nodded to Ned. "That was fancy work with the daggers."

Ned flicked one out, tossed it, spinning, from hand to hand several times, then put it away. "It impresses the court ladies and discourages trouble. A worthwhile skill to develop, even if one has the formidable Percy clan behind him."

John Percy blushed, hearing the tease in Ned's words.

Owen grinned into his cup. It was good to be on the road with Ned. He felt alive.

• • •

Scarborough was walled on three sides, the forth being the harbor; but it had long ago outgrown the walls. Almost 200 years earlier a wide, deep ditch had been dug to encircle a new outer wall, but funds were never forthcoming to build it, and now houses straggled far outside the old ditch. Within the walls the timbered, gabled houses squeezed one atop the next, down steep streets that ended abruptly at the sands of the harbor. Crowding was such that solars and stalls stretched out over and in the harbor; in every generation there were fools who built out onto the sands and foreshore and had their homes and shops washed away by the fierce storms of the North Sea. It did not stop them rebuilding; everyone wished to be within convenient reach of the lucrative pirate trade and the fairs and markets that set up on the sands of the harbor.

As the company rode along the top ridge of streets to the castle walls, Owen stared down at the townspeople going about their business seemingly unaware of the steep incline, the growling sea below. Were they spiders that this dizzy slope bothered them so little? Or was it peculiarly disturbing to him, with his one-eyed balance? He did not ask the others, for to ask would be to admit his weakness. It was hard enough to know it himself. He just hoped that Hugh Calverley lived up in the castle precinct so he would not need to spend much time on the steep, narrow streets.

The way from the outer gatehouse of Scarborough Castle to the inner bailey climbed steeply heavenward. Sir William Percy had given orders that the company be shown directly to his parlor when they arrived. He had been expecting them since Lancaster's messenger arrived three days past. And this morning he'd had word of a small company putting on a show in an inn outside the city gates; one of that company had sounded like his son John.

Sir William studied Owen with interest. "You have been described as a one-eyed giant who held Tom Kemp off the ground while another of your company threw a dagger at John of Whidby, attaching him to a beam and frightening him so thoroughly he agreed to sleep out in the stables with his horse."

Owen laughed, nodded toward Ned. "The two men wished to fight for the room. We merely wished to warm your son after a tumble in the bogs and to get a good night's sleep. So Ned and I convinced those two to oblige us." He shrugged. "As you can see, I am no giant."

Sir William was shorter than Owen, but looked no less a soldier, sturdy and battle-scarred. He nodded at Owen. "I'd not call you a giant, 'tis true. But I can tell you keep the strength of an archer." He gestured to the travelers with a large, beringed hand. "I am pleased to welcome you all, though I admit to being ignorant of your mission. My lord duke did not enlighten me in his message. Obviously business of a delicate nature. But I shall help you as I may. My lord duke is a good friend to my cousins Henry and Thomas. First, however, you must break your fast." He clapped the servants into action, setting up a small table. "And John must attend his mother who is most anxious to see how he fares."

Ned slapped John on the back. "He's a fine lad, Sir William. Led us straight and true and carried on even when soaked and bruised."

When the company had eaten their full of brown bread, cheese, a hearty broth and cold venison, the servants cleared the table and left the room. A shorter, wirier version of Sir William entered the room.

Sir William motioned for the newcomer to sit. "My brother, Ralph."

Ralph Percy nodded to the company without lifting his eyes to them.

Sir William leaned into the table. "Now. Tell us what the stewards of Scarborough can do for you."

Louth cleared his throat and bowed slightly to the two Percies. "We hope to find three men, one of whom is in your service, Hugh Calverley of Leeds."

Sir William grunted, frowned over at his brother, shrugged back at Louth. "I can show you where we buried him."

"Hugh Calverley is dead?"

Sir William nodded.

"How did he die?" Louth's disappointment rang in his voice.

"Servant found him lying in a puddle of blood in front of his own fire. House had been searched, everything turned over, out of place. Someone looking for booty, no doubt." Sir William shook his head.

Louth looked to Owen.

"When did this happen?" Owen asked.

Sir William closed his eyes, screwed up his face. "I recall something in the service at his grave about St. Ambrose." Early April.

"Shortly after Will Longford disappeared," Louth muttered.

Ralph turned beady eyes on Louth. "Longford?"

"Aye," Owen said. "The man Hugh tried to catch for you."

Sir William nodded. "Was a time he came often to Scarborough, disappeared into the town with uncanny ease. We set Hugh to catch Longford in his game. Too slippery. Knew Hugh was up to something before the boy learned a thing." He downed some ale. "You think he came after Hugh? After so much time?"

Owen shrugged. "Perhaps."

"What else do you know about Longford?" Sir William asked Owen.

"Little more than that. We are here to discover what we may about him."

Sir William sat back, arms folded, one of his pointy eyebrows cocked. "Perhaps you should just tell us all of your business."

Owen nodded to Nicholas de Louth, who did not look pleased with the request. But he complied, giving a brief, clear account of the peculiar events of the past year.

Sir William shook his head over the tale of Joanna Calverley. He nodded enthusiastically at Lancaster's connecting Captain Sebastian with the soldiers Joanna had seen. "I would fain know where she saw them. We had word of Sebastian and his company crossing the Channel to recruit men. We have looked for their gathering place. Hugh searched for it. How is it his sister knew of it and he did not tell us?"

"How well did you know Hugh?" Owen asked.

"He was not a boon companion, if that is what you ask. I never looked into his heart. But he dug a few Frenchmen and Scots out from under the rocks hereabouts. Did well for me."

Owen had not thought they would know Hugh well. He'd been a lackey, expendable. They were Percies, above everyone else in the town. "Your son had some trouble with him."

Sir William frowned, displeased. "John whined about it?"

"No. I had asked what he knew of Hugh Calverley. He told me

of the incident."

"It was a lesson John needed to learn. Hugh was not openly connected with the castle."

Owen nodded. "We have told you of Hugh's sister. Did Joanna come looking for Hugh this past year? A red-haired woman? Green eyes. Pretty."

Sir William looked to his brother.

"Hugh said nothing about a sister, but he was a quiet one." Ralph frowned, drew his brows together. He had no right earlobe and a scar on that side of his neck told the tale of a near fatal sword blow. "But Hugh was away round that time. Perhaps he met her somewhere else."

"Away?"

At last Ralph looked Owen in the eye. "He was gone for ten days or so not long before his murder. Said he was hunting down a man might lead him to Captain Sebastian. He was always looking for folk he thought would lead him to the captain. Got a bit single-minded about Sebastian." Ralph shook his head. "Good luck to you in finding Sebastian." Ralph Percy gave an ill-humored grin, looked down at the floor. It was obvious he had done with them.

Sir William made a conciliatory gesture. "It is possible Hugh was murdered because he had got close to Sebastian, but he had not found him. Or if he had, he had not yet told us."

"Where had Hugh gone?"

Sir William shook his head. "He came and went all the time. I never felt the need to watch him."

"Who went with him?"

"His two men."

"They are your men also?"

"No."

"Unusual practice."

Sir William took another drink.

"I should like to speak with Hugh's men."

Sir William looked down at his boots. Ralph Percy was left to explain. "They did not return with him, far as I know. He came back without his quarry and without his men."

Owen sat with his back pressing against the wall, his long legs stretched out to the side of the table. Sir William and his brother Ralph were fighting men. He understood them. He could tell that at the moment Sir William was uncomfortable and angry with his brother. "Tell us about Hugh, if you would, Sir William. What was he like?"

Sir William raised puzzled eyes to Owen.

"You're wondering why I ask such a question about a soldier?" Owen said.

"Most folk do not wonder about a soldier's character, just his strength, his skill with weapons, his courage, his trustworthiness."

"A good place to begin. I assume you would not have used Hugh had you not trusted him."

"He proved eager to do my bidding. I tried him sorely with the Sebastian seal. He failed, but he did not tuck his tail between his legs and cower away. He asked for another chance to prove himself. Courage. Perseverance. Good soldierly qualities."

"You never doubted his loyalty?"

Sir William tucked his chin in and frowned up through his eyebrows. "Should I have doubted it?"

Owen shrugged. "Did he ever do anything to make you doubt him?"

"Nay." His voice went up at the end of the word—with doubt?

"But there was something about him that made you pause."

Ralph snorted. "Pause? Nay, run, by God. The man had a temper. Never cross him, that's what we learned. Not us, mind you, his partners. So we let him choose his own men."

"He killed partners?"

"No," Sir William said quickly, silencing his brother with a stern look. "No," Sir William repeated, this time softly, pleasantly, with a smile to Owen. "He fought with them. Came to blows. Afterwards they preferred to work with someone else. Said his temper flared with no spark that they could see. They were—uneasy about him."

"Word gets round the barracks and no one will partner him." Ned nodded. "I've known some like that."

Sir William looked grateful. "But we never had reports of his turning on us, if I understand that to be your question."

Owen nodded. "Where did he find the two who disappeared?"

Both men shrugged.

"You were not concerned?"

"They looked as if they would fight well," Ralph said. "'Twas enough."

Owen decided to ignore their puzzling indifference for now. "Hugh lived alone, did he?"

"Aye," Ralph nodded. "A small house up on the bluffs south of here. Well hidden."

"Did he have a woman?"

Sir William shrugged. "We would not know that."

"Servants?"

"Harry, his manservant. He's round here somewhere. Want to speak with him?"

"I do indeed."

Owen leaned over toward Ralph. "You did nothing about his murder, did you?"

Ralph looked up, startled. "What do you mean?"

"You did not ask round about it, try to piece it together. You thought it was one of his old mates, didn't you? Perhaps the two missing men?"

Ralph snorted. "And who would have cared?"

"Why have you said nothing to his father about his murder?"

Ralph reddened.

Sir William coughed. "We have not had a messenger headed for Leeds since then."

Owen grinned.

Louth looked at him, puzzled.

Owen shrugged. "Can you find Harry for us?"

Sir William nodded to Ralph, who departed without a word.

The middle-aged Harry was hard of hearing. Owen sat close to him and spoke loudly into his ear. "Was there any trouble at the house before Hugh Calverley died?"

Harry grinned a devilish grin. "A pretty redhead. Aye."

"He doesn't understand," Louth said softly.

Owen ignored him. "A woman visited him?"

Harry nodded. "Called him brother." He rolled his expressive eyes.

"What was her name?"

Harry shook his head. "Never gave it."

Or Harry never heard it. But Owen had watched him when he first came in the room. He seemed to get the gist of what people were saying by watching their lips. "Any other trouble?"

Harry chuckled. "Always trouble round Master Hugh. He was watching a house, I can tell you that. I can even show you. Got interested when I told him I'd seen that one-legged man there."

"Longford?"

"Aye." Harry nodded. "That'd be him."

"How long ago did you see Longford there?"

Harry shrugged. "A few years past."

Owen sat back, frowning. "Do you mean to say Hugh watched this particular house for a few years?"

Harry held his hand up to his ear. "What?"

Owen leaned closer and repeated the question.

"Oh, aye. On and off, you see. I'd tell 'im when I saw folk he might find interesting."

"What sort of folk?"

"Soldier types. Or folk who seemed out of place."

"And who was it most recently?"

"The redhead."

"You will take us to the house?"

Harry nodded. "This evening. Better then. In the dark."

Louth knocked on the door to the small room Owen was sharing with Ned and Alfred. Being a canon of Beverley and clerk to Prince Edward, Louth had been offered his own chamber, equally small, but private. Ned had gone off with Alfred in search of amusement, and Owen had been lying on his cot, thinking over the morning's business. He did not welcome an interruption and sighed at the second round of knocking. "What is it?"

Louth opened the door only wide enough to poke his head in. "I would speak with you."

Owen nodded.

Louth settled on the edge of Ned's cot. The flesh on his round face was slack, as if the trip was taking its toll. "You were on the heels of something about the Percies' not reporting Hugh's death. Why did you veer away?"

"I want to worry them."

Louth blinked. "Why?"

"People do foolish things when they worry."

"What do you expect them to do?"

Owen shrugged. "We shall see."

Louth lowered his eyes. "You do not trust me." Petulant.

Did he trust Louth? Owen had little confidence in him, but he believed Louth meant well. "I don't know what they are hiding, Sir Nicholas. It is but a feeling I have."

Louth met his eye again. "You might have gotten it out of them right away."

"No. They have no reason to confide in me, much less confess to me if it comes to that. Not now. Not yet."

"What do you think we shall learn seeing the house Hugh was watching?"

"Perhaps nothing. But Harry himself is interesting. Joanna came to mind when I asked him about trouble. Why?" Owen nodded. "Harry will be far more helpful than the Percies, I think." He slapped his thighs, rose. "I need a good walk, fresh air. Want to walk the battlements with me?"

Louth's eyes widened in horror. "Faith, no. I shall go to the chapel."

Owen grinned. He had guessed that Louth would shrink at the suggestion. Now he would have time alone to think. Though he was not himself easy about going up there, which was the point.

16

NEAR DEATH

Daimon ran to keep up with Lucie, who marched down Davygate, hurrying after Brother Sebastian, her pale shawl fluttering behind her. It was so early that few folk were about, and the river damp intensified the stench of sewage in the narrow streets. At this moment Daimon was not enamored of the great city of York; but he adored the woman who kept so many steps ahead of him, and he would gladly live and die in this crowded, dark, stinking city if it meant he could be near her. He had lost his heart just moments ago when Lucie Wilton wakened him in the shop and whispered her request that he accompany her to the abbey without waking Sir Robert.

"Sir Robert sleeps so soundly," she had said. "I would fain let him get his rest."

Daimon had not been able to take his sleepy eyes from her hair, strands of red and gold shimmering in the lamplight. Mistress Wilton crouched on the floor beside his pallet, leaning close. She had a warm, sweet scent. Lord. He had thought her lovely before, but at that moment, her hair loose, her body warm from bed, her breath so sweet… Jesu, give him strength to control himself.

She had had to repeat what she had said to him.

Daimon had with great effort pulled his eyes away from her and considered. "Leave Sir Robert?" He shook his head. "He will not like it."

"Please." She touched his shoulder. So gently. "We must go quickly, Daimon. Brother Sebastian waits in the kitchen. Dame Joanna is injured."

"Badly?"

"Would they send for me at this dark hour otherwise?"

That had seemed a good reason to risk Sir Robert's anger. Daimon had agreed. He saw now how wise that had been. Sir Robert would have lagged far behind. Mistress Wilton glanced back as she turned into Lop Lane, paused, waited for Daimon to catch up, grabbed his hand. Glory to God on the highest!

"Come, Daimon. We do not want the gate warden at Bootham Bar to give up on us and return to bed."

Her hand grasped his with surprising strength. Daimon hurried along with her, hand in hand, marveling that his feet could still brush the earth.

Tildy had awakened Lucie with a frightened face. "'Tis Brother Sebastian from the abbey, Mistress Lucie. He says you must come."

Lucie had looked up at the window, confused. "Is it such a dark morning?"

"It is very early, Mistress."

Brother Sebastian. The Abbot's secretary. Lucie sat up quickly at that. Something must have happened that Abbot Campian wished to keep quiet. Tildy helped Lucie dress. Shivering in the morning air, Lucie grabbed a shawl. She could not stop yawning and shivering. Down in the kitchen Brother Sebastian waited. He looked very pale.

"What has happened?" Lucie asked.

"Dame Joanna tried to kill herself, may God in His mercy forgive her." Sebastian crossed himself.

Lucie did likewise. "But she is alive?"

The monk nodded. "There is much blood."

Lucie tried to keep her teeth from chattering. "Who found her?"

"The Reverend Mother woke to an odd sound. Coughing. Choking."

"Brother Wulfstan is there?"

Sebastian nodded. "Our infirmarian says Dame Joanna is alive, but has lost much blood. He wants you to try to speak with her, see whether you can wake her. He says you are best with her."

Lucie scooped up some fennel seeds from a shelf by the door and chewed them to freshen her breath. "What about Dame Isobel?"

"She fainted."

Ah. How like Isobel.

Now, as Lucie hurried through the postern gate dragging Daimon behind her, she wondered what self inflicted wound could be so horrible as to make the prioress faint. She shivered and took a deep breath. Her stomach was not as strong as usual in her present condition. Would she embarrass herself?

Brother Oswald and Abbot Campian waited for them on the guest house steps. The hospitaler held a lantern up to Daimon's face.

"The lad should stay with Oswald," Abbot Campian said. "Bless you for coming, Mistress Wilton, and at this early hour. Brother Wulfstan particularly wished to have you here."

"Has she wakened?"

The abbot shook his head. "Please go up. Sebastian will wait for you here and escort you to my parlor when you have finished. I shall have food and wine for your troubles."

Lucie gathered her skirts and hurried up the stairs. Through the doorway to the right of Joanna's room she could see flickering lamplight. She paused, stepped inside. The serving girl bent over Isobel.

"She is still in a faint?" Lucie asked.

The girl raised her head, her eyes large with fear. Lucie stepped closer, noted Isobel's bloodstained hands. A pitcher and cup sat on a small table beside the bed.

"Wine?" Lucie asked.

The serving girl nodded.

Lucie poured some into the cup and drank. Her shivering ceased. She drank again, welcoming the warmth that crept from her throat outward.

"Keep the Reverend Mother warm," Lucie said. "I shall see to her after I have seen Joanna."

The girl nodded.

Lucie left her, stepped out into the corridor, took a deep breath, pushed open Joanna's door—and stepped back at the lingering smoke and the strong, sweet stench of blood. *"Deus juva me,"* she whispered, crossing herself and gulping the cleaner air of the corridor. Then, getting herself firmly in hand, she entered the room and joined Brother Wulfstan, who sat nodding beside Joanna's curtained bed, an oil lamp burning on the table beside it, the flame dancing in the breeze from the window.

Lucie squeezed Wulfstan's shoulder. "Brother Wulfstan. It is Lucie Wilton. I am come to help you."

He started, woke, rubbed his eyes, looked up at Lucie, pressed the hand still on his shoulder. "Bless you, Lucie. I think it best we try to wake her, see whether she can speak, where she has pain." He stood up.

"She wounded herself?" Lucie said.

Wulfstan pressed his fingers to his brows, released them, nodded. "She is not a pleasant sight."

"Why did she do it?"

Wulfstan shook his head. "She has slept most of the time since we bled and purged her. I had no idea she was alert enough to do such a thing."

"Dame Isobel has been no help?"

"The Reverend Mother was in a faint when I was called. I have not spoken with her."

Lucie nodded. "Open the curtain."

Wulfstan gave her a worried look. "I hesitated, considering your condition. Owen would not like you to be exposed to this."

Lucie clenched her fists at her side, trying not to express her impatience. Brother Wulfstan had once done her a favor that went far beyond common friendship. She would not lose her temper with him. "Please, Wulfstan. Open the curtain."

Lucie held up the lamp. Wulfstan pushed the curtain away. The stench of blood intensified. Unable to help it, Lucie took a step back, turned her head away.

Wulfstan steadied the lamp. "Are you all right, Lucie? Do you need to go outside?"

She shook her head. "I shall be fine. It is just such a lot of blood."

"Had she been weaker, she would not have survived, I think."

Lucie turned back to the bed, moving the lamp closer to Joanna's still form. She lay with her right hand raised up to her shoulder, clutching a bloody knife.

"Where did she get the knife?"

"It is from the kitchen. She must have kept it after one of her meals."

Across the bloody neck a wound gaped, a jagged wound. Joanna had made several tries, Lucie guessed. She turned away, took a deep breath, turned back. Joanna's hands were smeared with blood, as was her face. Lucie had noticed a bowl of water and some cloths on the floor beside the bed. "Would you moisten a cloth for me?" Wulfstan did so, pressed it into her hand. Lucie dabbed at Joanna's face. She had no wounds on her face, thanks be to God. She went to dab at Joanna's neck, but Wulfstan reached out to restrain her.

"Do not touch the wound. It must clot," he said.

"Holy Mary, Mother of God," Lucie said, crossing herself and trembling at what she had almost done. "I am not skilled in this."

"No matter." Wulfstan gestured at the blanket, at the bloodstains farther away from the neck. "Would you examine her beneath the blanket? I pulled it back, but could not bring myself…"

Lucie nodded.

Wulfstan turned away.

Lucie pulled the blanket down. Joanna's shift was bloody at the pelvis and the upper thighs. Lucie pulled up the shift, gave a little cry.

"What is it?" Wulfstan whispered. "Do you need me?"

"No. It is just—Sweet Heaven, why does she hate herself so?" Lucie bent down to Joanna, dabbed at her stomach and thighs with the cloth. The thighs were untouched. But there was a deep wound in Joanna's womb. Jagged, as if Joanna had stabbed and then moved the knife back and forth to do more damage. How could she inflict such a wound on herself? "She has stabbed herself in the stomach," Lucie said, turning away and covering Joanna. "We must clean and pack the wound."

"I have sent for Dame Prudentia. Try to rouse Joanna, Lucie."

But try as she might, Lucie could get no response from Joanna. At last, exhausted and faint with hunger, Lucie left Joanna in the care of the two infirmarians.

• • •

Joanna's ragged wounds haunted Lucie as she followed Sebastian to the abbot's parlor. How had the woman mustered strength enough to inflict such wounds? What could bring Joanna to such an act of violence on herself? Had Magda's therapy worked too well? Had Joanna wakened, alone, confronted by a memory she had tried to bury, vivid now because her mind had cleared? Or was it perhaps Owen's telling her of her mother's death that had driven her to despair? It seemed too extreme an act for the mourning of a parent, but Lucie knew so little of Joanna's heart that she could not say that it was not so.

Brother Sebastian opened the door into a cheery room with a fire just right for the cool morning and a tempting scent of fresh bread baked with herbs. Abbot Campian rose from a chair where he had been reading. He was not a young man, but his face was smooth, neither laugh nor frown lines adorning it. A man who took care to keep emotions at bay. He signed the blessing over Lucie and welcomed her to sit at the small table. Sebastian backed out of the room and closed the door softly. Campian poured wine for both of them. Lucie noted his white hands. Owen had told her that Abbot Campian had the cleanest hands he had ever seen. They were remarkable. Lucie glanced up at Campian's eyes, expecting to see them, too, devoid of anything untidy. But his eyes watched her with keen interest and concern.

"Were you able to rouse Dame Joanna?"

"No. She is in a faint after losing much blood."

The abbot sat with his cup of wine untasted, his hands folded in front of him on the table, his eyes focused on his hands, perhaps to give Lucie privacy in eating.

She sipped her wine, trying to erase the memory of the blood scent. It revived her. She must take care to stop before it dizzied her. Magda had told her that one of the greatest dangers in pregnancy was falling, not just because she might injure the babe in her womb but the midwife had observed that women's joints seemed more easily overstretched and strained when they were with child, perhaps readying the body for birth. Lucie sighed. Her every move was restricted by an ever growing set of rules and cautions—not as onerous as those at St. Clement's, but frustrating all the same. Was that what Joanna had run from? Rules? Eyes following her every movement? She had run to her brother. Did he seem to enjoy more freedom?

Of course he did. Owen certainly did.

Lucie sighed, took a piece of bread, nibbled at it. Warm and flavorful. It stirred her appetite. She must eat, must put the nauseous sight of Joanna's wounds out of her mind.

"You are not hungry?"

Lucie was startled by the abbot's soft voice. She found him regarding her thoughtfully.

"What I just saw—It is difficult to put the scene from my mind."

Campian nodded. "God help her find the peace she seeks in a less sinful way." He shook his head. "My stomach liked neither the odor nor the sight. For you it must be far worse. I am in your debt for coming. Your husband would not be pleased with me."

"He would understand."

"I do not think Captain Archer understands anything untoward where you are concerned, Mistress Wilton." Campian smiled. A peculiar smile, causing no wrinkles, expressed only on the mouth and in the eyes.

Lucie thought it would be difficult to like Campian, but she knew that he and Wulfstan were old friends.

"Will she live, do you think?" he asked.

"If we can keep her from injuring herself. I wish I knew what horror it is she runs from. I would like to help her."

"What do you see in her that makes you wish to help her?"

Lucie considered the question. "In truth, I cannot say. Except that she is a fellow sinner, suffering something so horrible she wished to end her life. I have felt despair like that. I have come to wish for death at times. But I have never acted on it. How much more must she suffer to not only conceive the act, but try until she fainted from loss of blood to carry it out."

"You think that is what stopped her? The loss of blood?"

Lucie nodded. "That and exhaustion from the terrible strength she called up to inflict those wounds."

"Is it possible they were not self-inflicted?"

Lucie shook her head. "I think not."

"How can you know?"

"I said I *think* not. I do not *know* it is not so. I do not have the skill. But having spoken with Joanna, having seen some way into her heart, I can believe she did this to herself." Lucie lifted her cup of wine in trembling hands.

"I am sorry I asked such questions."

"You have a right. She lies in your guest house."

Lucie gazed round the small, comfortable room. On the far wall was a fresco of a Benedictine monk kneeling before a woman in a deep blue mantle, kissing her outstretched hand. Presumably the Blessed Virgin Mary, to whom the abbey was dedicated. The painting was simple, almost childlike, but for Mary's eyes, which somehow expressed an immense sympathy and kindness.

Campian noticed where Lucie's eyes lingered. "A clumsy painting, but I have grown fond of it."

"The Virgin's eyes. Were they painted at the same time as the rest of the fresco?"

Campian looked surprised. "So you notice it, too? How Brother Peter's gift blossomed when he reached her eyes?"

"It is as if the rest of the fresco were merely a background, an explanation of the expression in her eyes."

Abbot and apothecary looked at one another with a fresh appreciation.

"Has he painted anything else?"

Campian shook his head, his eyes sad. Lucie looked, startled, at his eyes, then those of the fresco. The expressionless face, the soul revealed only by the eyes.

"What is it?" the abbot asked.

"Nothing," Lucie said, sipping her wine to hide her smile.

"Jasper is coming along quickly in his studies."

"I look forward to the day when he is back with us," Lucie said.

"I think he will be a good apprentice. He is quick and levelheaded."

"He is fond of Captain Archer."

"They have spent much time together. Owen has been readying Jasper to master the longbow."

"Your husband possesses an odd mix of talents."

"Indeed he does." Lucie's eyes kept returning to the blue mantle on the fresco. "You have of course heard of the furor over the blue mantle Joanna keeps by her?"

Campian smiled. "Ah yes. Rumors of miracles."

"Are they all—the holy relics, I mean—are they all—" Lucie could not say it.

The abbot nodded, understanding her unvoiced questions. "Are they what we claim?"

Lucie waited.

The abbot folded his hands and studied them. "We pray that they are, Mistress Wilton. And if they perform a miracle or two, it must be so, must it not?" He raised his eyes to hers.

"Do you ever doubt? I am thinking of the fuss at St. Clement's."

Campian sighed.

"Forgive me for that question."

Campian's eyes looked sad though his mouth smiled. "We would not preach so much of faith if we expected the faithful never to doubt, Mistress Wilton."

A far more honest answer than Lucie had expected. "Thank you, Father."

17

VENGEANCE INTERRUPTED

The house that Hugh Calverley had found so intriguing was a house like any other, wattle and daub, waxed parchment windows that would hum and thrum in a North Sea gale, a jutting second story, a heavy oak door. A wrongheaded attempt at security, the door; beside it were patches in the wall where intruders had found the wattle and daub easier to break through.

Harry had led Owen, Ned, and Alfred to the house the previous night. They had sent Harry back to the castle and settled in for a long watch, crouching in the shadows, alert to every sound in the street, the skitter of rats, the splash of night waste, the hesitant steps of drunks and thieves out after curfew. But no one showed an interest in the house. No one entered, no one left. It appeared deserted.

Tonight was different. Early in the evening a pale glow through a rear window suggested occupation. When the darkness was complete and the street deserted, Owen motioned Ned to one side of the door, stationed himself on the other side. His ear to the narrow opening, Owen listened, his dagger ready. Ned leaned toward him, pointed to himself, Owen's shoulders, the upper story.

Owen nodded. Ned took off his sword belt, handed it to Alfred, put one of his daggers in his mouth. Owen crouched down, hands on knees. Ned climbed onto his shoulders. Owen rose slowly. With his dagger, Ned poked at the waxed parchment, puncturing it, then sliced slowly, trying to be quiet. It was not a silent procedure, requiring some sawing of the waxed and weathered hide, but it was not a noise that the listener would necessarily find alarming. When

Ned judged he had a sufficient opening, he tapped for Owen to lift him higher. Owen grabbed Ned's ankles, lifted. Ned tumbled through the parchment, over the sill, and rolled to the floor.

Down in the street, someone else had judged the night to now be sufficiently advanced for stealth. He slipped toward Owen and Alfred, dipping in and out of doorways. "Is there some way to warn Ned?" Alfred whispered. Owen shook his head and pulled Alfred with him into the deep shadow across the street. The man checked round the house, then pressed his ear to the wall beside the front door and listened for a long while. At last he moved to the door, crouched down, slipped his dagger in the crack in the door, moved it up slowly, slowly, and at last gently pulled. The door opened silently. The man knew the workings of the door, that was plain.

When he had slipped inside, Owen and Alfred crept toward the house. A cry came from within, the sound of a struggle. Fearing it might be Ned, Owen rushed in. Two men stood in the middle of the room, daggers in hand, circling each other. One bled from a slice high on his arm. Ned was up above them, crouched at the top of the ladder; he nodded to Owen. The bleeding one suddenly noticed Owen and gave a shout, then dashed into the back room. Owen dashed after him while, with a shout, Ned leapt down, knocked the other backward.

Alfred took off after Owen, but they were both too late. The bleeding man had disappeared down the dark back alley.

When they returned, Ned was busy tying his captive's hands.

Owen picked up the lantern that lit the room, opened its shutter all the way, and went off to search the house for more intruders or clues as to who belonged here. The house was simply furnished, a pallet in the upper sleep loft and a chest—empty; downstairs a trestle table and two benches in the front room, two pallets and another chest in the back room. The latter chest held a man's clothes. Nothing to give Owen any idea why Hugh had watched the house or who the two men were.

Owen returned to the front room. "Time for a walk up to the castle." He shined the lantern on Ned's captive. Ned yanked the man up by his tied hands. He bled from the nose and mouth. Owen found a rag and wiped his face.

"Come on, stand up," Ned said, jerking the man off his knees.

The man stood, but kept his head down, as if hiding his face. He was average height, but stocky, broad-chested, with muscular arms and legs. He was the one who had stolen into the house while Alfred and Owen watched. The other had been tall and skinny. "What's your name?" Owen asked. The man did not respond.

Alfred grabbed him by the hair, jerked his face up. "Murdering bastard!" Alfred shouted and got in two punches, one in the mouth, one in the groin, before Owen got him off the man.

"I cannot have you silencing him, Alfred. We need to talk to him." Owen put the lantern down on the table and helped the man back onto his feet, wiped his face again.

"You killed Colin, you bastard," Alfred shouted, lunging toward him again.

Owen pushed Alfred away, walked the man over to the lantern light. "So you are the man who was watching St. Clement's?" He studied the man. Dark, thinning hair, bushy eyebrows. That was about all he could tell at present, with the swelling and bleeding. "Perhaps you would tell us your name so we can call you something other than bastard."

"What good will that do you?" The man's words slurred round his swollen tongue. He coughed. "I was not the one killed his friend."

"What was your purpose here tonight?"

"Unfinished business."

"Are you one of Captain Sebastian's men?"

He stared at the floor.

Owen shrugged. "Someone at the castle will know you."

Hugh Calverley's manservant identified him as Edmund, one of Captain Sebastian's men. He guessed the other one to be Jack, often in Edmund's company. Harry knew nothing else of use.

"So what is this unfinished business between two of Sebastian's men?" Owen asked.

Edmund's dark eyes were wild with fear. "You have killed me, breaking in before I could finish him. Letting him escape."

"You meant to kill Jack?"

"Or die in the attempt."

"On Sebastian's orders?"

Edmund pressed his lips together and said nothing, but his eyes burned into Owen.

Two of Percy's retainers took Edmund off to clean his wounds and keep him under guard.

While Ned and Owen slept, Louth went down to the house with some of Percy's men and searched it. They found a jacket with a St. Sebastian emblem sewn inside; in a small chest hidden behind paneling they found gold coins and a St. Sebastian seal. All in all, proof of little except that they were on the right track.

Ned, Louth, and Owen summoned Edmund to a meeting.

Louth presented the jacket. Edmund shrugged. "Folk put all sorts of patterns on their clothing. I favor a plain fashion, myself. As you can see."

Louth showed him the chest with the seal. Owen noted that Edmund looked less comfortable. "A nice piece of metalworking."

Louth pretended to study it for the first time, holding it up to a lamp, turning it this way and that. "Indeed. Quite skillful." Sir William Percy had noted it was not exactly the same as the one they had lost to Longford.

Owen grew impatient. "We believe it belongs to a Captain Sebastian, whom the King has sent us to find. You can point us toward him."

Edmund's eyes widened. "King Edward sent you?" His tone was less surly.

Louth nodded.

"Captain Sebastian must be important."

Louth shrugged. "There are many ways in which to be important. Your captain is about to fight on the wrong side of his King. An unpleasant sort of importance."

"What is that to me?" Edmund's face was round, almost childish, though his thinning hair refuted youth. His voice was low and soft. His manner, now that he was not attacking, almost courteous. His thick brows arched now as he tried to keep his face impassive. A futile effort, for his eyes were expressive.

Louth held up the King's letter.

Owen noticed that Edmund's eyes roamed over the letter, stopping nowhere. "You cannot read?"

Edmund blushed. "I'm no clerk. Neither are you, I'd wager."

Owen grinned. "You are right that I am no clerk, but wager I cannot read and you would be out some money." He sat close to Edmund, stretched out his legs, folded his arms across his chest. "So you're no clerk. What are you, then?"

Edmund shifted his eyes back and forth, as if remembering a rehearsed answer, which came after too long a pause to be believed. "A shipwright."

Owen looked Edmund up and down. On his face, neck and hands, his fair skin was freckled from the sun and his hands were calloused, but he did not look weathered enough for a shipwright. Owen noted another usefully readable part of Edmund's anatomy, his mouth, which puckered when he was not comfortable with what he had just said, as now. But Owen pretended to take his reply seriously. "A shipwright. I suppose that is a common trade here. And you were in York watching St. Clement's for—Let's see. Perhaps the sisters owe money on a ship you built them?"

Edmund looked down at his feet, pressed his lips together.

Louth looked from Owen to Edmund, puzzled.

Owen let the silence drag on.

After several minutes in which nervous sweat slicked down the sparse hairs at his temples, Edmund lifted his troubled eyes and asked, "What does the King offer Captain Sebastian?"

Owen nodded toward Ned, who came forward with a leather money pouch, shook it.

Edmund tilted his head, considering the weight. "Show me."

Ned opened the pouch, shook a few gold coins into his hand.

Edmund raised an eyebrow. "The King is so generous to a would-be traitor?"

Ned put the coins back in the pouch. "The King allows that the captain might not realize this is a treasonous act," Ned said. "And, in truth, Captain Sebastian and his men are of more use to the King fighting for Don Pedro than hanging from a gibbet."

Edmund took a deep, shuddering breath. "The King is wise."

Ned grinned. "So you admit to knowing Captain Sebastian?"

Edmund wiped his forehead. "What would it be worth to me?"

Owen leaned back, looked up at the ceiling, scratched his tidy Norman beard. "Your life?" He brought his eye back down to Edmund. "Would that suit you?"

Edmund hunched his shoulders, looked down at his hands. "I do not know how this game is played."

Dangerously honest for the role he had taken on. Owen stood, looked out the high, recessed window, hands clasped behind him.

Louth, uncomfortable with silences, took over. "You killed one of the archbishop's retainers as he was escorting you to a meeting with the archbishop, Edmund. Your life was not threatened. So you murdered a man for no cause, a man who wore the livery of the archbishop, who also happens to be our King's Chancellor. Such a deed is punishable by death. But if you assist us in the matter of Captain Sebastian, we shall perhaps spare your life."

Edmund's eyes shone with fear. "I tell you I did not kill him. I merely ran to the men who were to help me if I got caught."

"You *led* him to his death then," Owen said quietly.

Edmund hung his head.

Owen resumed his seat, leaned toward Edmund confidentially. "What was it you wanted at St. Clement's that you did not dare speak with the archbishop?"

Edmund crossed his arms, clenched his jaw.

Owen smelled his fear. "Why did you attack Jack? Was he with you in York?"

"What will you do with me?"

"That depends. Will you help us, Edmund? For the freedom to

walk down into the town on your own?"

Edmund, eyes still fixed on his feet, sighed. "That you cannot do for me. Once Jack tells the captain that I attacked him, I will be marked for death myself."

"Why did you attack him?"

"He is a murderous devil."

"Some folk might say the same of you."

Edmund shrugged.

"So what do you want from us, Edmund? Protection from Jack?"

The expressive eyes slid sideways. "I no longer know whom to trust."

Owen decided to change the subject for now. "Where is Will Longford?"

Edmund's eyes shifted from Owen to Louth to Ned, back to Owen. "You do not know where he has gone either?"

"You have not seen him since you came searching for him in Beverley?"

"No."

Owen believed him. "When did you last see him?"

"Last time I saw him in Beverley." Edmund tried a smile.

"You think to charm us with your wit?" Owen did not smile.

"When did you last see Longford in Beverley?" Louth asked.

Edmund stared at his shoes.

"Who owns the house we followed you into last night?" Owen asked.

"Captain Sebastian."

Owen cheered up. "Indeed. Does he ever stay there?"

"The captain is no fool." Edmund studied his dirty nails. "What is your interest in Will Longford?"

"Sir Nicholas found a letter in his house from Bertrand du Guesclin, the French king's Constable. I should like to talk to Longford about du Guesclin."

"As I said, Longford's disappeared. I don't know where he's gone."

"When did he disappear?"

Edmund pressed his hands together to keep them still. "Longford and his man Jaro were expected here in late April and they never arrived." He took a deep breath. "Captain Sebastian sent me to Beverley to remind them. But they were not there. No one had seen them."

"So you went to Longford's house," Owen said. "Did you search it?"

A pained look passed over Edmund's face. He nodded. "After—" He dropped his head, put a hand to his forehead. "Yes. I went through the house."

"After what, Edmund?" Louth's voice was sharp with tension.

Edmund sat there for a few minutes, head in hand. The guard opened the door to a servant carrying a pitcher and four tankards. A table was set up between Edmund and his questioners, the pitcher and tankards placed on it. The servant bowed and backed out, the guard closed the door. And still Edmund sat. Owen poured the ale, offered one to Edmund.

Edmund took it with shaking hands, held it up to his mouth with both hands, drank, set it back down, wiped his mouth on his sleeve. "The maid. Jack killed her." Louth moaned. "Acting on no one's orders. To clear the way for the search, he said. She was not important, he said." Edmund's eyes were haunted.

"Who is this Jack?" Owen asked.

"That bastard you let flee last night."

"And he was your partner?"

"No. Well, of late I have worked with him. I did not know him well, and I sent him in first, never thinking—" Edmund grabbed up the tankard, took another, long drink.

"It was not because Maddy was wrapped in a mantle and mistaken for Dame Joanna?" Louth asked.

Edmund shook his head. "How do you know when such a devil crouches in the shell of what seems to be an ordinary soldier?"

"Captain Sebastian sent him with you?" Ned asked.

Edmund nodded.

"Have you told him what Jack did?" Owen asked.

"I have. He said that it was in the nature of a good soldier to act ruthlessly when needed, that I was too womanly in my aversion to such acts."

"The unfeeling bastard!" Louth hissed.

Owen had heard such theories before. The old Duke had not tolerated such captains; he'd said that such an attitude was an incompetent captain's substitute for good sense and courage. In Owen's experience, it might also hide a deeper motive. Perhaps it *had been* the mantle that signed Maddy's death warrant. Perhaps Captain Sebastian had ordered Jack to kill Dame Joanna; no need for Edmund to know. "Did you find what you sought in Longford's house?" Owen asked.

"No."

"What was it?"

Edmund was silent.

Some loyalty to Captain Sebastian remained? "And then you followed Dame Joanna to St. Clement's?"

Edmund drew himself up, looked Owen in the eye. "I have been thinking all night. As you see, the captain is unhappy with me. And will be more so when Jack gets to him. I cannot bring Captain Sebastian to you. But I will tell you what I can."

"What do you ask in return?"

"Information about Joanna Calverley."

Owen cocked his head to one side. "What do you want to know?"

"Has a man been to see her in York? Fair-haired. Handsome."

"No."

"No one has been to see her?"

"As far as I know, the only one who tried was you, Edmund. Why do you ask?"

Edmund watched a spider moving toward him, reached out with his foot, crushed it. "She disappeared with my partner."

Ah. Now they made progress. "And would this partner's name be Stefan?"

Edmund looked surprised. "How did you know?"

"Did you and your partner bring Joanna to Scarborough?"

Edmund fidgeted uneasily. "What has she told you?"

"Very little."

Edmund frowned. "She is a strange one. I cannot see why Stefan is so taken with her."

"Was it Stefan who gave her the blue mantle, told her it was the Blessed Virgin's?"

Edmund smiled a little. "I did. We thought we would have a bit of fun. That was when Stefan was still playing with her. You could get her to believe anything."

"Did you take part in the false funeral?"

Edmund rubbed his face, threw his head back.

Owen recognized the signs of exhaustion. Good. "How did she get you to help her?"

"Longford got us to help." Edmund shook his head. "I have done strange things in my time, but when he came up with the idea to playact her death and burial..." He shook his head.

"So it was Longford's idea?"

Edmund thrust his chin out in a defensive pose. "She asked for it, make no mistake. She wanted the trail to end in Beverley. Didn't want her kin or the Church to come after her. I don't know whether it was the relic she'd stolen or what, but she wanted to vanish." Edmund fidgeted, rounding his back, then straightening and stretching his arms out in front of him, pulling on his hands, stretching his upper back.

"And Joanna liked the idea of the burial?" Owen asked.

"By that time she had no choice. Longford had a use for her, so she would do as he said or else."

So she had not been pleased with the scheme. Probably frightened. "Tell me about the burial."

Edmund shrugged. "Little to tell. Stefan and I slipped her out of the shroud while Jaro got the gravedigger drunk. The gravedigger passed out, we filled in the grave, rode off with Joanna hidden in a cart."

"Was she drugged?"

Edmund nodded. "Jaro concocted something. I think he gave her too much. It took a while to wake her."

"So Jaro was still alive when you left?"

Edmund frowned, looked round at the solemn, intent faces. "Why? He isn't now?"

"Jaro is buried in the grave you filled in on Joanna's shroud," Ned said. "Neck broken."

Edmund fell silent over this news. He scratched his knee. "I knew nothing of this."

And why would he say otherwise? "Who would want to kill him?" Owen asked.

Edmund rubbed his temples wearily. "I hardly knew him. He was a good cook, seemed loyal to Longford. They were not gentlemen, Captain Archer. I am sure they made enemies wherever they went."

From what Owen had heard from Louth and Ravenser, that seemed true. Enough of that. "How did you meet Joanna Calverley?"

Edmund straightened up. "She came to Longford with a relic to sell. We arrived the next day."

"This was another trip ordered by Captain Sebastian?"

"Yes. To summon Longford."

"Summoning Longford has become a regular task."

Edmund nodded. "The way grows familiar."

"And he introduced you to Joanna?"

"Not immediately. He had given her something to keep her asleep while he thought how best to use her." Edmund looked round at the men. "You see why I say they made enemies."

"How did he involve you?" Louth asked.

"He had come up with a plan. We'd use her to get to her brother. Longford was obsessed with Hugh. He thought since he had once made a fool out of Hugh, well, Hugh being so crazy, he must be just biding his time, plotting his revenge. So Longford wanted us to get Hugh out in the open where Captain Sebastian could find him."

"And you agreed?" Owen asked.

"Stefan and I, we thought we might have some fun with it, see what Hugh would do. And we did not want to leave any young woman with Longford."

"What did you mean to do with Joanna after Hugh was sufficiently teased with her?"

Edmund shrugged. "Abandon her, I suppose. She is very fair. She would not be without a protector for long. As it turned out, Stefan wanted to keep her by him."

Owen winced at the cold-bloodedness of it. "So what happened?"

"She was trouble from the first. She cast a spell over Stefan. He has been a fool since we took her from Beverley."

"So where is Stefan now?"

"That is what I want to find out. Joanna is back in York and Stefan's gone. I want to know what happened."

"What do you think happened?"

Edmund shrugged. "The fool's gone off to fight a dragon for her, that's what I think. He cannot do enough for her. Fine clothes. Feather beds."

Owen frowned. "Fight a dragon?"

"He saw himself as her defender. Got funny about the Hugh Calverley part of the plan. Told her not to go near him, that Hugh would be blamed for her escape from the convent and the sham burial. That either Sebastian or the Percies would punish him severely. Stefan knew she would not wish to hurt Hugh. He told her they would find some other way to reunite her with her brother."

"You had nothing to say about that? Seems to me he was going against your plan."

"He kept assuring me he had a new, better one."

"And you believed him?"

Edmund hesitated, shook his head.

Owen settled back, stretched his legs. "So Joanna did not know Stefan before she met him at Longford's?"

"No."

"Are you sure of that? Strange that you would arrive the day after she did. A rendezvous?"

Edmund shook his head. "Stefan and I have been partners a long time, Captain."

"You are certain they had not planned the meeting at Longford's?"

"I am certain they did not. He'd never seen her before. I told you she has cast a spell on him. I have never known him to bed another woman more than once."

"Why?"

"That is how he is faithful to his wife."

"Wife? So Stefan is a citizen of Scarborough, not a member of Sebastian's Free Company?" This could be the reason Joanna chose to return to the convent.

Edmund shook his head. "Stefan is of Sebastian's company. His wife and family are in Norway. He sends them money."

An interesting circumstance. "He prefers to be away from them?"

"You judge him without knowing him. Stefan had trouble there. He is waiting for better times. Perhaps a pardon."

Owen had known men in that position. Their loyalties could be difficult to judge. "Do you think Joanna found out he is married?"

Edmund shrugged. "I was not a part of their private conversations."

Owen pushed that thought aside for a moment. "So you traveled to Beverley in May, seeking Longford?"

Edmund nodded. "We did not find him. But we did hear of Joanna's return."

"Did you speak with her?"

"By the time I got there, she was locked up in the nunnery."

"So you followed the company to York."

Edmund shrugged.

"What did you mean to do with Joanna when you found her?"

"Find out what has happened to Stefan."

"Why did you not approach Sir Richard de Ravenser or Sir Nicholas and ask to speak with Joanna?"

Edmund glanced at Louth. "With the death of the maid I did not think I would be courteously received."

"You hate the fact that Joanna came between you and your partner," Owen suggested.

Edmund groaned. "You are intent on thinking the worst. I can tell you and Ned have fought together. How would you feel if he disappeared suddenly? And his leman? Then she showed up somewhere else and was shut away and guarded so you could not even ask her what had happened? You couldn't find Ned, you couldn't speak with the only person who might tell you where he was?"

A cry from deep in the heart of the man. He was not at all the outlaw Owen had thought. He would provide no simple answers. "I would feel much as you seem to."

They did not speak for a while. Owen stood, looked up at the sky visible in the window, stretched his back. He felt a sadness about this man and his friend. Stefan, exiled from his country, leaving behind a wife and children. And Edmund. What of Edmund? Where were his true loyalties?

It was Edmund who broke the silence. "I care about Stefan. I want to see him at peace with himself. He has not been so. He told me he felt his soul was in peril, that his love for Joanna was a grievous sin, but he could not help himself."

"A grievous sin because she was a nun?"

"All of it. Her vows, his marriage vows, his children, our using her against her brother—and I suppose he was thinking more about not using her against Hugh."

Thorny. But such complications were part of love, at least in Owen's experience. He had wanted Lucie from the moment he saw her, when she was still married, and Owen was apprenticed to her husband. "You must have a theory about happened between Stefan and Joanna."

Edmund had fallen to scratching his knee again. He stared down at the blood seeping through his leggings. He turned his head this way and that, finally looking up at Owen, his eyes sad. "They disappeared about the time that Hugh Calverley was murdered. At first I thought Stefan took Joanna away so that she would not hear. But when I discovered that she was traveling alone—" He threw up his hands.

"Joanna was fond of her brother?"

Edmund rolled his eyes. "She spoke of him as if he were the perfect soldier, the perfect brother. God had blessed him with all virtues befitting a man."

"An opinion you did not share."

"Hugh Calverley was a beast, plain and simple."

"But Joanna did not feel that way."

"Not at all."

"How about Stefan?"

"I think he was trying to see Hugh from Joanna's eyes."

"Then you would not think it likely that they murdered Hugh Calverley, ran away, then decided to separate for a while, or forever, for their souls?"

Edmund shook his head. "No. I am certain that is not what happened."

"Who do you think murdered Hugh?"

"The man had many enemies, Captain Archer."

"And what of Stefan's disappearance? What has Captain Sebastian done about it?"

"Precious little. A few half-hearted searches." Edmund sighed. "I believe he thinks Stefan murdered Hugh." He nodded at Owen's raised eyebrow. "Another reason I am out of favor. The captain thinks I helped, and then Stefan ran away with the sister." Edmund pressed his palms to his forehead. "Ever since that woman came into our lives, nothing has gone right. I want to return to York with you. I want to speak with Joanna and find Stefan."

Owen glanced at Louth and Ned. Ned shrugged. Louth shook his head. "How do we know we can trust him?"

18

BARTERING

Owen climbed the stone steps round and round, higher and higher, to the battlements of Scarborough Castle. Sir William de Percy had invited him for a private talk up near the heavens, where eavesdropping would be difficult. Owen wondered if Percy had any notion how heights bothered a one-eyed man. Not that Owen had ever meant to decline; he sought to train himself out of his skittishness. Reason and experience should make up for depth perception—with practice. He had forced himself up onto Knaresborough's battlements once a day and several times at night. But Owen had not walked Scarborough's battlements yet; he expected that Knaresborough's dizzying height would be nothing compared with this, high over the North Sea.

Owen reached the top of the tower warm with the effort, but breathing comfortably—until he faced into the wind. Sweet Jesu, the force was so strong he had to duck and gasp for air; surely a slighter body would be blown over in this gale. And it was yet summer. What must the watch on these battlements suffer in winter? A handrail would be appreciated on the inside of the ledge on which he stood, but Owen refused to let anyone know how vulnerable he felt. He was grateful as he looked out and down that the drop-off from castle wall to bluff to sea was no more dizzying than Knaresborough's prospect of the River Nidd.

Owen spied Sir William at a guard station on the next tower. He made his way toward Percy, forcing himself to saunter, look about as if enjoying himself, and not clutch the wall beside him. Fortunately,

Percy had chosen a spot sheltered slightly from the wind. "Sir William."

The stocky man spun round, fixed his beady eyes on Owen. "How did you fare with Edmund?"

An abrupt beginning. "He cannot help us with Captain Sebastian."

Percy nodded, looking perversely pleased. "No matter. Perhaps I can help you there. The men of the Free Companies are a greedy lot. My men will pass rumors through the town that the king has a tempting proposition for Captain Sebastian; I wager the captain will send word. You watch—with a sizable bribe, you will succeed where Hugh failed."

Owen looked out at the North Sea, gray-blue in the summer sun. "Surely that is not why we are up here, Sir William?"

Percy leaned against the wall to Owen's left, trying to see his companion's expression. "What does your prisoner say about Hugh Calverley's death?"

Owen only sensed Percy on his blind side; he could not see him, nor would he satisfy the man's curiosity by turning toward him. He did not want Percy at ease. "Edmund claims no knowledge."

"We were not responsible." The voice was defensive.

Now Owen turned toward Percy, feigning surprise. "You? But of course not."

Percy snarled. "Do not play the innocent with me, Captain Archer. You made it plain yesterday that you thought the Percies had been negligent in seeking out Hugh's murderer and notifying his family."

"It puzzled me is all." Owen smiled, turned back toward the sea. "So who are you so hesitant to implicate?"

"I do not know who killed him."

"But you suspect, Sir William. You sit up here, steward of Scarborough Castle, and you watch the goings on below. You have eyes all about. You admit as much by offering to lure Captain Sebastian to a meeting. Who do you think killed Hugh?"

Percy came round to Owen's good side, though it placed him in more wind. "You must understand Scarborough. 'Tis home to smugglers, pirates and spies. Scots, Flemings, Zealanders, Normans—" He blinked against the wind, but stood his ground.

Owen looked south toward the harbor, north toward Whitby. A

coastline rippling with coves and harbors, bluffs pocked with caves.
"I can see it would suit them."

"To keep the King's peace among such folk requires compromise."

"No doubt."

Percy moved back into the shelter of the tower wall and settled
with a grunt on a stone bench. "Two of the three powerful families
who supply most of our bailiffs—the Accloms and the Carters—
are bold thieves."

Owen leaned against the wall facing Percy, arms folded.
"Your point?"

"Hugh was warned to turn a blind eye—but he did not always
do so."

"You think he crossed either the Accloms or the Carters once
too often?"

Percy looked down into the castle yard, where a group of boys
screamed in mock battle. "Should I put all who live in this castle in
jeopardy for the death of a man whom few mourn?"

"But you do not know for certain these families were involved?"
Percy shook his head.

"What do you intend to tell the Calverleys?"

"Hugh died for King and country."

"Tell me, Sir William. If you disliked him so, why was he here
in Scarborough?"

Percy looked surprised. "He was good is why. Rounded up
spies, traitors, trouble-makers—and Sebastian's recruits. Many of
them are now in my service. A good soldier is often the last man
to whom you would marry your daughter. You should know that."

Owen and Ned took advantage of the long evening to see Hugh
Calverley's house. Deaf Harry showed them how he had managed
to run messages between the castle and Hugh's dwelling all those
years without being caught by Sebastian's men. He led them on such
a fiendishly circuitous route that neither would have sworn they

still looked out on the North Sea. The house was a squat, thatched cottage that would be taken for a peasant's house by all except the wary, who would note the absence of children, animals, crops. Two rooms, packed mud floors, in one room a fire circle and a sleeping loft, in the other a stable to one side. The place had been stripped of all signs of Hugh Calverley.

"His men slept here, too?" Owen asked.

Harry, who tended to bend very close while reading lips, jerked back and nodded. "Aye. They slept in t'other side, with horses."

"And you slept below, Hugh above?" Owen asked.

Harry straightened again and shook his head. "I slept above. The master had a curtained feather bed below."

"Fancy for such a hovel," Ned remarked.

Harry had not been watching Ned. "What?" he shouted, turning to Ned.

Ned repeated his comment.

Harry nodded. "My master and his women liked their comfort, sir."

"And you, Harry, did you find it comfortable?" Ned asked.

Harry beamed. "Master Hugh promised the Percies would see to me if aught happened to him, and they have. That's a good master."

Owen saw the doubt on his friend's face and wondered what he was up to.

"They say your master beat you about the head." Ned mouthed the words dramatically. "And that is why you're so deaf."

Harry tugged an earlobe, shrugged. "Master Hugh had a temper, true enough. But he was patient wi' me most times. I had threads and bread, sir, and a goodly fire. And now in my decline I work at the castle." His blackened teeth formed a grim smile. "I never looked for such riches."

Owen stared into the fire in the hall until his vision blurred. A cup of wine in his hand attracted flies that he absently swatted away. He could not get deaf Harry out of his mind, the gratitude expressed in those watery eyes for the bare necessities and beatings that had bloodied his ears too often. Owen had grown so accustomed to his comfortable life that he had forgotten folk like Harry. Owen's family had been freemen, but poor. They would see his home in York as luxurious. And Sir Robert D'Arby was offering to expand it twice over. Why was he so fortunate? Should he return to Wales, see how his family fared? Lucie had once accused him of being cruel, not returning to show his family he had survived his years as an archer for Henry, Duke of Lancaster. But what might Owen do for his family? Would he shame them by offering help? Were any of them yet alive?

Sir William Percy entered the hall and made for Owen. "You have it."

Owen lifted his eye to his host, slowly focusing on the man. "Have it?" He shook his head, not understanding.

"Captain Sebastian will meet with you and Ned tomorrow, midday, the church of St. Mary the Virgin, right below the castle."

Owen sat forward, now alert. "In truth?"

Percy grinned from ear to ear. "I've done well by Lancaster, eh?"

"You have done well indeed, Sir William." Owen rose. "I shall tell Ned and Sir Nicholas."

Percy stayed him with a large, beringed hand. "You heard what I said, eh? You and Ned. Sir Nicholas later, if the captain is satisfied."

Owen turned his good eye dead center on Percy's face. "Why?"

"You are soldiers. He is comfortable with soldiers. Sir Nicholas is an ecclesiastic. The captain says they talk in circles."

Owen and Percy shared a good laugh over that observation.

Owen paused to admire the new carvings flanking the door of St. Mary the Virgin, heads of King Edward and Queen Phillippa. The royal couple had taken their marriage vows in York Minster, and all Yorkshire had embraced them. Owen wondered if the gargoyle on the waterspout directly above Phillippa might be modeled after Alice Perrers. He had never seen the King's mistress, but he knew that stonecutters often entertained themselves with such subtle jokes, and Thoresby had described her as very much the gargoyle.

Ned nudged Owen and nodded toward two richly caparisoned horses in the churchyard held by a squire in a jacket much like the one Louth had found with the Sebastian emblem hidden inside—a subtle livery. "Our man is here betimes."

Owen nodded. The squire glanced nervously about, and from round the side of the building Owen could hear a horse snort impatiently. "He has prepared for trouble."

Ned grinned. "As we knew he would."

They entered the west door. After the glaring noon sun, Owen's eye took a moment to adjust to the dark church nave, dimly lit by wall torches. A huge man in dark clothing rose from a camp stool, snapped his fingers. A boy opened a lantern.

"By your patch and height, you must be Owen Archer." Captain Sebastian was a shaggy bear of a man with a booming voice. Owen was accustomed to being the tallest in any gathering. Sebastian was no more than four fingers taller than Owen, but his girth made it seem as though he towered.

"Captain Sebastian." Owen held out his hands, showing he held no weapon.

Sebastian did likewise, then turned his dark eyes on Ned, who quickly lifted his hands.

"Good," Sebastian thundered. "John!" The boy scurried to open two more camp stools. "Sit," the captain said. His smile exposed healthy teeth.

But for the height, he reminded Owen of Bertrand du Guesclin. Owen commented on the resemblance.

Sebastian looked pleased. "But your memory has softened his appearance. Du Guesclin is much uglier than I." He threw back his head and roared. A chantry priest glanced their way. Owen could imagine the sniff and frown. Sebastian was clearly a man who saw no reason to whisper merely because he was in a church. "So." Sebastian sat forward, hands on knees. "You carry a letter from King Edward?"

Ned drew it out of his belt pouch.

Sebastian nodded, but made no move to take it. "About Don Pedro the Cruel, eh?"

"You are the last of the English knights to hear the warning," Ned said. "Our King has vowed to win back the throne of Castile for Don Pedro, the rightful king. Any English knight fighting against Don Pedro commits treason."

Sebastian wagged his head from side to side impatiently. "And he offers gold?"

Ned held up the purse.

"Our King is puzzlingly misguided in one fact, gentlemen." Sebastian sat up straighter. "Though I deserve it more than anyone I know, I am not a knight."

Ned frowned, tapped the letter against his hand. "But you are the Sebastian who made a pact with four English knights?"

"Aye. They sorely needed me."

Owen knew where this led. "So you will not change your allegiance in this struggle?"

Sebastian scratched his beard. "I cannot read, 'tis true, but I understand law well enough to know the King's letter holds no power over me. It states knights, if you represent it properly. So I am still free to follow my conscience."

"You would trip your King on a detail?" Ned's voice was sharp with disapproval.

Sebastian made a face. "A detail to you, far more to me."

Owen glanced at Ned, expecting his friend to pursue this. But instead Ned tucked away the letter and the purse with the jerky motion of anger.

Owen and Sebastian exchanged puzzled looks.

Sebastian snapped his fingers. The groom hurried over. "Wine!" The boy brought forth a wineskin and handed it to his master. Sebastian threw back his head and squirted a generous gulp into his mouth, passed the skin to Owen. Owen drank, passed to Ned.

Sebastian took another squirt, handed the skin back to the boy. Elbow on knee, he leaned closer to Owen. "So you have seen du Guesclin?"

"I was captain of archers for Henry of Lancaster when he fought du Guesclin at Rennes."

Sebastian grinned from ear to ear. "Ah! A glorious moment for the Capital."

True enough. Owen had heard many versions of the story, each more glorious than the last. The plain truth was, during the war of the Breton succession, in which the English supported the challenger to the French King's appointee, du Guesclin had planted a prisoner in Lancaster's camp who warned of a large company on its way to relieve the French. While Lancaster led his army off to waylay the company, du Guesclin plundered Lancaster's camp, then sent word to the Duke on his return offering to bring back some of the wine for his dinner. The old Duke, admiring the Breton's nerve, had indeed invited du Guesclin to bring the wine and share it with him. "Du Guesclin is a master of trickery," Owen admitted, "with a dash that delights the troubadours." The Breton captain successfully held Rennes against Lancaster, but had allowed the old Duke to save face by giving him enough time in the city to plant his banner on the wall. "And he is a fair-minded man."

Sebastian nodded vigorously, snapped his fingers for the wineskin. "Which is why he—and I—support Enrique de Trastamare against Don Pedro. Trastamare might be a bastard, but Don Pedro is far worse in God's eyes—he is a murderer. Right is on Trastamare's side."

"Don Pedro is the born king," Ned reminded him.

Sebastian drank, passed the skin on to Owen, shrugged. "So was our King's father—yet we put him aside for the good of the realm."

"True enough," Owen said, "but King Charles plays this hand to free his countryside of the *routiers*, not because he believes Trastamare is God's chosen." Owen drank, passed on the skin.

Sebastian shrugged. "Then Charles does it for the good of his people."

Now was the time for Ned to begin bargaining, but Ned showed no signs of doing so. Owen did not wish to lose the opportunity. "Captain Sebastian, I trust you would obey King Edward's command if knighthood were added to the gold."

Sebastian beamed.

Ned choked on a mouthful of wine.

"Your friend does not deem me worthy of knighthood," Sebastian said. "Yet he mistook me for a knight earlier."

"We have no right to offer it," Ned protested.

"Rest easy," Owen said. "I merely ask it so that we may know the terms to report to Sir Nicholas."

"Prince Edward is to lead the expedition?" Sebastian asked.

Owen nodded.

Sebastian held out his right hand. "The gold and the knighthood and I shall fight alongside my Prince no matter my personal opinion of the cause."

Owen grinned. "I thought so." They shook. Ned and Sebastian shook.

As Owen rose to leave, Sebastian asked, "What of Edmund of Whitby? I hear you bloodied him and dragged him to the castle."

"He must answer in York for the death of one of the archbishop's retainers. I shall take him there."

Sebastian's eyes narrowed. "A retainer? Foolhardy Edmund." He shook his head. "The Percies cannot try him here?"

"No."

"A waste of a good horse, riding him to York. They will surely execute him."

Owen shrugged. "I merely obey orders."

Sebastian snapped at the groom to gather his things. "There are two men we share a desire to find, Captain Archer. Will Longford and Edmund's friend, Stefan. If you should find them, tell them I have need of them."

Owen promised to do so.

On their return to the castle, Ned headed for the practice yard and spent a long time hacking at a straw dummy with his sword. When he was stumbling with fatigue and soaked through with sweat, Owen approached him. "What is it, friend?"

Ned turned on Owen, sword poised, then relaxed, sheathed it, sat down hard on the ground. "I cannot do as you do. And that is what he wants, you know. I am to replace the spy stolen by the Lord Chancellor."

Owen crouched beside his friend, searched the pained eyes. "What nonsense are you talking?"

"Lancaster. He thinks to create another Owen Archer of me, and I cannot do it. Not once did it occur to me that Sebastian was never called 'sir.'"

"And you think I saw it? He *told* us, Ned."

"But you caught his purpose at once. Knew he would tumble for the knighthood."

True enough. "It was not the old Duke taught me to think so, Ned. It took a churchman and lawyer to do this to me, see the twists in a man's purpose." Owen stood up, stretched. "A large tankard of ale will keep your joints from aching. Come along, Ned. Let's get drunk once more before I'm off to York and you to the king."

Sir William and Ralph de Percy seemed pleased to hear of Owen's intention to leave the following day; but they were puzzled by his request to take Edmund along.

"He will walk me round Longford's haunts in Beverley," Owen said, "mayhap loose the nun's tongue. We must satisfy my lord Thoresby."

Ralph spit into the fire. "He will kill you in your sleep."

"I think not. And Alfred will watch him with murder in his heart— he still holds Edmund responsible for the death of his partner."

Louth and Ned were to take a more direct route to the king with Sebastian's demands.

"Joanna, stop! Joanna, look what you have done!" Lucie grabbed at the nun's arm, but Joanna shrugged her off, kept on digging. Lucie, great with child, lost her balance and fell to her knees. Struggling to rise, she stumbled again as Hugh's terrified scream rose from deep in the earth. "Listen, Joanna. He is not dead! Why are burying your brother alive?" Joanna had dragged Hugh to the edge of the impossibly deep grave, so deep that mists in its depths concealed the bottom, and had rolled him into it with a casual motion of her booted foot, all the while looking distracted, as if she were hurrying through a repetitive chore while thinking of something else. And now in the same manner she shoveled the dirt on top of her living, writhing brother. Lucie wanted to close her ears to the malevolent scraping of the shovel through the piled earth, the whispered descent, the faint thump of the clumps of earth and gravel landing on Hugh. Over and over again. And still he screamed. "Joanna, for pity's sake!" But Joanna kept up the rhythm as she looked off in the distance. How could Hugh scream so? Joanna had ripped open his neck with her teeth. Lucie crawled to Joanna, tugged at her skirt. "For the love of God, Joanna, if you will not stop, at least be quick about it." As Lucie grabbed Joanna's ankle, the shovel came down on her head. She was falling, falling toward the screams. "My baby! My baby!"

Lucie clutched her stomach and breathed deeply. A cramp from thrashing in her nightmare, nothing more, please, God. She breathed deeply, slowly, breathing round the pain. It eased. She rolled to the edge of the bed and sat up. Fine. Stood up. No pain. Thanks be to God.

Lucie walked sleepily to the window and gazed out on the first glimmer of dawn on the rooftops of the city. Whence came such a dream? Why would she dream of Joanna injuring her brother and burying him alive? Holy Mary, Mother of God, pray for us sinners…

19

"...BEFORE DEATH'S SLEEP"

On the evening of Corpus Christi, Owen sat in a tavern staring into a tankard of thick country ale. He did not want to be up on the moors, headed toward Beverley. He wanted to be in York watching the pageants with Lucie. Ever since he knew he was to be a father, he had imagined events that were to come. One of those was the Corpus Christi celebration this midsummer; he and Lucie would watch the pageants and smile at the thought of sharing this with their child in the future. They would hope for fine weather next year so the infant could sit outside with them. He or she would be nine months old by then. Not old enough to be aware of the wondrous event they were watching, but who could say what a baby remembered?

Owen also worried about Jasper. Corpus Christi last year was when all Jasper's troubles began. His mother had collapsed while watching the pageants, his master had been murdered the following evening. The boy would find this time painful. Owen hoped Lucie had thought to bring Jasper home from the abbey today to feel part of a family at this sad time. How much better if Owen could be there, too.

And Lucie. She would be great with child by now. She needed Owen to be there. He wanted to be there, his arm round her, steadying her. Keeping her warm at night. Helping her up the steep, shallow steps to their bedchamber.

Not here, in a greasy, smoky tavern in the midst of the moors, drinking ale made from barley so poorly ground he must chew the chaff that remained after he swallowed. A second drink did not wash it down, but left more chaff—and more and more as he drank his way down to the bottom.

Edmund slumped sullenly over his tankard, too, looking up only to check round the room for Jack. With each day of the journey Edmund grew more obsessed with the feeling that Jack rode along behind, just out of sight and hearing. Neither Owen nor Alfred had seen any evidence of pursuit, although once or twice Owen thought he heard an echo of their hoofbeats.

Only Alfred seemed in good humor, grinning at the taverner's daughter, who kept glancing over her shoulder at him while she passed among the trestle tables. She was young and plain, with a sharp tongue for the grabbers and pinchers who slowed her down, and an amazing kick that landed true every time. Alfred was smitten. "Now there's a woman knows her own worth, keeps to her business."

Edmund closed his eyes and shook his head. "She's probably bedded more lovers than you ever will and is riddled with disease."

Alfred just laughed. "You are jealous that she smiles at me, not you."

Edmund gave him a disgusted look. "You haven't a brain in your head."

The taverner's daughter put Owen in mind of Bess Merchet. "You might find her harder to bed than you think," he warned Alfred. "A woman with such a backbone does not fall into the arms of the first man who flirts with her."

Alfred shrugged. "I can but try." He rose.

Owen grabbed his hand. "We must rise early, ride in to Beverley. I do not want to dawdle on the road because you had little sleep and cannot sit your horse in a gallop." Nor would he be of any use if they must turn and fight.

For a moment, Alfred's face changed, hardened, his eyes narrowed, his color rose. He moved his eyes slowly to Owen's hand on his. "I never liked you much. 'Twas Colin worshipped you."

Owen squeezed the hand harder and gave Alfred a look that warned he was not amused. "I am not asking you to like me. But you are mine to command on this journey. We have business in Beverley and York. And Edmund to keep an eye on. You shall leave off the lovemaking until we finish our business. Then be damned if you will."

Alfred backed off, not liking the look in Owen's eyes. "I was just having some fun. Meant nothing by it."

Owen let go Alfred's hand. A hush had spread round them as folk eyed the two men with curiosity and apprehension. "We are calling unwanted attention to ourselves," Owen said softly. He picked up Alfred's tankard, shook it, and said loudly, "Empty? Is that all you're bellyaching about?"

Alfred lifted his hand and balled up his fist, turned suddenly to the room at large and belched. He grinned, relaxed his hand. "Better now." And sat down, banging his fist on the table. "So I'll have another, now you've asked."

Edmund shook his head. "You're a pig."

"But not an ass. I know an eye that threatens bloody murder when I see it." Once Alfred had drunk down his ale, he went stumbling off to bed.

Edmund soon followed. Owen stayed below until he had made a thorough study of each face in the room. He would remember them if they turned up again on his journey.

But for all their growing unease, they arrived without incident in Beverley at dusk the following day, pushing their way against an opposing force of folk leaving town after the Corpus Christi pageants, picking their way through the guild members disassembling the pageant wagons. By the time they reached Ravenser's house, they wanted only something to drink and then bed. Ravenser recognized their condition and showed them to a bedchamber. The provost held Owen back while Alfred and Edmund went in.

"The stocky one. You did not set out from York with him."

"No. He is one of Captain Sebastian's men. Come along to help us question Joanna."

Ravenser's eyebrow went up, just as his uncle's would. "Unbound?"

"We have come to an agreement," Owen said.

Ravenser gave him a look that clearly said he thought him a

fool. "I must hear about this. But first, let me give you this letter and leave you alone to read it." Ravenser drew from somewhere in his fine houppelande a sealed letter. The Wilton's seal, now Lucie's, with a mortar and pestle. "I received one as well," Ravenser said.

Owen went back down to the hall with an oil lamp and read of Joanna's self-mutilation and her eerie refrain, "No one should suffer the grave before death's sleep." Lucie thought Joanna's attack on herself was her response to her mother's death. Owen tucked that idea in the back of his mind and read on, how Lucie grew large and clumsy, Sir Robert proved a patient, helpful gardener, Jasper was to come stay for the eve and day of Corpus Christi. And Lucie had adopted a stray kitten, an orange tabby, whom Melisende disliked. Owen groaned. Melisende was intrusive enough in their small house. Why was Lucie adopting another cat? She wrote that she hoped Owen would take time to see Beverley Minster, which was said to be almost as beautiful as York Minster. By now she trusted he would desire a peaceful place where he might think. Owen smiled. She was right. And her concern was a comfort; a man could feel so alone.

Ravenser joined Owen. "You have read about Dame Joanna?"

Owen nodded. "Bad luck she has been unable to speak."

"The woman is dangerous. My uncle sees no difficulty in returning her to St. Clement's once we know all is safe, but I do not agree."

"His Grace is in York now?"

Ravenser shook his head. "At Windsor or Sheen on the king's business, but he hopes to return shortly after you arrive. What do you think about the nun's obsession with someone being buried alive?"

"Jaro could not have been alive when they buried him."

Ravenser frowned at the memory of the corpse. "I agree. I cannot see how one's neck could be broken in the grave. So it is her own burial that haunts her?"

"According to Edmund, she was not long in the ground. A few shovels full of earth over her. Can a momentary experience leave such a scar?"

"Edmund told you this? The man who sleeps upstairs?"

"He took part in the ruse." Owen rubbed his eyes, weary from days of journeying with the tension of Edmund's spectral pursuers. "I have much to tell you. But Joanna's obsession with someone buried alive—it makes me uneasy, Sir Richard. How thoroughly did you examine Jaro?"

"We opened the grave, cut open his shroud, noted the broken neck." Ravenser tilted his head to one side, leaned back in his chair. "What are you thinking?"

"That I should take a look at that grave. And speak to the gravedigger."

"You doubt our thoroughness?"

"They tell me Jaro was huge. Fat. Much could be hidden with such a corpse."

Ravenser pressed the bridge of his nose. "I confess my own doubts on the matter." He closed his eyes, leaned his head back. "I shall attend you. When do you wish to proceed?"

"Tomorrow?"

"Tomorrow," Ravenser whispered to himself. He opened his eyes, lifted his head. "I ask you to wait one more day, until the Corpus Christi revelers are safely gone. It is so crowded in the city at present that nothing can be accomplished without an audience."

Owen agreed. "Tomorrow I shall speak with the gravedigger and the priest who buried Joanna."

Ravenser nodded. "I shall arrange for them to come here."

Owen tucked Lucie's letter in his belt, slapped the arms of his chair, and rose, stretching.

Ravenser smiled. "You are not comfortable sitting in a chair for long, are you?"

"True enough. Years of campaigning. Gets the body out of the habit."

"I look forward to hearing about Scarborough in the morning."

Alfred and Edmund were up long before Owen. He slept like the dead, finally waking when a servant came in with a cup of spiced wine and Ravenser's request that Owen join him as soon as possible in his parlor. He would find bread and more wine in there.

The parlor walls caught Owen's attention, hung with embroidered panels in vibrant colors. No stories were depicted, rather the panels looked like the edges in illustrated manuscripts, particularly one with animals forming an alphabet. Owen had long ago given up any effort to be inconspicuous when he examined a room, his single eye making it necessary to turn his head this way and that like a bird.

Ravenser stood by the window, the shutter opened to let in a lovely breeze, and smiled at Owen's study. "You like them?"

Owen sat down, poured more wine, pulled apart a small loaf of pandemain, took a bite, washed it down, sighed and settled back. "I do, but with reservation, Sir Richard. They draw me in, invite me to turn myself on my head to see all the fine features."

"Too distracting?" Ravenser took a seat opposite Owen.

Owen nodded. "I should accomplish little work in this room."

"Perhaps that is why the Irish are so difficult to rule. They are too distracted with their dreams."

"These are Irish embroideries?"

"I was up in Ireland with Sir Lionel for a short time."

"They say the Irish are much like us."

"I forgot. You are Welsh."

"Also difficult to rule. Also dreamers."

Ravenser shrugged. "I want to hear about Captain Sebastian."

Owen told him of the conversation in the church.

Ravenser sniffed. "Arrogant traitor. Why should such as he expect knighthood?"

"He is an excellent captain, they say. Men have been knighted for less."

Ravenser studied Owen. "But not you, eh? Ever resent that, Archer?"

Owen laughed. "A Welsh longbowman? Knighted? I was never fool enough to expect it."

Ravenser did not join in the laughter. "Yet the old Duke and my uncle entrust you with delicate business. You are an odd one not to resent that."

"I have a good life, Sir Richard. Far better than I ever dreamed. What do I need with the responsibilities of paying for the mount, arms and livery of squires and soldiers?"

Ravenser grunted. "What of the stewards of Scarborough, the Percies? How did they behave?"

"They have learned, I believe with the help of gold, to look away from the transgressions of the Accloms and Carters, the governing families of the town who happen to be smugglers and thieves. Sir William explained the need for compromise. If he did so with them, most like he also did so with Sebastian. And Sir William has not informed Matthew Calverley that his son, Hugh, was murdered. I think he believes it was Sebastian who ordered Hugh's death."

"I see." Ravenser pressed his fingertips together and closed his eyes. "You speak of a powerful family, Archer." A vein on one eyelid twitched.

"Put aside what I have said if it disturbs you, Sir Richard. I offered it as an explanation, not a battle cry." Owen had no desire to take on extra tasks in this matter. He was ready to be done with it.

Ravenser nodded, then glanced round to make sure no servants were present. "And what of Maddy's murder?"

Owen told him about Jack. "I am sorry I let him get away. Edmund believes the man is following us, awaiting his opportunity to attack. Alfred and I are beginning to believe him."

"You have seen signs of pursuit?"

"No. 'Tis just a sense of eyes at our backs."

"Good." Ravenser pushed his chair back from the table. "It is time we were off to St. Mary's."

"I thought the vicar was to come here."

"It appears that Thomas has an ague. We must speak with him in his bedchamber."

Neither the priest nor the gravedigger had been forthcoming with any new information, though both recognized Edmund, which removed any doubts Owen might have had about Edmund's story.

"He stood there with his friend, very respectful, and I had the notion the friend was her lover, so sad he looked," the priest said.

Edmund had seemed shaken by this accurate guess.

Before returning to Ravenser's house, Owen chose to walk from North Bar to Longford's house with Edmund as guide. One of Joanna's stories had been that she had lost her way. He wanted to see if that was likely. It was just Owen and Edmund on this pilgrimage. Alfred had been sent off to a tavern to sit quietly and hear what he might hear.

Edmund led Owen off the main street into a small churchyard. An oak shaded it, and a well tempted the thirsty. "This is where she lost the Magdalene medal. Stefan came here and retrieved it from the priest."

"Now there is someone might have something interesting to say. How did Stefan find him?"

Edmund shrugged. "I did not accompany him. I never thought to ask."

Owen stepped into the church, a cool, dark womb smelling of candle wax, incense, and damp stone. It reminded him of Lucie's suggestion, to seek quiet in the minster. He would do that later. An old woman knelt by a statue of Mary.

"God be with you, Goodwife," Owen said. "I seek the priest of this church. Do you know where I might find him?"

"He'd be at minster most days, being a canon," the woman said, never moving her eyes from the statue.

Owen had forgotten the priest might be a canon of Beverley. He could ask Ravenser about him. Back outside, Owen nodded to Edmund to lead on to Longford's house. The way was not complicated. If Joanna had become lost, it was for some reason other than a few false turnings. The house was visible from the main street they had followed from North Bar.

Edmund stood by the door, watching Owen pace the main room. "What do you expect to find?"

"Nothing. I am sure what is to be found here has been found. I just wanted to see it. See whether I might learn anything of Longford from his house."

"So what do you learn here of him?"

"The walls are scarred and pocked; the chairs and table have been mended more than once. I would guess he has a fierce temper. Perhaps when he drinks alone."

Edmund nodded. "You have learned something of him. Will feels God cheated him with the leg. All those years of soldiering and then to fall off his horse escaping a cuckolded husband and crush the leg." Edmund grinned at Owen's look of surprise. "You didn't know?"

"No one has talked much about Longford the man, just his connection with du Guesclin, with Captain Sebastian, Joanna and Hugh Calverley..." Owen shook his head. "Fleeing an angry husband. An embarrassing end to a career."

"Will brags about it, his wild wenching, his derring-do. But it is a curse to him."

Owen had seen enough. "Is there good ale to be had in Beverley?"

"I shall show you my favorite inn."

They had not far to go. The taverner paused as they entered, eyeing Owen's patch and scar. Then he recognized Edmund. "Been a long while. Is Longford back, too?"

"Nay. I am on other business. Traveling with Captain Archer here, former captain of archers for the old Duke of Lancaster."

The taverner's eyes opened wider. "You fought with Henry of Grosmont?"

Owen was accustomed to this response. It usually earned him excellent service in hopes of a good tale or two. "That I did."

"Then why in God's name are you traveling with the like of Edmund here? Outlaws they are, same as the one came asking about you."

Edmund tensed. "Who was that?"

"The one came with you last time. When you were looking for Stefan."

"Jack?"

The taverner shrugged. "Can't say as I remember a name."

"When was he here?" Edmund asked.

"Yesterday. Early in the day."

"Have you seen him since?"

The taverner shook his head, turned back to Owen. "So why are you traveling with Edmund?"

"The king has welcomed his friends back to his service."

The taverner's eyes opened wide, shifted from Owen to Edmund and back. "Then 'tis true what they say, our king is desperate for gold to fight King Charles." He shook his head. "Hard times are upon us when our king needs the likes of Will Longford."

After Owen had sent off the taverner with a firsthand account of one of the old Duke's lesser known exploits, he and Edmund settled down to judging the ale.

"Too bitter, but smooth, clean." Owen nodded. "I could drink another."

Edmund drained his cup, called to the taverner for another round. "Told you he was behind us."

"He's in front of us now. Biding his time, I think."

When the taverner came with the pitcher, Owen asked, "This man asking after Edmund. Did he ask after anyone else?"

"A one-eyed archer—yourself, I should think, Longford, Stefan—and a nun, God help us. I asked did he mean the one who died and was resurrected in Our Lady's mantle. He said was none of my business, which I took as a yes."

Owen thanked him for the information.

Edmund fell to his drink while Owen studied him. He'd been on the road with Edmund for days now. What had he learned of him? Edmund was quiet, thoughtful, steadfast in his loyalties, or Owen was no judge. "You don't seem the sort who joins up with someone like Sebastian."

"I suppose I'm not."

"What will you do after this?"

"If I find Stefan, my life will go on as it was. But without Stefan"—Edmund wiped his mouth on his sleeve—"I'll go back to building ships, I suppose."

"You *were* a shipwright? Really?"

Edmund nodded. "I was young. An apprentice in Whitby. Working on a ship for Sebastian. Met Stefan, listened to his stories. It sounded like a man's life, fighting, wenching, drinking, sailing, more fighting." He smiled sadly at his balled up fist, scarred knuckles. "But the taste for all that weakens with experience. I'd like a wife. Children. A home." He shrugged. "Still a dreamer, you see."

"But if Stefan wishes to continue in this life, you will do so?"

"Aye."

"Why?"

Edmund pounded the table lightly with the balled up fist, then opened his hand, pressed it palm down on the table, fingers splayed. He took out his dagger and began the dangerous game of stabbing the table in between each finger, going back and forth on the hand, faster and faster. When the dagger grazed a finger, he stopped, lifted his hand, wiggled the bleeding finger. "Your friend Ned is far better with a dagger than I am, eh? So is Stefan. He never misses. Ever."

Owen did not see. "And that is why you would stay in this life? Because you admire your friend's skill with the dagger?"

Edmund shook his head. "Because as a shipwright I shall not meet such a man again. Not likely. I shall meet only cautious men, out to make money and keep their families fed and housed. I can always go back to that. I could not find another Stefan." Edmund sucked on the finger. "Or you. It's been interesting meeting you. You looked such a rogue. I was sure one of us had to kill the other. And you decided to trust me."

Owen shook his head. "It was you decided to trust me, to bargain with me."

"A shipwright never needs to make such choices."

"Nor does he have to watch his back."

"That is your fault, Captain Archer. I had Jack cornered. He would have been dead if you had left me to it."

Owen did not need to be reminded of that.

At dawn the town was cool and full of intriguing shadows. Owen walked to St. Mary's graveyard with Ravenser, Edmund, and Alfred, expecting nothing to come of this deed. But he must try it, must put to rest the feeling that there was more in that grave than Ravenser and Louth had noticed.

Old Dan was already at the site, digging, his son with him. The grave was at the edge of the yard, shaded by a tree. Owen looked up at the buildings facing the grave. Sides and backs of houses at a slight distance, no main street nearby. Unless a neighbor had been out relieving himself in the dark, a burial at night might be accomplished here unheeded.

"There he is, just as we left him," said Old Dan, stepping back.

Owen stepped forward, covering his lower face against the sickeningly sweet smell of rotting flesh, and looked down at the huge, decomposing body. The man had been taller than average and fat, with a barrel-shaped torso and muscular legs. The face was decomposing. It was damp here between the Beck and the Walkerbeck. The bodies would go quickly. The head was at an unnatural angle. "Jaro?" Owen asked, glancing at Edmund.

Edmund nodded. "Jaro indeed. I told you he was a good cook."

Owen averted his head and took a deep breath, then crouched down at the top of the grave, motioning for Alfred and Edmund to go to the feet. "He will be heavy. Let's lift him out by the shroud if we can, if it's not rotten yet."

Old Dan knelt down beside Owen, gasping at the stench. "With four it'll be easier."

They heaved, the shroud held, they lowered and got better grips, then heaved and swung the body to the side of the grave. It landed with a moist thud.

"Sweet Heaven," Ravenser said. Beneath Jaro was a bloodstained shroud, spread open, empty. But round the top edge curled fingers, torn and bloody. The outline of a man's head and torso was plain beneath the sheet.

Owen lifted the sheet from the side, avoiding the hands. It was a man, his face distorted in terror, mouth wide open—tongueless, eyes bulging, torso arched upward in the middle. The man had only one leg. "I think we have found Joanna's nightmare. The man buried alive—Will Longford." He turned aside, took a deep breath.

"Deus juva me," Edmund whispered, falling to his knees beside Owen.

"Whoever did it used Jaro's bulk to weigh Longford down," Owen said. "And he was not alone."

Ravenser made the sign of the cross and said a prayer.

"Now what?" Edmund asked.

Owen stood up, dusted his knees. "Now I am most anxious to return to York and find out how Joanna knew of this."

Scaffolds and tents of stonemasons and other artisans cluttered the front and south side of Beverley Minster. Owen walked past the foundations of the front towers and passed into the nave. It was high and long, filled with summer light.

A stonecutter working inside pointed him toward the north aisle. "My father did his best work down there."

Owen discovered intricate carvings of musicians, human and animal, fashioned with a sense of humor. Their expressions and gestures were so lively he strained to hear the music.

He moved slowly down the nave, studying the figures. At the shrine of St. John of Beverley he paused, knelt down, said a prayer.

"You were looking for me?"

Owen rose to greet the priest who had found Joanna's medal. "I wished to ask you about a nun you may have encountered a year past. She lost a medal in your churchyard."

The young priest nodded. "I know you are somehow connected with her. An odd story, her death and resurrection."

"She did not die, Father. You do know that?"

The priest shrugged. "We all believe as our conscience leads us, Captain Archer. Yes, I do remember her. She had removed her veil and knelt in the mud when I found her. I had no idea what had happened. The man who came for the medal told me a boy had tried to steal it, she had frightened him, it had dropped in the mud. But she told me only that she must catch up with her companions."

"Companions?"

The priest shrugged. "A nun never travels alone."

"But you saw no companions?"

The priest shook his head.

"The man. Tell me about him."

"Tall, fair, built much like you. I guessed him to be a soldier. Perhaps her lover." He closed his eyes and clucked his disapproval. "It happens all too often."

"And yet you think she died and was reborn?"

The priest spread his hands wide. "Christ brought the Magdalene into a new life. This child valued her Magdalene medal. Perhaps her patron saint interceded to save Dame Joanna's soul. I have heard of the miracle of St. Clement's."

Owen ignored that. "You know nothing more of the man?"

"Nothing."

"Did anyone else ever come seeking the medal. Or the nun?"

The priest shook his head. "She is back at St. Clement's now?"

"She is in York, under the archbishop's protection."

"St. Clement's will be the richer for her return. In every way. God is benevolent."

Owen stayed in the minster after the priest had gone, watching the dust dance in sunbeams. This fascination with Joanna's supposed miracle made him uneasy, made him doubt all miracles. Were they all such wrongheaded rumors? How could one ever know which ones were true? Which ones false? And what about the mantle? So many thought it truly Our Lady's mantle. How many other relics were frauds? He crossed himself and tried to pray, but went back to staring at the stone musicians. At least they felt right and true.

20

HOMECOMING

Lucie was in the shop, bent over her mortar and pestle, crushing lovage root.

"Mistress Wilton!"

Jasper de Melton stood in the doorway, his blond hair almost white from summer days in Brother Wulfstan's garden learning herb lore along with his reading and writing.

"Have you completed your errands?" Lucie asked.

"I delivered the rosemary to Mistress Merchet. She gave me a meat pie for my troubles. And Mistress Katherine, the laundress, says the kitten is most likely from her cat's litter, and we are welcome to him."

"Him? Is she certain?"

"She says all the orange and white cats from her litters are male. Always."

Lucie smiled. "I have know an orange female to sneak in from time to time."

Jasper shrugged, took a few steps into the shop. "Are you busy?"

"Of course I am busy, Jasper, but with no customers in here I should welcome your company."

Happily the boy came round the counter and hoisted himself up onto a stool. He leaned close to the mortar and sniffed. "Strong."

Lucie nodded. "Can you guess what it is?"

Jasper sniffed again, shook his head.

"Lovage root. Do you know what it does?"

"Makes you look fair to the one you love."

Lucie bit back a smile. "Did Brother Wulfstan tell you this?"

"No. Mistress Fletcher did."

Ah. The woman who owned the room Jasper and his mother had lived in. "And why did she tell you this?"

"Not me, my mother. She said mother should bathe in lovage to be even more beautiful, so Master Crounce would marry her."

"So what has Brother Wulfstan told you of lovage?"

"I cannot remember."

Lucie glanced up, hearing the hush in Jasper's voice that signaled tears. It was the memory of his mother. "I am making this up for Thomas the Tanner, who is long married with four children. Do you think he wants to look more fair to Mistress Ann?"

Jasper shook his head.

Lucie had hoped for at least a smile, but this past week, so full of memories of his mother's last illness, a smile would be difficult. Lucie too had a time of year when she found it difficult to stop thinking about the past—late November, when her first husband had been struck down. "Thomas has swollen hands and feet by day's end, so I am preparing something to help rid him of water."

Jasper nodded.

Not a time for instruction. Lucie touched his shoulder, pointed to the corner of a shelf behind her. A ball of white and orange fluff was tucked into the spot where she had removed the jar of lovage. Jasper jumped up to pet the kitten, who at once began a loud, rumbling purr. The boy rubbed his forehead against the kitten. "He is soft as down." The voice was calm now, gentle with affection.

It was just the reaction Lucie had hoped for. "What would you like to name him?"

Jasper lifted his head, looked at Lucie with surprise. "I am to name him?"

"I should like that."

"Why?"

"I thought you might take particular care of him in these next months, when I shall be quite busy."

Jasper glanced at her widening middle, then quickly turned back to the kitten.

Lucie winced at her clumsiness. She had brought up another

topic that put him in mind of his mother. At least she recognized it. At first she had not understood why Jasper reacted oddly to any mention of the baby; it was Bess who reminded Lucie that Jasper's mother had been pregnant when she died, and worse, it had been the baby who poisoned her.

"What other herb lore did you learn from Mistress Fletcher?"

Still stroking the kitten, Jasper said softly, "That 'He who would live for aye/ Must eat sage in May.'"

"Live forever? I had no idea."

"And she gave Mother sprigs of St. John's Wort to keep under her pillow and dream of her future husband."

"In case it was not to be Will Crounce?"

Jasper nodded.

"What else?" Surely there were some that did not remind him of his mother. "What about rue? Such a powerful herb, she must have had some words about rue."

"Rue grows best when it's stolen."

Lucie laughed. "No! Truly?"

Jasper turned round, gave a tearful smile. Lucie dropped the pestle and put her hands out. He ran to her and hugged her tight.

"I shall be fine, Jasper. Magda Digby says both mother and child are healthy, she sees no signs of trouble. I am not going to leave you." She stroked his flaxen hair. His arms tightened round her.

"Now that's a fine thing to come home to. My wife in the arms of another man."

Lucie and Jasper both looked up with smiles as Owen filled the doorway.

Dusty and smelling of horse, Lucie thought she had never loved him more than at that moment. She hurried round the counter. He dropped his pack, pressed his hands on either side of her face and kissed her hard. "I have missed you," he whispered.

Tears in her eyes, Lucie just nodded and took his arms, put them round her. "A hug will not crush me."

Owen hugged her with care, covered her face with kisses. Then he looked over at Jasper. "You have taken good care of my lady, Jasper. How shall I repay you?"

"Take me to the butts this Sunday to watch you train the men?" The boy's eyes were hopeful.

"Is that all you require?"

The boy nodded.

"Would that all debts might be settled so pleasantly."

Jasper's face lit up.

Lucie squeezed Owen's arm in thanks.

Lucie had fallen asleep as soon as she lay down on the bed, but she woke during the night and opened the shutters, letting the moonlight shine on Owen, the dark hair on his chest and arms, the way his hair curled about his temples and along his chin. *Blessed Mary, Mother of God, thank you for guiding him safely home.*

Owen's right eye fluttered open. Seeing Lucie sitting up, he asked sleepily, "Are you unwell?"

"I am well. And content. You had a long journey. Do not let me keep you up."

"You have trouble sleeping?"

"Now and then. Magda says it might become more frequent toward the end and is nothing to worry about."

"But you must keep up your strength."

"Owen, do not worry."

He propped his head up on one elbow. "You said in your letter that Jasper was to stay for Corpus Christi and then return to the abbey school. I did not expect him to be here still."

"He wished to stay a while longer. Wulfstan and I agreed that it is best to let Jasper decide for himself where he wishes to be. At present it is here."

Owen stroked Lucie's bare leg. "The moonlight makes your skin quite magical."

Lucie wiggled her toes. "It makes me feel quite magical. I like the middle of the night. Sometimes. When you are here." She was angry with herself the moment she said it. She had never been one to whine before.

"I promise not to leave again before the baby comes."

There. She had made him feel guilty about having been away on the archbishop's business. She had seen the light in his eyes today. He was tired, disturbed by what he had learned, but refreshed by the experience. It seemed a small price to pay to have him content when he was at home. "You were wonderful with Jasper today. Try as I will, I cannot bring such a smile to his face."

"I am glad he wants to stay."

"I have asked him to name the kitten."

Owen shifted onto his side. "I confess you puzzle me with the kitten. Melisende seems enough cat for anyone. We are never plagued by mice."

"The kitten will follow Melisende and learn to be a good mouser." Lucie ran her hand down Owen's side. "You will like it."

"What is there to like or not like about a cat? When they have no mice to torment, they fuss and bother and go off hunting for days and worry you."

About to say that Melisende was good company while Owen was away, Lucie caught herself, thanks be to God, and just shrugged. "Jasper has taken to the kitten."

"I begrudge you and Jasper nothing that makes you happy." Owen sat up. "You have asked me very little about Scarborough and Beverley."

"I wanted you to choose the time. When you were rested, ready to think about it again."

"Hugh Calverley is dead. So is Longford."

"Jesu. The toll keeps rising."

"I want to tell Joanna. Can she speak?"

"When I saw her yesterday, she was able to whisper. By tomorrow her voice might be even stronger."

"Good."

Lucie frowned, picked at the edge of her shawl, remembering the horror that followed hard upon the news of Joanna's mother's death. Another thing she could not speak of to Owen. She had purposely been vague in her letter about whether she had seen Joanna's wounds. "I suppose we cannot delay telling her."

Owen slipped an arm round Lucie. "You are thinking about what happened before, when we told her of her mother's death."

Lucie nodded, snuggled against Owen's warm body. "We must tell her."

"We must confront her with it, Lucie. She has spoken of someone buried alive."

Lucie crossed herself. *Let it not be Hugh.*

"You are not asking me," Owen said, trying to see her expression.

Lucie took a deep breath. "I want to know, but it is such a horrible question." *Which one was alive when they buried him?* She shook her head.

"It was Longford."

"Will Longford." Lucie crossed herself again, grateful the dream had been wrong. "I am glad it was not her brother."

"Hugh was not a kindly person, Lucie. No better than Longford it seems."

Lucie clutched her shawl tighter. She had also not told him about her nightmare. She could not rid herself of that vision of Joanna burying her brother alive. "Where was Longford buried?"

"Beneath Jaro."

"But they had opened Jaro's grave."

"And had not looked closely. He was not visible without shifting Jaro. It took four of us to lift Jaro from the grave—he was one of the fattest men I have ever seen. Longford must have been unconscious, they spread a winding sheet smoothly over him, put Jaro in a shroud, covered them with dirt."

"Even so, Longford was a strong man, wasn't he?"

Owen took her hand, kissed the palm. "Perhaps I have told you enough, Lucie."

"It is that horrible?" Oh Lord, she sounded like a weak, silly fool. "I have seen horrible things, Owen. Tell me."

He gently smoothed her hair back from her face. "But in your condition…"

"I must know everything if I am to speak with Joanna."

Owen pressed her hand. "True enough. You are right that Longford was a strong man, and a large one; but he weighed far less than Jaro. To ensure that he stayed in the grave, they had crushed his only leg—and he had injuries to his back that might have made it impossible to move. His hands are bruised and his fingers torn, so perhaps only his leg was affected. And just to be safe, in case all that did not keep him buried, they had removed his tongue so he could name no one."

Lucie dropped her head in her hands, horrified at the brutality. "What sort of men did this?" It was plain that Joanna could not have done all this.

Owen shook his head. "It was as cold-blooded a murder as I have seen. Do you know, I hope we learn that it had something to do with his support of du Guesclin, that it was something political, not personal. I do not want to know that someone hated Longford enough to do that."

Lucie considered the effort that had gone into such a deed. "I do not think you will get your wish. If you had been ordered to get rid of someone like Longford, would you have taken such time, exercised such cruelty?"

"There are men who delight in cruelty. Like the man who murdered Maddy."

Maddy. She had forgotten to ask about her. "You know who did it?"

"A worm of a man, Lucie. According to Edmund, the man killed Maddy just to make it easier to search the house."

"Jesus, Mary and Joseph, watch over Maddy's soul," Lucie whispered. "Who is Edmund?"

"One of the men who helped Joanna escape Beverley."

"Stefan's partner?"

"Aye. One of Sebastian's men. As is Jack, Maddy's murderer."

"Will this Jack be punished? Even though Maddy was just a servant?"

"If Sir Richard and Sir Nicholas have their way, yes. But to show you what a fool I've been while away, I stopped Edmund in the act of attacking Jack."

"What?"

"I heartily regret it, believe me. He now shadows Edmund."

"You must catch him, Owen. He must pay."

"I am hoping he does something foolish. Alfred is trailing after

Edmund, watching."

"Is Jack alone?"

"I do not know. But I doubt it."

"This is all such a nightmare."

Owen hugged Lucie. "God grant me the wits to resolve this quickly. Joanna has much to tell us. We must find out how she knew about Longford's burial."

Best to do it soon. "Shall we go to her in the morning?"

"I should like to. And then I want Edmund to see her."

"I am curious to meet him."

"Then you will tomorrow."

"Why did Stefan not come?"

"He has vanished. That is why Edmund was willing to come with me." Owen put his arm around Lucie. She rested her head on his shoulder. "Are you strong enough yet to go on with Joanna?"

With all her whining, of course he would ask. "I am quite strong enough."

"Good. I want you to use all your wiles to reach her, find out what she is hiding. Where is Stefan? Who murdered Longford and Jaro?"

Lucie tried to push the horror aside and think clearly. "Longford and Jaro were murdered by strong men."

"Soldiers, I would guess. Perhaps some of Sebastian's men. But why?"

Lucie bit her lip, thinking. "Might Edmund and Stefan be the murderers?"

Owen shook his head. "I think I know Edmund, traveling with him all this time. He would kill quickly, wishing to be done with it. And then he would run to a confessor."

"But does that not depend on what Longford had done? Might it be revenge for a similar act?"

"I cannot say for certain that I know his heart, Lucie. But I think such a deed would haunt Edmund, and he would have been driven to confess it to me."

Lucie sighed, squeezed Owen. "Now let's talk of pleasant things so I might go back to sleep."

• • •

The hospitaler shook his head at the sprig of mistletoe on the floor just inside Joanna's door. "Dame Prudentia is sadly superstitious." Mistletoe placed so ensured quiet, pleasant dreams. When Lucie was a little girl, her Aunt Phillippa had used mistletoe to ward off nightmares. But Lucie did not comment. Nor did she mention the angelica that she and Wulfstan had sprinkled in the four corners of the room to exorcise the demons that troubled Joanna.

The curtains had been removed from Joanna's bed to give her more air in the warm July weather and to make it easier to watch her. Dame Agnes, the subprioress, sat the watch this morning. She turned her cheery face toward Lucie and Owen.

"Joanna slept peacefully through the night. She woke at dawn, drank some watered wine, and fell back into a peaceful sleep."

Lucie was pleased. "May we be alone with her for a while? You might wish to walk out in the fresh morning air."

Agnes needed no coaxing. She blessed them and hurried away.

Dame Joanna lay with her hands crossed over her chest. The white bandage round her neck looked like a gorget, nothing more, it was so clean. Her face was pale from loss of blood and a month in bed, but the haggard look was gone.

"'Tis a shame to wake her," Owen whispered.

Joanna opened her eyes. "I am thirsty." Her voice was raspy, not unusual in one who has just awakened.

Owen sat on the stool beside her bed, reached over and poured her some wine and water. "Shall we lift you to drink?"

"Yes."

Owen handed the cup to Lucie, who went to the other side of the bed. As Owen lifted Joanna, Lucie put the cup to her lips. She sipped the wine, frowning a little with each swallow.

"Your throat—is it still very sore?" Lucie asked.

"Better," Joanna whispered.

Lucie met Owen's eye, explained. "She pressed down so hard with the dull knife she bruised her throat. That is taking longer to heal than the cuts."

Joanna pushed the cup away. "Enough."

Owen gently lowered Joanna's head.

Joanna closed her eyes.

Owen leaned toward her. "I am returned from my pilgrimage of disgrace, Dame Joanna."

She opened her eyes, so startlingly green. "A pilgrimage?" Her face was expressionless, her voice too hoarse to read the nuances.

"You called it that, do you remember? A pilgrimage of disgrace?"

"I say foolish things."

"I have been to Scarborough. Where you traveled with Stefan and Edmund."

Joanna closed her eyes. "I have been ill."

"You tried to take your life. I know."

The eyelids shot open. "I am bedeviled. The Devil is strong. Even wrapped in the Virgin's mantle he reaches me." Joanna's eyes flashed with anger, her cheeks flushed.

Owen thought it odd she felt anger rather than fear. He glanced up at Lucie, who raised her eyebrows and pressed her lips together as if to say, "Who knows?"

"A pilgrimage of disgrace. Whose disgrace, Joanna?"

Still angry. "You do not listen."

"I do. I listen well, and I remember. Perhaps it is you who forgets. Let me remind you of something. Hugh was murdered. In his house near Scarborough."

"My knight. My champion." Joanna's eyes filled with tears.

It was a quiet response, sad, not shocked. "Who is your champion, Joanna? Hugh?"

She closed her eyes, looked away. Tears wet her lashes, dampened her cheeks.

"Who are you thinking of as your knight and champion?"

Joanna took a deep, shuddering breath. "Hugh is dead. There is nothing more."

"You and Stefan left Scarborough at the same time that Hugh was killed. Why?"

Joanna turned back to Owen, looked at him, offended. "You

cannot think I wished him dead."

"What should I think?"

"The Devil wants me dead, too." Her eyes challenged him.

"Who killed your brother?"

Joanna blushed. "I am thirsty."

She played with them. Owen would have liked to withhold the wine, make her uncomfortable. But she needed the wine to speak. He sighed, lifted her up, Lucie helped her drink.

When Joanna was settled again, Owen tried another path. "You have spoken of someone buried alive. Who did you think was buried alive, Joanna?"

"I was."

"Who else, Joanna?"

She frowned, dropped her eyes to her hands. "He used me."

"Who did?"

Joanna rocked her head back and forth on the pillow. "I should never have left St. Clement's."

Owen touched her head gently, stilling it. "Why should you not have left? What happened to you while you were away?"

Tears again. "I am not worthy to be called Dame Joanna. I cuckolded my divine bridegroom."

She moved away from Owen's purpose. "It is Longford who was buried alive. But I am certain you know that," he said.

Joanna's eyes changed, grew wary. She clutched the Magdalene medal. "Will Longford?"

"He was buried beneath his servant, Jaro."

"No." Joanna turned away.

Owen grasped her chin, made her face him. Her neck was rigid with fear. Owen did not let that stop him. "Longford's leg was crushed and his spine had been damaged. I think he could barely move from the waist down, if at all. His tongue had been cut out so he could not reveal his torturers if someone found him."

Joanna's head trembled in his hand. She gasped for air.

"We must lift her chest and head, Owen," Lucie said, leaning over to help.

While Owen held Joanna up, causing a coughing fit, Lucie

added pillows, then helped her sip some wine. Owen lowered her.

Joanna still clutched the medal. "Why do you tell me this?"

"About Will Longford? Because you knew that he had not been dead when he was put in that grave. How did you know, Joanna? Who told you? Who committed this careful, cruel murder?"

Joanna held the medal up to Owen. "Christ was cruel to Mary Magdalene."

Owen bit back a curse. "You may rest now, Joanna. But I shall be back tomorrow." He went to the door, called for Dame Agnes.

But it was the Reverend Mother who came hurrying down the hall. "I have sent Agnes to bed. I shall stay with Joanna today."

"She is agitated, Reverend Mother. Perhaps someone should stay with you."

Isobel peeked in the room, saw Lucie patting Joanna's face with a damp cloth. "No doubt you are right, Captain. Would you ask Brother Oswald to send for Prudentia?" As Owen turned to do so, Isobel stayed him with a touch on his arm. "But first, please tell me what has agitated her. Agnes said she had had a peaceful night."

Owen told her of the news they had been forced to impart.

The Reverend Mother crossed herself, whispered a prayer, then tucked her hands in her sleeves, shook her head. "This is a terrible business. I thought I was a strong woman, but this has given the lie to that. It is your wife who is strong. Called out so early in the morning, in her condition, to deal with the horror of what Joanna had done. All that blood…" Isobel took a step backward. She had never noticed what a piercing eye Owen had. Perhaps that is why God took one away.

Owen trembled with rage. "Lucie was called in the middle of the night to tend Joanna?" He worked hard to keep his voice low. "Do you realize that my wife is with child? And you called her out in the middle of the night to a woman around whom people have been dying in unusual numbers?"

Isobel crossed herself. "I make no excuse for my weakness, Captain Archer. But it was Abbot Campian who sent for Mistress Wilton, not I."

"He sent an escort?"

"I do not know."

• • •

Lucie would have been blind not to see Owen's anger as they walked back to the shop. The expression on his face was murderous, the hand that did not support her was balled into a fist, his strides kept lengthening until she was forced to ask him to slow down, and all the way the ominous silence. It had not taken her long to guess what had transpired. Owen had returned to Joanna's room with Dame Isobel. By then his temper had flared. The Reverend Mother must have told him of Lucie's early morning visit. It was the very thing that would put him in such a temper, which was why Lucie had not told him. There was nothing for it now but to let him stew about it and finally burst out. To bring it up would only make it worse.

Lucie was perversely relieved when Tildy met her with the news that Thomas the Tanner was worse, and the physician, Master Saurian, had been called in. He had left a prescription for her to fill, a poultice to be applied after bloodletting.

"I must do this at once, Owen."

He nodded, turned on his heel, left the shop. Lucie and Tildy exchanged a look.

"He's in such a temper, Mistress Lucie."

"That he is, Tildy, but it's naught to do with you, so don't fret about it. I shall be in the shop."

As Lucie scurried about the shop gathering the ingredients, she began to hum. When Owen was in such a temper, it was a blessed relief to be away from him.

Tom Merchet brought two tankards to the table in the kitchen and invited Owen to sit, "Before you put one of those big hams through a wall. Sit down and have your say. Bess is upstairs teaching Kit the proper scrubbing of a floor or some such. She'll not bother us."

Owen lowered himself onto a bench. "There are things I should be doing."

Tom pushed the tankard under his friend's nose, then paused, his hand hovering above it. "Pity, wasting good ale on one who is not of a mind to appreciate it." He shrugged, settled his hands round his own tankard. His round, pleasant face was creased with worry. "Though if it's to do with the baby, I shall be of no use to you, having none of my own. As the babe gets older I might be useful. Bess came to me with little ones. I know what they're about." Tom smiled into his cup. "As well as a man ever does."

Owen finally looked up at his companion. "What are you going on about?"

Tom shrugged, took a long drink, nodded with satisfaction as he lowered his tankard. "Never you mind, just tell me what's to do."

"Lucie went to the abbey in the middle of the night to take care of that nun."

"Last night? When you'd just come home?"

"No. While I was gone."

Tom pulled on his bottom lip, thinking. "Middle of night, you say? But abbeys have infirmarians and all manner of folk about. What did they need with Lucie?"

Owen shook his head, disgusted. "And in her condition, Tom."

Tom made properly indignant noises.

"Worse than that, Lucie did not tell me. I thought she had seen Joanna once she had been cleaned and bandaged. But Lucie examined her, Tom. Got her hands in all that blood. What will that do to the child, Lucie looking at all that blood? And the horror of it all? The nun stabbing herself." Owen put his head in his hands. "Dear Lord, Lucie is impossible."

"Drink up, Owen."

Owen raised the tankard to his lips, stopped. "Do you remember when she took a boat over to the Riverwoman in the midst of the flooding last year?"

"At night." Tom nodded. "I remember. Drink up, my friend." He smiled as Owen tilted the tankard and drank deep. Another good gulp like that and the man would feel a bit smoother. Tom knew just how Owen felt. Lucie and Bess were nothing alike and every bit alike.

Stubborn, clever women. Bess's sturdy body and loud mouth did not inspire quite the same protective feelings Owen felt for Lucie, so thin and pretty and quiet, but a good wife was hard to come by and Tom had his moments of wishing Bess were not so forward with strangers. When Owen clanked the tankard down, empty, Tom reached for the pitcher and filled it again. "Now. Did Lucie go of her own accord, just having a feeling that something was wrong, or was she summoned?"

"Summoned. But that—" Owen paused as Tom shook his head.

"It makes all the difference, my friend. Lucie is an apothecary. She has the cure of bodies as the vicar has the cure of souls. Not like a physician, I grant you that, but Dame Isobel and His Grace ask for Lucie because she calms Joanna as no one else can. 'Tis a God-given gift, Owen, and Lucie must not hold it back." Tom took a breath. It was an uncommonly long speech for him. He winced as the hawk eye bored through him. "I just say what you know yourself."

Owen leaned his head back against the wall, rubbed the scar, grabbed the tankard and took another drink. "At least I had the sense to come to you before I opened my mouth to Lucie and let my spleen come tumbling out. I would not let her see that, not now." He stretched his foot out and rested it on a stool.

Tom judged it time to change the topic. "I saw Sir Robert head over to the garden a while ago. How does he get on with Lucie? About Corbett's house?"

Owen made an embarrassed face. "I've not asked." He sat up straighter, frowning. "Now why did Sir Robert not stop her that night?"

Tom sighed. His ale had been wasted in this effort to calm Owen. "That one I cannot answer. You must needs speak with your wife."

Lucie was closing the door to the shop when she saw Owen outside, leaning against the wall. "Why are you standing out there?"

Owen shrugged and followed her in, closing and barring the door for her. Lucie, smiling, kissed him.

He frowned. "What was that for?"

"For worrying about me as you do." She picked up the broom to sweep the stone floor behind the counter.

Owen grabbed the broom from her. "How do you know?"

"You were angry after speaking with the Reverend Mother. I know what she might tell you to make you so. And I am sorry I did not tell you."

Owen paused as he began to sweep. "Jasper should be doing this."

Lucie shrugged. "Either of you. You are both my apprentices."

Owen shook his head, went back to sweeping, stopped again. "Tell me this. Why did Sir Robert not stop you?"

"Because I convinced Daimon that Sir Robert need not know. In truth, Brother Sebastian led us with such urgency that Sir Robert could not have kept up with us."

"And you in your condition? Are you to be running down the streets in the middle of the night?"

"I did not run." Lucie took off her apron. "And now I must go up and lie down before supper. If you wish to continue this, you must come up."

Owen followed her.

She lay down on the bed and asked him to pile several cushions under her feet. He sat down beside her, took her cap off, smoothed back her hair.

"Tell me what you saw."

Lucie described the room, the overwhelming odor of blood, the neck, the womb.

"Why her womb?"

"I do not know, Owen. I feel that I know nothing about Joanna. I have spoken to her so often, yet I cannot even tell you what makes her laugh, what she likes to eat… I do know what she hopes for—death."

"You should not be with such people now."

Lucie closed her eyes. "I am not about to break apart, Owen."

"She will give you nightmares."

"She already has."

"You see?"

Lucie propped herself up on her elbows. "Stop a moment, listen." She described the dream.

"You see? What will the baby be like with you dreaming such dreams?"

"Owen, for pity's sake, you are going to drive me mad! Can you imagine what sort of thoughts my mother had while she carried me? Do you think in all that time she did not remember the soldiers raping and torturing the women in her convent? And her brother impaled on a pike? What of all the women of Normandy who gave birth while they trembled in their houses wondering if their village would be the next one put to the torch? I am not ill! Your mother had many children. You tell me she barely paused in her daily chores to give birth."

"She was not dealing with madwomen."

"She was dealing with you!"

"Well, if I am mad, it's you who has driven me to it."

Lucie suddenly felt laughter bubbling up from deep within. She grabbed either side of Owen's beard and pulled him down to kiss him.

He raised himself a little, stared into her laughing eyes. "It is *you* are going mad."

"No. I am just content. This is more in the tradition of your homecomings." She pulled him down again.

Dame Isobel jerked awake. Joanna moaned and squirmed in her sleep. Brother Wulfstan had advised a strong sleep potion tonight, and Isobel had duly give it to Joanna. Her dream must be troubling indeed. *Merciful Mother, do not let her harm herself.* Isobel leaned over Joanna, took her hands. "'Tis but a dream, Joanna. Mary and all the angels protect you. And the mistletoe. We have put the mistletoe in the doorway."

Side to side, side to side the head thrashed. "Evil. Evil. Evil. Evil. Evil. Evil. Evil…"

21

STEADFASTNESS

It was early morning, and Tildy bustled about the kitchen while Lucie, Owen, and Edmund argued about Edmund's meeting with Joanna.

Edmund sat stiff and rigid, carefully groomed for the occasion, his thinning hair smoothed down with perfumed oil. He wore a houppelande of light brown, plain, but well cut and almost new. "I would rather be alone with Joanna. She will be distracted by others in the room."

Lucie admitted that might be true, "But Joanna is easily thrown into confusion. She is comforted by my presence. You will be the better for it." She wondered about Edmund's feelings for Joanna.

"I should be there," Owen said to Lucie. "I know Edmund's story."

And had perhaps become too fond of him to judge him. "You are too abrupt with Joanna," Lucie said. "She will be agitated, no matter how well we plan this. But with me there is a chance she will stay calm longer."

Edmund tapped the table nervously. "It is a private matter. I wish to speak with her alone."

Owen shook his head. "Nothing in Joanna's life is a private matter until we learn what she knows about the deaths that have occurred in her wake. She teases us with knowledge of them. We must come to an understanding."

Lucie should have more faith in Owen's ability to handle Joanna, but she could not shake the feeling that he would frighten her deeper into her shell and they would be back where they had begun. "We must not swoop down on her like hawks," Lucie warned, "or we will frighten her." She turned from Owen's irritated glare and faced Edmund. "Still, you must see that either Owen or I should be there. We must observe how Joanna behaves when she sees you, what she says. Perhaps she was not so when you were with her, but now she speaks in riddles and digressions. It would be difficult for you to remember all of it, and you might forget something of great significance to us. Your purpose is different. You seek your friend; we seek to learn much more."

Edmund looked down at his hands. "I had hoped to see her alone." His voice rang with disappointment. Again Lucie wondered about his feelings toward Joanna.

Owen stretched his legs out beside the table, leaned against the wall, his arms folded. Lucie noted that he had removed his earring, a sign that he was settled back into his life in York. She smiled to see it. Owen caught her eye, nodded. "You are thinking that it is most appropriate that a woman be with Joanna in the room, and thus you win your plea."

How wrong he was, but how dull she would sound if she told him her true thoughts. "There, you see? We are agreed without further argument."

Edmund shrugged.

Brother Oswald greeted the threesome with news of the Reverend Mother's long night with Dame Joanna. "Not, praise God, as before. This time it was a bloodless wakening, a whispered chant of 'evil, evil, evil.' The Reverend Mother apologizes that she is not here to greet you, but she required sleep."

"Who now sits with Dame Joanna?" Lucie asked.

"Dame Prudentia. And Brother Wulfstan has been within for a short while. You will find him there."

Owen folded himself into a bench outside the door to wait.

Lucie knocked. Prudentia opened the door and cheered up at the sight of the apothecary. "God be with you, Mistress Wilton. Our poor Joanna has just now wakened and Brother Wulfstan has coaxed her to drink some broth. She will be ready for you soon, thanks be the Lord." She spoke in a loud whisper, with much glancing back at the old monk sitting in the chair by Joanna's bedside. "I had worried that she was given far too much sedative last night to ever waken this day, but Brother Wulfstan assures me that the tisane is mild."

Brother Wulfstan turned round, saw that it was Lucie, and rose, giving a blessing in greeting. Lucie motioned him over to her, introduced Edmund in a hushed voice. "How is Joanna? Do we waste our time trying to speak with her today?"

The morning sun shone on Wulfstan's face, lighting up the white stubble where the razor met the myriad wrinkles ever more visible on his face. His eyes were kindly. "It is a good day for her, strange to say. At least I believe I have had the first clear speech with her this morning. She asked me whether God understands that we can be mistaken in those we love, and whether God would accept her repentance for deeds done unwittingly for the Evil One."

Lucie glanced over at Joanna, who lay back against the pillows, eyes closed. "The Evil One?"

Wulfstan nodded. "May God lead you to the truth, Lucie." He blessed Lucie and Edmund, then touched Prudentia's arm. "Come. Let us leave them to their work."

There were two chairs by the bed, one on either side, the far one by the window, the near one by the small table that held the spirit lamp and Joanna's medicines. Lucie motioned to Edmund to sit in the far chair, so that Joanna could clearly see him in the daylight. He crossed the foot of the bed without Joanna's notice. Lucie sat down and called Joanna's name.

The green eyes flickered open. "Mistress Wilton." Joanna looked beyond Lucie. "The Captain has not returned with more terrible tidings?" Her voice was hoarse, but rose above a whisper today. Lucie helped Joanna to watered wine.

"I have brought you a different visitor today. He has come a long way to speak with you. I hope you will be kind to him."

Joanna frowned, reached with her stubby fingers for the Magdalene medal. "Where?"

Lucie nodded toward the other side of the bed. Joanna turned her head, frowned, then her eyes opened wide. "Sweet Mary in Heaven!"

Edmund, looking solemn, gave Joanna a little bow. "Joanna. Or is it Dame Joanna again?"

"Would that anything could be as it was." Joanna's eyes shimmered with tears. "Have you come to bury me again?"

Edmund earnestly reached out to her, "Faith, I never wanted any part of that pretending."

Joanna shrank from him, turned back to Lucie. "He must leave," she said firmly.

"Why?" Lucie asked. "He befriended you once."

"No!" Joanna spoke now in a loud whisper, stretching her right hand across the covers to Lucie. "None of them befriended me. They lied. They stole my soul."

Lucie put her hand in Joanna's, but resisted when Joanna tried to pull her uncomfortably close. "No one took your soul, Joanna. You lie here before me alive, with your immortal soul still to answer for."

Joanna shook her head in an exaggerated manner, like a spoiled child. "No. I have no soul. No longer."

"Joanna, please tell me where Stefan is," Edmund implored. "Then I shall leave you in peace."

Joanna turned to him, suddenly smiling. "Leave me in peace? Truly, sweet knight, what peace might I have?"

Edmund hesitated, frowning in puzzlement over Joanna's shifting mood.

Joanna clutched the medal, bowed her head to it.

Edmund reached for her, touched the mantle.

Joanna pulled it away from him. "Do you understand what you touch?"

Edmund smiled engagingly. "'Tis the very mantle I gave you when we were on the road to Scarborough."

"You?" Joanna looked shocked. "Never!" She sat bolt upright, wrapping the mantle more tightly round her. To Lucie she said, "You see? Pernicious liars. We must not trust them. We can neither sleep nor turn our heads. They must die. What else is there for it?" She turned back to Edmund, who was looking alarmed. "The Blessed

Virgin Mary draped it round my shoulders when my soul was taken away. I was very cold."

Edmund crossed himself. "God forgive me, I did say it was Our Lady's. You were so frightened and cold. I wished to comfort you."

"And now you try to trick me and take it from me. You have heard about the miracles the mantle has performed and you covet it."

"'Tis not Our Lady's mantle, Joanna," Edmund cried. "I had it from a weaver in Beverley."

Joanna hunched her shoulders and drew up her knees. With both hands she held the Magdalene medal up to her forehead.

Lucie understood Edmund's frustration. "We must be patient." She smoothed Joanna's hair. "All Edmund wishes to know is where Stefan is, Joanna. He is missing."

Joanna peered up at Lucie. "Stefan was evil. So was Longford."

Lucie could see that Joanna used her to avoid speaking to Edmund. Lucie moved the spirit lamp so that it would light up Joanna's face, and then stood. "I shall leave you two to speak." She moved to the chair by the door, far from them, in the shadow.

Joanna lay still for a time, then turned to see whether Edmund was still there. When she saw him waiting patiently, she laughed at him. "I know you. Steadfast Edmund."

"Steadfast is Stefan's virtue, not mine."

"Was a time I thought so. But when Hugh told me…" Joanna leaned toward Edmund with a solemn expression, as if about to reveal something of great import. "You see, Edmund, he told me everything."

Edmund shifted on the stool, looking uneasy. "Hugh? What did he tell you?"

Joanna wagged her finger at him. "Everything."

"What is everything?"

"Stefan meant to use me and then discard me." Joanna lay back against the pillows, covered her eyes with her hands for a moment, then dropped her hands at her sides as if exhausted.

"That had been our plan, I confess, but Stefan changed his mind. You know that. You left Scarborough with him. He would not have left with you if he still meant to discard you."

"And why not? We went down to the sea to watch the ships depart. Sebastian's ships. We often did that. And now. Now Stefan will ever and anon watch the ships go sailing off…" Joanna held the Magdalene medal up to Edmund. "Do you remember this? See this?" She held up the side depicting Mary Magdalene standing with Christ before His tomb; she pointed to the inscription. Edmund frowned at it. Joanna laughed. "You cannot read. Of course. Neither could Stefan. But he understood what it said. *Noli me tangere*. He knew that phrase full well."

Edmund looked honestly confused. "I do not understand."

"'Touch me not.' Christ said that to her. She had given everything for Him and He said that to her." Joanna's tone was neither amused nor angry, but rather indignant. "Mary Magdalene had found His tomb empty. Mine is not—did you know?"

Edmund leaned toward her, bringing his face so close to hers that she could not turn away. "Where is Stefan?" he asked, pronouncing each word distinctly.

"He destroyed my love," Joanna cried, her voice breaking. "And then I could not touch him."

Edmund sat back a little. "Stefan?"

Joanna studied the medal with sad eyes. "Stefan was not steadfast."

"He loves you, Joanna."

"*Noli me tangere*," Joanna whispered, holding the medal to her face.

Suddenly Edmund rose, grabbed the medal and yanked. "So help you truth and God, you shall answer me!" The chain broke.

Joanna screamed and lunged at him, raking his face with her fingernails.

Edmund grabbed Joanna's shoulders and shook her. "Tell me!"

Lucie ran to them. Owen burst through the door, saw the two locked together and Lucie's dangerous proximity, quickly pulled Edmund away. Joanna lunged for them. "Brother Oswald!" Owen shouted.

The hospitaler, who hovered in the doorway, rushed over and grabbed Joanna's hands, pressed her back against the pillows.

Owen, still holding Edmund by the shoulders, noticed the bloody streaks on his face. "What in God's name, Edmund?"

Edmund stared at Owen for a moment, unseeing. He touched his face, brought away a blood-speckled hand, looked down at the medal in his other hand. He sank down in the chair. "Holy Mary, Mother of God," he whispered, dropping the medal and covering his face with his hands.

Lucie did not know whom to attend first—Edmund, with his bleeding face, or Joanna, who sobbed hysterically. But Owen resolved Lucie's dilemma by asking for a damp cloth. He knelt down and dabbed at Edmund's scratches. Edmund submitted with embarrassed silence.

"Shall I stay?" Oswald asked. He had let go of Joanna but remained at the foot of the bed, watching her closely. "She is not yet calm."

"And she will not be for quite a time, I fear," Lucie said. "But I do not think we shall have any more violence. Perhaps if you wait in the corridor."

The hospitaler nodded and shuffled out.

Lucie knelt to Joanna, pulled damp strands of hair from her tear streaked face. Owen handed Lucie the Magdalene medal. Lucie placed it in Joanna's hand. Joanna clutched it to her heart. Her sobs subsided into hiccups. Lucie helped her to wine. "Lie there quietly for a while," Lucie whispered. Joanna nodded, lay back against the pillows. The bandage about her neck was bloodstained. Lucie unwrapped it, cleaned the wound, put a salve on it, wrapped it in a clean bandage.

Owen leaned against the bedpost, looking down at Edmund, who dabbed his own face now. "We shall see to those scratches by and by. For pity's sake, Edmund, what demon drove you to attack her?"

"She teases me. She knows what has become of Stefan and she will not say." Edmund pressed the cloth to his hot face, then balled it in his fist. "But no. She means none of it. She is surely mad."

Owen poured a cup of wine; Edmund took it gratefully and drank it down.

Joanna suddenly reached for Lucie's arm. "We needed but the seal was all," she whispered, her eyes imploring. "Why should he be so cruel? Faith, they did not bury me. Not truly."

"Who, Joanna?"

"Mother was right. She understood." Joanna glanced over at Edmund. "If Stefan loved me, why did he never offer marriage?"

Edmund, who held a cloth to his stinging scratches, shook his head. "How could he, Joanna? What of his wife and children?"

Joanna's green eyes were heavy-lidded. The sedative and her outburst were pulling her back down into sleep. "Wife and children? He never told me." She laughed weakly. "What a curse, to love so wrongly."

Lucie thanked God Joanna was too drugged to react emotionally, but she wished to ask one more thing before the eyes closed. "You mentioned a seal, Joanna. Tell me about it."

Joanna sighed. "Such a pathetic thing, to waste so many arrows on a frail man." The eyes closed; the words slurred.

"Saint Sebastian?"

Joanna smiled sleepily. "The captain is not so frail." She touched Lucie's arm. "Edmund the Steadfast asks after his friend, does he not?"

Edmund rose, hopeful.

"Yes," Lucie said, "he asks only that. Where is Stefan, Joanna?"

"Adrift on the sea. Adieu, sweet Stefan." The fingers on Lucie's arm went limp.

When Edmund stepped into the sunlight, Lucie shook her head at the welts rising round his scratches. "We must take you to Brother Wulfstan. A night in the infirmary would do you no harm."

Edmund kept glancing back at the guest house. "Did you hear her? Stefan is dead."

"'Adrift on the sea' might mean many things," Owen said. "Are you in pain?"

"It does not matter."

Owen and Lucie exchanged a look, nodded, headed Edmund to the infirmary.

• • •

After the night office, Wulfstan stopped in the infirmary to check on Edmund. Henry had done an excellent job of applying the plaster to the scratches and Edmund appeared to sleep peacefully. Sleep was the best restorative. Since Edmund had shivered as the sun set, owing more to his refusing food than a result of the scratches, Brother Henry had built a fire in a small brazier. The infirmary was now much cozier than Wulfstan's cell. Begging God's patience with his self-indulgences at his advanced age, Wulfstan pulled a chair near the brazier, settled down and fell asleep.

He was awakened by Brother Oswald. The hospitaler shook Wulfstan's shoulder and explained in a loud whisper, "The Reverend Mother asks you to attend her. Dame Joanna thrashes and cries out in her sleep. The Reverend Mother wishes to sedate her, but fears she might do harm."

"Where is Dame Prudentia?" Wulfstan asked and yawned sleepily.

"She is abed. She had sat with Dame Joanna since dawn yesterday."

Wulfstan rubbed his eyes. "In a moment. I shall come in a moment." He muttered to himself as he dashed water on his face and rubbed the sleep out of his eyes.

He did not notice, as he hurried out after the hospitaler, that he had gained a second shadow.

Joanna truly did thrash about. The scent of her sweat hung about the bed. And yet her eyes were closed, her motions those of one dreaming.

"Can you calm her?" Dame Isobel asked with an anxious wringing of the hands. "I fear she will hurt herself."

Wulfstan stood back from the bed, his hands tucked up his sleeves. He shook his head. "I do not like to give her more. Not until she wakens."

Dame Isobel moaned. "Sweet Jesu, what am I to do with her?"

Wulfstan leaned over Joanna, touched her forehead with the back of his hand. "She is so warm."

Suddenly Joanna's eyes opened. She placed her hand on

Wulfstan's and moved it down to her mouth, kissing the palm.

Wulfstan tried to pull his hand away from the unseemly closeness, but Joanna tightened her grip. In her other hand she held the Magdalene medal.

"Mary Magdalene is the patron saint of repentant sinners," Joanna said.

"Indeed she is, Dame Joanna. May St. Mary watch over you."

Joanna gripped his hand ever tighter, her eyes pleading. "I wish to confess to you, Brother Wulfstan."

"My child, I am but the infirmarian. Let me send for Abbot Campian."

"No! I cannot. I do not know him. You have been kind to me."

"He, too, is kind. And a just man, Dame Joanna. I fear—"

She shook her head adamantly. "You must shrive me."

Blessed Mary and all the saints, how did she come to choose him? "Why now, child? Why have you left it so late?"

"I cannot rest, Father. Now that I know my error. I cannot rest."

Brother Wulfstan turned to the Reverend Mother for assistance, but she waved him on from her seat near the door. "If it will bring her peaceful, healing sleep, Brother Wulfstan…"

"God bless you for coming this night, Father," Joanna said, releasing his hand and making the sign of the cross. She folded her hands.

The elderly monk, unwilling confessor, sat down beside her, blessing her.

Joanna's expression was that of an innocent child, hoping to escape punishment with a promise to behave. "If I confess, and if I am truly repentant, might I save myself from damnation?"

Wulfstan did not like the sound of that. "What is the error of which you speak?"

"I trusted in the Evil One. I did not know. Not until I heard how Will Longford died. I meant to take it to the grave with me. But if by speaking I may save myself from the eternal flames…" Joanna pressed her hands to her mouth and began to weep.

Wulfstan turned again to Isobel, but she sat with her head bowed, praying. The flame of her oil lamp flickered in the breeze coming from the door, slightly ajar.

Outside the room, Wulfstan's shadow crouched, as close to the door as he dared stay.

Brother Wulfstan sighed, bowed his head, and prayed that God might help him through this. When he was finished, he blotted Joanna's forehead with a scented cloth. "I shall hear your confession, Joanna. Tell me of this sin that terrifies you."

Joanna closed her eyes. "I have lived as the Magdalene."

Wulfstan lowered his eyes from the earnest, tear-streaked face.

"I gave myself to Stefan because he was beautiful and kind. He lifted me from the grave. He took me to Scarborough. He promised to find my brother Hugh. I loved Stefan. Until he lied to me. And for that I—" Joanna shook her head. "No. Not for that."

Wulfstan hoped that might be the extent of the confession. He raised his hand above Joanna's head. "For your sins of the flesh, I absolve thee in the name of the Father, and of the Son, and of the Holy Ghost, Amen."

Joanna grabbed Wulfstan's upraised hand. "No! That is the least of it. You must hear it all."

Wulfstan gently retrieved his hand, tucked it up his sleeve, bowed his head. "Continue, my child."

"He seemed to me everything best in God's creation. Strong, brave, fair, free. I did not understand that he was evil. Even after he returned and told me he had buried Will Longford alive." Wulfstan raised his head sharply, amazed at what he heard. Joanna met his astonished eyes. She nodded. "Oh yes. He and his two men. Because I told him how frightened I had been in the grave. I woke. I woke and knew where I was. It was but a moment, but so horrible. No air. No light. My limbs were bound in the shroud to keep me rigid, like a corpse. Stefan said they lowered me in and the gravedigger shoveled some dirt over me before Longford distracted him. But Stefan did not know I had awakened to feel the earth raining."

Wulfstan frowned. "Yet Stefan waited so long to avenge you?"

Joanna shook her head impatiently. "Not Stefan. Hugh."

"You told Hugh."

"But I did not tell him that Longford could not know." Joanna clutched Wulfstan's arm. "Would he have been so cruel had he known?"

"Your sin was telling your brother and making Longford seem more guilty than he was?" Wulfstan could feel her icy hand through the cloth of his habit.

"My sin was far worse. While Hugh was gone. Oh, sweet Heaven, if he had only told me." Joanna closed her eyes on tears that rolled down her face, withdrew her hand to wipe her eyes. "I thought Hugh had deserted me again, as he had the first time we went to Beverley. We were to go on a great adventure. But all at once I was sent off to my aunt's house."

Brother Wulfstan fidgeted on the chair. Where was the sin in this?

"While Hugh was away, I told Stefan I had seen my brother in Scarborough. So Stefan followed me when Hugh returned."

Wulfstan shook his head. "I do not understand. I thought Stefan had taken you to Scarborough to find your brother."

"No." Joanna spoke impatiently, as if so confused she thought she had already told him this. "Stefan warned me against seeing Hugh. He said that he and Hugh were sworn enemies."

Despite himself, Wulfstan was being drawn into the story. "But he had promised to find your brother for you."

"He lied."

Wulfstan closed his eyes, took a deep breath. "Go on."

"Stefan followed me to Hugh's house and killed him."

Dear Lord, no wonder the child seemed mad. "Because Hugh murdered Will Longford?"

Joanna bit her lip. "That must be why." It was the frown of uncertainty.

Wulfstan hoped this was the last of it, though wherein was her sin? "And then you ran away?"

Joanna nodded. "We ran. Stefan and I. And then—" She turned away and was silent.

Wulfstan waited.

In a tiny voice, almost inaudible to Wulfstan, Joanna cried, "I could not let him live."

The sorrow in those words made Wulfstan cross himself. He knew what was coming. He knew now the sin. But she must say it. He could not say it for her. "What do you mean, Joanna?"

She turned back to him, her eyes frightening in their pain. "I led him to his death." She reached out for Wulfstan. "Help me! Help me ask Him for forgiveness. I did not know. I did not see what Hugh had done. How horrible it was. And Edmund says that Stefan did love me. He did love me." She broke down, weeping hysterically.

"Joanna. Before I may absolve you, you must confess your sin. What do you mean you led him to his death?"

But Joanna was too hysterical. She would say no more. Wulfstan added a few drops of milk of poppy to the valerian tisane, coaxed Joanna to drink. He did not leave her side until she slept quietly.

22

THE SCABBARD

"I led him to his death." The words pounded in Edmund's head as he ran from the guest house. At the bottom of the steps he paused, uncertain which way to go. He had no idea what he meant to do. He cursed the day Longford introduced Stefan to Joanna Calverley.

But what of Stefan? Why had he murdered Hugh Calverley? Hugh was trouble, and Stefan was a seasoned killer, as were all Sebastian's men, but Stefan had not been ordered to murder Hugh and had no cause to do it on his own—someone else was bound to do it soon enough. And Joanna had adored her brother. How must she feel about his murder at the hands of her lover? She had said she led Stefan to his death. That he was adrift on the sea. Because Stefan had killed Hugh?

Edmund hated Joanna.

And he pitied her.

Looking round as the sky silvered with dawn, Edmund saw that he had wandered to the west front of the abbey church. Glad of a decision made however absentmindedly, Edmund pulled open the door and went in. In the quiet peace he sank down on his knees before a statue of the Blessed Virgin Mary and wept for Stefan.

Isobel rose as Wulfstan approached the door. "God bless you, Brother Wulfstan. I shall watch Joanna now."

Wulfstan made the sign of the cross over her and was about to leave, then paused, rocking back and forth on his sandaled feet while he thought. "You heard all that Joanna said to me?" Their eyes met. Wulfstan saw the pain in the Reverend Mother's face as she crossed herself. She had heard.

Isobel dropped her gaze. "Forgive me, Brother Wulfstan, but I could not help it."

"There is nothing to forgive. I am thankful you heard. I begin to see God's plan in this."

Isobel frowned. "But Joanna was making her confession. There should have been no witness."

Wulfstan could not remember the precise rules of confession—he saved what was left of his memory for his work in the infirmary. What he did remember was that a confessor was not to repeat what he was told by the sinner—something he had never been tempted to do. Could the Reverend Mother speak out? Surely God wished the truth to be known. "It was fitting that you were in the room, Reverend Mother. And it works to our benefit. I cannot reveal what has been told to me in confession. But you can."

Isobel looked horrified. "Oh no, Brother Wulfstan! It is not right."

Did she know of some rule he had misplaced? He knew full well he was becoming forgetful. But in this Wulfstan was determined. "Please, Reverend Mother. This is not a matter of a few venial sins that harm no one but the offender—people have been murdered. Several. Please wake Dame Prudentia and have her watch while you rest a while. Then I shall escort you to Mistress Wilton's apothecary after high mass. You must tell her what you heard."

Isobel made a face as if about to protest again, then pursed her lips and bowed her head in acquiescence. "His Grace the Archbishop would agree. He is anxious to resolve Joanna's story and return her to St. Clement's." Isobel glanced back at her charge. "But Joanna must be watched. And Prudentia is so tired…"

Always a whining protest. "I added milk of poppy to the tisane," Wulfstan said. "Joanna should sleep peacefully into the morning. Dame Prudentia can surely sit with Joanna while she sleeps."

"If it is what you wish." Though Isobel bowed meekly, her voice crackled with resentment.

Her false humility irritated Wulfstan. Better to voice an opinion than seethe silently. Besides, what did Isobel want if not to get to the truth? But Wulfstan was not one to challenge. "I shall be grateful for your assistance in this, Reverend Mother. Go in peace."

As he left the room, Wulfstan was deep in thoughts of Edmund, what to tell him of his friend. "Adrift on the sea." That is what Joanna had said yesterday. And tonight she had confessed to leading Stefan to his death. Had she drowned him? Is that what she meant?

Brother Oswald stepped into Wulfstan's path. "Forgive me. I know you have much on your mind. But you should know that there was someone in the corridor. He ran past me just before dawn. It was too dark to see his face. But he did not wear monk's robes."

Wulfstan had difficulty grasping this fresh subject. A hazard of age. He blinked a few times. "In the corridor. Do you mean someone listening?"

Oswald shrugged. "I cannot say for certain. I saw him only as he ran away."

Wulfstan thought of the man from whom Alfred guarded Edmund. Perhaps he was loose on the abbey grounds. "Beware of him, Oswald."

Oswald pursed his lips and rolled his eyes. "I pray we are soon rid of this troublesome nun." He said it quietly, but with far more feeling than Wulfstan had ever heard from the hospitaler. "I knew she would bring trouble to St. Mary's."

Wulfstan assured Oswald that Joanna would leave as soon as they knew she would be safe at St. Clement's. Then he hurried off to find Alfred and warn him to keep a close watch on the infirmary, for Jack may have found his way into the abbey grounds—if so, Edmund was in danger. Wulfstan sighed. He had doubted the archbishop's confidence in the security of the abbey from the beginning. It would be simple for an intruder to insinuate himself into the grounds by claiming to be a pilgrim.

• • •

Owen woke long before dawn. Before he could slip back into sleep, he remembered something Lucie had said last night. She had expressed concern that Owen had grown too fond of Edmund. Owen had been puzzled. What was the matter with his liking the man? Lucie had been vague in her answers. *Perhaps nothing at all. I simply wonder whether you know him as well as you think you do.*

Owen had brushed it off as sleepy talk last night, but now he lay awake wondering whether Lucie had some insight that eluded him. He watched her sleep, curled up, her head nestled in her cupped hand. Such a deep, peaceful sleep. He must not wake her, not now that she so often did not sleep. But how he yearned to ask what she had meant.

How well did he know Edmund? Owen knew little of Edmund's life except that he had been an apprentice shipwright in Whitby when he met Stefan. How long had Stefan and Edmund been together? Owen had no idea. Had Edmund ever been married? Been in love? It had never occurred to Owen to ask such questions.

What was it Lucie had said? *What does Edmund feel for Joanna? She is beautiful. You say her father and brother described her as flirtatious. Consider how he groomed himself to see her.*

Owen sat up. True enough. But what did it mean? He regretted leaving Edmund at the abbey infirmary. Were he here, Owen would wake him for a talk.

And what of Jack? Was he truly Edmund's enemy? Why was he following Edmund? If it was to kill him, why follow him all the way to York? An ambush would have been simpler out on the high moors than in a city. And until they spoke with the taverner in Beverley, Owen and Alfred had doubted Edmund's uneasiness. They would have been caught off guard, an ideal situation for the attacker. So what was Jack waiting for?

Owen feared Lucie was right, that he had formed an idea of Edmund and the mystery surrounding him and was acting on a view that might be dangerously wrongheaded.

Careful not to wake Lucie, Owen eased out of bed and dressed.

• • •

Edmund stared at the brightly painted statue of Mary, Queen of Heaven. Her robe was a warmer blue than the mantle he had given Joanna, but otherwise it was much the same. Was Joanna truly so innocent that she believed he had given her a holy relic to keep her warm? Or did she pretend to believe in order to brag of miracles? Was she mad? He had sensed something strange in her from the beginning, but had thought it simply her uneasiness about breaking her vows. Yet Joanna's behavior had never been that of a cloistered sister reluctant to sin. She had flirted with Stefan from the start, and even with Edmund in a subtler way. Was all this a sad battle over a soul already lost to madness?

But Joanna was no longer his concern. He must see to Stefan. Edmund resolved to return to Scarborough and scour the coastline in search of Stefan's body. There was nothing more to learn here. He doubted that in Joanna's state she would be able to describe where she had left Stefan.

And he feared that if he got near her again he would be tempted to shake her until she lost her wits entirely.

So best that he leave now.

As the monks shuffled into the choir for prime, Edmund left the church, too heartsick to bear their chanting. He noted others leaving, too. It was sad to think there might be others so full of grief that they could not bear the beautiful harmonies of the monks.

Out in the abbey yard, God's alchemy was turning the silvery light to gold. Edmund walked slowly round the cloister buildings, headed for the postern gate into the city. He would need a horse, and hoped that he might sneak his out of the stables at the York Tavern before any of the help woke. Then he could be alone with his grief on the long ride home.

Owen met Brother Wulfstan scurrying back to the infirmary. "God be with you, Brother Wulfstan. You are out betimes." He did not like the monk's worried expression.

The old infirmarian made the sign of the cross. "You are the answer to my prayers. I fear I have done a foolish thing, leaving Edmund alone in the infirmary. Pray God Alfred has kept careful watch." He told Owen about his call to the guest house and the intruder.

Owen's long strides got him to the infirmary before Wulfstan, where he discovered Alfred napping beside the outer door. "Idiot!" he muttered, kicking him.

Alfred woke with a sputter, his eyes puffy with stolen sleep. He jumped up at the sight of Owen.

Wulfstan, who had just arrived, repeated the story of the intruder in the guest house.

But Owen was already doubting Wulfstan's fears. "If it was Jack, why would he be eavesdropping in the guest house? Would he not have taken the opportunity to attack Edmund in the infirmary, knowing you were away?"

Wulfstan frowned. "Alfred was out here, guarding this door."

"Counting on you being in there, guarding the door from within." Owen tried to keep his voice neutral.

Wulfstan looked stricken. "Sweet Jesu, I had not thought of that. I should have alerted Brother Henry."

They rushed into the infirmary.

"Dear Lord, let not the poor man pay for my foolishness," Wulfstan prayed.

But they found an empty cot.

Wulfstan spun round to Owen, wild-eyed. "What can we do?"

Owen made a slow circuit of the room, his eye wandering up and down, then examined the inner door. From his crouch by the door he turned to say, "What made you think the intruder in the guest house was Jack?"

Wulfstan spread his hands. "Who else?"

Owen stood up. "Edmund himself."

"But why?"

"To hear what Joanna had to say, no doubt. Brother Oswald came for you here?"

Wulfstan bowed his head. "Yes."

Owen nodded. "Edmund is set on finding Stefan. He believes Joanna knows where he is."

Wulfstan sat down on Edmund's deserted cot and rubbed his eyes. "What was it Oswald said? Not a monk." He looked up hopefully. "It is possible you are right. Thanks be to God."

"We know nothing for sure. And now that Edmund is out and unguarded, what was not true may come true. What did he hear?"

"I cannot reveal her confession."

"Brother Wulfstan, for pity's sake—"

"Perhaps—" Wulfstan frowned, thought a moment. "Perhaps I might tell you what Dame Joanna told me of others. That is not her confession."

Owen nodded excitedly. "Surely there would be no harm in that."

Wulfstan took a deep breath, crossed himself. "Edmund might have heard that Hugh Calverley murdered Will Longford, Stefan murdered Hugh, and then, well, someone led Stefan to his death."

Owen took a moment to digest the news. Someone was Joanna? Had all these weeks of effort been resolved in one confession? "What does that mean, 'led him to his death'?"

Wulfstan's expression was apologetic. "I do not know. She became hysterical."

Owen paced, thinking what Edmund might do. "He will be after a mount."

Wulfstan's face lit up. "Shall I come help you search?"

Owen shook his head. "No need."

Wulfstan sadly nodded. "I would slow your progress."

Owen saw his disappointment. Old age was a humiliation that took much prayer to bear. "You have helped a great deal, Brother Wulfstan."

"Pray God forgive me for interpreting the rules to suit my purpose."

The guard at the postern gate gave Edmund a curious look. "'Tis a busy morning. I've not seen you before, eh?" His hand hovered over his sword hilt.

"I am Edmund of Whitby. Captain Archer brought me here yesterday to visit Joanna Calverley. She scratched me for my troubles." Edmund stepped closer, lifted his face to the guard to display his wounds.

The guard grimaced, nodded. "Those nuns are worse than nursing shecats. Brother Wulfstan took care of you, eh?"

"Aye. 'Twas much uglier yesterday. Not that my face had much beauty to destroy."

The two men chuckled companionably.

"You're not waiting for Captain Archer to finish his business this morning?"

"Finish his business?" Edmund frowned at the guard.

"He came this way not long ago. Did you see him?"

Edmund wondered why Owen would be here, but he certainly did not wish to see him. "Nay. He is on other business."

The guard nodded, swung open the oak door, and stepped back to let Edmund pass. "I trust you'll stay clear of nuns from now on."

Edmund hurried off toward Bootham Bar, where a large party of well-dressed churchgoers crowded. He fell in with them and was through the bar and hurrying down Petergate before the gatekeeper blinked. But his way was blocked by an overturned cart, summer apples spilling across the street and the farmer shouting at two men who lazily discussed how they might right the wagon. A sad reminder— Stefan loved summer apples. Edmund turned with a shrug into Lop Lane. Lucky the spill had not occurred before the intersection.

Lop Lane was narrower and darker than Petergate. Better for his purposes of moving in secrecy. But it reminded him of that other dark lane, where he and Jack and their men had turned and attacked Colin and Alfred. Ever since Joanna had come into his life, Edmund had been on a precipitous path to Hell.

Owen and Alfred made for the abbey's postern gate. "Has a man come through here? Scratched face?"

The guard grinned. "Aye. He showed me the nun's handiwork."

Alfred snickered, but Owen did not laugh. "How long ago?"

The guard stood to attention. "Just moments."

"Alone?"

"Aye. Unless he was trying to catch up with the three who came through earlier."

"What three?"

The guard shrugged. "Said they were your men, coming to report on the nun."

Damn it, Edmund was walking right into a trap. "Armed?"

The guard dropped his head, rubbed his chin. "Aye. Daggers and swords."

"One of them fair-haired but foul of face?"

The guard nodded.

Owen and Alfred hurried out the gate, Alfred muttering that it was proof Edmund had murdered Colin and was using his friends once more to escape his punishment.

As they came through Bootham Bar, Owen spun round and snapped, "Stop judging him before you know the facts! You talk like a simpleton sometimes. I despair of you."

Silenced and sullen, Alfred trudged down Petergate behind Owen. But he perked up when Owen slowed and whispered, "Trouble ahead."

Two men were piling apples into a lopsided cart just past Lop Lane. Owen noted their clothing—the subtle livery of Captain Sebastian. He glanced down Lop Lane, wondering if they had tricked Edmund into heading that way. But the overturned cart was an old trick that Edmund should not have fallen for.

The men from the cart saw Owen's patch and froze, then leaped over the apples and came for him and Alfred. The four circled each other, daggers ready; but when the Bootham gatekeeper spied the trouble and came running, Sebastian's men tried to bolt down Lop Lane. Owen and Alfred gave chase, and by the time the gatekeeper reached them they had wrestled the men to the ground and were busy binding their hands.

"Where's Jack?" Owen demanded of one.

Despite his bound hands and Owen's dagger at his throat, the man sneered, his resistance unwavering.

Owen swore and sheathed his dagger. "We waste time, Alfred.

Come along." They left the men in the custody of the gatekeeper and turned down Lop Lane. In the dark, Owen paused, listened. He heard the grunts of wrestlers up ahead. Signaling Alfred to stay right behind him, Owen crept forward, his dagger drawn. At the Blake Street crossing two figures struggled, daggers flashing. Owen flattened himself against the corner building, shadowed by the second story overhang, and watched the two men.

As one of them twisted away from his opponent with a cry of pain, Owen recognized Edmund. The other man had firm hold of Edmund's arm and bent it behind him to pull him back, then throw him down on the ground. It was Jack, ugly Jack from Scarborough, little Maddy's murderer.

As Jack stomped on Edmund's back and tossed his dagger aside to grab his sword, Alfred started. "The scabbard at that bastard's waist," he hissed in Owen's ear. "Matches the dagger I had off Colin's murderer." Before Owen could hold him back, Alfred leapt out, his sword drawn, and with a blood chilling cry charged Jack, chopping down on the murderer's unshielded shoulder just as Jack's sword sliced into Alfred's side.

When Lucie opened the shop door, her face deathly white with fear, Owen cursed himself for coming straight here without first cleaning off the blood. "Thank Heaven you're alive," Lucie cried, throwing her arms round Owen. "How badly are you hurt?"

He felt her trembling. "I am unharmed," he lied. But she discovered his bleeding hand soon enough. "It is nothing. Edmund and Alfred need attention."

Lucie led them all back to the kitchen, where Tildy was already stoking the fire. "Jasper has gone for water."

"See to Alfred first," Edmund said, sinking down onto a bench. "My wounds are less serious and far more deserved."

Jasper struggled in with a bucket of water. With huge eyes he looked round at the bleeding men and crossed himself.

"We are not half as bad as we look, lad," Owen assured him.

"Come, Jasper," Tildy said. "Bring the water, then see to the captain's hand."

Jasper cleaned Owen's palm with a calendula astringent, then applied an adder's tongue poultice and wound a clean cloth round his hand.

Owen was amazed by the boy's gentle assurance. "You have learned much from Lucie and Wulfstan."

Jasper nodded, but did not take his eyes from his work. "I think this will heal quickly," he said solemnly.

Lucie and Tildy packed Alfred's deep wound with a blood stanching paste and bandaged it. But Lucie was not confident. "He needs Wulfstan's care, Owen. We must get him there today."

"I can go nowhere until I answer to the bailiff." Owen slumped on a bench beside Edmund. "We have broken the peace of York. A man is dead—we must answer for it." He turned to Edmund. "You must answer for it. What possessed you to wander the streets alone this morning? And to fall for that old trick! Did you not recognize your own livery?"

Edmund's face was as white as Lucie's. "I was not looking for trouble. I was thinking of Stefan, bobbing on the tide." He closed his eyes. "About myself I care naught."

"So Stefan is dead?" Owen asked.

"I have no doubt." While Tildy held a hot compress to Edmund's aching shoulder, he told Owen of his resolve after hearing Joanna's confession.

"What confession?" Lucie demanded.

Owen told her what he knew. Edmund added some details.

Lucie rose from Alfred's side, pressing her fists into the small of her back. "Sweet Heaven, there are still so many questions. What of the seal of St. Sebastian? Joanna said 'we needed only the seal.' What had Hugh intended to do with it? Was he carrying out the deed at which he had failed so many years ago? Why did she say 'we'? And where is the seal? Damn the woman."

Owen did not like Lucie's energy. "You will stay put while I am with the bailiff?"

But Lucie did not respond, busy tsking over Edmund's wounds.

23

MARY MAGDALENE

Lucie paced the kitchen, from the open door to the fireplace, while Bess sat at the table, stripping mint branches. Lucie sighed. "So many answers, yet still so many questions. If Stefan loved Joanna as Edmund claims, why would he have murdered the brother she loved so much?"

Bess put aside her work and brought a pitcher of ale down from a shelf. "You must be in need of this. I am." She poured a cup of ale, passed it to Lucie, poured one for herself, drank. Her nose and cheeks flushed with the impact of her husband's strong brew. "Thank the Lord for my Tom." She grinned at Lucie. "What are you thinking?"

Lucie stood by the window, cup in hand, frowning. "Of what did Hugh and Joanna speak when they met? I must know that."

Bess grunted. "'Tis curious, isn't it? She was so angry with her brother for leaving without a word, still begrudging his deserting her years ago. What were those two up to?"

Lucie slowly lifted the cup to her mouth, but paused, lowered it. "And the medal, Bess. Mary Magdalene. Such a curious patron saint for a girl of 13. The patron saint of repentant sinners. Of what sin was Hugh thinking when he gave her that medal?" Lucie began to pace again. "I assumed that Matthew Calverley was right, that his wife despaired of Hugh and Joanna because of her family taint. But might it have been something else? Something Hugh and Joanna had done?"

Bess took another long drink, her eyes faraway. She nodded. "And they meant to run off together."

Lucie finally sat down opposite Bess and sipped her ale, staring into her friend's face, seeing her own questions mirrored in Bess's shrewd eyes. "Why did Stefan kill Hugh and not just capture him? He made enemies, doing that." Lucie put the cup down, pressed the heels of her hands into her brows. What else? There. Just at the back of her mind. "Stefan would have spied on Hugh and Joanna before he went into Hugh's house. What did he see that threw him into a murderous rage?" Lucie met Bess's frank look and nodded. "'*Noli me tangere.*' Who said that to Joanna?"

Bess tapped Lucie's cup with hers. "Why did she run away with Stefan and then murder him?" A knowing nod.

"Where is Daimon?"

"He and Sir Robert went to St. George's Field. They will return soon."

Lucie found it difficult to wait for an escort, but it was no use to arrive at St. Mary's before Joanna woke.

Sir Robert returned early from St. George's Field exhausted, admitting his age. Bess rose from her seat. "Come, Sir Robert. Let us go back to the tavern and rest. Lucie has business with Daimon. Some heavy lifting." Bess winked at Lucie.

When Bess had led Sir Robert safely away, Lucie asked Daimon to escort her to the abbey. He agreed at once, eager to oblige her in any way.

The city was quieter on Sunday than on other days but for the church bells. People moved about the streets, but they did so in more measured paces. It was midday, the sun warm on Lucie's back as she crossed the abbey grounds. She noticed little of her surroundings, rehearsing in her head how she would confront Joanna.

Prudentia rose from Joanna's bedside as Lucie entered and hurried over, her hands outspread, her ruddy face crumpled in distress. "God help her, Joanna will take neither food nor drink today, Mistress Wilton. She says she must die now. That it is Our Lady's wish. You must reason with her."

Lucie assured the infirmaress that she would try. "And you must have some food and rest. Go now. I shall watch over her."

"I should stay with her."

"God go with you, Dame Prudentia," Lucie said firmly. "I wish to speak with her alone."

"Ah." Prudentia was suddenly all smiles. "Then I shall of course leave you with her." She shuffled off in good cheer.

Joanna lay on the bed with the medal pressed to her heart, her eyes fastened on Lucie. "I have confessed my sins. You have heard?" Her voice was hoarse.

Lucie took the seat beside the bed, dipped a spoon into the cup of wine the infirmarian had poured for Joanna, grabbed Joanna's jaw with one hand, pressed the spoon to Joanna's closed mouth. Joanna tried to turn away, but Lucie held her firmly. "You shall drink this, Joanna, for we must talk."

Joanna pressed her lips together.

"Must I bring in Daimon to pry open your mouth? For I shall, Joanna, so help me God. You should be grateful that I have discovered your secret, the sin you have not confessed. If you died without confessing it, you would die in a state of sin, not of grace."

Joanna relaxed her jaw, accepted the spoon, coughing as the liquid trickled down her dry throat.

Lucie nodded, sat back. "When you wish for more, ask."

Joanna studied Lucie's face. "What secret?"

"I speak of that sin which you repented all those years ago. Of which that medal is a symbol."

Joanna's eyes went cold.

Lucie took a deep breath. "How young were you when you and Hugh became lovers, Joanna?"

Joanna clutched the medal.

"Young enough not to know what you did? Incest is not a venial sin, Joanna. Did Hugh rape you?"

Joanna's eyes widened. She lifted her head from the pillow. "Rape?" She gave a surprised little laugh. "Did your captain need to rape you? I think not. I think you rejoiced when you saw the hunger in his eye." She lay back down with a conspiratorial smile. "And why not love my brother? Why should I be denied perfection because

I was his sister? You think your captain is handsome." She waved away anticipated protests. "Hugh was more handsome still. Strong, brave, everything a man should be. I adored him." Joanna shrugged her eyebrows. "That, too, is sinful."

Lucie wondered about this new mood. "Then you did plan to run away together?"

Joanna's eyes were teasing one moment, filled with tears the next, though she tried to keep the smile frozen on her face. "We were off to France." A sob escaped. Joanna dabbed at her eyes. The smile vanished. "But he was not perfection. What he did to Will Longford—" She shook her head, closed her eyes. Her paleness worried Lucie. Even Joanna's lips were chalky. Lucie offered her the cup of wine. Joanna drank with one eye on Lucie. "I could not confess this sin to Brother Wulfstan."

Odd that Brother Wulfstan inspired a timidity in Joanna. No one else seemed to. "You are attempting to commit an even more serious sin—to end your life."

"It is Our Lady's wish."

Lucie knew the futility of arguing Joanna out of her delusion. "What did Hugh want with the seal of St. Sebastian?"

Joanna looked surprised. "I have just told you my brother and I were lovers. Have I not shocked you?"

"I want the truth. At the moment, that is all my concern."

Joanna shrugged. "The seal would introduce Hugh as du Guesclin's man and get us a safe conduct to France."

"From Scarborough?"

"No. Farther south."

"Why France?"

"No one would know we were brother and sister. We could be wed."

Lucie marveled at the naivete. Joanna and Hugh had reckoned without the long reach of the Church. But perhaps the Church turned a blind eye to du Guesclin. So they had planned to marry. "What of Stefan?"

Joanna turned away. "He never offered marriage."

"I am surprised your brother did. Mercenaries rarely attach

themselves to a family. But then, Hugh must have loved you very much to be so angry with Longford."

Joanna's breath caught. She crossed herself. "I cannot forgive what he did to Longford. I thought it had been quick. But what he must have suffered! Dear God, when I felt the earth raining on me, I could not remember how to draw breath. I could not scream. The earth was crushing me, pressing into me."

"I did not think they had truly buried you."

Joanna shook her head. "But the *feeling*."

"You told this to Hugh?"

"He already hated Longford. What I told him was just the excuse. Longford had made Hugh look a fool to the Percies. I know Hugh. That is why he left without a word. He knew I would not want him to do it."

"He was a cruel man?"

"He once burned the hand of a servant for a silly mistake. Hugh laughed while the boy howled. I could not bear it. I grabbed the boy's hand and pressed it into the snow." Joanna's voice suddenly flattened. "My mother hated Hugh."

"Yet you loved him."

"It takes strength to be cruel."

Lucie thought the opposite. "Why did your mother hate her son?"

Joanna struggled to sit up, refusing Lucie's help. She drew her knees up to her chest, wrapped her arms about her legs as if anchoring herself. "The way she died, walking into the water, did she take her life? Because of him? Or because of us?"

Lucie said nothing.

"Mother came upon us. Naked, in my bed. Hugh and I. She did not punish us. She simply said that a child born of us would be cursed. She gave me a plant to chew, so that I should not beget monsters."

"Did you go to St. Clement's in repentance? Is that why you took your vows?"

Joanna pressed her forehead to her knees. "If I could not have Hugh, I thought I wanted no man. But I was wrong. I found Stefan."

So she had loved Stefan. At least cared for him. "Where is Stefan, Joanna?"

Joanna raised her eyes to Lucie's. The green eyes swam with tears. "He is no more." The voice a quivering whisper.

"What happened?"

Joanna closed her eyes, rocked from side to side, letting the tears fall. "He had a wife. Did you know?"

"Yes," Lucie whispered.

"Jesu, I am accursed. My love is always sin."

"Stefan followed you to Hugh's house?"

"Hugh told me what he had done. But not the whole truth, not like your captain said. Hugh only said he had returned to Beverley to bury Longford in my grave—alive. He promised to protect me. Care for me." Her voice broke. Lucie handed her the wine. Joanna drank. "He had the seal. He had written letters for our safe passage, sealed with Sebastian's emblem. We would go to France. But we must go quickly. Right then. He was gathering his things. He said the house was no longer safe. His men had deserted him."

"Stefan heard this?"

"I do not know what he heard. I think he heard much of it."

"Please, Joanna. Why did Stefan kill Hugh?"

Joanna's face was flushed with wine and emotion. "I told Hugh I did not believe that he meant to take me with him. He would desert me again. Stefan was better for me. He had saved me." She shook her head. "Hugh told me Stefan had not meant to save me, he had simply not liked the idea of burying me alive, which is what Longford meant to do. Stefan thought it was too untidy. He preferred poison. A subtler, painless way to get rid of me and still hurt Hugh."

This did not sound like the man Edmund described. "Is that true, Joanna?"

Joanna shook her head, still clutching her knees to her chest. "Hugh lied. He was jealous. I had told him that I was trying to have Stefan's baby. So he wanted me to hate Stefan. And I saw that." Her eyes softened with tears. "I saw the yearning in Hugh's eyes. I could not hurt him. Not Hugh. He pulled me to him and kissed me. That was all it ever took. In a few kisses we were naked and rolling on the floor. Suddenly someone grabbed me and pushed me aside. Stefan. His face was so dark. So angry. I had not seen that side of him. Hugh was naked and unarmed, weak from sex. I reached for Hugh's things—to cover him—but Stefan struck me on the head. I was stunned." Joanna sobbed. "Dear God, I wish I had been unconscious. I could not stop Stefan, I could not help Hugh, I could only watch. Stefan drew his dagger and fell upon my beautiful brother." She moaned. "He stabbed him again and again. His chest, his stomach, his throat, even his face." She covered her eyes with her hands. "Blood danced in the room. It sprayed Stefan and me. When I stepped onto the floor I slipped in it. Hugh's blood was in my mouth, on my eyes. My brother's blood. Stefan slapped me and shouted for me to stop screaming. I did not know I was screaming. He slapped me so hard I fell and hit my head. I could not stand up. I was so afraid. For myself—I knew with all that blood Hugh must be dead. Stefan wrapped me in something and carried me away." Joanna drank down the wine.

Lucie refilled the cup, gave it to Joanna, then walked slowly to the window in a daze of blood. She gulped air. Turning, not wishing to sit just yet, she asked, "Where did Stefan take you?"

Joanna looked oddly calm. "A cave. By the ocean." Her voice was steady. "He would not speak to me. Would not let me touch him."

"Why did you stay with him?"

Joanna frowned as if puzzled. "Why, to murder him." Her direct look, a challenge rather than an apology, chilled Lucie. "He had murdered my Hugh. He must die." A long, shuddering sigh. "I had much time to think. I remembered what Hugh had said, how they had meant to poison me. And I believed him. How could someone who had loved me do this to me? And I thought how Hugh had murdered Longford as Longford had meant to murder me. So I planned his poisoning."

"You poisoned Stefan?"

Joanna rubbed her eyes wearily. "I did not know how. Not with what little we had there."

"And yet you stayed."

"I—" She shrugged. "I still wanted him."

Lucie pressed her chilled fingertips to her eyelids.

"One night, after much wine, Stefan stripped me and beat me—with the hilt of his sword, his hands, his boots—shouting all the while that I was unclean, I had made him unclean, I had made him a murderer. When I was bleeding and bruised and retching, he tied my hands to a post so I could not touch him, and he took me. So violently I thought he meant to kill me. And then he beat me again. And took me again. When he was finished, spent, he left me there, tied up, naked, unclean. I do not know for certain how long I lay there. I know it was days—I saw the light come and go. I lay there waiting to die. I prayed that death would not be slow in coming. I was so cold. Naked upon the stones. The sunshine I saw outside the cave could not reach me." She paused, crossed herself. "And then one night she came to me." Joanna's voice changed, hushed.

"Who?"

Joanna smiled. "Our Lady. She told me she would not let me die until I returned the vial of her milk that I had stolen from St. Clement's. I told her I could not move. She said I could work the cord on my hands loose enough to slide it up the post. So I obeyed her. She had come to show me the way to peace. It was midday by the time I worked my hands free. My first movements were so painful. It was late afternoon before I wrapped myself in her mantle, took my clothes, and went down to the water to wash." She bit her lip, dropped her eyes. "And there he was, lying on the rocks."

"Stefan?"

Joanna's eyes focused on something Lucie could not see. "He must have slipped."

"So you did not kill him?"

Joanna focused on Lucie. "But I did. If I had run away, he might have come to his senses. But to have me there... And then what he did to me—" She shook her head. "It should be clear to you. I am guilty."

"He was dead?"

"I did not go too close. I washed myself and dressed. I had my mission for the Virgin. Then I could die in peace. That is all I wanted."

Lucie found it difficult to believe that Joanna had not gone near enough to Stefan to see whether he breathed, whether someone might yet save him. "You walked away without knowing?"

Joanna nodded. "It was over."

Who was crueler? Hugh or Joanna? "Did you go into Scarborough? Tell anyone?"

Joanna looked askance. "Tell whom? Edmund would have murdered me then and there. I could not allow that until I had found the vial and returned it."

"Can you be so unfeeling? Stefan might have been alive. Don't you wonder if he lies there still?"

Joanna shrugged. "I suppose he does. Unless he slipped into the sea. I hope that happened. It is a kinder death."

As she stared at the madwoman before her—for surely Joanna was mad—all Lucie wanted was the comfort of Owen's arms. She shivered with cold on this warm July day.

When she left Joanna, Lucie was grateful that Daimon asked no questions, just accompanied her to the abbey church. She sank down in front of the statue of the Virgin, put her head in her hands, and wept. Maddy, Jaro, Longford, Hugh, Stefan, Jack—all dead; Joanna yearning for death. Even Mistress Calverley seemed to have willed her death to escape the tragic truth of her children. Not just their forbidden love, their cruel insistence on their way, no matter whom it destroyed. For Lucie the overwhelming tragedy was that none of this could ever be put right. Even if Joanna and Hugh had managed to escape to France and live as a married couple, they would have earned their momentary happiness by three deaths, and they would have lived with that knowledge. A confessor might have shriven them of their mortal sins—all but one. And that sin, of brother and sister living as man and wife, would have damned them for all eternity. Unless they parted. And then all would have been for naught.

Now even Hugh was gone. And Stefan. Leaving Joanna alone with her memories. Memories that made death seem a kindness.

A long while passed as Lucie worked through the emotions that gripped her. The bells rang out for nones. In the choir, the monks chanted their office and departed. At some point in the afternoon, Daimon had brought Lucie a stool. Now she sat, leaning her tired back against a pillar, staring at Our Lady, uncertain how to pray for Joanna. As the bells rang for vespers, someone knelt beside Lucie, gathered her in strong arms.

"Lucie, my love," Owen whispered, "it is over. Come. Let us go home."

She wiped her eyes, looked up into Owen's face, dark with worry. "Over? No. Not for Joanna. It will never be over for Joanna." Owen pressed her head to his chest, but Lucie had seen Edmund whisper something to Daimon, who gasped, then crossed himself. She pulled away from Owen. "What do you mean, 'over'? What is over?" That look in his eye.

Owen shook his head. "Not now. Come home."

"What has happened to Joanna?"

Owen tried to lift her.

Lucie fought him. "You said it, Owen. Now tell me."

"Joanna jumped from the window. Her neck was broken."

Lucie's stomach lurched. "But she did not confess the deepest sin, Owen. Not to a confessor. Only to me."

Owen pulled her close, kissed her forehead. "Perhaps it was enough. We shall pray that it was."

Jasper and his friends from the school sneaked round to the archbishop's gaol to glimpse the men being led out in shackles.

"What did they do?" one of the boys asked.

"Killed a nun," another replied. "Pushed her out a window."

Jasper shook his head. "No one pushed her. She jumped."

They all turned to Jasper with wide eyes, remembering his authority.

"Did Captain Archer see it?"

"No."

"Did anyone see it?"

"Dame Prudentia, the infirmaress," Jasper said. "She cried a lot and said it was her fault. But the captain told her that when people are determined to do such things, no one can stop them, just delay them." Jasper gazed round at the attentive faces lifted toward him. This was a benefit of being an apprentice in the Wilton apothecary that he had not foreseen. "Those men wear the livery of Captain Sebastian of Scarborough. He was a traitor, but now he fights for our King."

"How did that happen?"

"Captain Archer went to Scarborough and convinced him to fight for Right."

All heads turned to study the livery of the shackled men.

"But look at the one coming out with Captain Archer. He's wearing the livery, but he's free."

Jasper ducked back behind the corner of the building. Owen might not be pleased to see him there. "That's Edmund of Whitby," Jasper told his friends. "He helped the captain a lot, so His Grace the Archbishop has pardoned him. But he must return to Scarborough and answer to the Percies. He'll be under guard, but unshackled."

His friends ducked back round the corner to watch for any further action. They were disappointed there were to be no beheadings or hangings.

24

FAREWELLS

The men riding ahead of Edmund talked of how Fortune smiled on them, to be ordered down to the shore on such a warm day. They were glad to escape the stinking city. Edmund rode silently behind them, trying not to look at the blue sky. It reminded him of the cursed mantle he had given Joanna Calverley, the mantle he now carried. He had asked the Reverend Mother for this small thing, the mantle; perhaps it *was* somehow blessed and might speed Stefan on toward Heaven. Dame Isobel had gladly given him the mantle, pleased to be rid of it. "For it was you who gave it to poor Joanna. It should go back to you."

Perhaps it *had* been blessed—it had carried Joanna, the cause of all this sorrow, to her own destruction. It remained a puzzle to Edmund why everyone had been so determined to keep Joanna alive. He had not flinched at the sight of Joanna's blood, her bruised and swollen neck. She had wished for death. But he was grateful, in the end, that the sisters had frustrated Joanna's attempts to starve herself. It was far more satisfying to him that she had died violently, with pain.

Now Edmund wound his way down a bluff on the North Sea to identify a body that had washed up on the beach below. If it was Stefan, Edmund would wrap him in the frayed blue mantle and carry him back to Scarborough. Before departing to join King Edward, Captain Sebastian had arranged for a search party and, if Stefan's body was found, it was to be buried under the aisle in the manor chapel. It was characteristic of the captain, this courtesy. It was this made his men so loyal. He had learned it from du Guesclin.

Ever since the word had come, Edmund had prayed it was not Stefan. As long as his friend's body was not found, there was hope. Edmund could imagine Stefan alive and thriving, perhaps fighting with the Free Companies on the continent.

Edmund's companions reined in their horses. "There," one shouted above the surf and wind, "down in that cave."

Edmund took the lantern from his saddle, draped the mantle round his neck, and walked across the sand to the cave. His companions followed, but waited outside.

Stepping inside, Edmund stood a moment, blinded after the sun-drenched beach. He took a deep breath, smelled high tides and another odor, man's mortality. He opened a shutter on the lantern, held the mantle up to his mouth and nose, and moved toward a makeshift grave of rocks crowned with driftwood, just cover enough to keep out scavengers. The stench grew stronger, overpowering the tidepool scents. Edmund set the lantern on a stone and shoved aside the driftwood cover, still holding the mantle to his face. Then he lifted the lantern over the bloated, half-eaten body. There was so little left untouched, but the hair was blond, the height and build Stefan's, and the broken front tooth unmistakable. One hand clutched a leather purse attached to a leather cord at Stefan's waist. Edmund set the lantern down and worked the purse loose, his hands shaking with emotion.

"You were a good friend, Stefan, and I mean to be one in return. I take ship in a few days for your homeland. All your earthly belongings will be delivered up to your wife, and I shall tell her what a fine man you were. Rest in peace, my friend. Your family shall not want."

Edmund called to the men waiting outside.

When Stefan's body was wrapped in the mantle and slung across the extra horse, Edmund looked in the leather purse. There, sadly intact, was the seal of Captain Sebastian. The seal that would have provided Joanna and Hugh safe passage to France and a cursed marriage. Edmund wished with all his heart that Stefan had been too late to discover Joanna with Hugh, had been left wondering why she had deserted him, heartbroken, but alive. He must now find a way to describe this tragedy to Stefan's wife as an honorable death.

. . .

Owen, Ned, and Thoresby rode out of York on a sunny August day, headed for Pontefract. Ned and Thoresby would continue on with the Duke's retinue to Windsor, Owen would return in a few days. Lancaster had invited him to a high mass blessing the new captains and their Castilian adventure, with an accompanying feast at which Owen would be a guest of honor.

He had thought to refuse. He wanted no more of traveling, no more of Thoresby. But Lucie had insisted, supported by Bess and Magda; Lucie argued that Owen should see his friends once more before they all embarked on their new endeavors, for who knew when they might all meet again in this life.

Lucie had, it seemed, been doing quite a lot of thinking since Joanna Calverley's death. "Life is short and precious, and happiness even more so. I think we should swallow our pride and accept Sir Robert's gift of Corbett's house."

Owen found this new mood strange. "This new philosophy has convinced you to accept him as your father?"

Lucie had looked uncomfortable. "He is an old man. I fear I might regret it if I continue to reject him."

"And I, too, must swallow my pride?"

"He means no insult, Owen. He says you are a good husband to me, and he is proud of you."

"Because of Thoresby."

She shrugged.

"And my time as captain of archers for the old Duke."

"Faith, what is the harm in that? Sir Robert was a soldier. Like you when I first met you, it is the life he knew best."

"Will you call him 'father' when you accept?"

"I shall try to."

With such a concession on Lucie's part, what could Owen say? "Perhaps with a larger house we shall find opportunities for quiet moments together."

Now he rode between Ned and Thoresby, contemplating

another unexpected offer. Just a few moments ago, while they had paused at an inn, Thoresby had proposed that he be godfather to the child on the way.

Ned had blinked at the archbishop in disbelief.

Owen had tried to be courteous, but he was at once suspicious. What did Thoresby want in return? "I am most honored, Your Grace. But such a responsibility. Particularly if our first child is a son."

The archbishop had nodded. "And if it is a daughter, I propose to act as godfather to her and to your first son."

"Your Grace," Owen had to ask it—"to what do my wife and I owe this honor?"

Ned had kicked him under the table, his large brown eyes wide with shock at his friend's bluntness to so great a man.

But Thoresby threw back his head and laughed. "What do I want from you, that is the question I see in your eye. I predicted this response when I discussed the matter with Sir Robert and Jehannes."

"You—Sir Robert said nothing to me."

"Because I asked him to keep his counsel. And Jehannes. You might find reassurance in their delight in the proposal."

Now that he knew his honesty would not be taken amiss, Owen drank down his ale and sat forward, elbows on the table. "You still have not explained…"

"I am an old man, Archer, full of aches and pains and failing parts that remind me constantly of my mortality. The thought of playing some part in a new life—why, it is quite a cheerful thing to contemplate." He had told Owen to think about it, to discuss it with Lucie.

Owen had much to think about as they rode toward Pontefract.

Wobbly with brandywine, Owen sank down on the stone shelf in a sentry post. It was a warm August night, and he, Lief, Gaspare, and Ned had come up onto the walls of Pontefract to get some air after hours of attacking tables groaning with food and drink.

"What am I celebrating, I wonder?" Owen muttered.

"A successful investigation," Ned said with a slap on the back that almost knocked Owen over. "You managed to please three, maybe four lords with it—Lancaster, Thoresby, the King, and for all we know, the Lord God Himself. Can you imagine a lusty, incestuous bride of Christ? It might be blasphemous to even speak of it!"

"You're drunk, Ned."

"So are you, Owen. But thank the Lord I'm a cheerful drunk. You just brood more than ever."

Lief and Gaspare joined them.

"What's our friend brooding about now?" Lief asked.

"He has nothing to celebrate," Ned crowed. "He has forgotten the honor offered by John Thoresby—the Archbishop of York and Lord Chancellor of England has offered to be godfather to Owen and Lucie's first child, and to their first son as well if a daughter comes first."

"Sweet Mary and all the saints," Lief muttered. "A child with such a godparent shall surely prosper."

Owen belched.

Gaspare slapped him on the back. "So what's the gloom?"

How quickly they forgot Joanna Calverley. Owen looked up at his friends' shadowy faces, then beyond to the stars. "She might have been up there. She might have died in grace. But suicides are the folk we know for certain burn in Hell for all eternity. Their very deaths are terrible sins."

Lief sat down with a grunt. "Ah. 'Tis the nun who haunts you. How do you know that she did not regret her act and pray for forgiveness as she fell? How do you know that?"

Owen frowned, too drunk to come up with an answer. It was possible... "I should like to think that."

"What I want to know is whether you and Lucie have come to your senses and accepted Sir Robert's generous gift," Lief said. "Alice and I would ne'er say nay to such a house."

Owen shrugged. "Sir Robert bought the house, and he says it will sit there empty until we come round, for he's had enough of the city for a long time to come. He looks forward to my return, when he can go back to Freythorpe Hadden and walk his fields. He says he cannot breathe enough air in the city."

Gaspare grabbed the brandywine and took a long drink, then handed it to Owen. "Drink to your new home, Owen."

"And to your child's fortune in such a godfather," Lief said.

Owen dropped his head. "I have had enough."

Gaspare and Ned both snorted. "Is it possible to have enough brandywine?" Ned asked.

"To live a long life," Lief paused to belch—"a man must know his limits."

Gaspare and Ned exchanged grins.

"Wives and children," Gaspare said. "How they tame a man."

They all tilted their faces toward the stars and let the night air cool them.

Down below, in Lancaster's private parlor, Thoresby and the Duke shared brandywine before retiring.

"Your man Archer is worth his weight in gold, Chancellor. I regret having lost him to you."

"Sometimes I think he regrets choosing me, my lord Duke."

"A man like him chafes at any authority, I should think."

Thoresby felt the duke studying him. "What is it?"

"You do not seem pleased with the outcome of this investigation."

"Dissatisfied. Not displeased."

"Because there is no one to punish?"

"God makes us such slaves to our passions. It seems a cruel twist to our natures."

Lancaster shrugged. "Well, I am most pleased *and* satisfied. You have been generous with your assistance, Chancellor. I must repay you in equal measure."

Thoresby sat back, studied Lancaster over the rim of his cup. A golden lion of a man, like his father Edward in his prime. And almost as powerful as his father at this age. He might not be King of England and Wales, but he was Duke of Lancaster, an inheritance possibly worth more coin than that of the King. So young to be so powerful. He might do a lot for Thoresby. "You know my desire, my lord Duke. Alice Perrers out of your father's bedchamber. Any spur you might give to that exile will be most appreciated." He would not be greedy, not with so much at stake.

Lancaster swirled the brandywine in his cup and stared down into the whirlpool. "Mistress Alice. I had heard of your mutual dislike. But since then I have heard she admires you."

That disturbed Thoresby. What was the bitch up to? "A new ploy, my lord Duke, nothing more, you can be certain."

"I confess I find her vulgar and unlovely, but she has a quick wit and a knack for cheering the queen—that I should think would endear her to you."

"She cheers the queen while she plots to usurp her."

Lancaster pressed his middle and forefinger to the bridge of his nose. "Death shall do that for her soon enough."

Thoresby regretted having brought up the subject. "Perhaps we should speak of Mistress Alice another time."

Lancaster waved away the suggestion. "Do not mind me. Too much food and drink often puts me in a grim temper. Mistress Alice also has a clear head when it comes to business matters. I believe she has counseled the king wisely in financial matters pertaining to the household."

"She hopes to keep the coffers full so that she might expect more gifts, no doubt."

The blue eyes bored into Thoresby. "What is your personal stake in this, Chancellor? Why do you take such a personal interest in Alice Perrers?"

How could Thoresby possibly explain when he did not fully understand the intensity of his dislike himself? "I am devoted to your mother the queen. She has been a friend to me since I came to court years ago. Mistress Alice offends your mother with every breath she takes. That is the passion that drives me in this, my lord Duke."

Lancaster relaxed. "My mother speaks very highly of you."

Now that Thoresby had neatly sidestepped that unpleasant topic, he must move the conversation away from the despicable Alice. "I understand the king favors William of Wykeham for the seat of Winchester."

The comment brought Lancaster's head up with a jerk. Now the blue eyes were cold. "Wykeham. There's one I should like to separate from court."

Interesting. Thoresby wished to hear more. "He seems an intelligent man, and talented," he suggested, "though lowborn."

Lancaster dropped his head back, closed his eyes. "I care nothing of Wykeham's birth but that it was one of the more unfortunate dates in my history." He raised his head, fixed his eyes on Thoresby. "It is nothing I can point to and say, 'Thus he means to destroy me,' but mark me, Chancellor, the man will do it. There is a look in his eye when he gazes on me."

Thoresby could not think how anyone but the king could destroy the Duke of Lancaster. He fingered the chain of office round his neck. "You believe as I do that Wykeham is next in line for this?"

"I should not let it out of sight if I were you." Lancaster leaned over, poured himself more brandywine, sipped, suddenly laughed out loud. "Now I remember. It was at Easter. Mistress Alice sat at the high table with the most extraordinary jewelry. You know how low her bodices tend to be. On the swelling of her left breast she had pearls pasted in a pattern meant to mimic tooth marks. As if someone had bitten her there and left their pearly teeth embedded. And to my amazement, she claimed that you, my lord Chancellor, had been her inspiration. With coy smile she did swear she could say no more. What was that about, eh? It had that bastard Wykeham quite red in the face—much as you are now. What is it? Some water? Would that help?"

Still choking, Thoresby poured water, drank deeply. Sweet Heaven, she had almost killed him with that one. What a clever solution to that troublesome wound. How damnably clever. He hated her. "I cannot imagine what Mistress Alice meant by calling me her inspiration. But she would know that to suggest I approved of her brazen style would embarrass me and my friends."

Lancaster nodded. "She wore it for quite a while, so I am told, then tired of it. But the paste had been an unfortunate idea. The pearls left scars. Pale, but unmistakable. So like tooth marks. But too perfect, actually. Who has such perfect teeth?"

"You do, my lord Duke," Thoresby said, feeling mischievous.

Lancaster gave Thoresby an odd smile. "So do you, my lord Chancellor." He chuckled at Thoresby's confusion. "So. What is your next move?"

Did he know? How could he? Thoresby kept his face blank. "I am not yet certain."

"If I am to do aught before I take ship for Castile, you must approach me soon."

Thoresby nodded.

"But I am about to ask you another favor. I intend to put my weight behind the opposition to Wykeham's appointment to the seat of Winchester. When the time comes, I hope you will assist me."

Thoresby gave a little bow. "We are confederates, my lord Duke."

EPILOGUE

On the tenth of October, the feast of Paulinus of York, Lucie went into labor at last. Magda had assured Lucie and Owen that it was not unusual for a child to be hesitant to leave the womb, but they had worried anyway, spending many sleepless nights pretending to sleep so as not to worry the other. But at last, at dawn, Lucie had announced it was time.

Bess, Magda, and Lucie's Aunt Phillippa were all in attendance. Owen and Jasper paced down below. It was proving to be a long wait. Magda had called down for them to open all doors, windows, and drawers to encourage the child to come forth. When hours passed and they still heard no cries, Jasper suggested that they open all the jars in the shop, too. The task was soon complete, and still the two paced to Lucie's cries, not the babe's.

Midday, Tom Merchet dragged them out of the house. "Come to tavern. 'Tis an old North Country custom to tempt the child forth by drinking to its health and long life."

Owen was almost certain Tom made it up—he saw the twinkle in his eye—but he was weary of pacing, and the shop was closed for the event. There was no point in refusing.

"Boy or girl, what think you, Owen?" Tom asked as he filled three tankards.

"Perhaps a smaller cup for the lad," Owen suggested.

"On such a day as this?" Tom shook his head and kept pouring.

"Boy or girl?" Tom repeated, joining them at the table.

Owen shrugged. "'Tis unlucky to predict, Tom."

"Well, I'm hoping for a fine lad. Then Tom gets to be second godfather to 'im. But if a girl, it's Bess will have the honor of joining your family before I do. She'll brag about it till the end of time. Worse yet, she's said 'tis a girl from the first." Tom took a long drink.

"What will I be to the baby?" Jasper asked quietly.

Owen nodded. He and Lucie had wondered about that, too. The boy was not their son, yet they thought of him as such. They had decided to leave the matter up to him. "Brother to Gwenllian or John would suit us, but 'tis your decision, lad."

In the end, it was Magda Digby, the Riverwoman, who decided the issue. She burst into the tavern beaming right at Jasper. "Well, lad, the gods have brought thee a sister to protect. Art thou man enough for it?"

Owen was out the door before Jasper could get the answer out.

Tom Merchet shook his head and sighed. "The wife has won again."

AUTHOR'S NOTE

The action of this tale unfolds against the broad canvas backdrop of the Spanish intervention: King Edward's sons are preparing to march on Castile and restore Don Pedro the Cruel to the throne. The incident affords a glimpse into the medieval economic machinery of war. The intermittent fighting of the Hundred Years War took place on French soil, and the common soldiers involved were not members of a standing army, salaried in war and peace, nor were they all English; they were essentially mercenaries, paid only during active campaigns. When the English retreated, many of these soldiers were left behind to find their way back to their homelands as they might. Some of them, who faced poverty or serfdom back home or had developed a taste for living off the land in the harrying companies of the Black Prince, chose to stay on the Continent. They formed organized companies of *routiers*, called Free Companies, and roamed over the French countryside seizing fortresses and running protection rackets, moving on when they had exhausted the resources in the area. Though they were Englishmen, Bretons, Spaniards, Germans, and Gascons, their captains tended to be English.[1] And young Englishmen, hearing of the fortunes and reputations made in the companies, saw career potential, as Hugh does in this novel.

Even some who later became heroes of France were drawn to these companies early in their careers. The Breton Bertrand du Guesclin honed his guerrilla skills among the *routiers*.

Understandably, the people of France wanted their king to rid them of the *routiers*, who terrorized the countryside. And in 1365 King

1. Desmond Seward, *The Hundred Years War: the English in France, 1337-1453* (New York: Antheneum, 1978), 105-106.

Charles of France saw a way. Enrique de Trastamare asked King Charles to assist him in a popular uprising against his half-brother Don Pedro the Cruel of Castile, a tyrant whose preferred method of persuasion was murder. Charles was predisposed against Pedro, as it was said he had arranged for the murder of his wife, a French princess, shortly after he had cast her aside. The Pope had excommunicated Pedro as an oppressor of the Church; it did not help that he had befriended the Moorish king of Grenada. Thus, encouraged by the Pope, King Charles asked Bertrand du Guesclin, by now a knight, to round up the Free Companies and lead them over the Pyrenees to oust Pedro and replace him with Trastamare. The engagement was a success.

But Pedro had no intention of quietly accepting defeat; he turned to England, seeking the help of the Black Prince in winning back his crown, offering him lavish payment. The English were highly motivated to keep the powerful Castilian navy as their ally.

The Black Prince readied himself in the Aquitaine, and John of Gaunt, Duke of Lancaster, began gathering an army of soldiers and archers to support the venture. In the novel, Owen works with his old comrades Lief and Gaspare to develop an efficient method for training the archers Gaunt needed.

The extent of Chaucer's espionage work is unknown; in the early 1360's he studied law and finance at the Inns of Court and perhaps also served for a time in Lionel's army in Ireland. By 1367 he was Esquire of the Royal Household; late in that year the death of Blanche of Lancaster inspired Chaucer's first great poem, *The Book of the Duchess*. For Chaucer's mission to Navarre I use Donald R. Howard's interpretation of a safe conduct preserved in the archives in Pamploma, allowing the poet to 'enter, stay, move about, turn around and go back'.[2]

Whence came Joanna? In *The History of Clementhorpe Nunnery*[3] is the following item:

> In 1318 there is mention of [an] apostate, Joanna of Leeds. Archbishop Melton ordered the dean of Beverley to return

---

2. *Chaucer: His Life, His Works, His World* (New York: Dutton, 1987), p. 115
3. R. B. Dobson and Sara Donaghey, York Archaeological Trust for Excavation and Research, 1984, p. 15

the nun to her convent... Apparently Joanna had defected from her religious order and left the nunnery. However, in order to make her defection credible, she had fabricated her death at Beverley and, with the aid of accomplices, even staged her own funeral there. The archbishop was prepared to take a lenient view of these excesses. He directed the dean of Beverley to warn Joanna of the nature of her sins and, if she recanted them within eight days, to allow her to return to Clementhorpe to undergo a penance. Melton further urged the dean to undertake a thorough investigation of the case, and to discover the names of Joanna's accomplices so that he might then take suitable action.

The story intrigued me. Was Joanna discovered, betrayed, or did she request to return to St. Clement's Nunnery? If it was her choice, why make such an about face? She had gone to great lengths to escape and make it permanent.

I moved the incident to 1365-66, putting it in Archbishop Thoresby's time, which provided me with a serendipitous relationship—Thoresby's nephew, Richard de Ravenser, was a canon of Beverley at this time, as was William of Wykeham. Nicholas de Louth is also a real person. Because I moved Joanna's story in time, none of the participants in the book had anything to do with the real story of Joanna of Leeds.

From the first, I envisioned Joanna to be an ambiguous character such as Mary Magdalen. As Susan Haskins describes in *Mary Magdalen: Myth and Metaphor,*[4] the saint had evolved from Christ's disciple and friend to a penitent prostitute who endured a long penance as a hermit in the desert: in fact, by the 14th century the biblical references to Mary Magdalen, Mary of Martha and Mary, and the prostitute who washes Christ's feet had been combined into one symbol, and the 5th century Mary of Egypt was also folded into the mixture. And thus the Magdalen medal that Joanna loses in the first scene, a gift from the brother she adores.

4. (New York: Harcourt Brace and Company, 1994).

The medal is a talisman, a good luck charm. It serves as a reminder that a character such as Joanna cannot be analyzed in modern terms; her belief in the protective power of the medal is part of her faith. So too is Joanna's remorse about stealing a portion of the Virgin's milk from the nunnery. St. Clement's did boast such a relic, a popular one in a time of great devotion to the Blessed Virgin Mary, and people believed in the power of such relics, going on pilgrimage to receive grace through homage to them.

In the book, Joanna refuses to discard the belief that her mantle is a gift from the Blessed Virgin, even when Edmund, who had originally told her it was Our Lady's mantle, admits to her that it is not. Joanna truly believes that Our Lady appeared to her and helped her return to St. Clement's. The mantle also causes a stir at the nunnery and when the cook believes the mantle has cured her skin ailment, Dame Isobel sees trouble ahead in trying to silence the rumor of a miracle. Indeed, she wonders whether she actually should silence it—such a relic could attract more pilgrims to fill the nunnery's coffers. Consider what P. J. Geary has to say about determining the authenticity of relics: "The most effective means available...was in reality a very pragmatic one: if the relics performed as relics—that is to say, if they worked miracles, inspired the faithful, and increased the prestige of the community in which they were placed—they had to be genuine."[5] Joanna's madness does not lie in her beliefs.

Why did Joanna choose the convent? As the daughter of a wealthy merchant and a high-born mother, her most acceptable roles would be those of either wife or nun. In late 14th century England women were making inroads into middle class occupations in the cities, but, then as now, not everyone can succeed in business. Joanna is not an entrepreneur like Bess Merchet nor has she been trained in a profession like Lucie Wilton. She considers the nunnery a safe haven until she comes up with a better plan. The life of a nun was seen as a respectable career; not all who took the veil had

5. *Furta Sacra: Thefts of Relics in the Central Middle Ages* (Princeton: Princeton University Press, 1980) p. 54.

religious vocations, and convent life could be quite comfortable. The number of documents reiterating the rule of enclosure (that a nun's place was in the cloister, not outside in the world) and admonishing sisters for wearing finery and keeping pets suggests less rigid establishments than we might imagine. And although St. Clement's was considered a small, poor nunnery, the description is relative; it could boast neither the size nor the wealth of Shaftesbury or Barking, but it was the third wealthiest of the Yorkshire nunneries and held considerable property. Joanna might have lived out her life in quiet contentment at St. Clement's—and perhaps the real Joanna of Leeds did.

THE OWEN ARCHER SERIES

THE APOTHECARY ROSE

In the year of our Lord 1363, two suspicious deaths in the infirmary of St. Mary's Abbey catch the attention of the powerful John Thoresby, Lord Chancellor of England and Archbishop of York. One victim is a pilgrim, while the second is Thoresby's ne'er-do-well ward, both apparently poisoned by a physic supplied by Master Apothecary Nicholas Wilton. In the wake of these deaths, the archbishop dispatches one-eyed spy Owen Archer to York to find the murderer. Under the guise of a disillusioned soldier keen to make a fresh start, Owen insinuates himself into Wilton's apothecary as an apprentice. But he finds Wilton bedridden, with the shop being run by his lovely, enigmatic young wife, Lucie. As Owen unravels a tangled history of scandal and tragedy, he discovers at its center a desperate, forbidden love twisted over time into obsession. And the woman he has come to love is his prime suspect.

Lovingly detailed, beautifully written, *The Apothecary Rose* is a captivating and suspenseful tale of life, love, and death in medieval England.

THE LADY CHAPEL

Perfect for fans of both Ellis Peters and CJ Sansom, *The Lady Chapel* is a vivid and immersive portrait of court intrigue and a testament to the power of the medieval guilds.

Summer in the year of our Lord 1365. On the night after the Corpus Christi procession, a man is brutally murdered on the steps of York Minster. The next morning his severed hand is found in a room at the York Tavern—a room hastily vacated by a fellow guild member who had quarreled with the victim.

Archbishop Thoresby calls on Owen Archer to investigate. As Owen tracks the fleeing merchant, he uncovers a conspiracy involving a powerful company of traders, but his only witness is a young boy who has gone into hiding, and his only suspect is a mysterious cloaked woman. When Owen discovers a link between the traders and a powerful coterie in the royal court, he brings his apothecary wife Lucie into the race to find the boy before he is silenced forever by the murderers.

THE KING'S BISHOP

From the marshy Thames to the misty Yorkshire moors, murder stalks Welsh soldier-sleuth Owen Archer and one of his oldest friends.

On a snowy morning in 1367, Sir William of Wyndesore's page is found in the icy moat of Windsor Castle, and some whisper that the murderer was Ned Townley—a former comrade-in-arms of Owen Archer. Burdened with a reputation as a notoriously jealous lover, Ned cannot hope to clear his name; even Mary, his ladylove, is unsure of the truth. Hoping to put Ned out of harm's way while solving the murder, Owen places his friend in charge of a mission to Rievaulx Abbey at the edge of the moors. But when the travelers receive news of Mary's drowning, Ned vanishes into the wild.

Riding out in search of his old friend, Owen does not know whether he will be Ned's savior or executioner. With his one good eye, Owen sees more than most, but now he must find a way to penetrate the curtains of power that surround the Church and England's royal court and discover the truth of Ned's innocence or guilt...

THE RIDDLE OF ST. LEONARD'S

In the year of our Lord 1369 the much-loved Queen Philippa lies dying in Windsor Castle, the harvest has failed, and the pestilence has returned. In York, the atmosphere of fear and superstition is heightened by a series of thefts and violent deaths at St. Leonard's Hospita, as well as rumors that these crimes are connected to the hospital's dwindling funds. The Master of St. Leonard's, Sir Richard Ravenser, hurries north from the queen's deathbed to summon Owen Archer, soldier-spy, to investigate the scandal before it ruins him.

While his wife Lucie faces the plague-panicked townsfolk at the apothecary, Owen encounters a seemingly random series of clues:

a riddle posed by one of the victims at the hospital, a lay sister with a scandalous past, the kidnapping of a child from the hospital orphanage, and a case of arson. The answer to the riddle of St. Leonard's lies in the past, and as Owen's family is caught up in the sweep of the pestilence, he must abandon them to race across the countryside to save the next victim.

A GIFT OF SANCTUARY

Under the pretense of escorting his father-in-law and the archbishop's secretary on a pilgrimage to the sacred city of St. David's in Wales, Owen Archer and Geoffrey Chaucer, in truth, are carrying out a mission for the Duke of Lancaster. England and France are at war, and the southern coast of Wales is vulnerable to invasion—Owen and Geoffrey are to recruit archers for the duke's army and inspect his Welsh fortifications on the coast, while quietly investigating whether the duke's steward at Cydweli Castle is involved in a French plot to incite rebellion in Wales.

But trouble precedes them in the cathedral city of St. David's. On Whitesands Beach beyond the city a young man is beaten and left for dead, then spirited away by a Welsh bard. Shortly afterward a corpse clothed in the livery of the Duke of Lancaster is left at the city gate, his shoes filled with white sand. Meanwhile, at Cydweli Castle, a chain of events begun by the theft of money from the castle's exchequer ends in a violent death and the disappearance of the steward's beautiful young wife. Owen and Geoffrey begin to see connections linking the troubles in city and castle, and learn they must unravel the complex story of betrayed love and political ambition to prevent more deaths. But in the course of his investigations in the land of his birth, Owen is haunted by doubts about his own loyalties...

A SPY FOR THE REDEEMER

Late spring in the year of our Lord 1370, and Owen Archer is anxious to leave Wales for home. His mission for the Duke of Lancaster complete, he attempts to arrange safe passage on a ship sailing for England, but the hanging of a stonemason interrupts his plans. On the surface it appears the young man was driven to suicide by a broken heart, but to Owen the signs all point to murder. As his investigation stretches on, however, Owen finds himself drawn into the influence of the leader of a Welsh rebellion whose manifesto speaks to his heart, and a choice is offered to him: join or die.

Meanwhile, at home in York, Owen's wife Lucie is troubled by rumors that her husband's long absence is permanent, as well as threats by a customer who claims she was poisoned by a physic from the Wilton apothecary. Meanwhile, Lucie is tempted by the attentions of a friend's steward, even as she uncovers a shattering betrayal in her own household.

THE GUILT OF INNOCENTS

Winter in the year of our Lord 1372. A river pilot falls into the icy waters of the River Ouse during a skirmish between dockworkers and the boys of the minster school, which include Owen Archer's adopted son Jasper. But what began as a confrontation to return a boy's stolen scrip becomes a murder investigation as the rescuers find the pilot dying of wounds inflicted before his plunge into the river. When another body is fished from the river upstream and Owen discovers that the boy Jasper sought to help has disappeared, Owen Archer convinces the archbishop that he must go in search of the boy. His lost scrip seems to hold the key to the double tragedy, but his disappearance leaves troubling questions: did he flee in fear? Or was he abducted?

On the cusp of this new mystery, Owen accepts Jasper's offer to accompany him to the boy's home in the countryside, where they learn that a valuable cross has gone missing. A devastating fire and another drowning force Owen to make impossible choices, endangering not only himself, but the two innocents he fights to protect. The bond between fathers and sons proves strong, even between those not linked by blood.

A VIGIL OF SPIES

Archbishop Thoresby of York, the second most powerful cleric in England, lies dying in his bed. The end of his life is seen by the great families of the North as a chance to promote one of their own as his successor, and Thoresby himself announces he will leave the matter to the dean and chapter of York. On the eve of this decision, the dying archbishop agrees to a visit from Joan, Princess of Wales, wife of the Black Prince, heir to the throne of England. Thoresby's captain of the guard, Owen Archer, has no doubt that trouble will follow.

As soon as the company rides into the palace yard he is proved right: they arrive burdened with the body of one of their party, and Owen finds evidence that the man's death was no accident. Within days of this discovery, a courier carrying an urgent message for the archbishop is found hanging in the woods. With guards surrounding the property, it is clear that the murderer walks among the palace guests. The powerful Percy and Neville families are well represented in the entourage, including a woman who remembers an afternoon tryst with Owen as much, much more. Even the princess' son is suspect. As Owen races to unmask the guilty and rid the palace of the royal party, his final wish for his lord is that he might die in peace.

THE MARGARET KERR SERIES

A TRUST BETRAYED

In the spring of 1297 the English army controls lowland Scotland and Margaret Kerr's husband Roger Sinclair is missing. He'd headed to Dundee in autumn, writing to Margaret with a promise to be home for Christmas, but it's past Easter. Is he caught up in the swelling rebellion against the English? Is he even alive? When his cousin, Jack, is murdered on the streets of Edinburgh, Roger's last known location, Margaret coerces her brother Andrew, a priest, to escort her to the city.

She finds Edinburgh scarred by war—houses burnt, walls stained with blood, shops shuttered—and the townsfolk simmering with resentment, harboring secrets. Even her uncle, innkeeper Murdoch Kerr, meets her questions with silence. Are his secrets the keys to Roger's disappearance? What terrible sin torments her brother? Is it her husband she glimpses in the rain, scarred, haunted? Desperate, Margaret makes alliances that risk both her own life and that of her brother in her search for answers. She learns that war twists love and loyalties, and that, until tested, we cannot know our own hearts, much less those of our loved ones.

THE FIRE IN THE FLINT

Scots are gathering in Murdoch Kerr's Edinburgh tavern, plotting to drive out the English forces. Margaret takes her place there as innkeeper, collecting information to pass on to William Wallace— until murder gives the English an excuse to shutter the tavern. The dead man was a witness to the intruders who raided chests belonging to Margaret's husband and her father, the latest in a string of violent raids on Margaret's family, but no one knows the identity of the raiders or what they're searching for.

Margaret's uncle urges her to escape Edinburgh, but as she flees north with her husband Roger, Margaret grows suspicious about his sudden wish to speak with her mother, Christiana, who is a soothsayer. Margaret once innocently shared with Roger one of Christiana's visions, of "the true king of Scotland" riding into Edinburgh. Now she begins to wonder if their trip is part of a mission engineered by the English crown...

A CRUEL COURTSHIP

In late summer 1297, Margaret Kerr heads to the town of Stirling at the request of William Wallace's man James Comyn. Her mission is to discover the fate of a young spy who had infiltrated the English garrison at Stirling Castle, but on the journey Margaret is haunted by dreams—or are they visions?—of danger.

He who holds Stirling Castle holds Scotland—and a bloody battle for the castle is imminent. But as the Scots prepare to cast off the English yoke, Margaret's flashes of the future allow her to glimpse what is to come—and show her that she can trust no one, not even her closest friends.

A Cruel Courtship is a harrowing account of the days before the bloody battle of Stirling Bridge, and the story of a young woman's awakening.

CPSIA information can be obtained
at www.ICGtesting.com
Printed in the USA
JSHW011800261020
9092JS00001B/34